Praise for

DEBRA SALONEN

"Debra Salonen captures reader attention with multifaceted
characters, layered conflict and fast pacing."
—Pamela Cohen, *Romantic Times*

"People who scoff at romances and accuse them of being
trite, frivolous or too predictable will be very surprised,
pleasantly so, I think—by the intensity, the depth and the
heat of (Debra Salonen's) *Back in Kansas*."
—Linda Mowery, *www.TheRomanceReader.com*

"...a wonderfully written love story with loveable characters.
The plot is engaging and certainly keeps the reader
riveted throughout the story. *His Daddy's Eyes*
is just the sort of book to curl up with to
while away some lazy afternoon hours."
—Jenna Richardson, *www.HeartRateReviews.com*

D1447334

Dear Reader,

The editors at Harlequin and Silhouette are thrilled to be able to bring you a brand-new featured author program for 2005! Signature Select aims to single out outstanding stories, contemporary themes and oft-requested classics by some of your favorite series authors and present them to you in a variety of formats bound by truly striking covers.

We want to provide several different types of reading experiences in the new Signature Select program. The Spotlight books offer a single "big read" by a talented series author, the Collections present three novellas on a selected theme in one volume, the Sagas contain sprawling, sometimes multi-generational family tales (often related to a favorite family first introduced in series), and the Miniseries feature requested previously published books, with two or, occasionally, three complete stories in one volume. The Signature Select program offers one book in each of these categories per month, and fans of limited continuity series will also find these continuing stories under the Signature Select umbrella.

In addition, these volumes bring you bonus features...different in every single book! You may learn more about the author in an extended interview, more about the setting or inspiration for the book, more about subjects related to the theme and, often, a bonus short read will be included. Authors and editors have been outdoing themselves in originating creative material for our bonus features—we're sure you'll be surprised and pleased with the results!

The Signature Select program strives to bring you a variety of reading experiences by authors you've come to love, as well as by rising stars you'll be glad you've discovered. Watch for new stories from Janelle Denison, Donna Kauffman, Leslie Kelly, Marie Ferrarella, Suzanne Forster, Stephanie Bond, Christine Rimmer and scores more of the brightest talents in romance fiction!

The excitement continues!

Warm wishes for happy reading,

Marsha Zinberg
Executive Editor
The Signature Select Program

SAGA

DEBRA SALONEN

BETTING ON GRACE

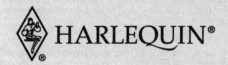

HARLEQUIN®

TORONTO • NEW YORK • LONDON
AMSTERDAM • PARIS • SYDNEY • HAMBURG
STOCKHOLM • ATHENS • TOKYO • MILAN • MADRID
PRAGUE • WARSAW • BUDAPEST • AUCKLAND

ISBN 0-373-83677-5

BETTING ON GRACE

This edition published by arrangement with Harlequin Books S.A.

® and TM are trademarks of the publisher. Trademarks indicated with
® are registered in the United States Patent and Trademark Office, the
Canadian Trade Marks Office and in other countries.

www.eHarlequin.com

Printed in U.S.A.

Dear Reader,

Families fascinate me. I start every book I write by investigating the backstory of my central characters. I need to meet their siblings, parents and grandparents. Sometimes, I bump into distant relatives who like to gossip. This "history" helps me understand both my characters and their world. I love this part of the process and am always sorry to type "the end" because it means saying goodbye to the family I've come to love. Fortunately, that didn't happen with Grace because her three sisters will have a chance to tell their stories in my upcoming SISTERS OF THE SILVER DOLLAR miniseries appearing in Harlequin American Romance in 2006. Kate's book, *One Daddy Too Many*, will be released in May, followed by Liz's adventure, *Bringing Baby Home*, in August and Alex's poignant reunion with her tarnished knight in *The Quiet Child* in November.

In researching the setting for *Betting on Grace*, I made several trips to Las Vegas. Marc and Lisa Wolpert graciously opened their beautiful home to me and showed me around Boulder City, Searchlight and Lake Mead. Bob and Joyce Peterson helped me "discover" Henderson. My cousin Carol Gregory and her husband, Kenny, were my guides to Mesquite. Les and Leona Bagby, my dear uncle and aunt, were all too happy to give me an insider's view of retirement life in Vegas. Many thanks to all. Also, I need to recognize Jan and Mom for introducing me to Ethel M. and nickel slots, and thank Paul for being my chauffeur on our "working" anniversary trip.

For a free bookmark, send a self-addressed, stamped envelope to: Debra Salonen, P.O. Box 322, Cathey's Valley, CA 95306. For writing tips, a new contest every month and links to other fabulous authors' Web sites, check out my "blog" at www.debrasalonen.com.

Wishing you all the best!

Debra

To my family, with love.
I'd also like to acknowledge the estimated quarter of a million
Gypsy/Romani who perished in Hitler's death camps.
From the tears of sorrow may hope and tolerance grow.

CHAPTER ONE

THE NOISE LEVEL WITHIN the small, crowded detective quarters was almost enough to mask the sound of the phone, but the flashing light, which blinked in time to the pulse in Nick Lightner's temple, caught his eye. The beat seemed to say, *Going, going, gone.*

The festive celebration was in honor of his father's long and distinguished career in law enforcement. Today was Pete Lightner's last day as chief of detectives in Clarion Heights, a Detroit suburb that Nick's family had called home for twenty-eight of Nick's thirty-four years.

In Nick's book, "retirement" was a four-letter word. He'd seen too many good cops turn into couch potatoes just months after handing in their badges. From the minute his father announced his plan to step down, Nick had started nagging his parents to plan exactly what they wanted to do with the rest of their lives.

His nagging had worked. Just last week, Pete had announced, "Your mom and I have decided we're through with Michigan's winters. We're selling the house and moving to Portland, so we can be closer to Judy and the girls." Judy was Nick's sister. His parents' *real* child.

Nick knew that his adoption played no part in Pete

and Sharon's decision to move. They'd loved him and provided for him as if he were their own child from the moment they'd taken him in. They had every right to want to be closer to their grandchildren. In the offspring department, the best Nick—whose last serious relationship had ended nearly a year earlier—could give them was Rip, a five-year-old collie mix named after Richard "Rip" Hamilton, the Pistons' star shooting forward.

In his head, Nick knew this move wasn't about him. But the five-year-old inside him—the little kid whose father had given him away to a friendly cop after Nick's mother was struck by a bus and killed—hated losing anything, from a silly bet to a major case. This tenaciousness worked in his favor on the job but was hell on relationships.

As was his habit, Nick hid his disquiet behind a short temper and withering scowl.

He picked up the phone and growled, "Nick Lightner."

The slight hesitation on the other end of the line put Nick's cop instincts on alert. "Oh, yes, of course," a woman's voice said. Unfamiliar, with just a hint of an accent Nick couldn't place. "I'm sorry. Your name threw me for a moment. I've always thought of you as Nikolai. Nikolai Sarna. But you would have a new name, wouldn't you?"

Tingles of apprehension raced down his spine. No one other than his parents and the attorney who'd handled the adoption in Los Angeles knew his birth name. He'd been Nicholas Lightner since the day before his sixth birthday.

"Who is this?"

"My name is Yetta Radonovic." The name meant

nothing to him. "I'm your father's cousin. Your *birth* father, I should say. Jurek Sarna. Most people know him as George. He was…is, I mean…my father's sister-in-law's nephew. That doesn't really make him my cousin, I suppose, but he's family, all the same."

Nick's mouth turned dry. He'd seen his birth certificate. His mother and father had been honest with him from the start about his adoption. Partly because they figured at five, he'd remember his past; partly because that's the kind of people they were. Up-front. Honest. Responsible. Unlike Jurek Sarna and Lucille Helson, the ex-con and the exotic dancer who had given birth to him then handed him off to another family when things turned sour.

"I don't know about your mother—I never met her—but your father was a Gypsy," Pete had told Nick when Nick asked about his past.

"Romani," Sharon had corrected. "I believe that's the proper term these days. Linguists have proved that the Romani came from western India. The name Gypsy stemmed from a mistaken impression that the people were from Egypt." Sharon was a teacher and never passed up an opportunity to share information.

Nick had no time for the past. He knew who he was—a thirty-four-year-old cop, no wife, no kids, no commitments. He lived ten miles from the house he'd grown up in. He loved his job, his dog and the Pistons. He had no interest in the hazy memories that crept into his dreams on nights when he'd had one too many beers.

He hadn't given his genealogy more than a passing thought since his eighteenth birthday when his mother suggested they try to locate his birth father. Nick had turned down her offer to help. "He didn't make any effort to keep me. He just handed me off to you. I don't have any use for a person like that."

A truly kind woman, Sharon had mentioned mitigating circumstances. "Your mother had just passed away. A tragic accident. I'm sure your father was reeling from the loss. Plus he didn't have a home or job to return to after he got out of jail. Maybe he thought he was doing you a favor by giving you to us."

Nick hadn't even tried to see her point. A decision had been made. His father had given him away. Like leftover pizza. Like a stray cat that was too much work to feed. Nick hadn't wanted to know this man sixteen years ago, and he didn't want to know him now. He assumed that was what this call was about.

"How did you get this number?" Nick asked the woman who had waited patiently while he collected his thoughts.

"From Jurek, of course. He's always had connections on both sides of the law that we don't speak about. I could be wrong, but I believe he's always known where you were."

The very notion made Nick's skin crawl.

"What's this about?"

"I...I'm not sure that calling you is the right thing to do, but Jurek said you were a policeman. Normally, that would make you...um, suspect. We Romani tend to solve our own problems without involving law enforcement."

"You don't trust cops."

"Exactly. But since you're family—"

Nick's bark caught the attention of his father, who was lifting a glass of champagne as someone toasted him.

Nick waved to signify the call wasn't anything serious. "Madam," he said, lowering his voice for maximum impact, "I am not anything to you or to the man y—"

"Of course you are," she said, interrupting him. "Just because Jurek made a bad decision thirty years ago doesn't change who you are. You're Nikolai Sarna. You're Jurek's son, which makes you half Romani. That blood runs through your veins, whether you choose to admit it or not. And right now, your Romani family needs your help."

Nick started to laugh. The woman's audacity impressed him. She sounded regal, as if used to giving orders and having people toe the line. "What kind of help? Money? I gotta tell you, I don't make enough—"

"Don't be absurd. I wouldn't call a stranger and ask for a handout, even if I were destitute. The simple fact is my youngest daughter, Grace, is in danger. She's considering entering a business relationship with a man who I'm convinced wants more than just her money. In my dream, he appeared as a snake that swallowed each member of my family whole."

A dream snake? What kind of bullshit is this? Maybe it was some kind of prank, he decided. "Where are you calling from?"

"Las Vegas. Where you were born."

He'd never denied the fact.

"On July twenty-ninth, nineteen-seventy. At four in the afternoon. I was the third person to hold you. You had such fine blond hair, I thought you were bald. My girls all had dark black hair."

Nick looked at the people grouped around his father. The plan was to move the party to The Grease Monkey, a popular watering hole where Nick's mother and the other spouses would meet them. He wasn't in the mood for a party, but at the moment it sounded better than this nonsense. "Yes, well, that's very interesting, but I'm a cop, not an exterminator and your...um, snake...is two thousand miles away from here."

His sarcasm must have come through loud and clear. She said haughtily, "Jurek warned me not to expect your cooperation. I thought twice about calling you, but in addition to this matter of Charles Harmon..."

Charles Harmon? How do I know that name?

"...a mutual friend told me that your father is entering the hospital next week for an operation. I'm sure Jurek would rather you didn't know that, but I learned the hard way that it's much healthier to clear up unresolved issues before a person dies than wait until it's—"

Nick sat up abruptly. His feet hit the floor with a snap that made several heads turn his way. "Did you say Charles Harmon?"

He pawed through the files on his desk for a fax that had come through a day or two earlier from his counterpart in Toronto.

"Yes. Grace insists he's just a friend...and, to be fair, he was my husband's lawyer when Ernst was alive. Charles also helped me handle some financial matters a few years back. But he's changed since he bought into that casino. And I've seen the way he looks at Grace—like a gambler counting his chips for some high-stakes bet."

What was that alert about? White slave trade? A possible link to an international drug... "Ha," he said, snagging the sheet from the middle of the stack.

The woman on the other end of the line made a huffing sound. "Well, if you're not interested in helping us and meeting your father before it's too late, then I'll leave you with my good wishes and say goodbye." She hesitated for a fraction of a second then added, "You've been in my prayers since the day I learned of your mother's passing, Nikolai."

The name rattled him, but Nick ignored the odd flutter in his chest. He quickly scanned the bulletin. "Wait. Hold on. I didn't say I wouldn't help."

"Yes, actually, you did."

Nick started to grin. "Well, maybe I changed my mind." He couldn't care less about his long-lost relatives, but a chance to nail a scumbag like "Lucky Chuck" Harmon was too sweet a gift to pass up. "Tell me more about your daughter and the snake."

"GRACE, GRACE, Grace, tell me you're joking."

Three Graces. Never a good thing. When her eldest sister Alex, short for Alexandra, started repeating herself, Grace Radonovic knew it was time to change the subject.

"So, what do we know about this long-lost cousin of Mom's—other than the fact that I'm supposed to pick him up at the airport in an hour?" Grace asked, cramming a too-large wedge of Danish in her mouth. "Why can't he take a taxi?" she mumbled, chewing and talking at the same time. "You know what traffic is like in February. All the snowbirds in the northern half of the country have descended on Vegas in their giant RVs."

Alex reached across their mother's faux lace tablecloth to grasp Grace's hand. "Sweetie." Her melted-

chocolate-colored eyes were filled with gravity and concern—a mixture Grace and her other sisters called Alex's preschool-teacher look. The combination always
made Grace feel about five. "Don't change the subject.
No one is knocking your ambition, but you have to be
realistic, too."

"She's right," another voice said from across the room.

Liz, short for Elizabeth. Sister number two. A true
healer, Liz was a physical therapist, who had regularly
worked in poor and war-torn countries with WorldRx,
an international medical team of volunteers. These days
she had a job at DesertWay Medical—a small private
hospital in Vegas.

"I can't believe you're even suggesting this. We're
spread too thin as is," a third voice chimed in.

This came from Katherine, or Kate, as she preferred.
Third-born, just two years older than Grace. Together,
they owned Romantique, a neo-Mediterranean restaurant located in an upscale strip mall on West Charleston Boulevard. Kate, an accomplished chef, ran the
kitchen; Grace handled the marketing and bookkeeping.

Not giving up on the hope of deflecting her sisters'
attention from her impetuous—and obviously prema-
ture—announcement, Grace said, "Delicious pastry,
Kate. Did Jo make it? Maybe we should promote her to
assistant chef. I know you're finicky about who you let
work at your side, but she does have a way with cream
cheese." She spoke so fast a bit of raspberry filling
lodged in her throat, causing her to cough.

"Don't talk with your mouth full," Alex scolded, giving Grace a look designed to stop even the most fear-
less four-year-old in his tracks. "Besides, diversion isn't

going to work. You can't casually toss out, 'Oh, by the way, I'm thinking of opening a second restaurant with Charles,' and not expect us to react."

Grace knew that. She'd planned to share her idea in full once she'd ironed out the details with Charles, but his call this morning had left her wondering if she'd made a mistake by suggesting they could do business together.

Charles Harmon was an old family friend and Grace's occasional dinner date. He was also a lawyer and part owner of the Xanadu, a small, shabby off-Strip casino where Grace had hoped to locate her new venture. She'd been in the shower when he'd called and he'd left a message asking her to drop by the casino to discuss her plan. Nothing in his tone could have been construed as ominous or threatening, but a chill had passed through her body as if she'd been dunked in Lake Mead in January.

"If you didn't want our feedback, why'd you say anything?" Liz asked, filling the electric teakettle with water. Four sisters, four beverages of choice: coffee, tea, cola and whatever strange brew Liz currently favored.

"Because…well, because you know me. I have a bad habit of speaking before I think things through, right?"

Her sisters agreed with a combination of groans and sighs.

Before any could comment, she continued. "Last week, I floated an idea past Charles. Why not remodel the Xanadu's ridiculous excuse for a coffee shop into a satellite operation of Romantique? Can't you see it as a hip bar with an exposed kitchen where Kate could really show off her stuff? I even came up with a name for it. Too Romantique."

Alex and Liz, who were six and a half and five years older than Grace, respectively, exchanged a look Grace had seen many times.

"It's a very clever name, Grace," Alex said. "But I have to go on record as being against this. I'm not comfortable with you doing business with Charles. There's something about that man that makes me nervous."

"Yeah," Grace said, snickering softly. "We know. That's why you set him on fire."

The standing joke for years had been that their father, Ernst, had brought Charles home to meet Alex, who'd accidentally dropped the cherries jubilee and singed Charles's beard. Charles had been clean shaven ever since.

"I agree with Alex," Liz said, tapping her foot as she waited for the water to boil. "You're talking major remodeling. That isn't going to be cheap. Where are you getting the seed money? I know Charles is pretty well-off, but he does have two partners. Are they game for this?"

Leave it to Liz to ask the tough questions. Everything about Liz was functional, from short-sleeved denim blue shirt with a rainbow embroidered just above her name to khaki pants and thick-soled shoes. Her shoulder-length ebony hair was pulled back in a scrunchy.

She poured boiling water over several scoops of some greenish powder resting in the bottom of a juice glass. Grace didn't bother asking what medicinal properties the concoction contained. Liz went through health fads the way some people did diets.

"Well..." Grace said, stalling. "That particular issue didn't come up. But since I'm the one who brought the idea to Charles...I thought I'd ask Mom to let me invest the money in my trust fund."

Alex groaned. Liz choked on her partially swallowed swill. Kate let out a sound of pure disgust.

"Are you nuts?" they said simultaneously.

Grace felt her cheeks burn. "Like I said, this is just in the chatting-up stage. I tossed the idea on the table last week when Charles took me to dinner. His call this morning is the first I've heard back from him. Didn't MaryAnn tell us he was wrapped up in some pro bono insurance claim business?"

MaryAnn Radonovic, their cousin Gregor's wife, had been Charles's personal secretary for just over a year. Gregor, who was Liz's age, was the girls' paternal uncle's son. In addition to being part of the family, Gregor and MaryAnn were also neighbors, living just two houses down from Yetta.

Liz blew out a sigh and turned to the sink to rinse out the green residue in her glass. "I can't vouch for the pro bono aspect of his business, but I know we've been seeing a lot of referrals from Charles's group lately at DesertWay Medical." She'd joined the staff at DWM after her ten-month sojourn in India. "But you're trying to change the subject again and it's not going to work. You know what Dad had in mind when he set up the trust accounts."

Grace knew. A wedding. As old-fashioned as it sounded, Ernst had always referred to the four trusts he and Yetta had established for their daughters as "dowries."

"Well, none of you used your trust money for that purpose. Why should I have to?" Grace asked.

She'd known the question would come up and she'd given the matter some serious thought. Alex's money had been earmarked for a wedding until her plans fell apart at the last minute. Then she'd drawn from the fund to buy a house and set up The Dancing Hippo Day Care and Pre-school. Liz's nest egg had paid for grad school, several trips abroad and the down payment on her house. Kate's money had been invested—and lost—by her scoundrel ex-husband. Only Grace's trust remained untouched.

"Listen," she said, trying to sound businesslike, "Mom has final say on how I spend the money since she's the trustee. I just thought I'd feel you guys out first. You know how distracted she's been lately."

"Boy, that's true," Alex said. "I wonder how much of that has to do with our new guest."

"Yeah," Kate said after taking a swig of Coke, which, as usual, she'd tried to disguise by putting it in a coffee mug. "I have to say I'm not wild about some stranger moving next door."

"Did anybody do an Internet search on him?" Liz asked.

"I did, and nothing came up. Nada. Which is proba-bly a good sign, right? But I still don't know why *I'm* the one picking him up," Grace said, relieved that the focus of conversation had finally shifted away from her obviously unpopular declaration.

They might not approve of her idea, but, at least, she'd managed to keep mum about the weird dreams she'd been having lately. Talk about disturbing. In one, a sinkhole opened up in the street and was slowly swal-lowing the entire neighborhood. Grace was frantically trying to talk Kate out of her car, which was slipping trunk first, down the hole, when a stranger grabbed Grace from behind and pulled her to safety. She'd awoken, heart pumping and breathless—not because of the catastrophe but because of the stranger. She came from a long line of Gypsy fortune-tellers and she knew one thing: Strangers were never a good omen.

CHAPTER TWO

Y<small>ETTA</small> R<small>ADONOVIC</small> <small>PAUSED</small> just outside the threshold of her kitchen, where she'd been listening to her daughters' weekly breakfast summit. Eavesdropping, she'd learned, was by far the best way to find out what was going on in her family.

"The reason you're meeting Nikolai's plane, Grace, is because Elizabeth is taking me shopping," she said, walking into the room. Her daughters all stopped what they were doing to look at her. "Alexandra has a doctor's appointment and Katherine will be busy preparing a feast to welcome Nikolai."

Her daughters. Her four beauties. Each a unique individual with her own strengths and weaknesses. Of course, Ernst had never believed his princesses were anything but perfect. For a smart man, he could turn a blind eye to the truth when it suited him, she thought, frowning. *And, now, we might all pay the price for that foolishness.*

"Mom's right, Grace," Elizabeth said after greeting Yetta with a smile. "You're the logical choice and it would seem kinda cold not to meet his plane."

Her second-born daughter rarely passed up a chance to help others, although those altruistic tendencies had changed since Liz's last trip to Eastern Europe. Yetta had yet to get to the bottom of that, but she pushed the thought aside. She had more pressing issues to worry about at the moment.

"Besides, aren't you the one who was carrying on the other night about our need for new blood in the family?" Katherine chimed in. "Like we were a vampire cult or something."

"I was only making an observation," Grace said stiffly. "Mom, tell them. In olden days, four unmarried daughters would have been considered a liability. It would have been our duty to marry strong, wealthy men with big oxen."

Even Yetta had to laugh at that, although she didn't feel much like smiling. Her most recent dream had been vivid, if not easily interpreted. One of her daughters had been in great danger. Help from the outside was their only hope, even if that meant keeping secrets from her girls. She only hoped they'd forgive her when the truth came out. As it would.

"Oh, Grace, you are too much," Alexandra said with a laugh. Yetta looked at her eldest daughter with pride. Others might have given up or turned bitter after being cheated out of the life they had planned. Not Alex. But such bravery came at a price.

"Yeah," Elizabeth agreed. "No offense, but when it comes right down to it, we're descended from a group of nomadic wayfarers who were in the wrong place at the wrong time and wound up spending several centuries being slaves."

Grace looked at Yetta and sighed. "They're hopeless, aren't they? Tell them, Mom. You're the one who's imported a long-lost family member from Detroit. This guy must have something special going for him if we're letting him move in next door."

Oh, he had *something*. He had a badge and a gun and the right connections to local law enforcement. But for Nikolai's safety, her daughters would need to remain unaware of his true identity and his reason for coming to Las Vegas. At least, until the threat to the family had been eliminated. Then Yetta hoped Nikolai would make peace with the past and her daughters would understand her need for secrecy.

"Nikolai was lost to us as a child," Yetta said, recalling Jurek's suggestion that she stick as close to the truth as possible. "I've hoped for years that he might return to us. And now that he is coming back, I expect you to do whatever it takes to make him feel welcome."

Yetta waited for someone to speak. She knew her strident tone probably surprised them, but she'd been muffled by grief long enough. She blamed herself for the current state of disharmony within her family, and she'd taken steps to rectify the situation. She only hoped she wasn't too late.

Alexandra cleared her throat and said, "I might be a few minutes late to lunch. I have an appointment with my ob-gyn this morning." A sudden presence—fear—entered the room. "Just routine," she added, with the barest quiver in her voice.

Yetta walked to the cupboard so no one would see her face. Alexandra had been the first to disappear in her dream. Not swallowed by the snake, like the others, she'd simply faded away. Almost as if she'd never existed. At no time in her life had Yetta felt so impotent and frustrated, not even as she'd watched her beloved husband give up on life. She refused to lose another member of her family. And, though she doubted she could make her daughters—or Nikolai, for that matter— understand, Nikolai's arrival signified hope.

Grace concentrated on folding her napkin into a perfect triangle. Alex put on a brave face, but Grace knew that her sister was worried. For months now, Alex had been experiencing severe pain and nausea around the time she was ovulating. Six years earlier, she'd undergone surgery to remove a cyst on her ovary. The relatively routine procedure had been a success but Alex had developed a serious infection at the wound site. Now she dreaded the thought of another surgery, but the possibility was all too real.

As her sisters debated whether women made better ob-gyns than men, Grace thought about her current dilemma. Did she dare gamble on a second restaurant? Her instincts said yes.

In just two years of business, Kate and Grace had turned a profit with their restaurant, a feat most had claimed was impossible. Kate's reputation was steadily growing, but the only way for a chef to play in the big leagues in Vegas was to move closer to the heart and soul of the tourist industry: The Strip.

The Xanadu offered that possibility.

The only impasse to her plan, as far as Grace was concerned, was Charles. Lately, he'd been acting differently. And the last time they'd dined together he'd seemed a little too attentive. Almost as if he was interested in taking their friendship to some other level.

Grace didn't understand why, since there'd never

been even a hint of *sizzle* between them. Plus, as Charles knew, she was on a hiatus from romance.

Thanks to Shawn Bascomb. Her first love…and first heartbreak.

Shawn. Drop-dead gorgeous snowboard instructor and white-water raft guide. Free spirit. A Prince-Charming-in-the-making just waiting for Grace's love to bring out the hero in him. Or so she'd convinced herself. Only after Kate revealed that Shawn had cheated on Grace several times during their relationship had Grace been able to admit that shoulder-length dreads and well-defined muscles were his most charming attributes.

In part, Grace blamed her mother for Shawn. Yetta had filled Grace's head with nonsense at the impressionable age of ten. "You're going to marry an honorable man who doesn't know he's a prince. Your love, Grace, will help him find his true self."

Had Grace believed this? With all her heart. After all, her beloved father put complete faith in her mother's visions, so why shouldn't Grace?

And she had. Until recently…

Grace studied her mother as she moved around the sunny, east-facing kitchen. Petite and fine boned like Liz and Kate, Yetta was a study in contrasts. Shoeless, yet dressed in a tan, Anne Klein business suit with a skirt that stopped an inch below her knees, she seemed a regal peasant. The dull fabric was offset by the vivid scarlet, gold and teal of her flowery blouse, which wasn't tucked in. Her lush silver hair fell well past her shoulders.

"Are you hungry, Mom?" Liz asked. "Grace—the pig—left you a small piece of pastry."

Grace dabbed at the corners of her mouth with her folded napkin to prove her sister's dig didn't bother her.

Yetta waved away the suggestion. "I ate hours ago with Maya. She helped me organize the seating chart for the luncheon today. I want Nikolai to meet everyone."

Maya was Kate's daughter, who'd turned four a few days earlier. Grace glanced at Kate, who had complained to Grace only yesterday that Maya spent more time with her grandmother than she did with Kate. Grace had tried to be sympathetic, but mostly she was relieved to see Yetta returning to her old self. If hanging out with Maya helped, then Grace was all for it.

The family was fast approaching the second anniversary of Ernst Radonovic's death. For the better part of a year after he passed away, Yetta could barely bring herself to leave her bed before two in the afternoon. She'd wander around between television talk shows and games of solitaire on the coffee table in the living room—sitting in the chair Ernst had favored.

Grace missed her father and visited his grave often, but she hadn't been allowed the luxury of disappearing into her grief while the world spun around her. She immediately felt guilty about her mean-spirited thought. Her mother was starting to come out of her fog and some of that renewed energy had to be credited to Nikolai Sarna's impending arrival. Grace wasn't sure she understood why it had taken a stranger to lure her mother out of her depression.

As if reading Grace's thoughts, Kate said, "You're

making quite a fuss about this guy, Mom. He's not visiting royalty, is he?"

"He's family," Yetta replied. "He's six months younger than Alexandra. I took care of him when his mother first went back to work. She was a dancer."

"A dancer? Really? What kind?" Alex asked. Back when the Sisters of the Silver Dollar—as Grace and her siblings had called their amateur dance troupe—had performed for their father, Alex had been the best.

Yetta peered into her mug, as if the answer were to be found in the chamois-colored liquid. "It was a long time ago. Lucy was very beautiful. Long legs and blond hair. All the men in the compound fell in love with her."

"Even Dad?" Grace knew her sisters were thinking the same thing, although none of the others voiced the question.

"No. Ernst was too busy with his job and his beautiful new daughter," Yetta answered, giving Alex a tender smile. "And he had his hands full keeping Jurek—Nikolai's father—out of jail, as well." She shook her head sadly. "Trouble followed that man like a worthless dog."

"Are you talking about George?" Alex asked. "He's the one you just went to visit in Laughlin, right? Didn't you tell me he spent time in a Nazi concentration camp?"

Yetta nodded. "Jurek changed his name to George when he came to America, but he's always been Jurek to me."

"How come we've never met this guy?" Grace asked.

"He's pretty much kept to himself. Except when he first married Nikolai's mother. If things had been different…" Yetta's voice melded into a sigh. "Well, it's his way."

"It's not the Romani way," Grace insisted. "What turned him into a hermit?"

After a slight hesitation, Yetta said, "Shortly after I was born…back in the old country…there was a fire in our family's camp. Jurek was partly to blame. As punishment, he was sent to live with his grandmother. His mother was Polish, not Romani. His father was my uncle's wife's nephew."

Grace tried to picture their family tree but gave up when her mother went on with the story. "A few months later, Hitler invaded Poland." Yetta shook her head sadly. "The Americans liberated the camp where he was held, and, eventually, the Red Cross helped him reach New York where my family had settled. My parents invited him to live with us, but he was practically an adult by then. He took a job in Atlantic City instead."

She looked around the table. "Jurek has never asked for a thing from this family, but his health is not the best. I'm afraid if we miss this chance to reunite him with his son, we won't be given another."

Grace understood. She even felt sympathy for both men, but she was uneasy, too. Last night in her dream, the stranger who'd rescued her had held her gently and whispered the most intoxicating promises in her ear. Safety. Security. Hope. Grace hadn't felt any of those things since her father died.

"That's a nice sentiment, Mom, but how do we know the son is an okay guy? He could be a hit man for all we know," Kate said.

Grace looked at Alex, who made a face. Everyone knew that Kate's trust in men was below zero, but this quantum leap sounded extreme, even for Kate.

Yetta made a dismissing motion with her hand. "Well, he's not. You'll just have to take my word. I'm still the matriarch of this family and I do have some say in how it's run."

Grace's jaw dropped in shock. She hadn't heard her mother use that tone in years. Possibly not since her father's stroke.

"Grace will meet Nikolai's plane then we'll all welcome him at a family luncheon today. Is that understood?"

Grace didn't look at her sisters. "Sure—" she started to say, but before she could get the word out, a child's voice echoed from the hallway. "Gramma, Gramma."

A moment later, Maya danced into the kitchen, dragging a Dora The Explorer backpack. Kate's choice of husband may have been questionable, but at least, she had Maya to show for her ill-fated marriage. Born ten months before Ernst's first stroke, the baby girl had been the ray of hope that helped the family look ahead.

"Good morning, Maya," Liz said.

"Hola, bambina," Alex chimed in, extending her arms to the child.

Kate beamed with obvious parental pride and love as she watched the curly-haired cherub who, Grace thought, held the wisdom of ages in her huge black eyes, hug her aunts. After bestowing kisses to all, the little girl finally made it to her mother, who was sitting with her back to the window. "Are you ready to go to school, baby love?"

"Si, Mommy." Maya was a sponge. She never seemed to forget a thing. When told that she couldn't enter preschool until she was potty-trained, she'd replied, "Okay." And that was the last time she'd used a

diaper. "Great-Uncle Claude and MaryAnn are coming to walk me. Do you wanna come, too?"

Grace wasn't sure if this was something that had been arranged earlier or if Maya was offering a prediction. Although Kate refused to admit the possibility, occasionally Maya would say something that made everyone wonder if she'd inherited her grandmother's well-recognized ability to foresee the future.

"There he is."

The shout made Grace's ears ring. She looked at the open screen door where Claude, their father's younger brother, was standing. At sixty-eight, Claude still seemed childlike in many ways, probably because of his short stature. His big ears and ready smile made him popular with children.

Grace remembered her father saying Claude was a throwback to the little people. A reference to spoken lore that linked the Romani ancestry to the Celts, although Grace knew that the original Gypsy lineage started in Asia when Turkish invaders pushed the tribespeople from their lands in northwest India. Over the centuries, the various lines had broken apart and become absorbed by other cultures.

Her family called themselves Roms or Romani, but in fact that connection had weakened over the years. Grace had researched her family's genealogy, but she'd always sensed an unspoken rule that said the information was best not shared with strangers.

"Are you accompanying us, Alexandra?"

Claude's tone was formal, appropriate for addressing a princess, as Ernst had dubbed his daughters.

"Not this morning, Uncle," Alex said, shaking her head.

Her short, thick, nearly black waves were a feature Grace had always coveted. Of all the girls, Alex most resembled their father. Blue-black hair and thick brows that had troubled her no end until she'd discovered laser treatments.

Tall and thin, with a milky-white complexion, Alex was gorgeous—although Grace could tell she was in pain. "I have a doctor's appointment. Rita is covering for me, but I meant to ask if you'd help out at story time."

Uncle Claude was as gifted a storyteller as their father had been. In some ways, he was even more entertaining than Ernst because he was smaller and more nimble. "I'd be delighted to do so. And after lunch perhaps Maya could join us at the ranch?"

Claude's eldest son and his wife owned a small acreage west of town near Red Rocks where Claude raised and trained Shetland ponies.

Kate and her daughter were still discussing the matter when someone knocked on the door leading to the garage. Liz opened it. "Hi, MaryAnn," she said. "Come in."

Grace studied the woman in the ill-fitting business suit who stood on the stoop but didn't cross the threshold. MaryAnn was literally the girl next door. Six months younger than Alex, MaryAnn had been around for as long as Grace could remember. In the background at parties. A friend. Not quite a part of the family—until she married Gregor.

"Hello," MaryAnn said, fiddling with the waistband of her navy-blue polyester skirt. Unbuttoned, Grace noticed. MaryAnn was always on a diet, but nothing seemed to help her lose weight. "Are you ready, Maya? Luca and Gemilla are waiting outside."

Her children were eight and four and a half. Luca rode the bus to school, but he started his day at The

Dancing Hippo since MaryAnn left for work before his regular school started.

"Are you coming to lunch today, MaryAnn?" Yetta asked, helping Maya into her backpack.

MaryAnn looked startled by the question. "Oh," she exclaimed. "I almost forgot. Things have been so busy. But, yes, I think I can make it."

"Was Charles invited?" Grace asked. The idea made her oddly uncomfortable. She didn't know why. He was often included in family gatherings.

That was before you decided to go into business with him, a voice said.

Yetta started to answer, but MaryAnn interrupted. "I don't know, but he has a prior commitment."

She didn't expound on the statement. At times Mary-Ann acted a bit proprietary where Charles was concerned. At other times, she almost seemed to loathe him.

"No problem," Grace said. "He left a message asking to see me today, and I figured if he was going to be at the luncheon, I wouldn't bother stopping by the Xanadu after I pick up our guest of honor."

MaryAnn looked at her intently. "Charles called you? About what?"

"Some business we've been discussing," Grace said evasively. The last thing she wanted was to bring that topic back to the table. "But it's really no big deal. I'll be at McCarran, anyway."

MaryAnn didn't respond. Instead, she turned to Maya and said, a bit sharply, "Hurry up, Maya. You don't want to miss circle, do you?"

Grace watched as her niece dashed away, eager to join her cousins. Once the entire group was out of ear-shot, she said, "Is it just me or does anyone else think MaryAnn is losing it?"

"Well, she's married to the laziest man in town," Kate said. "And he has a gambling problem."

Liz gave Kate a stern look. "Actually, MaryAnn told me Greg's been very good about not visiting the casinos lately and he's been working for Charles for a good six months. But I do think you're right, Grace. MaryAnn has seemed kind of spacey lately."

"Personally, I think she's in over her head as Charles's personal assistant," Alex put in. "I warned her not to take a job with him, but she said the money was too good to pass up. And his company offers great benefits."

"Speaking of benefits," Grace said, snapping her fingers, "did you find out whether your new insurance will cover another operation? If you need one, that is."

"No. Because I'm not going to have one. Period," she said, taking a sip from her mug. Grace could tell by the little square label that dangled over the side that the beverage was green tea. "And speaking of Charles, we never finished discussing your plans."

Grace made a face. Talk about a blatant change of subject.

Charles had been involved with their family for so long that she tended to regard him as a fixture, but Alex and Charles had a different kind of relationship, probably stemming from Alex's rejection of him. Plus, Grace had to admit, Charles could come off as quite pompous and self-involved at times. Still, she felt obligated to defend him—in case their new business worked out. "Must you always say his name with such obvious bias? Charles has always been pretty generous about helping out any Romani who got in trouble with the law or needed a job."

Liz let out a long sigh. "I agree, but can't we show our gratitude without risking your trust fund?"

Yetta frowned. "What does Grace's dowry have to do with Charles Harmon?" When nobody answered right away, she added, "If you're suggesting that Grace might marry Charles, you're very much mistaken."

"No, Mom, that's not part of the discussion," Grace said, giving her sister a dirty look.

Before she could say anything else, Yetta nodded. "Good. Because Charles Harmon is many things, but he is *not* a prince."

The room went so still Grace could hear the low drone of a television in one of the bedrooms. Her stomach felt queasy—and she knew it wasn't from too many pastries. She was embarrassed for her mother. Although no one wanted to hurt Yetta's feelings, the fact was none of them believed in their prophecies anymore.

Too much had happened to undermine their faith. First, Yetta had had no premonition whatsoever of Ernst's stroke. Second, she'd insisted that Mark was Alex's soul mate. Mark Gaylord—a gaujo cop who'd broken Alex's heart when he'd gotten his partner pregnant and married her instead of Alex. Then, there was the matter of Yetta's blind faith in Ian Grant, Kate's ex-husband, who went to jail for embezzlement.

Nope, Grace thought, the future was a murky, unexplored vastness where anything could happen. She wasn't about to pin her dreams on some iffy, unproven prince who needed her help to find his nobility. She planned to put her money on something more tangible. Charles didn't set Grace's heart atwitter, but he did have something she coveted: location, location, location.

CHAPTER THREE

NICK LIGHTNER CLOSED his eyes and let his head tip back against the padded headrest. After his call from Yetta, it had taken the powers that be a week to set up his cover story and necessary connections, but this morning he'd left snowy Detroit behind and was on his way to Vegas. Flying wasn't his favorite means of travel, and his sore calves and aching shoulder muscles didn't appreciate the cramped space of coach.

He'd spent the previous day repairing a thirty-foot section of fence in his parents' backyard that had succumbed to high winds and too much snow. The ground was all but impenetrable and the single-digit windchill factor hadn't made the task any easier, but Nick had finally managed to make the enclosure escape-proof. He hoped.

Rip was a good dog, but turned wily when left alone too long. Normally, Nick's parents jumped at the chance to dog-sit, and they'd insisted Rip stay with them while Nick was in Vegas, but Nick had been tempted to board Rip at the vet. He didn't want to do anything to add to his dad's stress level.

Although Pete hadn't advertised the fact, one reason for his sudden decision to retire had been a cautionary medical report. "Slow down or your body will slow you down in a way you aren't going to like," his doctor had told him.

That was another reason Nick was against his parents' radical move. That and the fact he hated change. Period. His mother blamed this on abandonment issues he'd never completely resolved, but Nick disagreed. He'd had an extremely stable childhood. He simply liked things to stay the same. What was wrong with that?

But his parents had made their decision. Oregon—and their grandchildren—beckoned. They'd expressed a hope to have the house on the market by the time Nick returned from Vegas.

Nick's stomach made a low, rumbling sound. Airplane food, he figured, sitting up a bit straighter. To get his mind off home, he put on his headphones and turned on the small tape recorder he'd brought with him. The Las Vegas Metropolitan Police Department, or Metro, was already investigating Harmon for insurance fraud. Internal Affairs had been called into the picture because of allegations that several police officers were suspected of filing false or inflated accident reports and taking kickbacks from the insurance adjusters who were on the take from Harmon. When informed of Nick's "insider" status, they'd whipped up a covert plan to get Nick close to Harmon's inner circle.

Nick hadn't expected to be asked to do more than provide a contact number for Yetta Radonovic, but then his father had intervened. Pete saw this as Nick's avenue to promotion, and he'd contacted an old buddy of his on the Metro force. Zeke Martini, who'd dealt with the tight-knit Romani community in the past, had been happy to welcome Nick aboard.

"The insurance fraud is just the tip of the iceberg where Lucky Chuck is concerned," Zeke had told Nick on the phone. "Your primary goal will be to identify the dirty cops who are facilitating these phony accidents, but I want you to keep your eyes open for any evidence of money laundering, drug deals or white slave traffic."

Zeke's voice was one of two on the tape Nick was listening to now. The other belonged to an assistant district attorney.

"Harmon is smooth," the A.D.A. said. "Never been caught with his fingers in the till, but he's been mentioned as a 'person of interest' going back ten years."

Martini's gruff bass added, "Probably studied the law so he'd know the best way to break it without getting caught."

"That type always makes a mistake sooner or later. And getting cops to do his dirty work was a very bad idea."

"But he's kept himself pretty well insulated in the past," Zeke added. "That's where Pete's boy comes in."

Nick almost smiled. He hadn't been a boy in many, many years. Maybe never. That's what happened when your mother died and your dad handed you off to strangers, who, though kind and welcoming, couldn't completely erase the sadness and sense of loss.

Even after his move to Michigan, certain memories followed. Elusive images of laughter and music in the warm glow of firelight. Figures dancing. The rapturous feeling of being enveloped by warm loving arms.

His brain insisted a baby wouldn't retain anything from birth to almost three, which is how old he was when his parents left Vegas for Los Angeles. But his recurring dream was strangely seductive; it made him curious about his paternal relatives.

In an effort to keep the focus on his reason for flying to Vegas, Nick opened his eyes and started to leaf through the material he'd brought with him. The more he learned about Charles Harmon, the less he bought Harmon's squeaky-clean image.

Although he didn't talk about it, Nick had a sort of sixth sense about certain people that was almost never wrong. His dad had taught him not to say anything that could be construed as suspect profiling, but Nick still trusted his gut instinct when it came to reading people.

Nick's mother speculated that his gift came from his Romani heritage, but Nick knew it was something even simpler. In Nick's world, everything came down to trust. And he only trusted himself.

He picked up a second photograph in the file. Grace Philippa Radonovic. Age twenty-eight. College graduate with a degree in business. Restaurant owner. Single. Living at home. Two speeding tickets before she turned twenty. Three minor fender benders.

Those were the facts, but they told him little. Her picture was another matter. Hair a cascade of loose, highlighted brown waves that framed her heart-shaped face, brows a bit too bushy to be fashionable, large dark eyes. Brown, according to the fact sheet, but Nick would have called them tawny. A nicely shaped nose that fit her face.

His gut said *civilian*. But something about this woman triggered a reaction he couldn't quite read. It made him uncomfortable, which meant he needed to be on high alert once he stepped off the plane. Because, according to Yetta Radonovic, Grace would be picking him up at the airport.

As if on cue, the large jet touched down with a screeching jolt.

"Please wait until the airplane has come to a complete stop…."

Nick couldn't wait. He pulled his carry-on bag from underneath the seat in front and dug in the side pocket until he found his phone. As soon as the flight attendant announced that passengers were free to use electronic devices, he flipped it open and said, "Dad's cell."

While he waited for Pete to answer, the seat-belt light was extinguished. Nick stood up and reached into the overhead bin for his coat, which he shrugged on while juggling his phone.

The line hummed, unanswered. This would be Nick's last public call using his phone. Zeke and Pete had agreed that in keeping with Nick's cover story—jobless ex-con who needed a leg up in a new town—he shouldn't carry a cell phone.

"Pete Lightner. Leave a message."

The passengers near the front of the plane began to disembark. Nick looped the webbed strap of his carry-on bag over one shoulder and followed. "I just landed. You forgot to give me Zeke's contact number. You're slipping, old man." He added a chuckle so his father would know he was kidding. "Well, if Zeke's half the cop you said he is, he'll find me, I guess. Talk to you later. Give Mom a hug for me. And tell Rip I said to behave."

He pocketed the phone and marched up a gangplank into an open, brightly lit terminal.

"Holy shit," he softly exclaimed, taking in the neon, the glitter and, most remarkable of all, the slot machines. "I'm not in Michigan anymore, am I?"

Moving out of the way of hurrying passengers, he rested his tote on the back of a bench and buried the small phone deep in the cheap canvas bag. In his closet back home sat matching leather luggage. Those he'd agreed to leave behind, but his leather flight jacket was another matter. He loved his coat. It felt like a second skin after three winters in Detroit. If anyone asked, he'd tell them he got it at a consignment store.

Nick followed the signs to the luggage area. While he walked, he looked around—curious about this town where he'd been born. He knew nothing of Las Vegas, except what he'd seen in the movies. Several of his buddies made annual pilgrimages to Nevada casinos, but Nick preferred tropical beaches or cities that interested him, like New York, New Orleans and San Francisco. If asked to join his pals in Vegas, his standard answer was "Sin City? Are you nuts?"

Except for the shadowy images in his dreams, he had no tangible memories of Vegas or the Romani community that he'd apparently been born into. All he knew about his early years is what his parents had told him: "Your mother was killed in an accident and your father was so grief stricken he wasn't able to care for you anymore, so he generously let you come and be our little boy. *Adoption* is another word for chosen."

Nick couldn't remember if he'd bought that line at the time or not, but when Judy, who was the Lightners' natural child, told him the *real* story behind his adoption, Nick had believed her unequivocally. "Your parents were Gypsies. They stole you from your birth family and when they got tired of you, they left you on my parents' doorstep. Mommy and Daddy felt sorry for you so they let you stay with us, but someday the Gypsies are coming back. They're going to sneak into your room some night and take you away. That's what Gypsies do."

From that point on, Nick had refused to go to sleep without a light on and he'd suffered terrible nightmares for years. The family's move to Detroit had helped. Nick liked Detroit and had felt reasonably safe from the threat of his past catching up with him.

Until last week.

Over the years, Nick had met other adopted kids. Many had expressed a need to find their birth parents. Not Nick. Although mildly curious about his mother, he hadn't even looked into the circumstances surrounding her death. But from the reading he'd done to prepare himself for this role, he'd learned that family was extremely important to the Romani. If that was so, he wondered, then why hadn't any member of his birth family intervened when his father had given him up?

Not that he planned to ask Yetta when he saw her. But, he had to admit he was curious about her so-called second sight. They'd talked twice on the phone since her initial call. Each time, she'd opened up a little more about her abilities.

"I used to feel more confident about my gift," she'd told him last night. "But after my husband died, my brain turned fuzzy. Like someone had dropped a blanket over my head. I could see images, but couldn't make sense of them.

"I thought my gift was gone, but Elizabeth explained that the pills the doctor gave me—antidepressant pills, I believe they were called—somehow disconnected me from the person I know myself to be. I'm feeling stronger now, and the visions are starting to return."

"A vision," Nick had repeated. "That whole snake thing, right? You're sticking with that story?"

"Nikolai," she'd scolded, although her tone was indulgent, "you didn't grow up Romani or you'd understand. In this case, you're just going to have to take my word for it. Charles has something my Grace wants, which has made her blind to the danger he presents."

"He's a scumbag. She has to be more than blind to consider going into business with him."

Yetta had been quick to defend her daughter. "If you're implying that Grace is somehow involved in any wrongdoing, you're completely off base. Charles is wealthy, handsome and successful. Grace isn't the only one who can't see beneath the facade that he shows in public. Blackness is more than the absence of light, you know."

No, Nick didn't know what the hell she was talking about, but he was going to find out. That was his job. And in a few minutes, he'd meet the first of four "princesses."

Alexandra, Elizabeth, Katherine and Grace, he repeated from memory. Yetta's late husband must have been some kind of egomaniac.

As he entered the large, noisy baggage claim area, he looked around for his *royal* cousin. The Lightners didn't have much extended family. Pete was an only child whose parents had died within a few years of each other when Nick was a toddler. Sharon had two sisters but wasn't particularly close to either. Nick's aunt Emily lived a mere six or seven miles away from his childhood home, but he only saw her once or twice a year. Her children, who were all older than Nick and Judy, were virtual strangers to him.

A voice on the speaker announced where passengers from his flight could find their suitcases. Nick hung back from the milling crowd to scan the room once more. Maybe she wasn't going to show up. Maybe she was late. Maybe she planned to pick him up curbside.

He'd just taken a few steps when he heard a voice call, "Um, hello? Excuse me? Are you by any chance Nikolai Sarna?"

The name sounded strange to his ears, but he turned to look. The woman from the photo. Same large, slightly rounded eyes—a warm brown, as he'd guessed. She was a bit taller than he'd pictured, but then he looked down and saw four-inch heels. Her hair was artfully streaked with strands of gold and copper. The colors brought out the tan in her complexion.

She was beautiful in a way he couldn't describe. All Nick knew was that her photograph didn't do her justice.

"It is you, isn't it?" she asked, smiling.

Her smile produced a gut-level response that took him completely by surprise. What the hell was this about? a part of him wondered. So she's pretty. Get over it. She could be evil, too. Don't forget, if she isn't part of Chucky's scam she's exceedingly stupid for getting involved with a criminal, right?

"Mother said to look for tall, dark and blond. An oxymoron, of course. But, now I see what she meant. You do have a certain dark brooding quality despite the blond hair. Sort of Heathcliff meets Surfer Boy."

"I beg your pardon?" He tried to keep his tone neutral, but she made a face that a parent might give a child who's just scraped his knee. She put her hand on the sleeve of his leather coat. "Oh, dear, I've offended you.

I'm sorry. Didn't mean to, of course. I babble. It's what I do when I'm harried. And I just got flack from the parking guard. You'd think this was a maximum-security prison." She gave him a mortified look and her cheeks flushed. "Another inane thing to say. Can I start over?"

Nick nodded because she seemed to expect it.

She pivoted on one heel and walked three steps away then turned dramatically, held up her hand as if just spotting him and called, "Hello. Is that you, Nikolai? It's me, Grace, your father's mother's second cousin twice removed…or something. Here to pick you up and bring you back into the fold."

He knew she was only pretending. This was just a joke to her. But the words connected with a place he never liked to acknowledge. In that place there lived a little boy who believed he'd been handed over to strangers because his mommy and daddy didn't want him anymore. Tiny shards of glass pricked along his sinuses. *Cry? Me? Are you out of your mind?* a voice in his head shouted.

Nick's only recourse was to turn away and march to the baggage claim where he spotted his pathetic, secondhand-store suitcase. Most of his fellow passengers had long since escaped. Only one elderly woman was still at the moving ramp, wrestling with a much too large trunk.

Nick let his beat-up Samsonite weekender continue on its journey while he hoisted the woman's old-fashioned steamer trunk off the carousel. "Can I call you a porter, ma'am?"

She gave him a grateful smile. "Thank you, but no. My grandson is coming for me. He's always late, but he'll be here. He knows his mother will take away his car if he doesn't show," she said, winking one watery blue eye.

He nodded then caught up with his bag before it could disappear again. When he turned around to look for Grace, he found her still in the same spot, her expression misty.

He approached her warily. "What's wrong?"

"That was so sweet," she said. "I'm a soft touch for kindness. Although I have to say, at first glance, I wouldn't have pegged you as the type to help an old woman in need. I'm impressed."

The last was said with a saucy wink that told him she was kidding, but to Nick's ire a swift, silly rush of pleasure coursed through him. He let out a warning growl. "I'm nobody's hero. Don't forget it."

She made a moue with her plump pink lips. "Ooh, I stand corrected. Well, if you're ready we can go. Although you might want to lose the leather jacket. This is the desert. We probably have four or five days a year that would warrant a heavy coat like that. Today isn't one of them."

Her clothing seemed to support her point. Her short black skirt was made of some material that looked like leather and adhered to her shapely butt and thighs. Above that she wore a relatively demure sweater with sleeves that stopped just below her elbows. Black and white. Her purse and shoes were fire-engine-red.

"Not that the coat doesn't look great on you," she said, giving him a toe-to-head perusal. "Wait till Kate sees you. She already thinks you might be a mob hit man, and you do look the part."

Nick's antennae went up. As part of his manufactured bio, they'd alluded to underground connections and a history of violence in and out of prison, but surely, Katherine wouldn't have access to that kind of information.

"So, is this really all your luggage?" she asked. "Wow, talk about traveling light. I thought Mom said you were moving here permanently?"

"You've got stores, don't you?"

"Tons," she said with an effusive gesture. "I just heard the other day that Vegas had surpassed New York as the current shopping mecca. Art, jewelry, fashion—if you can afford it, you can get it here."

With that, she turned and started off. Motioning for him to follow, she said, "It's a bit of a hike. I apologize, but it's not my fault. Some guy in a Hummer cut me off, and I pulled into the wrong parking lot by mistake and they wouldn't let me change without paying. Which just isn't right, is it?"

She went on without waiting for Nick's answer, which was a good thing since he was having a hard time keeping his mind on her story and off her legs.

"It's not the money, it's the principle. And I firmly believe in sticking up for your principles…unless you're wearing four-inch heels. If I'd known I was going to have to walk a mile, I'd have worn different shoes."

Nick was glad she'd picked the shoes she had on. They showcased her great calves and ankles. Shapely. Not pencil thin like the models in the magazines. This woman had substance. Hips that made him want to run his hand from her waist to her… *Good Lord, I'm lusting after a perfect stranger, who could be a suspect.* He frowned.

Grace had stopped to extract her keys from her shiny red handbag and was scrutinizing him. She hesitated as if debating something, then told him, "A word of advice. Personally, I think that dark, squinty look is rather sexy, but my sister, Alex, runs a day-care center and there are always a lot of kids around the compound where you're going to be staying. So you might want to tone it down when we get home. Alex will hurt you if you scare Maya, my niece, or any of her friends."

Nick gave her a look that always worked on junkies, informants and crooks. Grace's eyes widened. Her bottom lip disappeared for a moment then she put her hand to her chest and laughed.

"Brilliant," she said shaking her head. "Oh, my, that was Dirty Harry and then some. Kate's going to love you. She's big on wilting glares, too."

With that, she marched away. "Do you mind if we hurry?" she called over her shoulder. "I have to make a quick stop at the Xanadu before your welcome-home lunch. And I thought we'd take the long way around so you can see some of the sights."

Welcome-home lunch? Nick's stomach lurched until his cop sense zeroed in on the first part of her statement. Xanadu was the name of the small casino that Charles owned an interest in.

In one of his e-mails, Zeke wrote that he felt Chuck was positioning himself to buy out his partners so he could introduce a more "exotic" venue for guests, one that included sex for hire.

"What's the Xanadu? A bar? I could use a drink."

"It's a casino. Just off the Strip. My friend is part owner." She stopped suddenly and looked at him. "You know what? Charles might give you a job. He has a number of family members working for him. My uncle, my cousin, my cousin's wife. In fact, MaryAnn is his personal secretary. I should have asked her this morning if she knew of any openings in personnel."

"Would he hire an ex-con?"

Her smile seemed so compassionate, she reminded him of his mother, who only saw possibilities whenever she looked at a student. "Absolutely. MaryAnn's husband, Gregor, has had a couple of brushes with the law. Nothing terrible, but not the kind of thing a potential employer would necessarily welcome. Charles put Greg right to work when he opened his insurance center. Most of the work is pro bono, but he pays Gregor very well."

Pro bono? She actually believes that? He could tell she did, because she launched into a discourse about how an insurance company had made life more difficult for her family after her father's stroke. She apparently thought Harmon was some kind of saint who looked out for the little guy when insurance companies tried to bully a victim into settling for less than a claim was worth. Was Harmon that good an actor? Or was she the most gullible woman he'd ever met?

Nick figured he'd find out soon enough.

CHAPTER FOUR

"JUST RELAX, George. This will be over in a minute. We'll take the tissue sample and get out of here."

George. The gaujos, or non-Romani, all called him George. Only Yetta still used his given name: Jurek.

He closed his eyes and tried to picture Yetta. The image helped block his doctor's voice, the bright lights and antiseptic environment of the outpatient operating room. The drugs they'd given him that morning had helped take the edge off his fear, but they couldn't keep him from remembering.

Facedown on a table exposed to the steady hand of a man he barely knew was a bad, bad thing, a voice said.

A bead of sweat materialized along the neckline of his paper gown. *This man is my doctor. I trust him.*

But when it came to trusting others, Jurek didn't. He'd learned at a very young age not to put his faith in anyone.

In a few months—if he lived that long—Jurek would turn seventy-five. The vast majority of those years had been shaped by one childhood lapse in judgment. Guilt—not cancer—was now eating his guts from the inside out. He'd paid dearly for his mistake, first, at the hands of the Nazis, then through his own weakness and stupidity. Now, the finishing touch would come courtesy of an insidious disease that his body had chosen to host.

"This looks encouraging, George. These polyps aren't pretty and we're taking tissue samples, but it's not as bad as we feared."

Liar. Doctors were good at telling you what you wanted to hear. His doctor, a specialist, was stalling. When the lab reports came back, he would sing a different song. He would say, "I was wrong, George. I'm sorry. You were right. The Nazi doctors did plant a tiny cancerous seed deep in your bowels when they worked on you. Like one of those time-release pills you see in commercials, it was just waiting to erupt. And, now, it's too late to do anything about it. You're dying, my friend."

Jurek closed his eyes and blocked out the sounds of the machines, the ventilation system, and the nurses moving about. He stopped feeling the external stimuli and went to the one place that provided sanctuary— home. The camp where he'd once lived with his mother, father, sister and brother, cousins, aunts and uncles and other Romani relatives. Twenty-five people, perhaps, in their close-knit group. He knew them all and they knew him. They spoke a language that set them apart.

Life wasn't easy for the Romani. They weren't liked and they knew it, but in the circle of their campfires, a child felt relatively safe. Which was an illusion.

In the worst moments of his life—when he was being violated by the soldiers who made him march till he dropped, or surrounded by death and despair too harsh to fully comprehend, or, even weeping at his beloved wife's graveside—Jurek would reflect on how his life might have turned out if he'd listened to his conscience that morning, instead of his cousin.

The early summer day had begun like any other. The men gathered together talking seriously about grown-up matters that didn't concern a boy who was eight, going on nine. The women were still discussing the birth of two-month-old Yetta. "Child of the north wind," they called her because of the storm that blew up the night she was born. But when she cried out the next morning, the sun was bright, the day still. Jurek had loved her from the first moment he held her.

He told himself a boy should have no feelings for a tiny infant, but he did. He liked her far better than the other pesky girls in camp. Perhaps to reward his atten-tiveness, Yetta's mother had asked Jurek to watch over things while she went to an adjacent wagon for some dried herbs. Baby Yetta was asleep in the back of the wagon in a small box that had once held apples. Alba and Beatrix, her older sisters, were playing a game in the dirt not far from the open cooking fire. They ignored Jurek, which was just as well because three of his cous-ins, all older than Jurek, invited him to sneak off to see the new puppy they'd found.

The dog was a secret because they knew their par-ents wouldn't welcome another mouth to feed. The boys were keeping it squirreled away in a small pen by the horses. Jurek knew he should stay where he was. He told them no, but they pressured him. He was a fast runner. He could see the dog and return before the little girls even knew he was gone. Yetta was asleep. She would be fine.

He was only gone a few minutes, but as Jurek

learned, tragedy can strike in seconds. Alba's skirt caught alight. Beatrix tried to douse it with water from a nearby pot, but the pot contained oil. Both girls became coated in flames. They ran to the shelter of their wagon for help. The wagon caught fire.

Jurek heard the screams and ran as fast as he could. Alba was facedown in the green grass, her back ablaze. He rolled her over and over and left her lying in shock, faceup. Her lovely skin blackened. Beatrix had made it into the wagon, but had ignited the blankets and fabric that made up their bedding. He pulled her out and used the water that she should have used.

The wagon, now totally engulfed, was like a neatly constructed inferno. Adults appeared; several of Jurek's uncles took hold of the tongue of the wagon to pull it away from the camp circle. His aunt tried to keep Jurek back, but he broke loose and scaled the steps to reach inside for the new baby. The north wind had somehow kept the flames at bay. She wasn't burned. He pulled her free and they tumbled to the ground. She didn't cry. She didn't make any sound.

A gaujo doctor who came to help said Yetta had inhaled the smoke. He couldn't guarantee that she would live. Alba died a few hours later. Beatrix survived, but all feared she would be too deformed to ever have a real life.

Jurek's punishment? He was banished to Poland to live with his grandmother, whom he'd never met. Before he left for Poland, Jurek had cradled the sleeping baby one last time, and he'd whispered a promise to make this up to her any way he could. Someday.

He didn't see his family again for nearly ten years. A few months after he arrived at his grandmother's, on

September 1, 1939, Hitler invaded Poland. The borders were closed. Jurek's nightmare began.

His grandmother did her best to keep them safe in the countryside, but two years later they were caught in a sweep and forced into a labor camp where his grandmother perished. Eventually, Jurek was sent to Sobibor. Each day was a challenge to stay alive. Many days he thought he'd prefer to die, but his promise to Yetta kept him going.

After Sobibor was liberated, Jurek set out to find his family. Surviving war-ravaged Europe took another set of skills. He learned how to lie, cheat, steal and kill. Eventually, he heard that his Romani family had immigrated to America just before the start of the war. Without funds, he had few options, so he signed up to work on a tramp steamer. His voyage took nearly two years of circumnavigating the southern hemisphere before he made it to New York. He was seventeen by the time he next saw Yetta and her family. And, although they'd welcomed him with tears of joy, Jurek found he'd changed too much to fit into their world. He'd moved to Atlantic City. He kept tabs on the family over the years, touching base with Yetta on occasion, but the only time he'd even come close to rejoining the group had been when he'd married Lucy. After her death, he'd drifted up and down the West Coast doing odd jobs until he'd finally landed in Laughlin eight years earlier.

Now, at the close of his life, he had a chance to make good on his promise to Yetta. When she'd visited him last, Yetta had been upset about a dream. He saw this as an opportunity to reach out, not only to help her, but to connect with the child he'd given up. His son. A boy with Lucy's fair hair and blue eyes who had deserved better than to be cursed with a worthless piece of trash for a father.

When a social worker came to the jail and told him his wife was dead, Jurek had understood that he wasn't done paying for his mistakes. Lucille Helson, the farm girl who dreamed of being a dancer, had been the best thing that had ever happened to him. And, for their son's sake, he'd made the most difficult decision of his life.

Now, he was dying—despite what his doctor said. A body could only take so much torture for so long, but he couldn't let go until he made sure that Yetta and her family were safe from this serpent that Yetta had seen in her dream.

And, selfishly, he hoped to see his son one last time.

"DAMN. I THOUGHT Detroit had a lot of cars and motor homes, but this place is a freakin' zoo," her passenger observed. "Why would anyone live here?"

Grace put on her blinker to turn onto Las Vegas Boulevard. The Strip, as it was known throughout the world. She'd circled around the back of McCarran Airport's industrial and business park to give Nikolai a bit of a tour, but so far, he didn't seem too impressed.

"Good question. Maybe you should ask one of the seven thousand new arrivals to Clark County—every month."

Grace didn't know why she took his rhetorical question so personally. Usually—at least whenever she got stuck in traffic—she agreed with his assessment. But something about this man got to her.

Good thing he isn't my type, she thought. She'd al-

ready done tall, blond and gorgeous—and had paid
dearly in the tender of a broken heart. Shawn Bascomb
taught her that shoulders made for portaging canoes
over rocky shoals were not necessarily broad enough to
carry a relationship of any substance.

Grace had been so sure that Shawn, a self-professed
ski bum with a penchant for white-water rafting in summer, had been the one from the moment they met. Although he'd proven as reliable as the seasonal snow he
lived for, Grace had been determined not to give up on
her errant prince.

After graduating from Mesa State College in
Grand Junction, she found a job in Ouray, Colorado,
to be near Shawn, who gave ski lessons at Telluride.
Grace took her responsibilities seriously; she had a
need to excel at her job. Shawn partied. Kate, who
was working as assistant chef at one of the resorts,
heard all the rumors Grace had turned a deaf ear to.
She finally told Grace, "Face it. Shawn's a frog, and
no amount of kissing is ever going to change him
into a prince."

"So, is it safe to say that you like living here?" Nikolai asked, leaning forward slightly as they passed the
Welcome To Las Vegas sign, which she'd just read was
one of the most recognizable icons in the world.

Startled out of her time warp, Grace stepped on the
brake for no reason, soliciting a nasty honk from the car
behind her. Flustered but determined not to show it, she
said, "Yes, I do. Most of the time. Vegas is several cities in one. You have this," she said, indicating the canyon of hotels they were approaching. "Touristy glam
and lots of jobs, but if you cross over the freeway and

head west, you hit Red Rocks and Mount Charleston. See that snowcapped peak?"

He looked around her to where she was pointing. This brought him close enough for her to breathe in his scent. A wholly masculine smell of leather and aftershave that made her mouth water.

Swallowing, she hastily inclined her head in the other direction. "Go that way and you run into Lake Mead and Boulder City. Hoover Dam. Well worth the trip. And sprinkled in between are neighborhoods, like the one my family lives in, which have a kind of small-town feel."

She checked to see if he was listening. His presence filled the car. Not just his body, but his energy. Something about him was edgy and exciting. He seemed attuned to what was going on around him. He probably never zoned out, she decided. "Most locals don't come down here unless they have out-of-town guests or want to see a show," she added.

"All these people are tourists?" he asked, as she slowed to avoid a crowd of pedestrians starting to cross the street in front of the glittering gold towers of Mandalay Bay.

"Oh, yeah. And snowbirds."

At the stoplight on Trop—short for Tropicana, she had a chance to study his profile. Long, slender nose. Thick but finely shaped brows a few shades darker than his hair. Lower lip was fuller than the top and sexy as hell, she realized.

Sitting up a bit straighter, she asked, "So, if you find the right job, do you plan to stay here permanently?"

The shoulder closest to her lifted and fell. "I guess."

She frowned. He didn't appear to have much ambition. But the cost of living here was reasonable, if one didn't have a gambling problem. "Do you gamble?"

His chin turned slowly, and the look he gave her made a shiver pass down her spine. "Do you?"

His response told her to back off, but as her sisters knew, Grace never let a little thing like privacy keep her from poking her nose into other people's lives. "Now and then. When I have out-of-state visitors to entertain," she said, returning her attention to the road. "Fortunately, my father taught me how to play. Most people don't do it right. Which, of course, is what casinos count on."

When he didn't respond, Grace kept up the chatter. Silence shared with Nikolai Sarna was not comfortable. "I'll warn you ahead of time, though, if you ask people that question, you probably won't get an honest answer. Gamblers have a tendency to fudge. My father used to say that gambling is like drinking. If you can't stop, then you shouldn't start."

As she slowed to turn at the next intersection, she caught the look of bemusement on his face as he tilted his head to gaze up at the replica of the Eiffel Tower. *Maybe I could take him up to the observation level sometime. It's got a great view. And it's romantic.*

The thought made her cut the corner a bit too sharply, drawing glares from several sightseers poised to cross the street. *No romance. Nix. Nada. None.* Especially with a perfect stranger.

"What do you do if someone in your family is spending too much time at the tables?" he asked, leaning forward to peer at the vast white complex that made up Caesars Palace.

Something about his question struck her as odd.

Maybe it was his use of the phrase "at the tables," which Grace recognized as gaming lingo. He was a player, she decided. "We try to be aware if someone in the family is losing too much. Then we talk to him or her."

"Most families go their own ways and don't mess with each other's lives," he said.

Did that observation apply to his own experience? Her mother said he'd been adopted by a gaujo family when he was a little boy. Grace didn't understand how that could have happened, but the thought made her sad. "Right. Well, that's the difference between Western thinking and Rom thinking. You may not be your brother's keeper, but you should be his support system, his conscience when he needs it, his collective memory."

He made a sound that seemed to embody all the skepticism Grace had heard from her sisters for years. They accused her of placing altruistic values on a way of life she only knew from fables and lore.

She turned the steering wheel harder than necessary and punched the gas to zip across traffic into the back entrance of the casino parking lot.

"Family means everything to the Romani," she said, tired of constantly defending herself and her heritage. "And because of what my ancestors suffered and what my parents and grandparents went through, I have an advantage. I don't *expect* the government to do anything to improve my life. If I want to make things better for my family, I have to do it myself."

She pulled into the parking space Charles had provided her in his underground lot. In the desert, shade was a privilege that usually came at a price. She turned off the engine. "This won't take long. Do you want to wait here?"

"Hell, no. This is my first time…in a real Las Vegas casino," he said.

Was that a tiny bit of humor beneath his deadpan demeanor? Grace hoped not. He would be easier to take if she could fit him into a neat little box labeled: rude, self-absorbed, jerk—who was occasionally nice to old women.

She glanced at her watch. "Xanadu isn't much of a casino by Strip standards, but there's a bar, if you're still on Detroit time," she added with a smile to show that she was over her snit. "But we only have about half an hour. Mother is expecting us at Romantique for your welcome party."

"I'll just follow you around. Don't want to get lost."

She laughed. "You won't. Not here. If this were Bellagio or Caesars or the new Wynn, there might be a problem. Even I get turned around when I'm in the big casinos."

They got out of the car. Without any prodding on her part, Nikolai took off his leather coat and chucked it into the back seat. Darned if he didn't look just as sexy without it, Grace thought as she waited for him to join her. Black jeans that looked well broken in, a pale blue, long-sleeved cotton shirt that had probably started the morning well-pressed, and ordinary hiking-type boots with thick soles and red laces. Nothing special about his clothes, but on him, everything looked fine.

"Damn fine," she muttered under her breath.

"Huh?" he asked as they walked to a door marked Employee Entrance.

"Nothing. I just realized how old and run-down the place looks from this angle. Of course, the place *is* old by Vegas standards. It used to be called The Shady Tree

Resort, but my dad told me locals referred to it as the Shady Lady because it was popular with hookers."

He opened the door for her, and she recalled her granny once telling her that good manners could compensate for a multitude of faults.

She walked quickly to get through the hubbub in the kitchen. "The second owner built this addition," she said, using her hand to encompass the building at large. "According to Charles, he was a moneyed gay man from back East, who had visions of Kublai Khan's pleasure dome arising from the desert. He went bankrupt."

She exchanged greetings with a few members of Charles's staff, but in all honesty, she didn't know any of them well. She rarely had time to visit the casino. She'd argued that putting her name on a parking space was a waste, but Charles had refused to budge.

"My partners have two stalls apiece. I'm entitled. If you don't use it, I'll park my boat there next winter instead of leaving it at the marina," he'd replied.

Once they stepped into the casino, the atmosphere changed. No drab white walls. No hushed frenzy or smells of cooking food. Instead, there was noise, red brocade wallpaper, sparkling chandeliers suspended from a much-too-low ceiling and a faint blue haze of cigarette smoke.

To complete the tour she'd started, Grace took Nikolai to the main entrance, which led into a two-story dome decorated in tiny blue-and-gold mosaic tile above a fountain that consisted of four naked cherubs supporting a basin upon which rested two nymphs with long hair strategically placed so there was no need for parents to shield their children's eyes as they registered for their rooms. Lush ferns and corpulent goldfish completed the water element.

"Charles's partners, two brothers who came from New Jersey right before the boom in the late eighties, bought the adjoining property and built the hotel," Grace said. "It links to the main facility via a walkway on the second floor, which is where the business office is located."

At the base of the escalator, she stopped and looked at him. "That's the end of the docent-guided portion of your tour," she said breezily. "My meeting shouldn't take long. Shall we meet by the fountain in, say, twenty minutes?"

"I thought you said you'd introduce me to your boyfriend so I can ask him about a job?"

Grace was beginning to wonder if that was such a good idea. What did she know about this man? Nothing. Heck, he really could be a hit man.

Which, a voice in her head noted cynically, Charles might welcome. At dinner a week ago, Charles had vented at length about his frustration of dealing with his partners. Ralph and Walt Salvatore were the septuagenarian brothers who each owned thirty-four percent interest in the Xanadu. Notoriously competitive, any decision one made was immediately countered by the other. If Charles met Walt's asking price for his shares, Ralph would ask for more.

"I'm not proud. I'll do anything."

Grace didn't believe him. Nikolai carried himself with pride and self-assurance. Much like her father had.

"Well, I guess you could ask if they're hiring."

They rode up the moving stairway without speaking. Grace covertly watched Nikolai scan the casino. He didn't just look, he took in, she decided. As if he might be called upon to testify about it someday. The thought made her shiver. Grace didn't like law enforcement. Probably a result of her Rom background. If one looked back at one's history and saw nothing but persecution from those in power, one tended to distrust governing bodies of any type.

"By the way," she said, "for the record, Charles is not my boyfriend. He's a friend, although he might become more in the near future," she added without thinking.

Was it her imagination or did the temperature between them just drop a degree or two?

"What does that mean?"

His judgmental tone compelled her to answer. "Not that it's any of your business, but my sister and I own a restaurant. She's a chef. An amazing chef and we've done well, but I want to branch out. The Xanadu is close enough to the Strip that we'd catch tourist dollars if we opened an ultralounge here. Something hip and chic. Theme bars are big business in Vegas right now."

She'd been arguing the pros and cons of this endeavor in her mind ever since leaving home for the airport. Her sisters might have legitimate worries, but Grace was certain the potential for success outweighed the risk.

"At the moment, Xanadu's coffee shop is more like Xanadon't," she said. "But with the right decor—something popping, sexy, maybe a little dangerous—we could attract a younger crowd. That means big bucks. The under-thirties drive this market, and I want a piece of it."

When she'd floated her idea past Charles, the concept had been just starting to take shape in her mind. "I want to call it Too Romantique."

"Ahh, very clever play on words."

She tried to hide her blush of pleasure by leading the way through the glass doors marked Headquarters. Charles and his partners each maintained an office that included a private bathroom, a bar and a sofa that made into a bed. Not that Grace had ever heard of either brother sticking around the office long enough to need a nap. Charles lived on the premises in a suite on the sixth floor.

She opened the door and stepped inside. The waiting room was large and rather opulent. Grace never tired of studying the collage of black-and-white photos of old Las Vegas that hung on the walls.

"Hi, Grace," a voice hailed. MaryAnn was at her desk, which always struck Grace as too modern. The chrome-and-glass ensemble matched Charles's office furniture—the effect he'd been trying for, no doubt.

"Charles is busy at the moment. Do you want to wait?"

Grace motioned Nikolai closer. "No problem. Mary-Ann, this is Nikolai Sarna. Fresh from frosty Detroit. Well, I'm assuming it was cold, given your coat," she said to him, suddenly embarrassed. Did her observation reveal too much interest in him? "Um…MaryAnn will be your neighbor once we get you settled. She lives two doors down from Mom." She turned to her cousin's wife. "Is Gregor here today?"

MaryAnn didn't offer to shake hands. In fact, she didn't even make eye contact with Nikolai, which struck Grace as odd. "No," she said shortly. "He's working the night shift at the legal defense office in North Vegas. A lot of accidents happen at night. Someone has to be on call."

She sounded upset, Grace thought, but she didn't want to go into family business in front of a stranger, even if he was family. Sort of. "Will Charles be long? We could wait downstairs."

"I'll ring him and ask," MaryAnn said.

But at that moment, the office door opened and Charles ushered two young women into the reception area. When he spotted Grace, he quickly scooted around the girls, who kept their chins down, making it hard to guess their ages. Young, Grace thought. Early twenties?

"Grace," Charles said. She couldn't tell by his expression if he was glad to see her or put out. "You're early."

He crossed the room to give her a peck on the cheek—his standard greeting. "Traffic was tolerable." She heard her guest's soft snort but ignored it. "Let me introduce you to Nikolai Sarna. He's a distant relative, newly relocated from up north, and looking for a job. I thought maybe I could send him to Personnel while we talk. But if you're not ready for me…"

Charles quickly shook hands with Nikolai then turned his attention to Grace. "I'll be free in a minute. Just let me make sure these girls—our new maids—are squared away. Why don't we meet in the coffee shop in ten minutes, eh?"

He started away but paused. "Oh, and MaryAnn can give you an application, Nick. She knows what jobs are open."

He left before Grace could correct him. "Nick" didn't fit this man at all.

She watched Charles escort the women away. He seemed inordinately friendly with the two. Not that she blamed him. They were beautiful. Long, nearly black hair. Smoky eyes. Thin enough to be models, but they weren't dressed stylishly. The two could be sisters, except they looked the same age and weren't enough alike to be twins.

"Is it standard policy for the boss to meet with all new hires?" Nikolai asked.

MaryAnn glanced up from the file drawer she'd pulled open. After pawing through some alphabetized folders, she withdrew a sheet of paper and handed it to Nikolai. "They're from Canada," she said. "Charles needs to be sure there aren't going to be any immigration issues cropping up." Looking at Grace, she added, "You know what a stickler he is about following the law."

Grace sensed some invisible reaction to that statement from Nikolai, but when she looked at him, he appeared to be studying the application. "Do you want to fill that out now?" she asked.

"You can fax it to Personnel. Or give it to me at lunch," MaryAnn said. "You're bringing him to Romantique, right, Grace?"

"Oh, yes. We're headed there after I talk to Charles. Do you want a ride?"

"No, thanks. Luca has a short school day, and Claude wants to take him, Gemilla and Maya to the ranch. He can't fit two child seats and a booster in the truck, so we'll switch cars at Romantique."

As the door closed behind them, Nikolai asked, "How long has she been working for Charles?"

"A year or so, I think." Her mind was on the two young maids. Something didn't seem right about them. "She used to be the girl Friday for a dry cleaner that went out of business. For the first time since she and Gregor got married, MaryAnn was out of work. Normally, that's what we say about Gregor. He's a nice guy, but he can't hold a job for love nor money. Charles hired them both, which was really quite sweet of him."

"You think he's a good man?"

Grace found his tone judgmental. "Charles *is* a good man. He was a friend of my father's, and my father was a very good judge of character."

He smiled for the first time and some kind of magic took place between his cheekbones and lips. Her gaze became fixed on the sexy slant of his mouth, the hint of even, white teeth. The rakish twinkle in his eye. She was so distracted she forgot she was on a moving staircase. Her heels snagged on the disappearing step. She would have fallen if not for Nikolai, who hoisted her to safety.

His hands remained fixed around her upper arms, as if to make sure she was capable of standing. "You okay?"

She pushed away too soon and wobbled drunkenly, but managed to stay upright. "Yes, thank you. I'm fine," she said, starting off toward the coffee shop.

But was she? Grace wasn't certain. She'd never in her life had such a visceral reaction to a man. Especially not with a stranger. Something about him struck her as too perceptive, too familiar. How that was possible, she didn't know, but she planned to keep tabs on him.

A tough job, she thought, hiding her grin behind her purse, but somebody has to do it.

CHAPTER FIVE

NICK SLID onto a bar stool to wait. Not by choice.

"Charles and I have business to discuss," Grace had told him seconds after he'd caught her on the escalator. Nick had felt something flash through him—a warning, he was certain. Grace was trouble, he'd be willing to bet on it.

She was also intriguing. And it pissed him off that she was now shutting him out. Not that she didn't have every right to. They barely knew each other. But even if Nick hadn't come to Vegas specifically intending to get the goods on Charles Harmon, he would have disliked the man presently standing shoulder to shoulder with Grace at a table across the room.

But Nick had to admit, he could see how someone might be taken in by Charles's patrician good looks. Just the right touch of gray at his temples. Thin but not scrawny. Rolled-up sleeves on a shirt that probably cost more than most cops made in a week. He exuded confidence and success.

And Grace had greeted him like a savior when he'd shown up at the doorway to the restaurant where she and Nick had been standing awkwardly, not saying anything. Nick had been tempted to apologize but he wasn't sure what for. He'd kept her from falling backwards off the escalator—and he hadn't taken advantage of the situation. Although he had been tempted.

Women, he silently muttered, furtively glancing behind him to keep tabs on the pair standing with heads almost touching, as they pored over some kind of blueprints that Charles had brought to show Grace.

All flash, no substance. That was Nick's gut opinion of the man. The first thing Charles did—after giving Grace a hug that seemed mostly for Nick's benefit—was express his regret over not being able to attend the family luncheon at Romantique. "Tell your sister I was tempted to risk contempt of court for one of her meals, but MaryAnn wouldn't let me."

His secretary. The one married to Grace's cousin. Nick made a mental note to have Zeke run a background check on MaryAnn and her husband.

"What can I get you?" a husky voice inquired. The bartender, a buxom fiftysomething Marilyn Monroe knockoff in a starched white tuxedo shirt and tight black jeans, gave Nick an interested look.

He leaned forward to rest his elbows on the bar. "Tonic with a twist," he said, laying a five-dollar bill just beyond the video poker monitor embedded in the bar.

"Coming right up."

The bar was exactly what Nick imagined a 1970s-era Vegas bar must have looked like—a rolled-laminate-and-chrome countertop with a dark brown tufted vinyl knee well. Suspended overhead were cheesy chandeliers. The mirror behind the bar was mottled with gold flecks. *Talk about a candidate for an extreme makeover.* The only modernization that he could see was in the form of the video poker machine in front of him. It looked state-of-the-art.

Nick wasn't a big gambler. He'd tried blackjack and craps in Atlantic City but had never won. He eyed the thing, wondering how it worked.

"It takes dollar bills."

Glancing to his left, Nick saw a tall, angular man in his mid- to late fifties leaning against the bar. His mostly gray hair was trimmed short the way Nick's father used to wear his. Nowadays, Pete Lightner shaved his head. And looked pretty damn good. This man didn't seem to have to worry about a receding hairline.

"I'm sure it does," Nick said drily. "Probably more than I want to give it."

The man chuckled as he sat down.

Nick glanced at the row of empty stools on either side of him and tensed. Was this some kind of pickup? Before he could discourage the stranger from crowding his space, the bartender returned with his drink. "And what can I get you this fine morning?" she asked the man, with a come-hither wink.

Nick gave the guy a second look. Ordinary. Clothes off the rack at Kmart. A navy windbreaker not unlike the kind the FBI used, except it was lacking the big yellow letters.

"Coffee, please. Black," the man said.

A tingle of awareness passed along Nick's spine. The man was a cop. Nick would bet his well-hidden Beretta on it.

"Are you a friend of Zeke's?"

In profile, Nick saw a smile slowly wrinkle the side of the man's cheek. His longish face reminded Nick of a beardless Abe Lincoln, only with a darker complexion. Latino or part black, Nick guessed.

The bartender delivered the mug and picked up Nick's fiver. "Both?" she asked, obviously assuming the two men knew each other.

"Sure," Nick said. "Why not?"

The man lifted his mug and nodded his thanks. After a tentative slurp, he lowered the cup to look at Nick. "Not bad. Thanks."

"You're welcome, but you didn't answer my question."

"Name's Zeke Martini. Yes, like the drink," he added in a tone that said he'd heard the unasked question a thousand times.

"Impressive timing. How'd you know I'd be here?"

"Had a tail on the princess for a week. She's not the greatest driver in the world, by the way. Hope your life insurance is paid up."

Nick chuckled to mask his surprise. He'd known Metro was interested in Grace because of her association with Charles, but he hadn't realized they were watching her round the clock. Would that change now that he was in the picture? "We should talk."

"We will. I'll let you get your sea legs first."

Zeke took another drink of coffee then stood up. Nick stopped him with his foot against his shin. "How do I reach you? Dial nine-one-one?"

"I'll be around," Zeke said cryptically. "Nothing's happening at the moment. Unless you know what that's about," he said, nodding ever so slightly toward where Grace and Charles were standing.

The spacious—some might say cavernous—dining room was mostly deserted so the couple had relative pri-

vacy in a sunny alcove with floor-to-ceiling windows
made of glass block.

"I'm not in that loop—yet."

"Positive thinking. I like that," he said. With a nod at
the bartender, he tossed down a couple of singles then
walked away, melting into the labyrinth of tables, slot
machines and gamblers on the casino's main floor.

So that's Zeke Martini. Not quite what he'd imagined, but something about the guy reminded Nick of his
dad. A cop thing, he figured. All job, no bull.

Staring into the distorted image of the mirror behind
the bar, Nick tried to make out what was happening at
the table in the alcove, but the only thing clear was
Grace's frown.

"AND I REALLY LIKE what he's done with the restrooms,"
Charles said, pointing to a spot on the plans he'd un-
rolled. "Get this—the only lights would be in the floors
and behind the mirrors. Sounds very hip, doesn't it?"

Grace fought to keep her temper under control. Yes,
this was exactly what she'd envisioned when she'd
blurted out her idea last week over dinner at Aquaknox,
her inhibitions lowered by a glass of primo Chardonnay.

Charles had appeared cautiously interested. Then,
not a word from him until now when he shows up with
a set of architectural drawings. Created with absolutely
no input from her.

"What do you think?"

She stepped back, hands on her hips. "You tell me.
Since you're so good at reading minds."

Charles's head went up so abruptly a shock of dark
auburn hair dropped across his eyebrows. He batted it

away. His long, classically handsome face took on a troubled frown. "Oh." His eyes widened in surprise. "Oh, dear. I believe I let my enthusiasm for the project get away from me."

His look of chagrin seemed real. Was it possible he'd simply been caught up in the moment? Grace had felt the same way when the idea came to her in the middle of the night.

The name, the concept, the location—everything about Too Romantique had made her giddy with expectation. Until that morning when her sisters voiced their concerns. Now, Charles was standing here practically gushing enthusiasm, and she was acting like a spoiled child because he'd taken her ball and run with it.

"I'm sorry, Grace. Really."

His apology seemed sincere, but Grace didn't like secret agendas. "If we do this, Charles, I expect to be more than the money man…um, person. It's my investment, my idea and my sister who will be putting her reputation on the line."

He nodded somberly. "Of course. You're absolutely right. I should have talked this over with you. But you've been so busy with your family…"

Grace couldn't argue with that. She'd babysat Maya two evenings last week and had filled in three afternoons at The Dancing Hippo when Alex was feeling under the weather. *But still…*

"I appreciate the fact that this is your building, Charles, so you have final say in the remodeling process, but, let's face it. Too Romantique is my baby. If it fails, you would still benefit from a badly needed face-lift, while I'd be out my entire trust fund."

"I would never let that happen, Grace."

Charles put his hand on her bare arm. His touch was cool and light. He wasn't a hands-on kind of person, which Grace liked. Shawn had proven that touch could lie, and trust was easily abused. "I know this appears as though I usurped your brainchild, Grace, but, in fact, these plans weren't something I commissioned."

"Then why do you have them?"

"Well, I happened to mention your idea to the contractor who's refurbishing some of our guest rooms. He was so impressed by what I described to him—all the things you'd mentioned to me—that he took it upon himself to put these sketches together on his computer." He used his free hand to make a sweeping gesture toward the thick, bluish white paper. "Nothing is written in blood. You can mark them up all you want."

Still feeling put out, Grace stepped back, ostensibly to view the plans from another angle. Normally, she felt comfortable with Charles occasionally holding her hand in public or even giving her a good-night kiss, but today, she felt an odd chill pass though her body whenever he touched her. The same feeling she got when she was out on the desert after sunset and the sharp cold of night first made its presence known.

"Well, I guess it's okay to have the basic size and scale down on paper, but Kate would kill me if I greenlighted a kitchen that she hadn't personally approved."

Charles nodded. "I understand completely. Take these sheets with you and show them to her. Use colored pens. Sticky notes. Whatever works. But keep in mind that the more we stay within the existing parameters, the more we can stretch our money."

Our money. Grace knew Charles didn't mean that the way it sounded. They weren't a couple and never would be. If she'd ever remotely entertained the idea of a more intimate relationship with him, the possibility had been blown out of the water the moment Nikolai Sarna had rescued her at the escalator. Friendship was one thing; wild, unprovoked lust was quite another.

She looked across the bar to where Nikolai was sitting. The silver-haired gentleman in a windbreaker who'd occupied the stool beside him was gone. Probably a tourist asking how to operate the video poker game.

"Is he someone I should be concerned about?" Charles asked, apparently following her gaze.

Grace ducked the implication behind the question. "He's someone I'm concerned about," she answered, keeping her tone flat. "Another mouth to feed until he finds a job and moves out on his own. I don't know what Mom was thinking when she invited him to stay with us."

"He's living at Yetta's? With Kate and the child right down the hall?" His thin eyebrows pulled together, almost touching. Not his most attractive look.

The child? He knew Maya's name. Didn't he? Kate had accused Charles of being self-absorbed and Grace had defended him, but maybe she'd been too hasty. "No. He'll be staying at Claude's, but I'm sure he'll eat at Romantique and borrow Mom's car and hang out in the backyard, like the rest of the family."

Charles put his hand on her shoulder and squeezed supportively. "I've always admired the way your family interacts. Loud, robust, opinionated. Just like in the movies." He smiled. "Not what I was accustomed to, but very entertaining."

Grace leaned over and started to roll up the plans. "Yeah, well, togetherness can get old, believe me. I love my cousins, second cousins and sort of cousins, but this big-family/one-boat thing only works if everyone is rowing together." She sighed. "And believe me, there are one or two who don't even have their oars in the water."

Charles laughed then gave her a quick, one-armed hug before she could protest. "Don't worry, my sweet. I'll take him off your hands and put him to work for me. Do you think he can mop floors?"

Grace looked at the man in question. Nikolai's back was broad, his shoulders obviously well developed. He looked fit and capable. "I'm sure he *could,* but will he?" She shrugged, dislodging Charles's hand.

"Let's ask," she said. A sudden, urgent need for fresh air sent her hurrying across the room. Too late, she remembered Alex's warning, "Full-bosomed women should strive to glide."

Nikolai turned when she was halfway across the room—prompted, she was sure, by some innate, male sensory organ that detected bouncing boobs within visual range. She saw his eyes widen appreciably.

Using the rolled-up plans as a pointer, she aimed one end at Nikolai. "Job interview. Don't blow it. I'll be in the car."

She paused just long enough to tell Charles, whose long stride made gliding his natural form, "I'll give these a look-see. Sorry about the lack of enthusiasm. You just caught me off guard." As an afterthought, she added, "Don't keep him too long. Mom would kill me if the prodigal cousin missed his welcome-home party."

Still responding to an urgent need to be out of the

building, Grace left the restaurant, the word *kill* echoing in her brain. She had no idea why. She had enough on her plate without fantasizing about murder.

CHAPTER SIX

"So, you're Grace's cousin."

Charles wasn't thrilled to put another Radonovic relative on his payroll, but he had little choice. His life had taken an unplanned and complicated turn a couple of weeks ago, and if he had any hope at all of getting things back on track, he needed Grace's help—and her money. Which, when it came right down to it, was rightfully his.

"Not really."

"I beg your pardon?"

"Supposedly my old man is related to Grace's mother. I never heard a word from these people until last week."

"Why is that?"

"I guess dear ol' dad started feeling guilty. First about being in jail when my mother got hit by a bus and died. And then for simply handing me over to some other family. After all these years this Yetta lady calls me up and says my birth father is sick and I should come to Vegas to meet him."

"So all is forgiven."

"Hell, no. Would you forgive the bastard? But my job just got sent overseas, and ex-cons don't get first pick at new jobs, if you know what I mean. So I figured, why not give Vegas a try?"

The man's nasal twang almost made Charles smile. On occasion, he could draw up a Southern drawl from his childhood. Both his father's cultured tones and his mother's trailer-trash lilt. But he preferred to keep the past in the past. His father had been a weak, mewling man who picked drink over work and died before his fortieth birthday. Charles's mother had been right when she said they were better off without the worthless piece of shit.

Charles would never forgive his father, either. He still remembered being in bed at night when his father would come home drunk and crawl under the covers beside him. Adoption would have been a godsend. But he didn't say so out loud.

"What were you in jail for?"

"Bar fight. I got a temper. So sue me."

Finally. A person with potential. Thank you, Grace.

Charles looked around the mostly empty lounge and restaurant. He detested having his name associated with such a seedy place. Ten years of refereeing petty squabbles between his partners, the battling Salvatore brothers, had convinced him the only way he was going to transform this casino into a viable, moneymaking proposition was by buying them out.

Unfortunately, the past six months had seen too much outflow of cash and not enough income. Start-up costs for his insurance scam had run over budget. The bribes alone had been ridiculous. Damn cops, he thought bitterly. And if Walt and Ralph didn't pony up to the escrow table soon, Charles would find another way to deal with them. Grace's money would cover his short-term needs, which included taking care of the person who was blackmailing him. One thing Charles refused to do was touch the nest egg he'd squirreled away in the Caymans.

"You've got an application, I see. Fax it back and you can start on Monday. If anything you put down doesn't check out, you're history. Got it?"

"What's the job?"

"Do you care?"

"Maybe."

Charles laughed. "Tough. If you want to work for me, you'll do what I say, and the fewer questions asked, the better." He stopped abruptly and turned to look the man in the eyes. "You may have heard the expression 'What happens in Vegas, stays in Vegas.' Well, the same thing applies to working for me. What happens on the job, stays here. Are we clear on that?"

"Sure. Whatever. Who am I gonna tell?"

"Your new *family,* maybe."

The man snorted as if that was the last thing that would happen. Charles was good at reading people. He'd learned from a master how to discern a person's weakness and make that work for you. Nikolai Sarna wasn't easy to read. The fact bothered Charles, but he didn't have time to worry about it. Lydia and Reezira, the Romani prostitutes he'd imported by way of Canada, were waiting in his suite. They were the cornerstone of his plan for an all-new, hip and pleasure-focused Xanadu. Too much money in the hands of twentysomethings who weren't afraid to test the boundaries of their sexuality was right there for the taking, and Charles wanted his share.

In the meantime, he planned to make sure his girls didn't lose their edge.

"So TELL ME about Harmon."

Grace was trying to concentrate on driving. Unfortunately, her passenger kept distracting her—with his scent, his energy, his presence. She reached overhead to open the moonroof. Street noise intruded, but she found it comforting.

"Did you know more pedestrians are killed in Vegas than any other major U.S. city?"

"If I wanted a travelogue, I'd have hired a tour guide."

"Just trying to be helpful."

"Then help me out by telling me about the guy who just offered me a job." He waved the form he'd brought with him into the car.

"I don't know what kind of boss Charles is, but you can ask Gregor and MaryAnn. And Uncle Claude. All three of them should be at your welcome-home party."

From the corner of her eye, she saw him frown. A big-screen, moody frown. The kind that could make a girl's heart go bing-bang-pow.

I need serious help.

"So, you've never worked for him. I get that. But you know what kind of man he is, right?"

Did she? Grace thought she did, but two nights ago she'd had a really disturbing dream. Charles had been slithering through the tall grass of a swamp like a six-foot-two-inch python. Grace and her sisters had been camping, and he'd slowly consumed each one of them, headfirst. Grace had been the last. She'd been in denial the whole time, insisting that what she was witnessing wasn't happening.

A blaring honk startled her. She made a face at the

rearview mirror. "All right, already." The car lurched forward narrowly missing a man on a bicycle. "Do you know how many people are killed on bikes in Vegas?" she shouted at the closed window.

She quickly checked over her shoulder then shot around the guy with a UNLV backpack. She started to make a comment about student drivers, but when she looked at Nikolai, he was smiling. A real, honest-to-goodness smile.

Her mouth went dry and her fingers tingled on the steering wheel. *Good Lord, no. Not this one. Please don't let me fall for him. How could I possibly turn an unemployed ex-convict who looks like a hit man into a prince? That's asking too much.*

Nick eased down in the seat of the small car, trying to get comfortable. He was determined to pick Grace's brain before they reached the restaurant, but she kept changing the subject. Did she know about Chuck's illegal activities? Was she protecting him?

"What did you do in Detroit before you lost your job?"

"How come you keep changing the subject? You won't answer my question about Charles. You're making me suspicious."

"Suspicious of what? Charles?" Her laugh told him she found the idea ridiculous. "Oh, please. He's far too…mainstream to do anything dastardly. He was a lawyer in a group practice that handled two of the largest casinos in town. He and my dad met while Dad was head of his union. I remember things being pretty tense around our house. Charles was interested in my older sister, Alex." Her hair bounced across her shoulders as she shook her head. "Like that match ever would have worked."

"It wasn't love at first sight?"

Her chuckle was low and sexy. She tapped the blinker. "Not even close. I was in high school at the time and I can still remember Alex giving Dad a hard time about trying to make an arranged marriage." She quickly added, "Not that that's what Dad was trying to do, of course. He just wanted the best for us. And when Alex started dating a guy who was a cop, I think Dad regretted not having picked her mate."

Really? "Why?"

"Cops and Gypsies…" Grace made a wobbly sign with her right hand. "There's bad blood between the two, historically speaking. My dad grew up on the Lower East Side of New York City. He had a pretty rough childhood and even got arrested once for something he didn't do—just because someone said he was Gypsy. An early case of racial profiling, I guess you could say."

Nick looked around. They'd crossed over a major freeway and were now in what appeared to be a newer neighborhood, blocks and blocks of two-story homes mostly hidden behind stucco fences. The architecture and landscaping reminded him of his last visit to southern California. Hummers and BMWs began to appear in the parking lots of increasingly upscale strip malls.

"We're here," Grace said, turning left on an arrow.

Contrary to the glitter and neon that adorned most of the storefronts they'd passed on the Strip, Romantique's sign was simple and elegant. A flowery font with touches of ivy on a burnt gold background.

Grace pulled into the parking lot and drove by the

canopied entrance. Nick noted the lush plants and small marble fountain near the door. A sandwich-style slate announced the specials of the day, but he didn't have time to read them because Grace whipped the car into a parking space at the rear of the building below a sign that read Bossy Person With Attitude.

Nick fought to keep from smiling. "Dare I ask?"

Grace's sigh reminded him of his sister when their mother asked her to do something she didn't want to do. "Kate's idea of a joke," she said. "Notice hers."

A flamboyant rectangle with palm trees and a Hawaiian sunset read The Big Kahuna. The space was occupied by an older Toyota station wagon, probably from the 1980s. The sun had done a number on its once silver metallic paint job.

Grace grabbed her purse from the back seat, along with the rolled-up plans she and Charles had been poring over in the bar at Xanadu. "We'd better hurry. Kate's not a patient person. She manages the chaos of a rush-hour kitchen better than anyone I know, but make her reheat something and…" She shook her head. "Well, just don't."

Nick opened the door and got out. He started to retrieve his belongings, but Grace rapped on the hood of the car. "Just leave your stuff. I'll probably be the one to drive you home."

He hesitated. His gun was in his bag, but he didn't want to make an issue over a cheap suitcase. She didn't wait to see if he complied with her order. With her back to him, Nick allowed himself a smile. He wasn't ready to write off her involvement with Charles, but he couldn't help liking her. She was bright, gregarious and adorable. She reminded him of Rip as a pup.

A puppy? You wish.

Grace paused beneath the arched navy-blue canvas canopy. "Brace yourself for total chaos. We're a loud, noisy bunch. Always a dozen or more people talking at once. Lots of hugging and kissing. But, trust me, you'll get used to it."

Nick doubted it. Even holidays at his parents' home had never usually amounted to more than four people, although that had changed after his sister got married and moved to Portland. Now, a family meal consisted of Nick and his folks.

He took a deep, fortifying breath as he followed Grace across the threshold into a lush, shadowy foyer that smelled achingly familiar yet looked totally unlike any place he'd ever visited. His mouth started watering even before his vision adjusted to the dim light.

The decor cried *gypsy caravan.* Faux paint on the walls gave a warm antique feel. Broad-leaved plants in rusted wash buckets. Church pews upholstered in copper-and-green-striped silk.

"Auntie Grace," a high-pitched voice cried with an excited shriek that reminded Nick of his nieces. Instead of the pitter-patter of little feet, he heard the squeaky thunder of sneakers against slate-gray tile.

Grace bent low to scoop a tiny munchkin into her arms. The child possessed a mop of chocolate-brown ringlets that framed her huge coal-chip eyes and round face. Nick felt something melt in his heart. His sister's children were fair-haired, blue-eyed clones of Judy and her husband. They'd never really warmed to Nick, who was slightly terrified of them. This child smiled as if she'd known him her whole life, which was probably no more than three years.

"Maya, this is Ni-ko-lai." Grace spoke slowly and distinctly. "Nikolai, I'd like you to meet my niece, Maya Grant. She's Kate's daughter. Can you tell him how old you are, Maya?"

"Four," the child said, as clearly as an adult. "Are you my uncle?"

"No, I'm sorry to say, I'm not."

Her tiny pink lips pouted prettily. "I need an uncle. Luca and Gemilla have two uncles."

She made the deficiency sound just plain awful. After a heavy sigh, she wiggled free of her aunt's arms. Once on the floor, she turned to the two older children who had followed her and whispered something. With a laugh, the group raced away.

"Hey, wait, I didn't introduce…" Grace's voice trailed off. To Nick, she said, "The other two are Luca and Gemilla. They're Gregor and MaryAnn's kids. Like I told you, they live on the other side of Claude's house, so they'll be your neighbors."

"One big happy family, huh?"

She paused, as if considering his words. "Big, for sure. Happy? Probably no more or less than other people, but since we live in close proximity to each other, we're privy to everyday ups and downs. Sometimes," she said with a wistful air, "we know way too much about each other."

Nick disagreed. He wanted to know more, but she didn't give him a chance to ask. "Let's go in."

Nick did a quick check in his head—like an actor getting into character. Nikolai, not Nick. Sarna, not Lightner. Unemployed.

Oh, crap. My ID. He'd forgotten to give his driver's

license and police ID to Zeke. He'd needed the permit to get his gun through security and had planned to ditch the real stuff as soon as he hooked up with his local contact.

"Something wrong?" Grace asked.

Nick didn't like it that she'd picked up on some involuntary signal. "Nice place. I like the ambience."

She gave him a funny look then shook her head slightly and turned away. Nick's *extra* sense told him he'd need to stay on his toes around her.

He followed her through the main dining area, which seemed filled to capacity. A marked difference to the dining room at the Xanadu, he noted. Grace waved greetings and paused every so often to exchange a word or two with both patrons and waitstaff until they reached what he assumed was a private dining room.

A curtain of multicolored glittery beads and tiny bells did little to block the hum of voices coming from the enclave. Nick had yet to see the kitchen, but he could smell it. Garlic, basil, spices like cumin and curry made his mouth water so much that when he swallowed, his lips made a smacking sound.

Grace looked over her shoulder and smiled. "Welcome to Romantique. I guarantee you won't go hungry."

The twinkle in her eye made him want something more than food. Satisfaction. Completion. It had been too long since he'd partaken of that particular dish. And, he reminded himself, it was going to be a lot longer. He was here on business and couldn't forget that.

The noise level within the room went from seventy decibels to two forks clinking the second Grace and Nick stepped through the curtain. He made a quick scan to get his bearings. Five round tables set in the pattern found on dice. Six adults at two tables. Three to four people—with booster seats and a couple of high chairs at the tables closest to the door. An older woman with silver hair was sitting alone at the table to his left, but purse straps draped across the backs of adjoining chairs told him she wasn't being shunned.

He concluded almost immediately that the man who had set this particular ball in motion, his father, wasn't in the group. Not that Nick had been expecting to see him. According to Yetta, Jurek was undergoing some tests for an undisclosed malady and had been told not to travel—even sixty lousy miles.

"Okay, everybody, we're here. I'm only a few minutes late…" Grace let the word trail as if expecting a response. She got one. Catcalls and whistles, a few stomped feet and jeers. She made a cutoff signal at her throat. "Yeah, whatever. If you want prompt, hire a cab. Anyway, here he is. Drumroll, please."

Nick gave her his most withering glare, but it was wasted on her back. The noise level rose once again. When it stopped, thanks to a small but imperious hand gesture from the woman he guessed to be Yetta Radonovic, Grace stepped to one side and put her hands out as if ushering in royalty.

"Nikolai Sarna. Son of Jurek Sarna, who most of you know as George. Fresh from Detroit. Please introduce yourself to him, since…I don't have any idea who you people are."

She gave Nick a wink then walked to Yetta's table and dropped her purse strap over a vacant chair. Nick started to follow but was forced to stop when the little curly-haired angel, Maya, blocked his path. She had something in her hand. A hand-painted card, he realized.

"I made this for you," she said, motioning him to bend down to see her artwork.

Nick leaned over to admire the bold slashes of color. As he pointed to a word he couldn't read, he felt a tingle of awareness shoot through him. He glanced under his arm and spotted her two cousins standing very close, almost touching him. Odd, he thought.

Maya shook the card to draw his attention back to her. Nick looked back and that was when he felt it. Tiny fingers lifting his wallet from his pocket. The whole thing happened so fast he wasn't even sure what he felt was real—until he checked.

He let out a loud noise—something between a hoot of amusement and a cry of outrage. Maya's eyes doubled in size and her bottom lip disappeared. Her two cohorts started to run, but Nick's arms were long and he couldn't let them blow his cover. He hauled them up against his chest and stood up.

The boy cussed and kicked. The girl burst into tears. Maya threw herself at his knees with a loud wail and clung tight as a limpet. The noisy babble around him stopped. Chairs scraped against the floor as people surged forward to protect the children from a madman, no doubt.

First to reach him was a bulldog of a man about Nick's age. Dressed in a white crew-neck sweater that emphasized the bulk of his shoulders and chest, the fellow was a few inches shorter than Nick. He might have made a formidable opponent if not for the slightly glazed look in his eyes and smell of alcohol coming from his lips.

Grace, who'd been about to sit down, dashed back to where he was standing. "Take it easy, Gregor," she said before turning to look at Nick. "What the heck are you doing?" she demanded, picking up her niece.

"Ask them what they were doing."

Nick lowered the children to the floor and let them go. The boy, Luca, stared at his shoes. His sister ran to the woman Nick had met at Charles's office. MaryAnn. Their mother.

"Nikolai," Grace said above the ruckus Maya was making. "What…?"

Nick scanned the floor for his billfold. He'd read a travel warning about pickpockets in Rome. He knew that the standard MO included dropping the evidence if a score went bad.

He lifted the corner of a tablecloth and spotted his black leather wallet resting against the leg of the table. He stretched to grab it, feeling instant relief. His oversight could have blown this entire operation. He needed to be more careful in the future.

"Who knew I'd encounter a roving band of pickpockets in Las Vegas," he said, keeping his tone light. "Bet they don't talk about that in the travel brochures."

Grace's mouth opened and closed like a fish out of water. Her eyes went from surprise to shock to anger. She scanned the crowd, obviously looking for someone in particular. "Uncle Claude?" she growled. "This is your handiwork, isn't it?"

A rotund older man with hair too black for his age stepped forward to stand beside his son. His jovial smile didn't appear forced, nor did he look the least bit abashed. "They almost pulled it off, didn't they?" the man said, reaching out to tousle the little boy's hair affectionately. "Good try, Luca. I could have sworn you'd gotten away with it. This fellow must have an extraordinarily sensitive butt."

Claude introduced himself and Gregor to Nick. After repocketing his wallet, Nick shook hands.

"Or maybe this one has the gift," Claude said. Increasing his volume as if giving a lecture to college students, he turned to face the rest of the group. "Everyone thinks that Gypsy women are the only ones with the sight, but, in fact, it was our forefathers who were the most intuitive."

He nodded with obvious pride. "They were the first to communicate with animals. They were the original horse-whisperers. And many were in touch with the spirit world."

"Don't you dare try to change the subject," Grace snapped after handing her niece to the older woman. "You taught these babies how to steal, didn't you?"

Claude threw out his hands in a gesture of helplessness. "It's a lost art, Niece. Part of our heritage."

She put her hands on her hips, eyes narrowed. "Stealing is not part of *my* heritage and you know perfectly well that my father would never have allowed this. He went to his grave trying to improve the image of the Rom in society and you're doing your best to undermine that."

"It's only a game, dear girl. Good manual dexterity will serve these children well through life," Claude insisted.

Nick almost smiled. The old man's sincerity seemed

palpable. A couple of voices in the crowd obviously thought so, too.

"Cut him some slack, Grace."

"No harm, no foul."

Grace's lips pressed together severely. She looked at the mother of the two older children. "Is that what you think, MaryAnn? Am I overreacting? Do you approve of your father-in-law teaching your children how to steal?"

MaryAnn seemed to shrink back from the attention. Now that she was out from behind her desk, Nick saw that she was about twenty pounds heavier and a couple of inches shorter than Grace. This made her pudgy but not unattractive, although compared to Grace and the two women who flanked her—Grace's sisters, Nick presumed—MaryAnn looked drab and unremarkable.

"I...um...I guess nobody got hurt. It was a joke. Right, son?"

Luca nodded, obviously hoping to deflect attention away from himself and his sister.

"Gregor? What about you?" Grace asked.

Looking as discomfited as his wife, the man ran a hand through his closely cropped black hair and said, "Aw...Grace, you know Dad. He didn't mean any harm."

Grace pulled herself to her full height and turned on one spike heel. She looked at her niece, who was watching the proceedings with hands clutching her grandmother's suit jacket. "Maya, I want your promise that you will never do this again. Taking other people's property is wrong. Do you understand?"

The little girl nodded.

"Good," Grace said softly, then she gave the child a

kiss on the forehead. A second later, she was gone. A word to her mother, a nod to Nick and she left the room, purse and rolled-up plans in hand.

"Is she coming back?"

"Probably not," the woman he'd decided was Yetta said. "Grace's heart is easily bruised, and she puts too much of herself into those she cares about. People like that are often disappointed when the mere mortals in their lives falter and fall. She'll need to lick her wounds in private."

Before Nick could say anything, a tall, thin woman with cropped glossy black hair approached him. She held out her hand. "I'm Alexandra. Welcome to the zoo."

The next two hours flew by in a blur of names, faces, histories, connections and amazing food. Each of the four courses was served family style by waitresses in black slacks, mauve shirts and white aprons that came to their shins. Heaping bowls of salad were accompanied by platters of pickled beef tongue, a sampling of olives, the creamiest goat cheese he'd ever tasted and large rounds of chewy bread. Oxtail soup was next with an array of toppings, including cracked pepper, chopped chives and stiff chips of hard Parmesan.

The main course consisted of the best homemade fried potatoes Nick had ever devoured and a delicious stewed pork dish. Pasta primavera was the vegetarian offering. Dessert, which Nick normally avoided, was an airy sponge cake drizzled with a raspberry chocolate sauce that made him want to lick the plate.

"I swear that was the best meal I've ever had," Nick said, pushing back from the table with a satisfied groan.

Katherine, whom everyone called Kate, stood in the doorway, hatless but wearing the standard black-and-white checkered pants and double-breasted shirt he associated with professional chefs. She was drinking a canned cola from a straw. Most everyone else was sipping high-octane espresso from tiny cups.

"I'm glad you liked it. Mom said we should have a typical Romani feast in your honor. Regular patrons get the same stuff only in smaller quantities."

"You're truly a culinary genius. I can see why your sister wants to open a satellite operation."

Kate frowned but didn't say anything. From the candid exchange over lunch, he'd discerned that Grace's sisters had reservations about the new endeavor…although he'd gotten the impression they'd toned down some of their opinions about Charles because of Mary-Ann's presence.

Yetta had actually said very little but appeared to watch everything.

"So, what now?" he asked. "Since my ride's left me stranded—" *And has my suitcase and gun.* "Do I walk the rest of the way? Probably wouldn't hurt," he added, patting his belly.

The women all spoke at once, and although Nick couldn't follow every thread, Yetta seemed to have no problem deciphering. She rose with regal grace. "Alexandra, you take Maya back to The Dancing Hippo. I don't believe her earlier behavior warrants a trip to the ranch. Elizabeth, you're on your own when it comes to installing the dishwasher. I still think you should have paid the extra thirty dollars to have a serviceman do the work. And, Katherine, dear, thank you for this. It was lovely. I'll remind Grace about payroll when I take Nikolai home. I'm sure she'll be over her snit by the time we get there."

After clearing her throat to gain the rest of the room's attention, Yetta said, "Everyone, thank you for coming. Nikolai will be staying with Claude, so please do your best to make him feel welcome."

Nick had been surprised that no one appeared to question his story and no one pressed for details of his youth. And, most surprising of all, everyone seemed glad to meet him.

He might actually have enjoyed himself if Grace had been there. Her absence disturbed him. He tried to convince himself that he was worried she might have run back to Charles. But he knew that wasn't the whole truth. He found himself watching the door like a teenager with a crush, for God's sake.

CHAPTER SEVEN

GRACE BRUSHED the potting soil from her hands and stood up, stretching her tired lower-back muscles. She used the sleeve of her mother's faded cotton shirt, which she'd grabbed from the nail beside the gardening tools in the garage, to wipe the sweat from her brow.

"Well," she said, stepping back to survey the results of her hard work. "Not bad for an amateur."

Gardening was her mother's forte, but Grace was the one who tended the plants here at her father's grave. Which probably explained why she'd needed to replace the two rosebushes that bracketed her father's headstone.

"Roses are one of the hardiest plants around," the clerk at the greenhouse had told her. "Even in the desert it takes a lot to kill a rose."

Somehow Grace had managed to do that. Maybe these two will do better, she thought, eyeing the leafy bushes skeptically.

"Okay, Dad, they're yours, now. See if you can take better care of them than the last two, all right?"

She'd gotten into the habit of talking out loud during her visits to her father's grave. Her sisters would have given her a hard time about it, but Grace found the one-sided exchange comforting.

She tossed the empty plastic containers into the gardening bucket she'd brought from home and set it to one side. "I suppose lunch is over by now," she said, placing the rubber knee pad on the grass near the base of the headstone.

She sat down, back against the marble marker, and stretched out her legs. If she positioned herself just right, the back of her head rested against the silver dollar that was recessed into the headstone. Everyone had warned the family that they'd be inviting vandalism by putting money on a gravestone, but Grace and her sisters had voted unanimously to include the token. After all, one of their most treasured collective memories was of dancing for their father. He'd called them the Sisters of the Silver Dollar and had rewarded them with the big shiny coins he always carried. So far, no one had disturbed the Gypsy King's resting place.

Grace looked beyond the neat metal and concrete column fence that encircled the cemetery. Traffic sped past on East Las Vegas Boulevard as usual. In the far distance, she could see the purplish outline of the mountains that surrounded the Vegas basin and a few man-made landmarks like the Stratosphere.

Surrounded by warehouses and busy streets, Woodlawn Cemetery was a small oasis in a not-so-great part of town. But Grace always felt safe and peaceful when she visited.

"I ran away, Dad. It was either that or blow up in front of a perfect stranger." She took a deep breath. The wind, a ubiquitous presence in the desert, held a slight bite, suggesting a change in weather. "Well, not *perfect*, but he is pretty darn good-looking."

She crossed her legs at the ankles and let her head rest against the stone. During the weeks following her father's funeral, she hadn't been able to visit his grave. The thought had been enough to make her physically ill, but eventually Yetta had coerced her into visiting. "Talk to him," Yetta had said. "It's good for the soul."

"Will he answer?" Grace had asked, only half-teasing.

"If you listen hard enough," her mother had promised.

And sometimes, he did. Whether the voice she heard was her father or her subconscious, Grace didn't know. Or care, particularly.

"What do you think about Nikolai?" she asked. "I'm not sure I'm comfortable opening a home for wayward Romani. Was inviting him here a mistake?"

The sound of traffic was her only answer.

Grace had learned that no answer usually meant she was asking the wrong question. "Okay, you're right. Forget that. He's here. There's no uninviting him. But can we trust him?"

Is he the one you're worried about? Or are you afraid you can't trust yourself when you're with him?

The question made her eyes pop open. "For heaven's sake, Daddy, I barely know the man. He's not my type. I wouldn't…couldn't…" She felt her cheeks begin to heat up and she reached for her hat, but at that moment a shadow passed over the sun. She blinked rapidly then felt an odd shiver pass through her. Not a chill, but a tingle of awareness.

Someone was watching her. She sat up straight and looked around.

The cemetery was nearly empty. On the opposite side of the driveway, a handful of mourners clustered near a freshly covered mound. A number of cars were parked along the side streets, but none appeared occupied. Feeling both foolish and unsettled, she gathered up her stuff to leave.

Her dad was wrong. Yes, she found Nikolai attractive, but she wasn't attracted to him. And even if she was, she didn't plan to do anything about it. Still, she was starting to feel guilty about abandoning him. Her sisters could be pretty nosy. The poor man was probably wondering what the heck had happened to her.

"ZEKE MARTINI, please." Nick spoke softly into the receiver of the pay phone near the men's restroom. The family was starting to disperse, but there appeared to be nothing speedy about the process.

The operator connected him. Nick wanted to know where Grace went after she left the restaurant. Was she back at the Xanadu with Charles? He hoped not. His bags were still in her car. He had no reason to think she'd go through his stuff, but that didn't keep him from worrying.

A recorded message instructed him to leave a message or call Zeke's cellular number, which wasn't provided. After the beep, Nick said, "This low-tech communication sucks. We need to talk."

He replaced the receiver and turned around to find Yetta watching him. "What kind of secret police are you? Anyone could have overheard you. Come along, we'll go where it's private."

Nick felt himself blush. He wasn't used to being critiqued. "Do you know where your daughter is?"

She made a shrugging motion with her shoulders.

"Probably at the cemetery. She blows off steam by talking to her father. Well, to his grave, of course."

Apparently interpreting Nick's look of skepticism, she added, "Grace and her father were very close. After Ernst died—even before that really, because of the stroke—Grace did her best to fill his shoes. She was our rock."

Rocks have been known to crumble. Maybe she's involved with Chuck because she's tired of shouldering the load for her family.

As if reading his mind, Yetta said, "Normally, that burden would fall on the shoulders of the eldest child, not the youngest, but Alexandra wasn't well at the time. Elizabeth had her hands full handling Ernst's rehabilitation. And Katherine was a young mother with a full-time job and a husband that—" she sighed weightily "—disappointed us all."

Nick knew there was more to the story. Zeke had filled him in on Kate's ex-husband, who'd waited until the family was most vulnerable then tried to abscond with the cash from Ernst's insurance policy.

"We were all in pretty bad shape, but Grace not only took care of us, she opened this restaurant," Yetta said, her tone filled with pride. "She's an amazing young woman, and your suspicions are groundless, as you will see." She held up a set of keys. "Shall we go? No doubt Grace left your bags at the house before she drove out to the cemetery."

"What makes you so sure she's not back with Charles?"

She smiled and a light he hadn't noticed before in her eyes twinkled. It made her look younger. "I have the sight, remember?"

"I thought you said it was broken?"

She shrugged eloquently. "Unreliable on occasion, but I do feel comfortable saying Grace isn't anywhere near Charles."

CHARLES STOOD at the window of his office and watched the traffic below. The day had proven a challenge in every sense of the word. From an unsatisfying meeting with Grace to the usual teeth-grinding session with his partners. As MaryAnn had predicted, neither brother was impressed with Charles's latest offer for their shares.

They'd agreed to think over the terms while vacationing in Hawaii, but Charles wasn't expecting any change of heart. If the two didn't start playing ball soon, he might be forced to take action of another kind. Accidents were common among the elderly, and something could be arranged pretty cheaply if one had the right connections.

A name popped into his head, followed by a face. Nick, Nicholas...Nikolai. Yes. An intense, edgy-looking fellow who definitely had something to hide.

Charles prided himself on being able to read people. He'd known the instant he met Ernst Radonovic that the man would prove an invaluable resource. To the world at large, Ernst had presented a model of honesty and propriety. He'd worked his way up to pit boss with one of the largest gaming consortiums in Vegas. During the great union wars in the mid 1980s, Ernst had been one of the few who'd been respected by both sides. But Charles had sensed the Gypsy King's weakness—his family. And when the opportunity to make a little

money under the table came during labor union nego-
tiations, Charles had argued that as a man with four
daughters—and four tuition payments and four weddings to look forward to—Ernst had no choice but to
play ball.

Charles had intended to take his half up front, but a
politically ambitious district attorney at the time had
been keeping tabs on Charles. Any sudden windfall
would have brought an immediate investigation, so Ernst,
whose gaming skills bordered on legendary, had claimed
the entire amount as winnings—no questions asked.

Distracted by…um, personal matters at the time,
Charles didn't find out until too late just what Ernst had
planned for the money. Four trust accounts in his daughters' names. Charles had been furious, but Ernst—a
most charming and likable man—had placated him with
promises of larger profits down the road—when any
hint of impropriety was gone.

Charles's patience—and trust—had been taxed as
first one daughter then another was given access to the
money. His money. He'd finally confronted Ernst. Tem-
pers had flared. Charles had snapped, and a pushing
match ended with Ernst unconscious on the floor.

The only reason Charles didn't let the old man die
was the fear that he'd lose access to his money. He'd
called 911 and Ernst had been rushed to the hospital. A
stroke, the doctors said. Everyone assumed that the
stroke had caused Ernst to fall and hit his head. Only
Charles and Ernst knew that the "fall" had come first.

And Ernst, although he recovered to some degree,
had returned home with no memory of the argument that
had triggered his decline. Charles had remained close

to the family, never giving up hope of one day gaining access to the remaining money in Grace's trust account.

When Grace suddenly suggested using the money to go into business with him, Charles had been so shocked he hadn't been able to reply. The irony made him want to do a jig on Ernst Radonovic's grave, but he didn't dare show his enthusiasm. Yetta still controlled the account, and she was the one woman who made him nervous. There'd been times when he was certain she could see every black mark on his soul.

Speaking of black marks, he thought, grinning at his reflection in the glass. Wasn't it time for another?

Lydia and Reezira, the prostitutes he'd "rescued," were waiting in his suite.

He'd read about the plight of Eastern European Gypsies on the Internet. Many had fled to Canada, where the immigration laws were more welcoming than in the United States. Although these young women were accommodated, in some cases, their lot in life was not much improved over the hardships they'd endured in their native lands. Some turned to prostitution.

Charles had put word out on the underground that he was looking for healthy, ambitious young women to work in his casino. And he didn't mean waiting tables or serving cocktails. He wanted women who knew how to pleasure men.

Once he was sole proprietor, he'd turn this place into a destination spot for people who knew what they wanted and didn't mind paying for it. Prostitution was illegal, but there were loopholes in the system if a person knew how to find them, and Charles had always been good at skating past trouble on lies, diversion and bribery. He didn't expect to have any trouble once he'd cleared up two small problems: his blackmailer and his pesky partners.

But both headaches could wait till tomorrow. Right now, he planned to lose himself in a world that met his very specific needs.

"Hello," he called, his anticipation growing. "Daddy's home, little girls."

YETTA INHALED deeply. For her, every breath was a gift. She'd struggled with breathing problems all of her life. As a child, her frequent colds and debilitating coughs had been shrouded with whispers and looks she didn't understand. Until she'd turned ten. Then her mother told her the story of the fire that had cost their family so dearly. One daughter killed. One deformed and destined to die young. Yetta's life had been spared, but her lungs had been permanently damaged.

Over the years, Yetta had slowly unraveled the threads of the story. An accident, for sure. But the person who'd shouldered the blame for it was Jurek Sarna, who had been just a child himself at the time. It broke her heart to think about the injustice done to him.

Now she had Jurek's son in front of her. Nikolai. The person who would help her rid her family of a threat. But Nikolai was more than that. He was the only one who could bring peace to a man Yetta had long since forgiven. A man who believed he was dying.

"Would you like me to tell you about your father?"

The question obviously annoyed him.

"I know my father. He's alive and well and recently retired from the police force."

They were sitting at Yetta's patio table protected from the sun by a large canvas umbrella that Nick had unfurled for her. Nice manners, she thought, but no trust. None whatsoever. Everyone was a suspect, including her.

Which meant Yetta would need to move slowly to build a connection between Nikolai and the very distant past. "You have questions for me about Charles, then?"

The change of topic seemed to surprise him, but he shifted position in the padded lawn chair and faced her, resting his elbows on the glass-topped table. "How long have you known him?"

"Oh, goodness, twenty years, at least."

His blue eyes reminded her so much of his mother. Beautiful, sweet, reckless Lucille, but there was the wariness of Jurek, too. Jurek, who never took anything at face value, including Yetta's love for him and his family.

"Ernst was forever bringing home wounded souls. Like a child brings a bird with a broken wing."

"How'd they meet?"

"Through work. Charles was a young up-and-coming attorney with the firm that represented the casino where Ernst worked. This was during a very turbulent time when unions were making a push for inclusion in the gaming industry."

Yetta could see him mentally comparing what she told him to what he'd undoubtedly read from some file.

"What do you know about his past? His family?"

"Very little. Charles has never been particularly forthcoming about his childhood. I've gathered he had a bit of a rough time. Ernst told me his father died when Charles was quite young. His mother remarried and had another child —a girl—later on."

"Who paid for law school?"

"I have no idea, but Charles is a very smart man. Cagey, even. He knows how to work the system, and he is most astute when it comes to making the right connections."

"How did your husband figure into this?"

"That's a very good question. At first, I thought he spent time with our family because he was lonely. Alexandra and Elizabeth were beautiful—eligible—young women. But, in hindsight, I wonder if I imbued him with too much humanity."

"What did your husband get out of the relationship?"

She could almost hear Ernst chuckling. *He's a smart one, Yetta. You may have gotten more than you bargained for when you invited him here.*

Or was that her imagination talking?

In her youth, Yetta had trusted the voices in her head, the visions that came to her. Her gift had set her apart, made her special. Ernst had revered her, called her his goddess, but after his stroke, the sight had failed her. She no longer trusted her instincts, which was one reason she'd asked Jurek for help.

And he'd directed her to this man, whom she didn't know but to whom she felt an overwhelming connection. And she alone knew why that was.

Perhaps it was time to share her secret. "I was the third person to hold you when you were a baby."

"Hmm. Now, about Charles's connection to your daughter—"

"Your parents were renting a little mobile home on Mojave. I remember because Jurek always called it 'Mo Jave' with a hard *J*. He was teasing, of course."

Nikolai didn't appear interested, but she sensed that

was a front. "Your mother was working in a stage re-view before she started to show."

"A stage review? Is that another name for a striptease?"

His snide tone made her angry. "No. She'd worked a razzle-dazzle show once, right after she moved here, but this was modern dance. Full of passion and grit. One reviewer said your mother 'danced with her heart, not her feet.'"

He still looked unconvinced. "Dancers don't get pregnant and have babies."

"That is true of many, I'm sure. And I will admit your mother wasn't thrilled when she found out she was expecting, but your father was over the moon. He was so proud. He thought your birth would make Lucy give up her dream of being a dancer."

"Obviously he was wrong." A statement, not a question.

"Lucy tried to be a stay-at-home wife and mother, as was expected of her. But the urge to dance was just too strong. She started doing exercises and fasting to get back in shape. Alexandra was just seven months old when you were born. I love babies, and since I was home anyway, I offered to babysit. What was one more?"

"Uh, double the work," he said drily.

"Double the treasure. You were a perfect baby. Alexandra was as imperial as her name. From the very beginning she seemed to assume the rest of us were there to serve her," she said, smiling at the memory. "But you...you were a gift."

"I doubt that."

"Don't. You see, I came from a family that put boys on pedestals. My brothers were young gods. My sisters and I...well, it was different for girls. It's possible I was suffering from a little depression because I didn't give my husband a son, even though he worshipped his daughters and always insisted that he preferred girls.

"When you came along, I could pretend that you were mine. That I'd had twins. I didn't love Alexandra less—she wouldn't have allowed it," she added. "But I had you, too, to feel fulfilled and complete. Which is why…" She couldn't say it. Even all these years later.

"Why what?"

"Why I did what I did."

His eyes narrowed. "What did you do?"

"I…nursed you."

"I was sick?"

She shook her head and looked at her hands in her lap. "No. You were healthy, but you weren't gaining weight like most babies do. Your formula didn't agree with you. You'd spit it up every time I tried to feed you, so I gave up trying. I had more milk than Alexandra could take, so I put you to my breast."

He seemed surprised but not repulsed. "Really?"

Yetta took a deep breath and let it out. "I never told anyone. Even my husband. I was afraid it would seem wrong. That someone might say I was slighting my child in favor of another. A boy child. I might have even thought that myself, but you were so happy when we nursed. Alex…she ate because it was time. You…because you needed me." She reached for his hand. "And I needed you."

"Why?"

"You helped me get over my blues. I only had you for six or seven months, then your father lost his job. Although it was unheard-of at the time, he became a stay-at-home father."

"You let me go."

"I had no choice. I…I was pregnant again. I'd trusted my cousins who said that a nursing mother can't get pregnant. They were wrong, of course."

"I…I meant after my mother died. Why didn't you…anyone…?"

"Come for you," she supplied, knowing how hard it must have been for a man like him to ask.

He nodded.

"I did, but I was too late. Jurek went into some place no one could reach him after your mother died. Emotionally, I mean. He was in jail for another four months. And the whole time, he wouldn't talk to anyone."

She pictured her cousin when she'd visited him in jail. He'd reminded her of photos she'd seen of prisoners of war—hollow cheeks and dead eyes.

"I know he's never forgiven himself for what happened," she said. "Lucy didn't drive and he'd been picked up for writing a bad check, so she had to take the bus to work. She'd just stepped out the door of the bus when some crazy guy ran the light and broadsided another car that struck her."

Yetta remembered feeling overwhelmed by shock and sadness when she'd learned of the tragedy. "I was back east visiting my parents when it happened. By the time I heard the news, you were gone. Jurek ordered me not to search for you, but I did anyway. Maybe because you'd been adopted by a policeman the authorities were more tight-lipped than usual. It wasn't until last week that I even knew Jurek had maintained a connection to you."

"Why didn't he ever contact me?"

"He said you were with a good family. You seemed well-adjusted and safe." She sighed. "Maybe he was afraid you'd hate him, and perhaps you do, but one thing I know for certain, the past is part of you, whether you want to admit it or not. You owe it to yourself to meet your father."

"He isn't my father."

She didn't argue. He was right. She wasn't his mother, either. She got up. "Nap time should be over at The Dancing Hippo and I need to pick up Maya. That little squirt brought me back to life, just as you did once. Babies are good for the soul."

He didn't refute the statement, but Yetta could tell he didn't believe her. He would. Someday. She'd seen it in his future. But she didn't tell him that.

CHAPTER EIGHT

GRACE PULLED into the carport beside her mother's eleven-year-old Lincoln. "Dang. If Mom's home then, no doubt, our guest is, too," she muttered, looking down at her grubby jeans and work shirt that she still wore.

She'd hoped to get back before the party at Romantique broke up. Fortunately, her home was situated in the rear corner of her parent's oversize lot. As long as Nikolai and her mother were in the house, Grace could slip through the backyard unnoticed.

Her 1950s era motor home was tiny, but it served her needs. The interior paneling was teak, the built-in features ingenious given the date it was manufactured. The only downside was its lack of insulation. Her father had used steel poles and existing trees as anchors to secure cloth webbing above it to provide shade. Liz likened the look to some of the bunkers she'd seen in Bosnia.

Grace had moved home shortly after breaking up with Shawn. She'd poured her heart and imagination into creating a haven that vaguely resembled the inside of *I Dream of Jeannie*'s bottle. "Too girlie," her male cousins had decreed. Grace didn't care.

She quietly closed the car door and unloaded her

gear. Still hoping her mother and their guest were sitting in the kitchen, Grace followed the flagstone path to the rear of the house. She was almost to the patio when she heard her mother's voice.

She couldn't make out every word, but Nikolai's reply was loud and clear. "Don't you mean stripper?" His question held a rawness that made Grace flatten herself against the rough stucco and slowly inch back into the safety of the garage.

She didn't approve of eavesdropping, even if she was dying of curiosity. She closed the door and pulled out her phone. A few seconds later, Liz's voice came on the line.

"Hi, do me a favor and call Mom on her cell and make up some reason for her to go into the house."

"What are you talking about? Why don't you call her?"

"Because I'm hiding out in the garage. She and Nikolai are having some big heart-to-heart and I don't want to interrupt, but the only way to get to my house is past them."

There was a slight pause. "I get it. You're attracted to him and at the moment you're looking less than stunning, but you're too embarrassed to admit that."

Grace let out a little yelp. "Nice call, sis. Maybe you *are* psychic."

Liz snorted skeptically. "And you're psycho. Just go back out there and breeze past. It's something you do with flare."

"You really think so?"

"Uh-huh. Now leave me alone. I'm busy installing my new dishwasher."

Grace closed her phone and looked around. Liz was

right. Nikolai was going to be here for a long time, most likely. There would be times when she wouldn't be at her best.

Squaring her shoulders, she opened the door and walked outside. She'd just reached the edge of the house when she heard Nikolai's laugh, followed by a harsh growl. "So much for your powers of prophecy," he said, his tone dripping irony.

"Hey," Grace said, unable to contain herself. "Nobody talks to my mother like that." She marched to the patio table where the two were sitting. A large ecru-colored umbrella protected them from the sun. Grace ducked slightly to get under it.

Nikolai sat at an angle to the table, one booted foot propped on his knee. Despite his casual pose, he seemed tense.

"You're back," he said.

Grace pretended to salute. "Yes, sir. Mission accomplished. No lives lost, although knowing my brown thumb there are no guarantees the new recruits will last long in the desert sun." A powdery shower of sand drifted across her nose. She blinked and blew out a puff of air, sending her bangs haywire.

Her mother pulled out a chair for Grace to join them. "Hello, darling. Nikolai was worried about his belongings."

Grace doubted that. Who would be crazy enough to take something of his?

"I dropped off his suitcase and coat at Uncle's before I left."

"For where?"

Something in his tone made her defensive. "I was

giving lap dances at the cemetery," she said breezily. "It's just something I do."

Her mother made a tsking sound. "Stop teasing the man, Grace. He doesn't know you, yet." Yetta stood up. "After I pick up Maya, I'll stop at Claude's to make sure he's prepared a room. He's such a pack rat the place is always a mess." She looked at Nikolai and said, "Wait here. I'll be right back."

Before Grace could say that she'd already checked on Nikolai's accommodations, her mother was gone. Yetta took her hosting duties a lot more seriously than Grace did, so perhaps it was best that she sign off on Claude's arrangements.

Instead of sitting down, Grace walked to the outdoor sink her father had built. She turned on the tap and washed her hands, using a little pink brush to clean beneath her nails. There wasn't a towel, so she wiped her hands on the back of her jeans.

When she turned around, Nikolai was standing a foot away watching her. The sun was bright and Grace squinted, wishing she hadn't left her sunglasses in the car. "How was lunch?"

His eyes didn't seem bothered by the strong light. And they looked even bluer than she remembered.

"Best I've had in a long time. They don't serve that kind of food in jail."

Grace wanted to ask what he'd done to land in the slammer, but she didn't want to embarrass him.

"I got in a fight. Put a guy in the hospital," he said, his tone mocking, as if he'd read the question in her hesitation.

"Oh." She couldn't think of anything to say. She started to walk toward her corner of the yard.

"You've never broken the law, have you?" he asked. His tone was serious and contained an element she couldn't quite define. Did he think she held his arrest against him?

"Actually, I once stole some nail polish from a drugstore. I'd left my wallet at home and I really, really wanted a new color of nail polish to impress this boy I liked."

"Did you get busted?"

"Oh, yeah. Big time. Not by the store, but when I got home, Mom and Dad were both waiting for me." She would never forget the look of disappointment on her father's face. "I didn't even bother trying to lie. Dad marched me right back to the store and made me replace the polish *and* pay for it. Then I was grounded for a month. I never broke the law again."

"How did they know?"

Grace laughed. "At the time, I thought Mom must have seen it. You know, her second sight. But years later I found out that Dad had been in the pharmacy picking up a prescription for my grandmother when I came in. I was so intent on my crime, I never even noticed him. He waited until I left, then drove home. Since I was on foot, he and Mom had time to talk about how to handle the situation before I got there."

He snickered softly. "Sounds like something my father would have done." Apparently as an afterthought, he added, "He was pretty ticked off when I went to jail."

Grace was curious about his adopted family. "Tell me about them. Your parents. Were they good to you? Do you have siblings?"

"One sister. My parents' real child. They're in the

process of moving to the West Coast so they can be closer to her."

Although his tone remained blasé, Grace sensed some hurt feelings. Probably something he'd never admit. "Are you looking forward to meeting Jurek?"

His forehead wrinkled in a way that made her want to touch his face. "Who said I plan to?"

"I guess I figured that was the real reason you came. After all, you don't have that look most newcomers have when they first move here. That giddy, we're-gonna-hit-the-jackpot kind of look. But then when things don't work out—and they generally don't—many of them can't take the heat, both literally and figuratively. They stay a few months, then move to Los Angeles or someplace on the Coast."

"Like my birth parents," he said under his breath.

"I guess so," she said. "How'd you end up in Detroit?"

"Gotta live someplace."

"Do you like it?"

"It's okay."

Grace laughed at his evasive answers. "If I'm being nosy, just tell me."

"You're being nosy."

Instead of being offended, she agreed with him. "I know. My sisters claim it's my worst fault. I doubt that. I have several contenders." She resumed walking toward the path that led to her trailer but only took two steps before stopping. She turned to look at him and said, "Listen, I'm sorry about running out on you earlier. My family—God love 'em—can drive me crazy at times. It's either split or blow up. I didn't want to ruin your lunch. Which was great, right?"

His expression softened. "I don't think I've ever eaten so much at one time." He pulled at the waistband of his jeans. If there was an extra pound of fat around his middle, she'd have had a hard time finding it. Although the hunt might be worth it, a devilish voice suggested.

Her cheeks turned hot. "Good. I'm glad. I have to get ready for work, but I'll take you next door first."

She reversed directions and led the way past the garage. It wasn't the most glamorous route, skirting the trash cans and recycling.

"What do you do?" he asked, sticking close to her.

"Meet and greet." Her mind was already racing ahead to what she expected the night to bring.

"Tell me more about your mother's clairvoyance. Is that for real?"

The unexpected change of topic nearly caused her to swallow what was left of the breath mint she'd been sucking on. "Well…she's had her moments."

"What kind of moments? Like that John Edwards guy on television? Can she contact the dead? Can she tell me what horse to bet on? Or who will win next year's Superbowl?"

Grace sighed. She'd tried over the years to explain her mother's abilities to nonbelievers. Most remained doubtful, to say the least.

"Nothing so practical, I'm afraid."

He waited for her to go on.

"A hundred years ago, Mom would have been called Puri Dye—the wise woman of our tribe. Even when Dad was alive, if someone had a problem, they'd come to Mom for guidance. Sometimes she'd warn someone not to travel, like when my sister Liz was going to board a plane for Costa Rica."

"Did it crash?"

"No. But it was delayed and she would have missed her connecting flight in LAX. Mom was sure something bad would have happened. There was no way of proving whether she was right or wrong because Liz took a different flight."

His half smile seemed to appreciate the irony. Grace gave him credit for not laughing.

"But after my dad's stroke, she didn't trust herself anymore because…well…we were all blindsided when it happened."

"Shit happens. Why should you get any warning?"

Outsiders had said the same thing in the past. Usually, she didn't bother trying to explain. "Because we're Romani. We're different. We've retained access to a metaphysical connection that the rest of the world gave up and doesn't trust. If we'd known about the stroke…"

His broad shoulders lifted and fell. "If I'd stopped after two beers, I wouldn't have gotten in a fight and landed in jail."

Grace had a feeling he was poking fun of her, and she resented it. "Listen, you don't know what it was like around here before this happened. Dad was healthy. Robust. He wasn't a candidate for a stroke." She looked away, feeling tears beginning to prick behind her eyelids.

"We were all devastated, of course," she continued after a few moments. "But Mom got hit the hardest. She not only lost her husband but all faith in herself. She's just now starting to come back."

"So who's head of the family? Claude?"

Grace shook her head. "Uncle is a sweet man, but you saw for yourself at lunch that he isn't particularly savvy about the world. Dad used to call him a throwback to another generation."

She checked her watch. She had hoped to go over Charles's plans with Kate before the kitchen geared up for dinner. Walking a little faster, she said, "Claude still believes it's okay for Gypsies to bend the rules."

"And he works for Charles."

"Off and on. He does odd jobs to support his ponies."

"Ponies? As in Thoroughbreds?"

"Ponies. As in four-foot-tall hay burners."

His half smile sent flutters where flutters didn't belong. She picked up the pace. "He puts on performances for children's groups and lets classrooms visit his stables. It's pretty neat to see the children interact with the pygmy goats, ducks, chickens, dogs…"

"He runs a petting zoo?"

Grace nodded. "Sort of."

"He makes a living at that?"

"Enough to augment his social security and disability check. Dad used to say that money washes through Claude's fingers like rainwater." She ran the backside of her nails along the four-foot-high chainlink fence that outlined Claude's small front yard. Instead of grass, Claude's lawn was nickel-sized chunks of white rock held in place by bender board. Two elongated diamond shapes of red bricks encircled a pair of stubby-looking Joshua trees. "Fortunately, his eldest son has taken over the ranch and makes sure all the bills get paid."

The home itself was a 1960s ranch-style, three-bedroom structure, with an attached single-car garage that was full of junk. Grace couldn't remember ever seeing a car parked in it.

"What kind of disability?"

The question seemed a bit nosy, but since he'd be living with Claude, she answered truthfully. "He served in Korea. Got a Purple Heart. Has a steel plate in his head. When I was little, I'd tap around trying to find it." Grace paused, picturing her uncle, who at times seemed as much a child as his grandchildren.

"Hmm. I knew an old guy inside who had a head injury from the war. Sometimes he'd black out for no reason."

Inside. Grace didn't like the sound of that. "Claude gets really bad headaches occasionally. Mom treats him with herbs."

"Your mother is an herbalist?"

Grace smiled. "The Romani traditionally lived close to the land and knew what plants held medicinal values. And Liz is a physical therapist. She went to India to study holistic medicine and hopes to open her own practice some day."

Grace looked over her shoulder. She could almost see more questions forming. She gestured for him to hurry. "I forgot my hat and my SPF is overdue for a touch up. Come on."

She dashed up the sidewalk and opened the screen, which was made of lightweight metal. The front door was solid wood, but the varnish was peeling.

She knocked once then walked inside. "Hello," she called. The small, square foyer was dark, thanks to walnut paneling. Family photos of Claude's three sons occupied one wall, with a couple of newer shots of grand-children resting on a decorator table.

"You met Greg," she said, pointing to a framed photo of her cousins. "He's the youngest. The guy in the middle is Enzo. He lives in Henderson. His daughter works for us at the restaurant. And Damon, the oldest, almost never leaves the ranch."

The place smelled musty, like old smoke and laundry waiting to be washed. To the right, Grace could see the living room and kitchen. Both looked fairly presentable. She wasn't surprised that the kitchen stayed neat since Claude took most of his meals out, either with his sons or at Romantique.

"Mom?" she called.

There was no answer, so Grace turned to the left. "Claude's bedroom is at the end of the hall," she said. "Mom thought you'd be okay here," she said, opening the first door they came to. "The two guest rooms share a bath, but since you're his only company at the moment, you can pretty much make yourself at home."

She stepped back to let Nikolai pass into the room. His arm brushed against her shoulder and she sucked in a breath to make sure that was the only part of her body that made contact. He glanced sideways as if reading her reaction all too clearly.

"I, uh, hope you'll be comfortable here."

Grace looked around the room. A brown tweed rocker. A double bed that looked inches too short to accommodate Nikolai's frame. Generic tan carpet and a couple of faded posters Grace's aunt had probably bought at a swap meet. The room didn't fit him. She closed her eyes and saw him standing in front of a bank of windows overlooking a green lawn where a young boy was playing fetch with a dog.

"Where's my coat? It's not in the closet." Nikolai's voice, which held a note of accusation, shattered her vision.

Grace blinked twice and took a deep breath to regain her composure. That hasn't happened in a long time, she thought. *Was it real? Too much sun? Hormones?*

"Well?" He was looking at her strangely. Could he tell she'd had a moment? The kind of moment she refused to talk about—even with her sisters.

"Front-hall closet," she said, her voice not quite her own.

Grace had been nine when she'd first experienced the odd sensation of seeing a door open to a scene nobody else could see. Had she been with her mother at the time, Grace might have reacted differently, but she'd been at school. Her teacher had acted as though Grace were having some kind of seizure. The school nurse had been called. The principal had come in to frown at Grace. The word Gypsy came up in the whispered conversations among the adults who surrounded her. She'd decided then and there that whatever this was, it wasn't a good thing.

"Are you okay? You went kinda pale all of the sudden."

"No. I'm fine. But I have to go."

He followed her to the door. "What about the fax?"

"What facts?"

"Your mother said you have a fax machine at the restaurant. Charles wanted my application back ASAP."

Grace opened the door and walked out on the stoop.

"Oh. Well, sure. I can send it to him tonight, if you fill it out before I leave for work."

His lips flattened pensively. "I might need a little longer. Gotta find a few numbers. He said he takes that sort of thing seriously."

Grace didn't know or care. She usually went with her gut when she hired someone to work at Romantique. "Well, drop it off later or we can send it tomorrow. I doubt if Charles will look at it till then. I seem to remember him saying something about some kind of banquet tonight."

"And you're not going?"

The question bothered her. Hadn't he been paying attention when she told him she and Charles weren't involved romantically? Or hadn't he believed her? "Well, not that it's any of your business, but Friday is Romantique's busiest night. I very seldom take weekends off. Plus, lawyer things are boring and I'd rather stay home and give myself a pedicure than hobnob with Charles's cohorts."

He appeared surprised by her frankness.

Before she could qualify her snippy answer, which had mostly been to put him in his place—she actually liked some of Charles's friends, just not the type that attended the annual I'm-more-successful-than-you-are dinner—a voice hailed her from the street.

"I'm glad we caught you, Nikolai," Yetta said, tugging on her granddaughter's hand. "Maya has something to say to you."

When the pair reached them, Maya took a big breath. Grace could tell her niece was resigned to doing something she didn't relish. Grace hid a smile.

Dark curls screening her face, Maya stared at the ground and said, "Sorry, Mr. Nick."

To Grace's surprise, Nikolai moved closer and knelt beside the little girl, who'd plastered herself against her grandmother's leg after delivering her apology. Nikolai touched his finger to her tiny chin and made her look at him.

"Apology accepted. As long as you promise never to do that again. What you and Luca and Gemilla did could get you in a lot of trouble. I wouldn't want to see that happen, okay?"

Grace was impressed that Nikolai got all three children's names right.

"Mom, we both know Maya wasn't behind this little stunt. Did you talk to Claude about not teaching them any more tricks?"

"Of course," Yetta said, "but you know your uncle."

Grace's phone rang. She wasn't done talking about the subject, so she ignored it. "Nikolai is right. What if they'd tried that on a stranger? They could—"

"Auntie Grace," Maya said, interrupting. "It's Mommy. And I need to talk to her. Please?"

Grace looked at the incoming number. Romantique. Her skin tingled. "Wow, Maya, you're right," she said, picking up the child. "How'd you know that?"

The phone rang again.

Maya rolled her eyes. "She always calls Grandma's after school and we're not there."

So she called me looking for you. Logic, not prescience. Grace felt her face heat up. Hopefully, nobody noticed her silly mistake. She glanced at Nikolai, who was grinning.

The phone rang again.

Grinning. As if he knew what she was thinking. As if he knew *her*. Damn. Damn, damn, damn. This was not supposed to be happening. She could not—would not—be attracted to an unemployed ex-con with zero prince potential.

"Hello," she barked, feeling practically choked by frustration.

"Jeesch. Bite my head off, why don't you?" her sister complained. "I'm looking for my daughter. Where are you? When are you coming in? You can handle dinner, right? I'm taking the night off."

Kate's words sank in. "You're what?" Grace exclaimed in shock. Kate never took the night off. Never.

"You heard me. I'm going to take Maya to Game-Works. She's been asking for weeks."

"But…who's cooking?"

"Jo. I took your advice and made her our new assistant manager. I'd planned to tell you at lunch, but you split. Where'd you go? What did you think of Nikolai? Quite the hunk, huh?"

Grace blew out a sigh, handed the phone to her niece and lowered Maya to the ground. "I've got to get to work before your mother loses the rest of her marbles." She glanced at Nikolai. Hunk, indeed. What happened to the hit-man theory?

JUREK DEBATED before picking up the phone to make a call. He was moving a bit stiffly, but outwardly there was very little proof that he'd been violated once again by a doctor's intrusive explorations. He'd been released with a smile and the reassurance that all was well.

"Go home and relax for a few days, George," his doctor had said. "I'll call you when the lab results come back."

Jurek wouldn't hold his breath. He didn't need tests to tell him he was dying. But he hoped to stick around long enough to make sure Yetta and her family were safe.

"Hello," a cheerful voice said.

Jurek's heart lifted in his chest. He loved and admired Yetta's sunny disposition. She'd been through hell the past few years, but somehow she'd regained her spirit and her optimism. Except when it came to her youngest daughter's affairs.

"Yetta. It's me."

"Jurek," she cried. "Where have you been? I tried several times. I was starting to worry."

"My battery won't hold a charge. Haven't had time to get a new one."

The pause told him she didn't buy that excuse, but she was kind enough to let it go. "Nikolai is next door at Claude's. Do you want to talk to him?" She rushed on without giving him a chance to answer. "I have to say I've been picking up some interesting sparks between your son and Grace. Wouldn't it be something if they wound up together?"

"I wouldn't count on that, Yetta. From what I know about him, he doesn't seem to be able to make long-term relationships work. He never gets too close to anyone." Except his parents, he didn't add.

Jurek found that comforting, but the realization bothered him, too. If he'd stayed in his son's life, would he and Nikolai have spent time camping, fishing, hiking the trails of Michigan's Upper Peninsula as Nick and Pete did? *If.* A word that only leads to heartache.

"You could be describing yourself, couldn't you?"

He didn't answer.

"Why are you all alone, Jurek? Is it because of what happened to Alba and Beatrix?"

Jurek squeezed his eyes shut. He couldn't believe she'd mentioned their names. No one had talked to him about the accident in more than thirty years. "Let the past stay buried with your sisters, Yetta," he said, his tone harsh.

"I would, but I don't think that's healthy."

The irony of her statement wasn't lost on him. "Perhaps not, but I'm fit as a violin," he lied. Just speaking on the phone had left him exhausted.

She didn't say anything, but he sensed she didn't believe him. When she spoke, there was a softening in her tone. "We can't undo the past, Jurek. But what we do today can amend the future."

His future was almost over, but he had one thing left to do. "Has Nikolai made contact with your serpent?"

A long sigh preceded her answer. "Yes. Grace introduced them on the way home from the airport. I believe Nikolai is planning to fax a job application from Grace's office."

She chuckled softly. "At least, that was the excuse he gave to follow her to the restaurant. Like I said, something is happening between them, even though they're both pretending otherwise."

Jurek thought about that statement after he hung up. Pretense had saved his life many times. Self-delusion had kept him from going insane after he lost his wife and son. But nothing was going to help him avoid what was coming. A reckoning. First, with his cousin and his son. Then with God.

CHAPTER NINE

"WE'RE ALL BASTARDS, you know."

Nick looked at the man sitting across from him. The two were alone in Claude's kitchen finishing off a pizza they'd brought with them. Nick's second day in Vegas had flown by in a haze of activity because kind-hearted Claude had taken it upon himself to show Nick around. The guided tour had included four hours at Claude's beloved ranch where Nick had met more family and lots of hirsute little horses. "Excuse me?"

"It's not our fault. Happened long before any of us were born."

Nick had hoped to use the time to pick Grace's uncle's brain, but that had proven more difficult than Nick could have imagined. The guy was either incredibly wily or a few marbles shy of a full bag. "Huh?"

"You've never heard the Gypsy version of creation?" Claude exclaimed. He stood up and carried the pizza box to the garbage can under the sink. "Pour us another toddy and I'll tell you the story as soon as I get back from the little boy's room. Damnable prostate…" His words were lost in a low mutter as he exited the room.

Nick almost groaned. He wanted facts not fiction, but talking to Claude was like reading one of his nieces' Dr.

Seuss books—there was rhyme and some reason, but mostly fantasy. He picked up the bottle of port.

Claude returned to his padded captain's chair and rocked back, resting his stocking feet on the cushion of the chair between him and Nick. "Let's see…where was I? Oh, yes. At the beginning of time." He took a drink from his tumbler. "Long before the universe settled down into its present comfortable pattern, it was a chaotic place, churning with energy and power. By combining forces, Sky and Earth managed to create a world, and their union produced five children."

He lifted his chubby hand and rattled off the names starting with his thumb. "Sun, Moon, Fire, Wind and Mist."

"Sounds like a rock band from the seventies," Nick said, unable to keep the cynicism from his voice.

"It's the story my father told me and his father told him. Your father probably told you, too, but you've forgotten. Bears repeating so you can tell your children."

What are the chances of that? Nick wondered. He'd never even come close to asking a woman to marry him. He'd had several girlfriends. Two had lasted over a year, but eventually they'd left him. And he didn't blame them. He wasn't the type to settle down and tell fantastical tales to his kids.

"Sky and Earth were happy, but even in the best of families, some children need more attention than their parents can provide. Such was the case with Kham, the Sun. He had big ambitions. He wanted to rise as high as possible so that everyone could see him and bow down to his glory. But at the same time, he was drawn to the gentle beauty of his sister, Shion, the Moon."

"He could get arrested for that."

Claude appeared not to hear Nick's comment. He had his hands folded on his rounded belly and was looking at the ceiling. "Sky and Earth knew that this attraction was doomed, so they set the two far, far apart in orbits that would never meet. But Sun has never given up his quest to behold his beloved sister, so Kham chases Shion across the sky, day in and day out."

"Sounds like a page from my love life," Nick said drily.

Claude looked at him. His bushy white eyebrows reminded Nick of Andy Rooney. "What few know is that Kham and Shion got together once before their parents sent them away." His tone was more resigned than scandalized, Nick thought.

"When Shion gave birth, her offspring were sprinkled across the earth just as the two lovers were cast into the sky. These were the earliest Gypsies, and like their celestial parents, Gypsy descendents became wayfarers who never stay in one place for long."

"Really?" Nick said, smiling despite himself. The man looked so serious. "But I got the impression your family has lived here almost thirty years."

Claude scratched a spot above his left ear. "Ernst and Yetta, yes. Ernst was an odd duck. Happy to stay put. Not me. I tried my hand at a bit of everything over the years. Construction. Ranching. Truck driving."

He pointed to a framed photograph on the wall that showed a short, burly man in a ball cap standing beside an eighteen-wheeler. "Sold my rig to buy this place when my wife got sick. She needed to be closer to her doctors."

"How long ago did your wife pass away?"

"Two years before Ernst's stroke. Brain tumor. Slow-growing kind. Took her away piece by piece. When I visited Ernst in the hospital and he couldn't talk…I thought the same thing had happened to him. I mean, what are the chances? I dropped to my knees and started to pray. No man should have to go through that twice in one lifetime."

Nick took a sip of Claude's nameless liqueur. It left a sweet but smoky taste in his mouth. He liked it. He liked Claude, too, he realized. Claude was the kind of uncle he'd once wished for. Jovial and irreverent. The kind of relative a kid could let loose with.

Too bad this shirttail uncle had picked the wrong man to work for. "So, Claude, tell me what I'm going to be in for if I start working for Charles.…"

"AND, FOR THE BAR, what if we tried something really off-the-wall, like mix your own drinks?"

"You're nuts."

"It was just an idea."

"Well, it sucks."

Grace was hurt. She'd come in early on a Saturday to talk with Kate, but her sister was in a bleak mood. From what Grace had gathered, Kate's outing with Maya hadn't been overly successful. "Do you want to talk about what's bothering you?"

"What's bothering me is this crazy idea of yours," Kate snapped. "I told you before I don't think we should be talking about expanding right now. I don't have enough time in my day as it is, and you're asking for more. What am I supposed to do—clone myself?"

"Good grief. When did you turn into such a drama queen? Running a second place wouldn't be that different from running one if we hire the right personnel. Look at Jo. She handled the kitchen very professionally last night."

Grace had made a conscious effort to observe the older woman in action. Jo had been serious, focused and formidable enough to scare the young servers, which wasn't necessarily a bad thing. She'd come through like a trouper, although after the rush, Grace had seen her sitting out back smoking, and her hand had been shaking when she put the cigarette to her lips.

"I'm glad you like her, but she's only one person. To set up a new kitchen, I'd need an entire staff. How long has it taken me to get this place on its feet so I could leave for a few hours?"

Grace didn't bother answering. They both knew the date of Romantique's anniversary. Three years in September.

"Are we a fluke or a success? You're the numbers person, Grace. How can you even think about risking your money on such a shaky record?"

"I'm not gambling on our record, I'm banking on you. You're the draw here, Kate, and you know it. You're too good for just one small venue. You have so much raw creative talent it's scary."

Kate swore. "Stop trying to stroke my ego, Grace. I know my limitations."

"Your limitations?" Grace shouted. "You're Katherine the Great. You may spell your name differently but you can do anything, remember?"

Kate glared. "That was before."

"Before Ian? Forget Ian, Kate. He was a frog. All princesses have a frog or two in their past. We move on. Look at all you've accomplished since he's been gone. This will be one more thing that you can look at with pride and say, 'So, there.' When…if you ever see him again."

Kate took a deep breath. "That's the thing, Grace. A part of me—the biggest part—hopes I never see him again. I pray every night that when he gets out of jail, he takes off for wherever he was headed with his clients' money, and leaves us the hell alone. But that means I will continue to be sole provider for our daughter. College. Braces. And maybe someday—sooner rather than later—a house of our own."

Grace closed the gap between them and put her arm around her sister's shoulders. "I know you're a teeny-weeny bit jealous about how close Maya and Mom have grown since you two moved home, but, sis, it's not gonna be forever. I went through the same thing when Granny Beran came to stay, remember? She and I were tight as ticks, but my feelings for Gran didn't change how I felt about Mom."

Kate sighed and rested her head against Grace's arm. "I know I'm being ridiculous for letting it bug me, but whenever Maya and I are together, all she can talk about is Grammy this and Grammy that."

"That's a good thing, sis. Pretty soon, she'll be all about boys."

Kate groaned and pushed Grace away. "You're a pain. Listen, even if I agree to get behind this project, Mom will never let you invest that money in something so risky. Never."

"She let Alex use hers to buy a house."

"That was different. Alex and Mark…well, you know what happened. Mom and Dad didn't want to see her lose the house. Not after losing Mark. Besides, property is generally a safe investment in this city. But Charles is only talking about a lease, right? That leaves you vulnerable. Why are you really doing this, Grace? Tell me the truth. No bullshit."

Grace hesitated. Secrets weren't easily kept among four siblings. "Promise you won't tell anyone. I had a…um…a vision. Sorta."

Kate groaned and put her hand to her forehead. "I figured as much. Go on."

"Plan A—Too Romantique is a smash hit and we earn back our investment in six months to a year. You make enough money to buy that house you want so badly, and I…"

Kate's eyes narrowed. "And you?"

"I meet someone. The right someone." Kate made a sound of pure dismay, so Grace quickly added, "It was hazy, but I had a sense of real need—on both our parts. I know it sounds crazy, but I did my homework, too. I promise you this imaginary someone is not the reason behind my plan. I'm a business major, Kate. I know how to crunch numbers and this makes perfect sense, given the economic climate at this time."

Her sister didn't appear impressed.

"If by some stretch of the imagination, our success is less than I'm picturing, we would still own the fixtures and our name. We could always sell the business and recoup most of our investment."

"Maybe if we owned the building, but Charles and his partners own the Xanadu. Wouldn't they have some say in the matter? There's a little thing called a lease."

Grace frowned. She had to admit she might have

glossed over certain details of this project. "If we make as much money as Charles thinks we can make—"

A crashing sound similar to the noise Grace imagined a gunshot would make ripped through the room stopping her midsentence. When she opened her eyes, she saw that her sister had thrown a fourteen-inch stainless-steel lid onto the floor.

"Listen to me, Grace. And listen well. You're not Mom. And even if you were, we both know how accurate her mystical powers have been lately. I can't believe you'd risk your trust fund on a crapshoot like this."

Grace, who'd been sitting on the counter, hopped to her feet to face her sister. "But the money is nothing compared to family and happiness. I know how hard you've worked to repay what Ian took. You refused my offer to help, but you can't refuse this. I'm investing in the future for all of us. And for Maya."

Kate didn't say anything for a minute, then she spoke softly. "I thought I was investing in the future with Ian and look how that turned out."

Suddenly Grace understood. She should have known what was at the root of her sister's unwillingness to take a chance on this project. Kate's ex-husband had stolen more than money when he made off with his investors' funds; he'd also robbed Kate of her ability to take risks.

"Kate, Charles isn't Ian. I don't love him and I sure as heck don't trust him. Or any other man, for that matter. Not after Shawn cheated on me." Grace knew Kate understood, but she still looked unconvinced. "If we do this, I intend to supervise every aspect of the remodeling and account for every dime. Yes, it's a gamble, but I'm willing to take it."

Kate let out a sigh. "Why now? Why can't we wait a year or two? Maybe when Maya is in school full-time."

Grace couldn't talk about the feeling she had that something bad was going to happen. Partly because she and Kate both had reason not to trust feelings, and partly because she was afraid that by opening her mind to the dark omen, she'd somehow let the catastrophe take place. To change the subject, she said, "Speaking of Maya, you still haven't told me how your mother-and-daughter night went."

Kate snickered softly. "Turns out the daughter half of that equation had other plans."

"She's four. What kind of plans can a four-year-old have?"

"Heather—Damon's youngest—is having a sleep-over birthday party at the ranch tonight. Mom insists I okayed it. If I did, I don't remember. We spent most of our time together shopping for the perfect present. You know how much I love to shop."

Grace gave Kate another hug then suggested, "So how about a real girls' night out tonight? We could go dancing and scout out the competition."

Kate smiled weakly. "Thanks. I know this sounds stupid, but I think I'm going out to the ranch to see how the party's going. I won't stay, but…"

"It doesn't sound stupid. She's your baby. I'm sure there's room if you wanted to spend the night."

"Why don't you call MaryAnn?" Kate asked. "She's home. I saw her car when I left, and she told me Gregor had to work late."

Grace felt a sharp sting, like a bug bite, on her shoulder. She scratched it absently, frowning. "I don't think so," she said. "She's been acting kind of weird lately. I can't explain it, but every time she talks to me, I get the impression her mind is somewhere else."

Kate leaned over to peruse the plans. "Well, what do you expect? Gregor's a sweetheart and a good father, but he's about as reliable as a slot machine. Which he plays far too much, if what Jo told me is true."

"What's Jo got to do with Greg?"

Kate frowned. Grace knew she wasn't one to gossip. "Jo's son is relocating here from California. He was in town last weekend to close escrow on his new house. Jo took him to the comedy show at the Riviera. They bumped into Gregor. He was pretty drunk, and he told them he'd just dropped a bundle at the casino."

Grace groaned. "Not again."

Kate put out her hands. "He's a big boy, Grace. His addictions are not your problem."

"I swear I just had this conversation with our new houseguest. I know Greg's an adult and what he does with his life is his affair, but we are all going to pay the price if he can't make his house payment or if he kills himself in a car accident. Isn't a little intervention better than the alternatives?"

"When you put it like that, I guess so, but just in case Jo had the wrong guy, would you please not mention my name when you charge in on your white horse?"

Grace stuck out her tongue, but she smiled, too. She was used to her sister's teasing. "Go study those plans somewhere else. I need to fax next week's produce order before things start going crazy around here."

Kate started to leave but paused. "Speaking of faxes,

wasn't Nikolai supposed to drop something off for you last night? I was sure Mom mentioned a job application."

Grace shrugged. "Yeah, I thought so, too. Maybe he got lost. Or sidetracked." She'd been on edge most of the night waiting for him to appear, and she had to admit she'd been disappointed when he hadn't shown up.

"You like him," Kate said.

"Do not."

"Do, too. I can tell by the way your cheeks turned pink when I mentioned his name."

"It's hot in here, okay? And I don't even know him. None of us know him. You could be right. He might be a hit man."

Kate studied her a minute longer. "Even so, you like him," she said, walking away. The door shut solidly.

"Do not."

Do, too. Grace didn't like the sound of that voice. Instead of her sister's, it sounded far too much like her own.

NICK STARED at the dark ceiling, unable to turn his mind off. He'd learned plenty today, but nothing very helpful. Normally, he would have accepted that the gathering of information was part of the process and eventually all the pieces would fall into place. But tonight he felt restless.

Maybe Uncle Claude laces his booze with caffeine, he thought. Although when he'd left him, Claude had been dozing in his recliner to the muted highlights from some ridiculous reality show.

Suddenly too wired to lie still, he jumped out of bed and pulled on his jeans. He grabbed his shirt and shrugged it on but didn't bother with the buttons. Instead of his boots, he put on the running shoes that he'd set out for the morning. Moving quietly, he slipped into the hallway and walked to the sliding glass door.

The hum of the city was different from Detroit, he noticed. Despite the streetlights in this part of town, there was more visible sky. He was far enough away from the unnatural glow of the casinos to spot a few stars. Scorpius hung low on the horizon.

For the first time in four years, he wished he still smoked. Quitting had been his gift to his mother. She and his father had been smokers until a routine X ray found an ominous-looking spot on her lung. As they waited for the results, everyone in the family made a pact to quit. Fortunately, the biopsy proved benign. Usually, he didn't miss the cigs. But tonight was different.

A quiet splashing sound caught his attention. He walked to the concrete-block fence that separated the backyards of the housing development. The fence was too tall to peek over but a conveniently placed boulder gave him the extra height he needed.

Grace. Doing laps. He watched her make a neat underwater turn. Someone should tell her that her pool was too small to support such an activity, he thought. She could bump her head. She might drown.

Swimming in an outside pool in February is just not natural, he thought as he hoisted himself up and over the fence.

There'd been two feet of snow on the ground when he'd left home. Generally speaking, Nick didn't mind winter. Especially around the holidays. Fall was gorgeous. He enjoyed the sights and smells. Summer in Michigan was never the same from year to year, and he loved the variety. In fact, he didn't know how people who lived in one-season climates could stand the sameness.

A surreal fog rose off the slightly heated water of the pool. A sunken light made the oval shimmer like a lava lamp. He stepped closer. Grace hadn't spotted him and was still intently pursuing her steady crawl.

"What the—" she said, splashing as if she'd just bumped into Jaws. "Are you trying to give me a heart attack?"

He stepped out of the shadows. He wasn't sure how she'd seen him, but obviously she had. "Don't you know it's not safe to swim alone?"

She'd come to an abrupt stop and was standing in chest-deep water. He could see the straps of her swimsuit, but he couldn't make out the color or pattern of the print.

"So this is you playing lifeguard? How chivalrous," she said, her tone dripping with sarcasm.

"I heard the splashing. I was curious. A swim sounded inviting."

"That's what gates are for. Gates that go *ding-dong*. More neighborly than hopping the fence and sneaking up on people."

He turned around and looked to where she was pointing. Sure enough, midway along the fence was a wooden gate. He'd noticed it the day before when he was talking to Yetta. "Sorry."

She didn't look convinced. "So where are your trunks?"

"Are they required?" He meant the question to be teasing, not provocative, but when her eyes narrowed just for a second, as if she were actually picturing him naked, Nick's body responded. He muttered a silent expletive and sat down on a nearby lawn chair.

Grace moved into deeper water so only her head was showing. He assumed her shoulders were chilled by the night air. He was glad he'd grabbed his hooded sweatshirt on the way out the door. "Do you do this often? Late-night laps?"

"Usually, I swim in the morning. When Dad was alive, he and I would race. Before his stroke. That's what made it so hard to believe when he was stricken. He was in such good health, fit and active. Then suddenly, he couldn't be in the water without help. It took two of us to help him in and out of the pool."

Nick's last partner had been in a car accident shortly before Christmas. Through physical therapy he'd managed to recover about two-thirds of his former mobility, but he'd never again walk without a cane. "I have a friend with a brain injury. I know how frustrating it can be for both the patient and the caregiver."

Grace parted the water in a graceful sidestroke and swam to the edge of the pool. "We were lucky Liz was here."

"Did he get better?"

"For a while."

Nick had no trouble imagining how heartbreaking Ernst's decline must have been for the family.

"Did Mom answer all your questions about your birth family when you two talked?"

He sat forward, shoulders hunched, hands linked. "She volunteered information that doesn't mean squat to me. It's ancient history. Who really gives a crap?"

She pushed off and kicked hard enough to create a

large splash. Her skeptical "ha" told him she didn't believe him. "I came here for work, not sentimental garbage. I have a family. I don't need another."

"Tell me about them."

"Why do you care?"

She turned abruptly and swam quickly back to the
side. Without pausing to catch her breath, she stiff-
armed a wall of water that broke a foot in front of him.
The residual splash dampened his shoes, ankles and
jeans, from the knees down.

"Hey…"

"No, hey, you. You're a guest here. I picked you up
from the airport, then didn't see you for the rest of the
day. Would it hurt you to play the friendly chatter game?"

That sounded almost as though she was disappointed.
Nick kicked off his shoes and walked to the edge of the
pool. Grace looked up, her eyes wide and mouth slightly
open. He stepped over the edge and sank down, fully
clothed. His feet touched the tile bottom and he pushed
off. When he opened his eyes, his face was a few inches
from hers.

"How friendly did you have in mind?"

Her mouth opened and closed the way it had when
her cousin's kids and her niece had tried to pick his
pocket. Nick had a feeling it took a lot to leave her
speechless. Instead of answering, she turned to swim
away, but he caught her arm.

She tensed as if he were a threat. Maybe he was—to
his own piece of mind, most certainly. To this case, very
possibly. He had to stop whatever was going on with his
libido before it got out of hand. And he would. After he
kissed her.

Just once. Because her lips were too tempting to resist. Even now, when her expression was one of consternation, her lips were ruddy and full. Her upper arm was soft, although the muscle seemed solid and ready to fight him off if necessary. But the slightly questioning look in her eyes told him it wouldn't come to that if he kept things civilized.

He kicked his feet. His jeans were heavy and cold on his skin even though the water was warmer than he'd expected. When he was close enough to detect the faint odor of garlic and spearmint on her breath, he said, "It would probably be uncouth to kiss you, wouldn't it? We haven't even dined together, yet."

She ignored his question. "I work odd hours. Sort of the split shift from hell."

"How 'bout breakfast?"

Even in the faint light, he could tell that she'd read more into the offer than he'd intended. "My treat," he added. "We could meet out front. You can take me to your favorite spot."

She laughed shortly, confirming her embarrassment. Oddly, this small vanity made her suddenly very human, and real. He knew without a doubt that she wasn't Charles's stooge or cohort. She was Grace Radonovic, her father's princess who was just trying to keep her family together.

He'd never met a woman like her, and if he had, he'd have pushed her away. This time, he pulled her closer. Her chest brushed against his.

"I think you might be crazy," she said, laughing. "And here we were worried about you being a hit man. You're really just plain nuts."

"That's one explanation. Dazzled by your beauty is another."

He lowered his head to kiss her, but she slipped, mermaid-like, from his hold and swam underwater to the far end of the pool. She pulled herself up and out of the pool, grabbing a towel from the back of a lawn chair. Even in the misty lighting. Nick could tell her breathing was shaky.

She started away but stopped and turned slightly. With a smile that made him groan, she blew him a kiss and said, "See you at breakfast. Any day but Saturday— I sleep in on Saturdays." Then she disappeared into the darkness.

As he sank under the water, he heard the sound of a door closing. Submerged, eyes blinking against the sting of the chlorine, he shook his head. She was right. He was crazy.

CHAPTER TEN

"HIT ME."

Nick watched the play at the blackjack table he was sitting at with minimal interest. He'd been in Vegas a week. Charles's reply to Nick's faxed application had been instantaneous—Nick could start bright and early that Monday morning. Which had meant no breakfast with Grace. Which had been a good thing, he told himself. In the clear, crisp light of day, Nick had no excuse for his behavior. None. He was here to do a job. And since he no longer considered Grace a suspect, there wasn't any reason to spend time with her. There would be no repeat of their near-miss in the pool.

"Is this table hot?" a voice asked from over Nick's shoulder.

Zeke. Nick felt a quick tingle of adrenaline but didn't shift his gaze from the pair of cards he'd been studying. Blackjack wasn't his thing, but he'd been trying to bond with two of his fellow janitors, who were sitting to his left.

"Not particularly, but feel free to change our luck," he said, nodding at the empty spot to his right.

"Don't mind if I do."

Nick pretended to study his cards: a jack of spades and a six of hearts. Not a good hand when the dealer had a ten showing. He eased them flat, indicating he planned to hold. Only then did he glance at his new neighbor.

Today, Zeke was wearing a gray windbreaker with broken-in jeans and a black golf shirt. The slogan on his cap read Golfers Do It On Par. Nick had to bite his lip to avoid smiling.

Zeke set out a small stack of chips and made eye contact with the dealer, a small, Asian woman whose name tag read Kim, Seoul, South Korea.

When Nick was sure the others at the table were distracted by giving advice to the beginner sitting in the wheel position, he said, softly, "Trash detail this morning. Caught a glimpse of some handwritten notes. But his secretary put them through the shredder before I could make copies."

In the five days that Nick had been working, he'd only been to Charles's office twice. Most of the time, he was emptying garbage in the casino proper or the public restrooms. He'd had worse undercover details, but his patience was being taxed. Particularly since nothing seemed to be happening at any level of the investigation.

According to Zeke, who had the ability to pop out of nowhere then disappear after a quick briefing, the two cops who were suspected of collusion had both been on vacation for a week. No new insurance claims had been initiated. Charles appeared to be lying low, almost as if he was aware of something.

"And the ladies?"

Zeke was referring to the women Nick had pegged as prostitutes the first day he arrived. He shook his head. "Nothing."

The dealer flipped over her hole card. A six. She had

to take a hit. Her next card was an eight. She went bust. The other three players—Nick's janitor pals and the stranger—cheered as the dealer passed out chips.

Nick's next cards were a six and a five. He turned them right side up and doubled his bet. His pals responded with loud hoots.

Since he'd started hanging around with the members of the janitorial staff, Nick had heard rumors galore, mostly about Charles's sex life: "He's a closet fag." "Charles is a trust-fund baby. Work is just a hobby for him. Sex is his real passion." "Charlie-boy likes little girls. He only dates women like Grace Radonovic for show. She's too old for him." "Charles is physically deformed in his privates—that's why he hires hookers."

The last had been from a woman who was reputed to have slept with both of Charles's partners, whom Nick had yet to meet. MaryAnn had told Nick the Salvatore brothers were in Maui for a family wedding. They were due back any day.

Nick watched as the dealer took hit after hit to finish with seventeen. He held his breath as she turned over his down card. A five of diamonds. He lost his bet. His pals groaned sympathetically.

He pocketed his remaining couple of chips and told his friends he'd see them later. When he turned to leave, Zeke did the same.

Before Nick could ask Zeke to run background checks on his co-workers, the detective asked. "What's happening with the princess's plans?"

Nick was embarrassed to admit he didn't know. They hadn't really talked since that night in the pool. Zeke wanted to know if she was still going through with her plan to open a nightclub with Charles, which meant Nick was going to have to swallow his pride. Because this was business. Just business.

GRACE HESITATED before opening the door of her trailer. She'd put off talking with her mother about Too Romantique for a week, but Charles wouldn't wait any longer. "You told me Kate would be done with the plan last night," he'd said just minutes earlier on the phone. "So? Are we going to do this or not?"

Grace had finally pinned down some design specifics from her sister by talking hypothetically. "*If* we opened a second place, what would you like to see—kitchen-wise?" she'd asked Kate and Jo. The two had bounced ideas off each other until they came up with a workable layout. Costly, Grace suspected, but one that even the Iron Chef would have drooled over.

Now, Grace just needed her mother to release the funds. *Not a problem.*

Grace took a deep breath for courage and stepped outside. The blue sky was dissected by contrails left from Nellis Air Force Base pilots. "Hi, Mom, what's up?" Grace called when she spotted her mother kneeling beside a small patch of exposed dirt. From the tools at her side, she appeared ready to plant petunias, a flower Yetta said reminded her of her childhood.

"Hello, dear. You're here late today."

"Comp time. I helped Jo steam-clean the walls last night after Kate went home."

"This Jo person seems very nice and helpful. I'm glad your sister found her. You should invite her to dinner some Sunday."

Romantique was closed on Sundays and Mondays.

"I could do that. You know she has a partner, right? Another woman," Grace added, feeling a bit embarrassed. Sexuality of any kind wasn't a subject she and her mother had discussed much. Growing up, that area of Grace's education had fallen to her sisters.

"Yes, I know. I'd like to meet her, too." Yetta sat back on her heels and rolled her shoulders. "You're not homophobic, are you?"

Grace nearly dropped the water bottle she was carrying...until she spotted her mother's playful wink. "No, Mother, I just didn't want to spring any unnecessary surprises on you, the way you did when you invited Nikolai to move in."

"But he's turned out to be such a delightful surprise. Don't you think?"

Delightful? Not the first word that popped up when she thought of him. Sexy. Worrisome. "I try not to think about him," she lied. Their almost-kiss had been on her mind the whole week. "I'm too busy. And I need to talk to you about this new project I have in mind."

"The spin-off restaurant. I heard some murmuring about it."

"I want to call it Too Romantique."

"Very clever name. You've always had a way with words."

The praise was nice, but Grace rushed on now that the ice was broken. "Thanks. I think it will attract a lot of attention and we can play up our heritage in the press release. Two sisters of Romani descent opening a hip bar and grill. We'll make back our investment in no time."

Yetta pushed the trowel into the powdery gray soil.

"Speaking of which, where are you entrepreneurs getting this money?"

Grace felt her cheeks heat up. "Um, well, I thought I might be able to use the money in my trust."

"No."

Grace scooted her chair a little closer. "Mom, you don't understand. This is a great opportunity. Charles will be matching my investment, dollar for dollar. He's even willing to sign something that reimburses me every penny if the restaurant goes belly-up."

"What if he goes belly-up?"

"Charles? Bankrupt? Never happen."

Yetta smiled. "So now you can see into the future, huh?"

Grace let out a sigh. "Mom," she said gently, "I'm a college-educated businesswoman. I've crunched the numbers. I know a good opportunity when I see one."

"And what does Charles see when he looks at you?"

Her tone made Grace blush. Surely her mother didn't think Grace was romantically inclined toward Charles, whose tepid hugs seemed almost fatherly when compared to a man like Nikolai who could start a fire in her veins with one brief touch.

"He sees a potential business partner, of course."

"Or an untapped bank account."

The sour tone surprised Grace. "Mom, Charles is one of Dad's oldest friends. Didn't he help Dad set up our trusts?"

Yetta looked away. "Don't presume to know what Ernst was thinking back then. Your father came into some money and wanted to insure that it would be there for you girls if anything happened to him. He and

Charles were not in agreement on how the money should be invested, which makes me wonder if Charles has an ulterior motive for supporting this idea of yours."

Grace frowned. Was that true? How come her father had never mentioned such a thing to her? "Mom, Charles has been good to you. He didn't charge you a dime to recover your money after Ian was arrested, remember?"

Yetta sighed. "I know you don't put much faith in my visions anymore, but, dear, I just don't completely trust Charles. You, of all people, should understand."

Grace looked away. She could lie and say she still believed in her mother's abilities, but even without extraordinary skills, Yetta would have sensed the truth.

Her mother touched her hand. "I understand, honey. I don't trust myself much anymore, either. But I can't agree to let you use that money for this purpose."

Grace jumped to her feet. "Mom, if this is about Dad's original intention for our trusts—as a dowry—I think that's a bit archaic. I'm twenty-eight years old. My flower-strewn-wedding days are just about over. Prince Charming disappeared down the rapids with a different princess in his raft. Now, my focus is on making money, and that trust fund could do me a lot more good if I put it to work in a new restaurant."

Yetta rose, as well. "Darling girl, you joke about what Shawn did to you, but I know how much it hurt. You pretend your heart is healed but it isn't. Not yet. It will be soon, though. I promise. You picked the wrong prince, sweetheart. That's all."

That's all? Like they grow on trees? "Mom, about the money. What if I borrowed against it? The way a person does with a life-insurance policy? I could slowly pay it back, and then when I'm forty or fifty, if my gray-haired prince shows up, we could throw a heckuva grand affair."

Yetta laughed, as Grace had intended. But her mother was right. Grace still felt betrayed by Shawn and fearful of putting her heart on the line. Maybe, subconsciously, she was using work and family to fill a void.

"I will think about it…if you do something for me."

"What?"

"Take Nikolai out on the town. He's had a humdrum life. Very little glamour. That can make a person bitter. I want him to have fun, live it up a bit. Can you do that for me?"

"You want me to show him a good time?" Grace asked, barely able to contain the shiver that raced through her body. She knew what kind of good time she'd like to show him.

Her mother looked at her, eyes narrowing. "Would that be so hard?"

Hard? She'd felt a certain hardness for a fleeting second in the pool. "No," she said, her voice squeaking.

"Are you well, dear? Your cheeks are flushed."

"I'm fine. Really. I just…well, I was thinking about where I'd take him. So many choices. A dozen great restaurants to pick from. All the sights, of course."

"Perhaps a show. His mother was a dancer, you know."

Grace nodded, but she recalled some of the conversation she'd overheard the day Nikolai had arrived. He hadn't seemed too happy about his mother's career. "I'll put something together, if you promise you'll think about letting me use my trust for this project, deal?"

Her mother put her arms around Grace and squeezed

her warmly. Yetta nodded, but Grace knew that a hug was not the same as a handshake.

NICK SLOWLY MADE his way back to the employees' break room after his plan to do a little private cleaning up in Charles's office failed. The door had been locked and one of Charles's regular security goons had been loitering in the hall. Neither Charles nor MaryAnn had been in the office.

He was halfway down the escalator when he spotted Grace. She'd started through the lobby with a purposeful stride then stopped suddenly and veered toward the restaurant where she and Charles had conversed the day Nick had arrived. Instead of going in, she pivoted on one heel and marched toward the elevator, a look of grim determination on her face.

He pushed off the wall and trotted across the foyer to catch her before the elevator door opened. Luckily for him, the elevators were as run-down as everything else in this place. He sidled up beside her and cleared his throat.

Grace was staring at the brushed-chrome doors and didn't look his way, so Nick nudged her. Her brows knotted and she turned as if to scold him.

"Nikolai," she exclaimed. "I was going to look for you next."

Nick couldn't get over how strange it was to hear her say his birth name. It sounded sexy and exotic. And he liked it. "I'm only second on your list, huh?"

Her cheeks colored slightly. "Better than last, isn't it?"

"Maybe. Who's first?"

"Charles. I have to tell him I need more time before

we can close our deal on Too Romantique. My mother is being extra cautious about money these days. I shouldn't complain after what happened with Kate's ex-husband but still—" She made a sound that told him she was embarrassed about having shared that piece of personal information with him.

She tried to escape his scrutiny by dashing into the elevator when it arrived but had to wait as five people, including Zeke, exited. Nick followed her in.

"Don't you have a job to do?" she asked.

"Yes," he said. *I'm doing it right now.* The thought served as a reminder that he needed to keep his head on task—unlike the last time they were alone together. In the pool. He pushed the dangerous image away. "But I'm on break. I thought Charles was pretty generous with downtime until one of my co-workers pointed out that the frequent short breaks meant you had no time to go anywhere so would probably spend money in the casino. Clever, huh?"

Grace nodded. "Oh, Charles knows how to work the system. The other day over breakfast Liz pointed out that while most people might construe Charles's efforts on behalf of injured casino workers as a good thing, some could argue that he was taking advantage of a fear of litigation to settle minor grievances out of court. Since he used to work for one of the biggest casinos around, he knows firsthand what the threshold is for nuisance complaints."

A week ago, Nick would have been surprised to hear this coming from her mouth. That was before he understood that she truly was an innocent where Charles was concerned. His fear at the moment was that she was also being set up to become a victim. But he needed proof.

"So much for Mr. Altruistic?"

She looked at him with eyebrows scrunched. "You know, sometimes you're not the person you're trying to convince everyone you are."

A sick feeling swept through his belly. "What do you mean?"

"You come off as blue-collar, tough, bitter and mad at the world. But other times, you're kind, sensitive and well educated."

He laughed shortly. "My jail had a good library."

She crossed her arms and gave a snort that said she didn't believe him. She wore a black business suit with dressy boots and a simple white wool sweater that lay sweetly against her neck. Her only jewelry was a heart-shaped gold locket. Her hair was piled in a twist atop her head.

"You look nice."

"Thanks. It's my professional look."

"You have an appointment with Charles?"

The elevator doors opened to the floor that held the business offices. She stepped forward but didn't exit. "Not exactly. But he's usually here this time of day. Why?"

Nick shrugged. "MaryAnn said something about a funeral. I guess I thought Charles was going, too. I could be wrong."

Grace let out a long sigh. "Darn. I forgot about that. Well, maybe I can catch him at his suite." She pressed a different button. "Aren't you going to be late for work?"

When the elevator chugged upward, Nick took a step closer to Grace. Her eyes widened with alarm and she put out a hand. "Look. We haven't talked about that night in the pool. I figure it's no big deal." Her smile looked forced. "No reason to feel awkward, right? You're in a new environment. You're lonely. I was handy."

Nick let out a low curse. "You think that's why I tried to kiss you?"

She readjusted the strap of her handbag and stiffened her shoulders. "More like you're not the kind of guy to pass up an opportunity when it presents itself. I just—"

He cut off her words with his mouth. It irked him to know she thought he was an opportunist who was looking for an easy piece.

She tried to twist away, but he took her jaw in his hand and held her still. Her skin smelled liked warm peaches, her breath was sweet and shaky. He closed his eyes and kissed her. She let out a small sound that he swallowed. A whimper? A sigh? He wasn't sure but he felt the moment she gave in to the spark between them. She looped her arms around his shoulders—for a heartbeat, then suddenly she pushed him back.

"Oh, no, not again," she exclaimed, smacking him solidly on the chest with the palm of her hand. "What is wrong with you? With me? I've never in my life kissed a man in an elevator." She pointed to the upper corner of the small box. "That's a camera, you idiot. There are probably half a dozen security people hooting and howling right this minute."

Nick cursed silently. The last thing he needed was for Charles to see him kissing Grace. Fortunately Charles's in-house security system left a great deal to be desired. Only occasionally monitored, the small screens were cloudy and often offline. "So you're here to see Charles on business, but you said I was also on your list?"

The door started to open but Nick hit Close, then waited for her to answer him. Her blush had spread to her neck.

"Um, well…this probably isn't the best timing, but my mother wants me to take you out on the town. Show you the fun side of Vegas. She says you deserve to live it up a little. Are you free tonight?"

Nick knew he should say no. He had no reason to spend time with her. She wasn't a suspect, but she did have Charles's ear. And she could give him inside information on Gregor and MaryAnn, both employees of Charles's.

"I get off at five."

"I'll pick you up at six."

He released the elevator door and she fled without a backward glance.

Nick dropped back to lean against the wall and watched her walk away. He wanted to believe that he was doing this for the sake of the job, but he'd never had to lie to himself in the past when it came to women. He liked sex. He liked Grace. He would have liked to make love with her, but that wasn't going to happen. Not tonight, anyway.

CHAPTER ELEVEN

NICK WAS USED to being in control. At the moment, he was anything but.

Grace had picked him up at six-fifteen. "Fashionably late," she'd claimed with a wink when he sat down in the passenger seat of her car. No excuses. No apologies.

"I've made reservations for dinner at my favorite seafood restaurant, but if that doesn't appeal to you, Delmonico's, which is renowned for its steaks, is right next door."

"I like fish."

"Cool. Since the real action doesn't start until later, we might as well take advantage of what's left of the sunlight. In fact, I thought you might enjoy a view from the top."

Nick had consented, more or less, to put himself in her hands for the evening which was why he was now following her to an observation platform atop the Stratosphere, some thousand-plus feet above the city. Belatedly, he wished he'd exercised some free will.

"You're not afraid of heights, are you? 'Cause I think we have time to ride the Big Shot, if you're up for a cheap thrill."

"What's the Big Shot?"

"If you have to ask, you've got to try it. At least once. There are a couple of other choices but this one is my favorite. The coaster is kinda tame by ride standards. X-Scream and Insanity—The Ride are fun, but they're the newest, and the lines are usually longer."

Nick had seen photos of the amusement-park rides that dangled over the edge of the tower. *Fun* wasn't the first word that came to mind, but he kept his opinion to himself. He didn't want to come off as a wuss, especially when Grace's eyes were alight with excitement. She obviously loved flirting with danger. She was flirting with him, wasn't she? Even though she didn't know he was a cop investigating members of her family, she had to sense he was no boy-next-door.

Nick bought the tickets—over Grace's suggestion they go dutch—and dutifully handed them to the man who strapped them into the molded seats that were equipped with well-padded shoulder harnesses. At his side, Grace, who'd volunteered to take the outside position, looked at him and said, "You're a bit green. I hope that's just from the colored lights."

"I'm not a huge fan of thrill rides."

She laughed. "But you were too macho to admit it when I gave you the chance to back out. That's delicious." She gave him a look that attempted to convey sympathy, but the mirth in her eyes ruined it. "At least, I haven't fed you yet."

Nick let out a low growl that set off another gigglefest, which only ended when the attendant came by to collect glasses, loose change or jewelry—anything that could become a lethal projectile during the ride. Nick's stomach began to do somersaults.

Around him the nervous chatter lessened. Even Grace seemed to take a moment to appreciate the peril in which they'd placed themselves. Or so he thought, until she said, "Doesn't Mount Charleston look beautiful with the last little bit of sunset behind it? I learned to ski there."

Nick studied the distant mountain range, which looked like an uneven construction paper cutout against a child's watercolor background. He'd made something similar for his mother when he was in grade school. He found that by keeping his gaze fixed on a point in the distance, his vertigo was less.

"You know what freaks me out about this ride?" she asked.

"That you paid money to risk your life?"

"No," she said with a laugh. "My friend, Kendra, who is in the army, told me that a combat-zone jump is made from eight-hundred feet. That's two-hundred feet below this."

Nick looked down. Beyond the edge of the platform, which was just a few feet away, the city was laid out in a grid of lines, angles and lights of all kinds. Headlights and taillights moved in a steady stream. The giant billboards that everyone associated with Vegas were the size of children's toys. The bold colors that would splash across the night sky were washed out in the dusky haze of twilight.

"I draw the line at a few things and jumping out of a perfectly good airplane is one of them," he said, the back of his head thumping solidly against the padded rest.

Grace laughed again, but whatever she'd been about to say was cut off by the voice on the loudspeaker that started a countdown. "Prepare to blast off. Five, four, three, two, one…"

"Keep your eyes…open," Grace said. The last word turned to a high-pitched squeal.

Yeah, right, Nick would have said, if his mouth worked, but his jaw snapped shut as the ride shot them skyward.

Just when he was sure the contraption was going to shoot off the top of the tower and sail into the night sky, the unit came to a quivering stop. Now Nick was an extra one hundred and sixty feet higher. The world had shrunk even smaller. He knew because he couldn't take his eyes off the view as the ride reversed direction and fell straight down to the launch pad.

It was over in a flash. The instant Nick realized he'd survived, he felt a rush of emotion. Something wild, crazy and powerful for the woman at his side. She wasn't laughing, but the dancing zest in her eyes made him want to kiss her till they fell off the ledge. The trip down couldn't be any more exhilarating than what he was feeling at this moment. He actually had to bite his tongue to keep from saying, *I love you.*

How crazy was that?

As SHE AND NIKOLAI WALKED toward the parking lot where she'd left her car, Grace mentally crossed off the items on her list. *The Stratosphere. Done. Walking along the canals and Saint Mark's Square at The Venetian. Done. The shark exhibit at Mandalay Bay. Done. Dinner at Aquaknox. Done.* She was full and quite pleased with herself, but there were still a couple more things her mother had suggested she add to the list.

"He needs to try a little gambling," Yetta had said. "And everyone should see the water show at Bellagio."

Grace doubted the dancing fountains, though impressive, would be high on Nikolai's "must see" list, but she'd suggest it. Along with taking in a dance revue. What red-blooded guy would turn down a chance to see gorgeous women in skimpy or, in some cases, nonexistent costumes?

"So," Grace said as they reached a relatively quiet stretch of walkway near Bally's. "Time for hard choices."

"How hard?" he said, leaning close enough to make his point.

She groaned as she would have if Gregor had teased her. "Difficult, I meant to say." She leaned back and crossed her arms. "You've been flirting with me all night. Do you mean to or is suggestive banter a sexy-guy thing? You can't help yourself?"

"You think I'm sexy?"

She let out sigh. "And now game playing. Listen. I was nearly engaged to a gorgeous ski bum once. We were this close to setting up house." She held her thumb and index finger up for him to see the tiny space between them. "But he couldn't give up the thrill of the conquest. He always felt terrible afterward and promised never to do it again, but his promises were lamer than his...well, you get the picture."

His chuckle was warm and inclusive. Grace had been fighting her attraction for him ever since he'd ridden the Big Shot with her. She hadn't actually planned the ride as a test, but he'd proven something to her by doing what anyone could tell was pure torture for him. He'd let down one set of his defenses and she'd wanted to reward him with a kiss. She hadn't, of course. But she'd wanted to. And the spark between them had only gotten more intense as they watched couples being serenaded on the gondola rides, something she hadn't dared suggest.

"I'm enjoying my evening out with you," Nikolai said. He took her hand. His was large and strong. "This is a date, right? Isn't flirting allowed?"

"It's not a date. Not exactly. You're family."

He dropped the hand he was holding to take hold of her shoulders. He waited until she made eye contact before saying, "Let's get one thing straight. We are *not*—" he stressed the word "—related. Not by blood, anyway."

"But—"

He shook his head. "But nothing. Whatever the connection is, it's not close enough that our children would be born with tails."

She knew he was just making a point, but his use of the word children made her pulse increase speed. "Okay. I won't refer to you as Cousin Nikolai anymore. Satisfied?"

He leaned in and stroked the side of her face with the back of his hand. "Not even close, but it's a start."

Grace was thankful for the dim light—well, dim by Vegas standards. "Um, then, we have to decide what to do next. How 'bout a show? Comedy, Broadway musical, topless revue?"

He appeared to be thinking over his options, so she added, "Charles is a big fan of the latter. I thought about calling him to ask which one he'd recommend, but I had to help out at The Dancing Hippo, which made me late. Alex was feeling a bit under the weather. I could try his cell—"

"No. That's not my thing. What else did you have in mind?"

His question was innocent enough, but Grace felt a clutching sensation low in her belly. She knew what she'd like to do with him but since that was not an option… "Um, Mom thought you might like to try your hand at poker, no pun intended. A friend of mine deals Texas Hold'em at the Orleans, but I'm not sure I can teach you everything you need to know to play in the time it takes to get there. It's not that far away."

"I've played a little poker. I can probably hold my own." He winked. "Pun fully intended."

Grace smiled. She tucked her arm though his in a friendly way, and marched beside him to the car. She kept up a running commentary about life in Vegas, but in the back of her mind a small voice kept saying, *Too fast, Grace. This is happening too fast. Slow down before you crash and burn.*

He might not be a blood relative, but he was a member of her family, at least, as far as her mother was concerned. Plus, Grace hadn't had a serious romance since the restaurant opened, so her family wasn't used to seeing men visit her little trailer. In fact, Nikolai was the first man to make her want to end her celibate ways.

Oh, well, she thought as she headed down Tropicana, the night was still young by Vegas standards. Anything could happen.

Two hours later, Grace decided if she had to describe what it was like playing poker with Nikolai, the only word that fit was *mind-blowing*.

He was so damn smart. He picked up the nuances of the game faster than any person she'd ever watched. He was unemotional and could bluff with a face that made you positive he held a straight flush every time.

Unfortunately, he bet too conservatively for her taste. Her father would have said the man had control issues.

"Sometimes when you're gambling, you have to step aside and let lady luck play for you," Ernst once told her. "This requires a leap of faith that the average person just can't make."

Nikolai lost several hands because he didn't bet aggressively enough to scare off the hangers-on. And she was one of them. Her cards were never particularly good, but she'd linger in a hand past the flop and twice picked up winning hands when the turn, the second down card, gave her three of a kind. Against a more experienced player, she'd have ducked for cover after the initial bet and raise.

She was watching now because she'd finally lost all her chips to someone else at the table when her bluff failed. The stakes weren't that high, but she'd played often enough to know that this wasn't her night.

Nikolai lasted a few more hands. In the end, he lost, too.

"Sorry about that," she said, when he joined her at the railing where onlookers stood to view the action.

"Are you kidding? That was worth every penny. I had fun."

"Really? You looked so intense."

He smiled. "That was my game face."

"I'll keep that in mind next time you're scowling at me."

He cocked his longneck beer bottle in her direction. His second of the night. She'd noticed that he drank moderately. They'd shared a bottle of champagne at dinner, courtesy of the sommelier who knew she owned Romantique. The sparkling wine had been just the right combination of dry and sweet to accent their fabulous meal of blackened ahi.

They headed toward the main part of the casino. Grace was reluctant for the night to end. "You know, I've really enjoyed myself this evening," she said.

"You sound surprised."

"I am. You're not an easy man to read. You gave up pretty quickly after I dodged your advances in the pool. I figured you were embarrassed or you had a girlfriend back home or…maybe I misread your intentions and you weren't into girls."

He nearly choked on his swallow of beer.

"Really?"

Grace felt herself blush. "No. But that would have eased the pain of rejection when you ignored me all week."

He took a step closer. "Tell me where it hurts and I'll kiss it."

She rolled her eyes. "That line doesn't actually work, does it? Please tell me Detroit women have higher standards than to fall for something that cheesy."

Nick pressed his mostly full beer bottle to his chest. If he was smart, he'd take the opportunity to call it a night, but flirting with Grace was…fun. "Now, you've wounded me to the core. How 'bout a nightcap? We can discuss what you can do to fix my…er, problem."

When she hesitated, he took her elbow and steered her toward a dimly lit bar where four musicians occupied a small, raised stage. An ornate marquee said they were the Masters of the Jazz Universe.

"Do you like jazz?" he asked after they were seated at a table.

Grace looked up from the drink menu she was studying. "I love all kinds of music. Especially if I can dance to it. Will you dance with me? I haven't been on the dance floor in ages."

"Sorry. I don't dance."

"I can teach you. I'm not as good as Alex, but I'm not bad." She gave him a coquettish smile that he'd seen turn snobbish waiters into obsequious attendants.

He was saved from answering by the arrival of the waitress. Nick ordered a scotch and soda; Grace asked for bottled water since she was driving. Nick approved, although he didn't tell her that. He'd been faking his alcohol consumption all evening and was stone-cold sober.

The room was overly warm and she shed her rhinestone-bedecked denim jacket, which she draped across the back of the chair. Her long-sleeved shirt reminded him of a painting by Toulouse Lautrec. The way it clung to her curves distracted him so that he missed her question.

"Sorry. What?"

"I said, 'I love this song. Are you sure you won't dance with me?'"

Nick had had similar conversations with other dates over the years. He usually wound up doing the gentlemanly thing, even though he hated to dance. Few things left him feeling more uncomfortable.

Before he could answer, Grace smiled and said, "It's okay. I can dance alone." She stood up and nudged her purse his way. "Will you watch this for me?"

She melted into the crowd of couples on the dance

floor, but Nick picked her out as if she had a spotlight on her. Eyes closed, arms lifted above her head as her hips rocked to the beat, almost as if she were making love to the music.

She didn't seem the least bit embarrassed to be dancing without a partner. She simply moved. Maybe the music spoke to her through her Romani blood—an instinct born from campfires and tambourines in generations past.

Nick swallowed hard and shifted in the seat. The melody was evocative, haunting. It coursed through his veins, leaving him slightly intoxicated in a way mere alcohol never could. He loved music, but it always left him feeling conflicted, partly because of his heritage, he supposed and partly because of something his adoptive mother once said. "Your birth mother was a dancer. Your family moved to Los Angeles so she could pursue her craft. I'm sure she must have been very good at what she did."

What Sharon didn't say, but Nick had sensed, was the fact that his mother had chosen dance over staying home to raise him. If she'd loved him as much as her career, she might still be alive. And his life would have been completely different.

Gradually his bitterness toward both his mother and her chosen profession had lessened, but he still avoided dancing whenever possible. Until now. His muscles hummed with an energy he couldn't ignore.

He stood up and reached for Grace's purse. Before he could take a step, he felt it quiver. Glancing inside, he saw her cell phone light up, indicating an incoming call.

Grace had worked her way to the middle of the throng. Nick tapped her on the shoulder. When she turned to face him, her eyes lit up with joy. A powerful pressure built inside him. Deep in his chest. He couldn't recall ever feeling anything like it before.

"You," she mouthed, although he couldn't hear the word.

She looped her arms around his neck and leaned against him, her hips swaying seductively to the beat. Nick swallowed hard. "Your phone," he said, the words garbled in his throat.

Apparently she hadn't heard, because she insinuated herself even closer, like a wisp of smoke, curling in and out with the pulse of bass. The drums seemed to block out all conscious thought. His feet shuffled awkwardly at first, fighting to find a rhythm to match the beat.

Grace's hand at the nape of his neck coaxed him closer. Her fingers played with the soft, short hair that was just starting to grow out. Her lips sang silent words to a song he didn't know.

He tightened his arms around her. One hand still held her purse, but the other was free to explore the silky softness of her blouse and the flesh under it.

Her hips rotated to the beat; their bodies touched in a way he hadn't experienced in too long. He closed his eyes and succumbed to the powerful energy around him and the awakening forces within.

Grace felt him succumb. She couldn't say exactly how she sensed his capitulation or that she'd even been aware of his resistance to the music until the muscles in his shoulders, where her forearms were resting, relaxed. A shared sigh passed between them. Their heads met, temple to temple.

She moved nearer, their bodies touching as intimately as possible given the crowd and their clothing. She wanted more and knew he'd welcome her invitation. She started to suggest that they go to her place, then she felt an odd sensation in the middle of her back. A tingle that didn't feel natural.

She shimmied slightly and tried to look behind her to see if she'd been poked. It happened again.

This time, she snaked one arm around to investigate and discovered her purse in Nikolai's hand. She hadn't even noticed that he'd been holding it.

"My phone," she exclaimed when the sensation occurred again.

Laughing, she turned in Nikolai's arms to take the bag from him. She peeked at the number on the screen. *If it's my mother...* She didn't finish the thought. *Kate.*

A sudden sense of dread passed through her. Ever since she and Kate had roomed together, they'd had a rule never to interrupt a date except for a dire emergency.

Nikolai's eyes were closed and his body was moving to the beat as if he'd been born dancing. She'd never seen him this relaxed, this loose. But she couldn't ignore Kate's call.

She put her lips close to his ear. His scent was so masculine and sexy, she was tempted to pull him into a dark corner and make out, but instead, she said, "Nikolai. I need to call home."

He stopped abruptly, arms collapsing at his side. "Huh?"

He looked around as if suddenly comprehending that he'd been dancing with her. His eyes narrowed. The space between them became a chasm of accusation.

Grace grabbed his arm. "It's pumpkin time, sweet prince," she murmured under her breath.

They paused at their table so Grace could put on her jacket and Nikolai could leave a generous tip for their untouched drinks. He was a confounding fellow but intriguing. Not really prince material, she told herself, but…

She studied him as they headed single file through the weekend crowd of gamblers. Black turtleneck, black jeans, loafers. An unremarkable style that looked GQ-cover-worthy on him.

We'd make beautiful Gypsy babies together, she thought. But even though she pretended to spurn her mother's prediction of a prince, in her heart of hearts, Grace still wanted the fairy tale. And, Nikolai—sexy and gorgeous though he was—didn't fit the image she had in mind.

"Thanks," she said as he opened the driver's-side door for her. "We might not have needed to leave, but Kate's pretty good about not calling unless it's an emergency."

She hit her sister's speed-dial number. The line was busy. "That was great fun," she said once Nikolai was seated beside her. She hit redial. "I haven't been dancing in ages. You're a natural."

Still busy. She frowned, her concern growing. It was too late to try Alex's, and Liz would kill her if she woke her up. With grim resolve, Grace pressed the home button. After three rings the answering machine came on. Where was her mother, a notoriously light sleeper?

Glancing at Nikolai, she saw his frown. "What's wrong? We probably didn't have to leave the bar but it was so noisy I didn't—"

He cut her off. "Not that."

"Then what? You didn't like me complimenting your dancing? Why? You're wonderful."

His scowl intensified. "No. I'm not."

The severity of his tone told her this denial went beyond mere modesty.

"My birth mother was a dancer," he said starkly.

"So?" Grace asked, hitting Kate's number again.

"So, how would you feel if your mother was a stripper who left you with a babysitter so she could go take off her clothes in front of men?"

The hostility in his tone surprised her. Normally, he was so good at keeping his feelings hidden. "Are you sure about that? My mom said—"

He didn't let her finish. "Your mother was her friend. But, think about it. A serious dancer would have gone to New York, not Las Vegas. And Yetta's the one who got stuck with me when my mother raced back to the clubs."

The beeping sound in her ear finally sank in. Still busy. Resigned to try again in a few minutes, she faced Nikolai and said, "So, your mother had a job. These days most women have to work to put food on the table. Aren't you being a little judgmental?"

Nikolai shrugged. "It's history. None of it matters."

"Yes, I can see you're clearly untouched by it," she said, laying her hand on his arm. Her attempt at humor actually won her a rueful smile. "I don't mean to be flip, and I'm not trying to trivialize your pain, but it doesn't seem fair to blame dance for what happened to your mother. Not unless you know this for a fact, which—" she hit redial "—in my opinion, means you need to talk to your father. At least, he was there."

The call went through. "Grace," her sister cried the instant she came on the line. "Get over to UMC right away. Mom and Liz had to take Alex to the emergency room. She spiked a fever and was in terrible pain in her abdomen. The cyst might have ruptured or it could be appendicitis."

There was more, but that was all Grace heard. She looked at Nikolai, who must have overheard because he jumped out of the car and raced around to her door. "I'll drive," he said, helping her to stand up.

She should have argued. He'd been drinking, after all. But he didn't give her the chance. He took her in his arms and squeezed her supportively without being asked. Then he whispered, "Alex will be okay. Trust me."

And she did.

CHAPTER TWELVE

"I HATE HOSPITALS."

Nick opened his eyes to look at Grace, who'd spoken the words with a heavy sigh. They'd been waiting for nearly an hour. He was restless and cranky and still unsettled, first about dancing with Grace, then about spilling his guts to her. What was it about her that got to him? He wasn't sure he wanted to know.

"You said that every time Dad was admitted," Liz said. She was sprawled in a chair across the room from where Nick and Grace were sitting.

Yetta, they'd been told on arrival, was with Alex. Kate had remained home with Maya.

He studied Liz, who was playing some kind of hand-held video game on her Blackberry. Of Grace's three sisters, he found her the most difficult to pin down. She didn't live in the compound nor did she regularly join the others for meals at Romantique. She seemed busy, serious and somewhat…haunted.

"You're probably quite used to this setting, given your profession, right?" he asked her.

She shrugged without looking up. "Not really. I'm a physical therapist, not a doctor."

"She's being modest. She's a healer. She's traveled

to Bosnia, Russia, India…where else, Liz? Dangerous places. She risked her life to help amputees in war-torn areas."

"That was before," Liz said, her voice flat and resigned.

Nick understood without asking that she meant before Ernst Radonovic died. He'd heard comments that alluded to that date as a turning point in the lives of the family and in fact, of the entire Romani community.

"So what kind of work do you do now?" he asked.

"The boring kind," she said abruptly. She jumped to her feet and stretched. "I'm going for a walk. Page me if anything changes."

After she left the room, Nick asked, "Is it me or is she prickly? I don't think we've had a real conversation since I got here."

Grace sighed. "Something happened to Liz when she was in Bosnia. She won't talk about it. Most of the time she's either working or holed up at her house in Henderson. Definitely not the Romani way, but Mom says Liz has always been a loner even as a child. The only person Liz is really close to is Alex."

"So she's taking this pretty hard," he said.

"Exactly." She rolled her shoulders as if the tension was getting to her. "Plus, I think she's struggling a bit financially. After Dad died, Liz went to India to study Ayurveda, a kind of holistic medicine. She came back suddenly after less than a year and bought a house. Now she works for a private hospital, but I know her heart isn't in it."

"Then why work there?"

"Good question. Last time I asked it, she told me to mind my own business."

She looked at him. "Did you own your own place before you…um…went to jail?"

He made a noncommittal grunt. Lying to Grace was starting to bother him. "I thought I heard someone say Charles's company refers a lot of clients to the hospital where Liz works."

Grace shrugged. "Maybe. All I know is she seems constantly strapped for cash."

Motive for playing ball with Chuck? He hoped not.

Grace stood up and started to pace. Her name suited her, he decided, watching her move.

She stopped suddenly and looked at him so intently he almost squirmed. "What if your aversion to dancing is really because you're afraid dancing well would make you seem too Romani?"

"I think you think too much."

She didn't smile. Instead, she sighed and said, "I had a dream a couple of weeks ago. In it, I was walking down the sidewalk when I met a wolf—the four-legged kind— at the intersection, waiting for the streetlight to change. At first, I was afraid, but he seemed very polite, almost human. When the light turned green, he trotted off. My mother, who was standing beside me, said, 'That wolf was raised by humans. He doesn't know he's a wolf.'"

Nick rose and walked to where she was standing. "You think I'm a wolf?" he asked, keeping his voice low.

She reached up and touched his cheek, her fingertips tracing the line of his jaw. "I think you're a Gypsy who doesn't know he's a Gypsy."

When she looked into his eyes, he could see that she wasn't making idle chatter. She really cared about him. "What was it like growing up in a gaujo world?"

Zeke had left it up to Nick to share as much or as little of his history as needed to create a successful cover. "Ordinary, I guess. The family that adopted me had a daughter and wanted a son to make a complete package," he said. "We made the perfect little family. End of story."

"What's your sister's name?"

"Judy. She's married and lives in Oregon."

"Are you close?"

"What is this? A police interrogation?"

She blushed so prettily, he answered her question. "Judy was nine when I went to live with them. I was five. She was an only child who suddenly had to share her parents with another kid. A boy, no less. So she pretty much hated me when we were kids, but now barely resents me at all."

Nick could tell she had more questions—ones he might not be able to answer, so he told her about Judy's version of how he'd landed up as her brother.

A look of outrageous indignation crossed her face. "That's horrible. And mean. And…and bigoted."

Nick laughed. "She was a kid protecting her turf."

"Humph," she snorted, crossing her arms at her chest. "We used to have cousins pop in and stay for weeks. I never terrorized another kid just because he moved into my territory. In fact, my cousin Rickie lived with us for two years when his parents were going through a rough time."

"Was he younger than you?"

"I was fourteen. He was twelve. Still is, if you ask his wife," she said with a grin. "My grandmother was living with us at the time, and she had to move into my room because Rickie, the only boy, needed a room to himself."

"You weren't jealous?"

"Heck, no. I was glad he came, because that meant I could go to sleep every night listening to Granny tell me stories. I still cherish the gift of my time with her."

"She passed away?"

Grace nodded. "Alzheimer's. She had to go into a facility at the end. That was real hard on my mom. Some of the family criticized her for not taking care of Granny at home." She paused a moment then added, "Which might be why Mom was so adamant about keeping Dad at home after his stroke. Liz came every day to give him his physiotherapy."

"Did he improve?"

"Some. Not enough to return to work, though. Which, in my opinion, is what killed his spirit."

Nick understood. For many men their sense of identity was closely linked to their job. Suddenly take that away and… He didn't want to think about the possibility. Nick was glad that Pete had decided to slow down a bit, but the idea of his father sitting on his butt doing nothing in Oregon scared him. And because he probably hadn't expressed his fears clearly, Judy assumed Nick was being selfish, trying to keep their parents from moving closer to her.

Grace, who still seemed lost in the past, went on. "Dad was with Charles when the stroke happened. They were walking through a parking lot to their separate cars. Unfortunately, Charles wasn't close enough to keep Dad from falling and hitting his head on a curb. At least, Charles called for an ambulance right away."

"Charles was the hero, huh?"

"Not in Dad's eyes," she said with a certain fatality.

"After he came home from the hospital, I could tell his feelings for Charles had changed. I don't think the two ever spoke again. I believe Daddy would have preferred it if Charles hadn't called for help."

"But you don't feel that way?"

"Not at all. None of us were ready to let go. Dad might not have appreciated living what he considered half a life, but that time between his first stroke and the one that finally took him helped us prepare for our loss, emotionally."

She turned to face the window. "Mom would probably disagree. She was completely devastated when Dad passed on. For months, she barely connected with the world. She made some rash decisions without consulting any of us." She sighed and was silent.

"Were you living here when all this happened?"

She nodded. "Thank God. I don't think any of us would have survived if we hadn't had each other. That's what family is all about, right?"

"You really buy that, don't you?" he asked, unable to keep the bitterness from his tone. "Because you're Romani."

"That's part of it," she said, turning to face him. "As a group, we've survived unbelievable adversity. Slavery. Genocide. Horrible atrocities. Instead of tearing us apart, it drove us closer. We share a unique bond. My father believed this was something to be proud of."

The look in her eyes told him she understood his unvoiced skepticism.

"You don't appreciate it because you didn't grow up hearing the stories and legends. My sisters and I weren't just little girls with Romani blood, we were Gypsy princesses." Her face took on a dreamy, wistful look. "Our great-great-grandmother was so beautiful a young prince fell in love with her. His parents wouldn't let them marry, but they had a child before her family was driven out of the country."

When she noticed his scrutiny, she blushed and made an offhand gesture. "My sisters call me gullible. A romantic. Maybe I am, but knowing I was descended from royalty helped shore up my self-esteem when other kids teased me."

"About being a Gypsy?"

"About my teeth." She gave him an artificial smile. "I had braces from the day my permanent teeth came in—sideways." She grimaced. "Something like that can scar you for life, but I had faith in my father's story and my mother's premonition, so I just ignored the teasing."

"What premonition?"

A flash of red colored her cheeks. "Oh, nothing."

"Grace," he said. "I told you about my sister."

She looked toward the ceiling and sighed. "Mom had a prophesy for each of her daughters. Mine was that I'd marry a prince."

That wasn't the answer he'd expected. "A prince, huh? The kind with a castle and a moat?"

She snickered. "I don't think so. In fact, according to Mom, he won't find out he's a prince until after he marries me." Her blush intensified. "Boy, I just realized how egotistical that sounds. 'Marry me, buddy, and I'll make you a prince.'"

She shook her head. "Well, it's my mother's dream, not mine."

Nick wondered if *his* mother ever had any dreams about his future.

Grace moved away, walking to the door to peer into the hallway. "I'm really worried that we haven't heard anything yet."

"I thought she looked pretty healthy," he said, although he had to admit Alex didn't always possess the same vivaciousness as her sisters. He'd assumed she was just more laid-back.

Grace let out a heavy sigh. "She's had…female troubles, as my aunt used to say, for a long time. Shortly after opening The Dancing Hippo, her doctor found a large cyst on her ovary. He removed it, but the incision became infected and Alex had to spend nearly two weeks in the hospital. It was really scary. And expensive."

"Wow. Did she have insurance?"

"Yes, but even the co-pay was a lot. And the worst part was her doctor couldn't guarantee the cysts wouldn't return. Alex vowed never to let them open her up again, but she's in pain every month."

Nick had never seen Grace look so bleak, but she tried to put on a brave face. "I offered her the money in my trust to pay any further hospital expenses, but she says money's not the reason she won't have the procedure done again."

"Then what is the reason?"

"I don't know. It may have something to do with Mark. Her ex-fiancé…uh…married someone else."

"Is your sister's bad luck with romance the reason you'd rather invest your money in a risky business venture than save it for a wedding?"

She frowned. "You've been talking to my mother, haven't you?"

Nick couldn't tell her that Yetta had asked him to investigate Charles. Nor could he tell her that any money she handed over to Chuck was sure to become frozen once the National Insurance Crime Bureau and the D.A.'s office got their hands on Charles's assets. But she was an innocent. He owed it to her to warn her. Right?

"Grace, you should think twice before you invest with Charles."

She gave him an odd look. "Why?"

"Because…" Nick wasn't sure what he planned to say, but he stopped speaking when a man walked into the room. A man dressed in a drab brown leisure suit that Nick had seen several times that week. Zeke.

Grace glanced at Zeke briefly without interest. Nick knew she was exhausted. She'd told him earlier that she'd worked her noon shift at the restaurant, then covered for Alex at the child-care center before picking him up.

"Why, Nikolai? I know why my sisters are against this idea, but what have you got against Charles?"

Nick could feel Zeke's eyes boring into him. What could he possibly say without blowing his cover? He was saved from answering by Yetta. She hurried into the waiting room. "Alexandra is better," she said, with a tearful smile. "Fine, actually. A nasty case of the flu, not her ovary. But she's dehydrated and her potassium is low so they're insisting she stay overnight—against her wishes, of course."

"Can I see her?" Grace asked, after hugging her mother.

Yetta took her hand then looked around. "Come. I'll take you. Where's Elizabeth?"

"She went for a walk," Nick said. "I'll let her know where you are when she gets back."

Once the women were gone, Nick looked at Zeke, who appeared to be reading a magazine. "Something you want to say to me?"

The magazine hit the table. "I guess I want to know what the hell you're doing? Dinner. Gambling. Dancing. Hey, a cop's got to do what a cop's got to do," he said, his tone sarcastic, "but that doesn't include warning one of the princesses away from our suspect."

Nick knew that. He didn't need Zeke to reprimand him. "Grace isn't part of Harmon's scams."

"That may be, but someone in this family is, and she probably talks to that person every day."

Nick knew that, too. He was a pro, and instead of acting like a pro he was behaving like an inept fool.

"You're here for a reason, Lightner, and you will play this game until—"

"Game?"

Both Nick and Zeke turned to find Yetta standing in the doorway. Nick dropped his head to his hands. Zeke rose and walked toward her. "My name is—"

"I know who you are," she said dismissively. "You are the police."

Nick looked up in time to see Zeke's complexion turn a ruddy hue.

"Ma'am, your daughters—"

"Are *not* suspects," Yetta said firmly. She had to lift her chin to look Zeke in the eyes. "I involved my family in this investigation because a person I trust promised me that you could remove Charles from our lives without involving my daughters."

"Mrs. Radonovic, thanks to your invitation, we've been able to stay on top of Harmon's activities, but we still don't have enough proof to arrest him."

"That's your problem, not mine."

"Actually, until Harmon is behind bars, he's both our problem…if your hunch is right. For some reason—we're not clear why—he's short of cash at the moment. Whatever he's got going may hinge on him having access to your daughter's money."

"Absolutely not. My husband put me in charge of that trust for a reason, and I will be in my grave beside Ernst before I let Charles Harmon touch a dime of it. That money—"

"Mom?" Grace rushed in, looking from her mother to Nick then back. "The nurse needed a couple of minutes alone with Alex so I came back here to wait. Tell me you weren't just talking about my business to Nikolai. A relative stranger."

A relative stranger? Nick felt hurt although he had no right to be.

"And why is everyone suddenly so down on Charles?" She raised her hand to keep Yetta from answering. "Wait, I really don't care. Because this isn't about him. It's about me investing in my future and at the same time doing something good for Kate. Don't you trust me?"

Nick pushed aside his bruised feelings to try to salvage the operation. He could tell that Yetta was on the verge of confessing everything to her daughter.

"It's my fault, Grace. I heard a couple of rumors this week at work about some kind of takeover. I asked your mother her opinion," Nick said, walking away from

Zeke, even though Grace hadn't shown any interest in the older man. "I don't want to see you get burned."

Grace stared at him a moment, her brow gathered. "Well, I appreciate the concern, but this really isn't any of your business."

Her tone was haughty. "Sorry. Just trying to help. I knew a guy in the joint who lost his shirt opening up a diner. He told me something like seventy percent of new restaurants fail."

Grace let out a tired sigh. "Yeah, well, statistics lie. Kate and I beat the odds with Romantique, and I plan to do the same with our new place." She took her mother's shoulders between her hands and said, pleadingly, "Can't you trust me to do the right thing?"

"I do trust you, Grace. It's Charles I'm unsure of."

"Why? He was Dad's friend. If Charles hadn't been there to call the ambulance, Dad might not have survived the stroke. And Charles helped you recover the money Ian stole. Give me one good reason why I shouldn't go into business with him."

Yetta looked tormented. Nick sensed he was missing something.

She lifted her chin and said, "Very well, Grace. Your father hoped that money would secure your future. If this is—"

Grace's hug cut her off midsentence. Nick should have felt relief—the game plan was still in play—but his gut told him something wasn't right. Yetta was keeping secrets. From her daughter. And from him.

"JUREK, ARE YOU THERE? Pick up the phone. I need to talk to you. I met the big-shot gaujo detective last night who is working with your son. It's obvious the man cares nothing about this family. You must talk to Nikolai."

Jurek forced himself to wake up. The drugs the visiting nurse had given him when she'd come to change the bandage on his incision had left him groggy. He reached deep for the strength to pick up the receiver. Yetta's voice must have been on his answering machine, but he hadn't even heard the phone ring. "Yetta?"

"Hello? Jurek? Is that you?"

He blinked against the daylight. The woman had left the blinds open despite his wish to be left in darkness. "I'm here."

"What's wrong? You don't sound well."

"Um…I was asleep. I had a late night."

"I tried your cell phone about eleven but there was no answer."

"I didn't have it with me. What's got you so upset? Something about a gaujo detective?"

"Zeke Martini. I met him last night. Not a scrap of humanity. Heart of steel."

Jurek frowned. He'd met Martini a few years back when Jurek helped the police track down a former business associate who'd taken a contract out on his wife. Zeke had been the first person he'd thought of when Yetta mentioned her concerns.

"Are you sure? He struck me as a by-the-book kinda guy, but fair." Had he lost his ability to read people? That was the one skill he'd credited with keeping him alive all these years.

"Well, he may know his job, but he doesn't know me or my family. We're not pawns in his little game."

He waited for her to continue. Her anger was evident in her tone, and he needed time to find the energy to respond.

"Jurek?" Yetta said. "What's wrong? You're not telling me something."

He closed his eyes. If he took a deep breath, he could still smell the antiseptic cleaner. The scent would follow him to his grave, which seemed to be looming closer every day. He'd returned to the clinic when he'd started passing large globs of blood. An exam had revealed a cut in his bowel wall, which must have happened when the polyps had been removed. The doctors had repaired it and sent him home.

"I'm fine, Yetta. Just tired. I'm on a new medication," he said, feeling an unexpected surge of energy. This last crisis had scared him, but he was determined to hold on long enough to see his son.

Yetta made a tsking sound. "Which is why I need to visit you. Bring some herbs, some restorative tea. When can I come?"

He looked at the array of pill bottles on his bedside table and the assortment of hospital paraphernalia he'd carted home. "Maybe next week. After my cleaning lady gets back from her vacation. I don't want anyone to see this mess."

She didn't say anything for a few seconds. "Even your son?"

"Now, Yetta, don't start. You know that's not why I gave you his number."

"Okay. I'll let it go for now, but eventually you two have to meet. For both your sakes."

Jurek didn't speak. To say anything would reveal how much he longed to see Nikolai.

Yetta sighed in a way that made him smile. "Maybe you're right about Zeke, but he rubbed me the wrong way."

"He rubbed you?" Jurek joked. "I might have to come visit you after all. A man can't go around rubbing my cousin and get away with it."

Yetta laughed. He liked her laugh. He wished he could be around to hear it more often. But in order for that to happen, he'd have to get well, and Jurek, seasoned gambler that he was, was afraid that wasn't in the cards.

CHAPTER THIRTEEN

A BLACK RAGE MADE Charles shove his keyboard off his desk. Too furious even to curse, he leaped to his feet and started to pace.

More money. The son of a bitch wanted more money. *Money I don't have.*

"Charles?" a voice asked. "Is everything okay?"

He froze. MaryAnn stood in the doorway between their offices, a worried look on her plain, round face. When was the last time anyone had shown him sympathy and concern? He couldn't remember.

"I just heard from the brothers," he said truthfully. Bad news always comes in threes, his mother used to say. First, Walter e-mailed to say he was rejecting Charles's offer but would reconsider if Charles threw in a permanent private suite. *Wishful thinking,* Charles thought scornfully. *As if the doddering old fool really needed someplace to conduct his clandestine affairs.* That blow had been followed by Ralph's outrageous demand for extra cash *and* a percentage of the gaming profits for ten years.

But both counteroffers from the Salvatore brothers, although annoying, seemed workable compared to the third e-mail in his private box. Charles had it memorized.

"A hundred thousand or I tell Grace."

"Bad, huh? I'm sorry," MaryAnn said. "I was afraid that would happen. Is there anything I can do to help?"

"Yeah, find me a hit man."

She startled visibly, then gave a small, uneasy laugh.

Scaring the help probably wasn't a good idea. Neither was sharing his secrets. But Charles was running out of options. He couldn't allow this predator to ruin everything he'd worked so hard to achieve.

He remembered all too clearly his mother's advice. "You gotta look after your own interests first. Nobody else is gonna give a damn, and a bloodsucking leech ain't gonna just drop off when it gets its fill. It sucks the body dry."

"What do you know about our new janitor? Nick What's-his-name."

"Sarna," she said. "Nikolai Sarna. He's living with my father-in-law, but I haven't really talked to him. I can get you his file." She started to turn away, eager to help.

"Just refresh my memory. Why was he in jail?"

She swallowed as if uncomfortable saying the words aloud. "Attempted murder. He almost killed a man with his bare hands."

Just my kind of guy. Charles stifled a smile.

"Do you want to talk to him?"

Perversely, Charles found a certain poetic justice in the idea of getting one Gypsy to off another Gypsy. He was convinced the blackmailer was a member of the Radonovic family. His money was on Liz, who had been a classmate of his sister's and was struggling to make ends meet. Although everyone thought of her as the altruistic do-gooder, Charles had sensed something dark about her since she returned from Eastern Europe. He wouldn't put it past her to resort to blackmail.

As MaryAnn started to leave, he asked, "You and Liz and my sister were in the same high school class, right? Did you know her?"

She appeared surprised by the question. "A...Amy? We...um...had a couple of classes together. I was really sorry when I heard she passed away. She seemed like a nice person."

Nice? Tragic would be more like it. Amy was one of those people who couldn't handle the cards they were dealt. Charles had had the same pathetic parents. A father who drank himself to death, and a mother who worked three jobs to keep food on the table—and fund her slot-machine habit. His life wasn't any bed of roses, but he hadn't taken the easy way out.

"Did you know she was a drug addict?"

"No. Not in high school, anyway. I heard rumors later on. That's how she died, right?"

Technically. He pictured her body on the table at the morgue where he'd been called to identify her. Emaciated. A thousand years old. Stringy hair and bad teeth. No trace of the beautiful child he'd once loved so dearly.

"Charles, are you sure there's nothing I can do to help?"

He shook his head. This was his problem. He would handle it. Or, rather, he'd find someone to do it for him. His new janitor, for instance, he thought with a smile.

"HE KISSED YOU? Where?"

The sisters were grouped around their mother's table on the Tuesday after Alex got out of the hospital for a breakfast meeting.

"On the lips, of course," Grace answered, making a face at Kate, who'd asked the question.

"She means where did this kiss take place?" Liz said, her tone impatient. She'd been reluctant to agree to this meeting, claiming she had other things to do, but Grace had made her feel guilty about not attending.

"And when?" Alex asked. "Before or after my little scare at the hospital? If he knew you were upset about me, it might have been a sympathy kiss."

Grace shook her head and groaned. "Oh, for heaven's sake. I can't believe I said anything. Why did I? I must be a glutton for punishment." When no one contradicted her, she went on, "Nikolai is…well, gorgeous. I'm wildly attracted to him. You know that's what I do—fall for handsome men who are totally wrong for me."

"Why is he wrong for you?" Alex asked. "He seems okay to me. He went right to work within a couple of days of arriving here."

Liz nodded. "Yeah. He didn't sit around for three months feeling sorry for himself the way Gregor did the last time he got laid off."

"But he's been in prison," Grace argued. "For fighting. That isn't good."

"No, but he paid his debt to society," Alex replied. "There are worse things, you know."

Grace guessed Alex was referring to Mark, her ex-fiancé. A cop. A terrific guy by everybody's standards— until he got his partner pregnant and broke Alex's heart.

"His record isn't the problem so much as all the blank spaces in his life story. If you were interested in a girl wouldn't you open up about your family, friends, goals, ambitions, likes and dislikes? That's what people do when they want to start a relationship, right?" She didn't wait for a unanimous vote. She'd thought this through and although Nikolai had shared a few things about his past, including that incident with his sister, he remained an enigma. And the fact that she was drawn to him despite this scared her.

"Maybe he had a lousy childhood," Alex said. She put her hand up. "Wait. Haven't we been down this road before? I swear I already said that. Am I losing my mind, or is it this new drug the doctor has me on?"

Grace got up and walked around the table to where her big sister was sitting. She leaned down and put her arms around Alex's narrow shoulders. "The pills seem to be working well. You look fabulous."

"She's right. Your color is almost back to normal, Alex," Liz added. She looked at Grace. "But when it comes to men, I think the Radonovic sisters are doomed to have this conversation again and again and again. What are the odds? You'd think at least one of us could pick a winner."

Kate, who'd seemed unnaturally quiet, let out a long sigh. "Speaking of bad choices, I got a letter from Ian on Saturday. I didn't want to upset everyone after Alex's scare, but apparently there's a good chance he's going to be released early. Soon, in fact. He wants to meet with me…regarding Maya. He wants to see her."

Alex sat forward. "Oh, Kate, no. Don't do it. He abdicated his parental rights when he stole Mom's money and tried to cheat our family and friends. You don't owe him anything."

"Surely he doesn't think we'd welcome him back into the fold, does he?" Liz asked.

Kate threw up her hands in a gesture of frustration. "I don't know what's going on in his head. I never did."

Grace frowned. "Do you know where you stand legally?"

"We're divorced and I have full custody of Maya, but apparently in this state unless you've signed papers saying you give up any claim of custody, you're a father till you die. He says he can petition the court for visitations."

The very idea made Grace queasy. Her ex-brother-in-law had a history of taking off. What if he grabbed Maya? "Have you contacted a lawyer?" she asked.

Kate nodded. "I've set up a meeting with Jo's son. He's new in town and Jo said he'd give me a discount since she works for me."

"Good," Alex said. "Hopefully, he'll find out Ian's threat is just wishful thinking. Personally, I don't blame him for wanting to meet Maya—she's the most amazing child on the planet, but naturally I'd never tell him that." Absently dunking her tea bag in the cup in front of her, she looked at Grace and said, "So, Grace, 'fess up. What's happening with your plans? I assume that's the real reason you called us together this morning."

She was right. Charles had phoned last night to tell her his contractor had a small window of opportunity and if they missed out, they'd wind up paying thousands more down the road.

"Um…Mom's agreed to give me the money."

Alex groaned.

Kate shook her head.

Liz pushed back her chair and walked to the sink.

Nobody said anything. They didn't need to. Grace could sense their unanimous disapproval. "It's a wonderful opportunity, guys," she said. "Primo location. The market's hot, and Charles is gung ho to make it happen."

"What about Charles's partners?" Alex asked.

At least this time Grace had an answer. "Charles said he's in the final stages of buying them out. And in case you're curious, I asked him how he can afford to purchase a multimillion-dollar property *and* remodel it at the same time and he said that's what loans and private investors were for. He's even drawn up a contract, although I haven't actually seen it."

Seeing the skeptical look on Liz's face, Grace blushed. She didn't want any of them guessing where her mind had been the past few days—far away from business. With Nikolai.

"It still sounds iffy to me," Liz said. "Contract or no contract, you're handing over a huge chunk of change to a man who *might* own the place by the time you open your doors *if* everything falls into place." She shook her head. "Doesn't that strike you as a little risky?"

Put that way it sounded downright foolish. Was she a fool? Not only where business was concerned, but in her personal life, as well. Both areas seemed to be headed in the same direction—expansion based on a leap of faith. Hadn't she done the same thing with Shawn? Jumped into a relationship without heeding the red flags? Hadn't her sisters tried to warn her that time, too?

"I'm an idiot, aren't I?"

"No, you're just trying too hard to make something positive happen," Liz said, her tone surprisingly gentle. "We've all been there."

Grace heard something sad behind the admission.

"You need to buy some time until we get an outside

opinion," Alex said. "Put off Charles for a week. If this offer is legitimate, it will still be doable in seven days."

"She's right," Kate said. "Give me a copy of the proposal and I'll show it to Jo's son. Jo claims he was top of his class in contract law."

Grace didn't look forward to breaking the news to Charles. She'd already suggested having an independent counsel represent her in the deal and he'd acted hurt and offended. "Your father trusted me—why don't you?" he'd countered when they spoke on the phone.

Grace looked around the table. She knew her sisters. They'd hound her for life if she made this deal without listening to them. And Lord help her if something went wrong, they'd hound her in the afterlife, too.

"You win. I'll tell Charles after lunch."

"Great," Alex said. "Now…about that kiss, where were his hands?"

Kate snickered softly. "More importantly, where was his tongue?"

Grace shook her head and groaned. *Sisters.*

CHAPTER FOURTEEN

"HEY, SARNA, they want you up in the big man's office."

Nick looked over his shoulder at his supervisor, a short Philippino with dreadlocks he wore tucked under his hat. Nick handed him his broom. "A raise already?" he said jokingly. "Must be my great work ethic."

"Hey, you'll be lucky if they don't fire your ass. I seen you talking to the boss's girl the other day. Word gets around, you know."

The boss's girl? Not according to Grace. Had news of their date reached Charles, he wondered as he made his way to the suite of offices?

To his surprise, MaryAnn sent him straight in.

Charles was seated behind his desk. "Sit down. I have a little problem, and I think you might be just the man to help me get rid of it."

Nick brushed off his dusty jeans. "For the right price, I'll do 'most anything. What's up?"

Charles made a bridge with his fingers. His expression was serious. Dead serious, Nick realized as he listened to Charles's proposition.

"You want me to off somebody? And you're not even sure who?"

"I've hired a computer expert to track where the

e-mail was sent from. The first two letters came in the mail. I ignored them because the threat wasn't specific. Just something like 'Pay up or you'll be sorry.' I put them through the shredder."

Nick forced himself to act nonplussed. Here was an undercover cop's reward for scrubbing toilets.

"Hey, I don't know much about computers, but just because you find the machine, doesn't mean you know who used it, right?"

Charles frowned. "It will give us a place to start. If I agree to meet the blackmailer's demands, he—or she—will need to contact me to set up a drop-off point. That's when you can nail him. Or her. At the moment, my money's on Liz—no pun intended."

"Grace's sister? What's she got on you?"

Charles turned sideways, his gaze fixed on something in the distance. "That is none of your business. Suffice to say, there are details regarding my sister's troubled life that I'd rather not be made public."

Nick remembered seeing some mention of Charles's sister in his file. A drug addict. Her body had been found in an ally in North Las Vegas. An apparent overdose.

"Why would Liz blackmail you?"

Charles's look said Nick was the stupidest person alive. "The money, of course. She's in way over her head with that house of hers. Grace has called it a money pit."

Nick's stomach clenched. He, too, had heard Grace mention Liz's struggle to make ends meet, but Nick would never have pegged her as the type to resort to extortion.

"Plus, something happened to her when she was overseas," Charles went on, more to himself it seemed than to Nick. "Grace told me the whole family has discussed it. They think it had something to do with a man, because Liz hasn't dated since she got back. Who better than a man-hater to want to bring me down?"

"What about your sister's friends? The people she hung out with."

Charles made a scoffing sound. "Those losers? They wouldn't dare cross me." Unblinking, Charles looked straight at Nick and a chill passed down his spine. "Not unless they want their well to dry up."

No shit. Zeke had been right about Charles's drug connection.

"Besides," Charles said, "whoever sent this knows I'm negotiating a deal with Grace. Today's note threatened to tell her if I didn't come up with the cash. That narrows the list of suspects. Someone who knew my sister and is privy to the Radonovic family gossip."

"Why would exposing details about your sister ruin your deal?"

Charles sighed. "Grace is young, idealistic and passionate about family. She'd never understand about Amy and me. We were…close. Not in age, of course. I practically raised her. But as she got older, she became more…troubled. She was mixed up and made some terrible choices for herself, including drugs. I know that Grace would blame me for that, if the blackmailer told her everything."

Everything. Nick wondered what that involved. To block his suspicions, he asked, "How much is this worth to you?"

They haggled over the price for a good ten minutes, then Charles said, "Are you sure you can handle it? I mean, I've heard that you and Grace have been hanging around together. Her last boyfriend was a good-looking loser, too."

"She's just a means to an end," Nick said, wishing like hell he meant it.

Charles nodded as if trying to decide whether or not to believe him. "And if the blackmailer is Liz? Could you do her?"

Nick knew the question was hypothetical, but it hit him harder than he would have expected. Liz was Grace's sister. If she was the blackmailer, he wouldn't kill her but he would arrest her. And the end result would be the same—he'd lose Grace.

GRACE'S HAND was shaking when she knocked on the door of Charles's suite. She wasn't big on confrontation. When she'd been dating Shawn, she'd given him third, fourth and fifth chances to make their relationship work. Finally, Kate told her, "He's the kind of guy who wants the woman to do all the work—even the breaking up. If he pushes you far enough, he can blame you for ending it."

The truth—and a couple of margaritas—had fortified Grace through that big ugly fight. Shawn had reversed her charge of infidelity. "What about you? You put your family ahead of me. Our relationship never stood a chance because you couldn't choose the man in your life over those damn Gypsies."

Grace had been devastated, but time—and the myriad problems facing her family—had helped her find some perspective. And a stranger's kiss had opened the door to new possibilities.

Another reason she was standing at Charles's door.

Charles was a friend. He'd been a safety net, of sorts, after her breakup with Shawn. A nice man who liked to take her to great restaurants. But there was no chemistry. Nothing like the heat that passed from Nikolai's lips to hers and made her realize she could never settle for platonic.

Even if nothing came of her attraction to Nikolai— Lord knows there were enough obstacles on that path— he'd at least made her evaluate what she wanted out of a relationship. Grace planned to clear the air with Charles, but first, she had to break the news to him that she couldn't finalize their partnership for another week.

She knocked a second time, harder. An odd murmur made her lean in and call, "Charles? It's me, Grace. Are you there?"

She was reaching for her cell phone, when she heard the click of the lock. She waited, curious.

The door opened a crack. The eyes that peered at her didn't belong to a man. "Um, hello. I'm looking for Charles. Is he here?"

The woman shook her head. Grace thought she looked familiar, but she couldn't place the face. "Is he downstairs in his office? I should have checked there first, but he said he planned to work here today."

The stranger looked over her shoulder as if silently consulting someone else. The door opened a tiny bit wider. Grace could see a second woman. Both were young and dressed in short satin robes even though it was afternoon.

It suddenly dawned on her where she'd seen the two before. The maids that Charles had hired. They were foreign, MaryAnn had said. Something about checking their documentation.

Grace wasn't stupid. These women hadn't been hired to clean toilets, and the fact that they apparently were living in Charles's suite, which only had one bed, told her he was more than their employer.

"Well, this pretty much proves my power of ESP sucks," she muttered. "Poor lonely Charles, my foot. He keeps not one, but two beautiful women on the side."

The pair exchanged a confused look, then the taller one spoke. Grace didn't recognize the language. Nothing sounded familiar except for the word Charles.

"Yes, Charles," Grace said, nodding and smiling as she muscled her way into the room. What was going on? Were these women here by their own choice? The door had been unlocked so apparently he wasn't holding them against their will, but still…something didn't seem right.

While not the grandest hotel suite she'd ever seen, the corner apartment was bright and tastefully decorated. Charles's expensive lithographs from an artist Grace found too persnickety for her taste occupied every spare inch of wall.

She marched from room to room, amazed by the mess. The Charles she knew was fastidious. The women followed, their expressions obviously worried.

"Listen, I'm not from Immigration. I'm not a cop."

"Cops?" the shorter one repeated, her tone panicky.

Grace pointed to her chest and shook her head. "Not me. Don't like 'em. Don't worry. They won't hear about you from me. Okay?"

The two looked at each other and seemed to understand her intent if not her words.

"What are your names?"

After a little more hand gesturing, Grace got them to say, "Lydia and Reezira."

"Grace," she said, but after that had no idea what to do. She thought about calling Liz. Perhaps she could communicate with these women, find out if they were here willingly.

But then it crossed her mind that the person to ask was Charles himself. She pulled out her phone and punched in Charles's number. He answered on the second ring.

"Where are you? We need to talk."

"In my office. I'm with someone at the moment, but give me fifteen—"

"Will five do? I'm just leaving your suite."

"My suite?"

"Yeah. You told me you'd be working at home today, remember? Guess we have different interpretations of the word *work*."

He didn't say anything for a moment. "Five minutes then." He hung up.

As she turned to leave, she paused to look in the small spare bedroom that Charles had converted to an office. A bank of built-in TV monitors which Grace had never seen before were tuned in to various spots around the hotel. This is new, she thought. After checking to make sure none of the camera shots included the elevators, she located the set that showed MaryAnn at her desk.

"I wonder who he's talking to," she murmured, lingering to see who would exit the office.

She didn't have long to wait. "Nikolai. Hmm. That's odd." The hair on the back of her neck stood up. A sign that usually meant something bad was going to happen.

No surprise there. Not only did she have to tell Charles their business deal was on hold, but she felt compelled to poke her nose into his arrangement with these women. Maybe there was a good explanation for keeping them half-dressed in his suite. But if there wasn't…she didn't know what she'd do. Probably go to the police, much as the idea turned her stomach.

On the elevator ride down to the second floor, Grace gathered her courage. She knew this meeting was going to be unpleasant. MaryAnn was gone when she got there. Since Charles's office door was open, she walked straight in.

"So Lydia and Reezira are maids, huh?" she asked when she was seated opposite him.

"Friends," Charles said, in a way that made Grace stifle a shiver.

"Really? The kind of friends who are free to come and go as they please?"

"The kind who entered this country illegally and need a place off the street while a kindly lawyer looks into getting them green cards. Young, vulnerable girls can fall prey to all kinds of heinous endings if they're not looked after properly."

His tone was patient and only slightly mocking. Grace didn't believe him, but the girls *had* opened the door for her. They didn't seem to be prisoners.

"That's good to know. Then you won't care if I introduce them to Liz. She should be able to teach them a little English so they can actually get a job once they're legal."

"Actually, I do mind. This is none of your business, Grace."

"I beg to differ. If I became your partner, and you were brought up on charges of say, kidnapping, then where would that leave me?"

"What do you mean *if* we became partners? I thought you were bringing me a signed contract and a wire transfer."

Grace looked over his shoulder at the scene out the window. A new, multistory parking garage was under construction across the street. She wished she were there.

"Kate has a stake in this, too. She's hired a lawyer to handle her ex-husband's custody claim and she wants to take the contract in for review when she sees him."

Charles let out a low epithet and stood up. "That doesn't work for me, Grace. I need that money now. Preferably today."

Today? He hadn't been this blunt on the phone. "Why? What's the big deal? So what if we have to pay the contractor a little more? Over time, the cost would be amortized and—"

"Typical," he said, cutting her off. "I should have expected this kind of runaround. Your father strung me along for years. Promises, promises. When will I learn that a Gypsy's word isn't worth shit?"

Grace sat back as if he'd slapped her. "My father? What does this have to do with him?"

Charles stomped around the desk until he was standing over her. "You want the truth? It's simple. The money in your trust account isn't yours. It never was. It's mine. Your father—yes, upstanding citizen that everyone thought he was—took a bribe that I arranged."

"No way," Grace cried. "You're making that up."

He went on as if she hadn't spoken. "Our deal was

fifty-fifty. Only there was this hotshot D.A. trying to earn a seat in Carson City. Ernst was a well-known gambler. For him to suddenly turn up with four or five hundred grand was no big deal. If I'd claimed the money…"

Grace got the picture, but she still didn't believe him. "Who would bribe my dad? And for what? He was a pit boss."

Charles backed off slightly. He settled his hip on the desk and crossed his arms. "During the late eighties Vegas was turned upside down by unions trying to establish a hold on the city. Ernst had a foot in each camp. The casino owners trusted him because he'd worked in the system for years. The union bosses trusted him because he had a way with people. You know that."

She did. Ernst was everybody's friend, but he was also highly respected. "He wouldn't—"

Charles cut her off. "He negotiated a couple of deals under the table. He called it 'finessing the situation.' The money was a payoff for certain concessions."

Grace jumped to her feet. "That's a lie. My father would never sell out."

Charles's snicker sent a chill through her body. "He saw an opportunity to make some sweet money that nobody could ever trace. He even claimed the winnings and paid taxes so the IRS couldn't come after him if someone did talk. The only problem was part of that money belonged to me."

"I don't believe you. How can you prove it?"

His face turned cold. His eyes went dead. "That's the same thing your father said…right before I pushed him in the parking garage. He wasn't too agile. He stumbled and fell. Hit his head on a concrete curb."

"No," Grace cried, suddenly seeing the image as if it were a video being played before her eyes. "You said the stroke made him dizzy. That he stumbled before you could catch him. That was how he hit his head."

"I lied, but…how can you prove it?"

Tears blurred her vision. Horror and impotence choked her. She stood there in shock until Charles grabbed her by the arm. "Listen to me, Grace. I want that money by tomorrow afternoon. For your family's sake, you can pretend we're still going into business together. And I'll continue to play the game as long as you keep your mouth shut about those two…ah, ladies in my suite."

Grace pushed at his hand. "This was all for show, then? You only agreed to build Too Romantique because it was a way to get your hands on my trust? But what happens when the construction doesn't take place?"

He dropped his hold and shrugged. "Such are the pitfalls of big business, Grace. Surely you learned that much in college. Building departments reject plans. Architects make mistakes. Water mains break. Any number of problems can slow up production. It's just part of the gamble one takes to play with the big dogs."

She tried to think but her mind kept going back to his threat. Her father was dead, but her family would be devastated if this revelation got out. Her mother was just starting to rebuild her life. Nobody could handle a blow like this one.

Charles returned to his desk and sat down. "Go home,

Grace. Deliberate on your options. Not that you actually have any. Your father screwed me out of my share and I'm through waiting."

CHAPTER FIFTEEN

NICK CALLED Zeke from the pay phone in the lobby. "Hey, it's me. I got a promotion. Wanna go somewhere and celebrate?"

"Front door of the Bourbon Street. Five minutes."

The line went dead.

Nick smiled. His boss wasn't the most talkative guy he'd ever met, but even Zeke would have to show some excitement over this development. Chuck was getting desperate. Desperate men made mistakes.

The meeting place was closer from the employee's entrance, so Nick slipped out the back door. His mind was racing with possibilities, but he knew from experience that any number of things could go wrong. He wasn't the type to get his hopes up.

A nondescript sedan pulled up just as Nick reached the entrance. The passenger door opened. Nick got in.

As the car pulled away from the curb, Zeke said, "So?"

"Chucky's being blackmailed. Needs a hit. Not sure who the target is, but Harmon seems to think it's a member of Grace's family. Might even be one of the princesses."

"You told him you'd do it?"

"Of course."

Zeke drove for a few miles without speaking then said, "Well, this should be interesting. Turns out we've been invited to the compound."

"Invited?"

"Okay, summoned. That queen mother is really something."

Nick agreed. So were her daughters. But what if Charles was right? Could Liz be the blackmailer? What would Yetta have to say about that?

"Utterly ridiculous," Yetta said twenty minutes later when Nick posed the question to her. The three of them were seated at Yetta's kitchen table where he'd observed her four daughters sitting earlier that morning. "No one in my family is trying to get money from Charles Harmon. In fact, just the opposite is true. He's been pressuring Grace to give up the money in her trust for this so-called remodeling project."

Nick knew that. "Wasn't that Grace's idea?"

"Grace is full of ideas. Charles saw his chance and jumped at it. If you're right about him being blackmailed, then isn't it obvious why he needs the money?"

Nick wondered if he was the only one who caught the irony of Grace giving Charles money to pay off another Romani.

"I know what you're thinking, Nikolai," Yetta said. "And you're wrong. If any of her sisters needed money, Grace would give it to them without question. We help each other out. That's our way."

So everyone said. "Well, that may be, but Charles is convinced someone in this family knows his dirty little secret and he's willing to kill to keep it from getting aired in public."

She looked at her folded hands. "It's time to tell my daughters the truth."

"No," Nick said, pushing to his feet. "Not yet." He had no trouble picturing the look on Grace's face when she learned not only that he'd deceived her but that he was a cop. However, risking Grace's wrath was only part of the problem. He couldn't jeopardize the investigation. "If word leaks, my name moves to the top of Charles's hit list."

Yetta looked at Zeke. "You have to give me your word of honor that none of my daughters will be in danger."

The sound of a car engine in the cul-de-sac prevented Zeke from answering. Yetta rushed to the door. "It's Grace. She looks upset. I hope she didn't notice your car in the street."

She grabbed Zeke's hand and pulled him to the side door. "Go quickly."

The older man disappeared like a shadow in fog.

Nick returned to his seat while Yetta poured a cup of coffee and put it in the microwave. "She was supposed to meet Charles after lunch. I didn't expect her back so soon."

A car door slammed. Grace walked in and stopped short when she spotted him. Even without special cognitive powers, Nick could tell she was upset. "Hi. I got off early. Your mom invited me over for coffee," he said, ad-libbing.

Grace looked at Yetta, who responded to the *beep-beep-beep* of the microwave. "Would you care to join us, dear? I could make a fresh pot."

"No. Thank you. I…I'll be in my house. Headache. Traffic. Gotta go."

She pivoted on the heel of her low-heeled shoe. Her dressy black slacks ended at midcalf. Beneath her suit jacket, the white shell she was wearing almost matched her skin tone.

Too pale, Nick thought. Something was wrong. Very wrong. "Did you talk to the boss man today?" he asked.

The hand holding her purse shook. She looked over her shoulder. "Y…yes. A quick business discussion." A telltale blush crept up her neck.

"Alexandra said you planned to tell him that Katherine's lawyer is looking over the contract," Yetta said as she delivered Nick's coffee. "I'm sure he wasn't happy. Sit down and tell us how it went."

Grace shook her head. "Later. I have a headache."

"Grace," Yetta said sharply. "Tell me what's wrong."

Nick took a sip of coffee, trying to stay in the background. He watched Grace over the rim of his cup and saw when she gave in. Her eyes filled with tears which she blinked away. "I don't know what to do, Mom. I went to Charles's suite because he told me he was going to be working at home this afternoon. He wasn't there," she said, swallowing loudly. "But Lydia and Reezira were."

Nick's pulse spiked.

"Who?"

"Two young women. Charles says they're illegal immigrants. He said he's helping them until they get work permits, but…"

"You don't believe him," Nick said. "I heard a rumor about a couple of working girls from Canada. I kind of laughed it off because Chuck comes across as such a cold fish. Who'd have guessed?"

"This isn't about Charles's sex life," Grace said. "I

don't want to get the women into trouble with the INS, but being here illegally makes them vulnerable, and men take advantage of vulnerable women."

Somehow he knew that applied to her, too. Now he was worried. Something happened today. Something beyond discovering prostitutes in Charles's room.

"So call the police," he said, just to gauge her reaction.

She pressed her hand to her heart. "Are you crazy? The heartless bastards would just throw the poor girls in jail or deport them. Charles would probably talk his way out of everything. No, I could try to find some kind of amnesty group, maybe. But never the cops."

He shrugged as if her answer didn't faze him in the least. "Yeah, well, whatever. I guess I'll go crash. Thanks, Yetta."

Nick took his time strolling to Claude's house. His stomach was churning—and not from Yetta's reheated coffee. Grace had made her feelings about his profession crystal clear. He had no doubt how she'd feel about him once he arrested Charles and took the two prostitutes into custody.

Unfortunately, he didn't have any choice. That was who he was.

"MOM? WHAT'S GOING TO happen? What should I do?"

Yetta heard the desperation in her youngest daughter's voice. She also was aware of how the question was phrased. Grace wanted her to look into the future for answers. But how could she when she no longer trusted her visions? What good was second sight when she'd had no warning of her own husband's stroke?

She walked to Grace and grasped her shoulders

firmly. "I don't need clairvoyance to know that you'll do the right thing," she said. "Listen to your heart."

"My heart is in worse shape than my head, Mom," Grace said, sadly. "If I do what I think I should do, the people I love most will be hurt. If I do what Charles wants me to do, everyone will be mad at me."

Yetta knew that Grace's agony wasn't just about two displaced women. Somehow the family was involved.

"Come and sit down, dear. We need to talk."

Grace tried to back away but bumped into the coat-rack. If Yetta closed her eyes, she could picture Ernst's jacket hanging on the first hook. His spot. Lord, how she missed that man. She'd loved him completely, despite his flaws.

"Grace," Yetta said softly, "your father predicted this day would come. In a way, he prepared us both for it."

Grace's expression changed from wary to curious. Of all her daughters, Grace had always been the easiest to read.

Once they were seated opposite each other, Yetta took a deep breath. Delving into the past was never easy. Although it was a cliché, times had changed. What Ernst had done back in the late 1980s was not what he would have done today. She was certain of that. But how could she make her daughter—the baby of the family who worshipped her father—understand?

Grace shifted uneasily in her chair. She didn't like the resigned look on her mother's face. She had a feeling she didn't want to hear what Yetta was about to say. What she really wanted—and had since the minute she walked in the door and spotted Nikolai sitting at the table—was to run to him. The enormity of her need had left her unnerved and flustered. Was it shelter in his strong muscles and broad shoulders that she sought, or escape of another kind? A chance to lose herself in sexual bliss? Neither option was possible, she told herself sternly.

"Grace?"

The question in Yetta's tone made Grace's cheeks heat up. Probably not a good thing to think about sex in the presence of an intuitive mother. "Sorry. I had a bit of a shock this afternoon. My mind is all over the place."

"A shock. Yes, I suppose finding out that your father was human could be pretty devastating to someone who always believed her daddy could do no wrong."

"D…Dad? Who said anything—?" She stopped midsentence. Even as a child she'd known it was useless to lie to her mother. The woman *knew* things. *Everything.* "You knew?"

Yetta shook her head. "Not at the time."

"How is that possible?"

"So many reasons. Excuses, I guess. My father had just passed on. And your grandmother was declining so fast. I had two daughters in high school. You and Kate were involved in so many activities. Dance, karate, soccer. Later, when I found out what Ernst had done, I realized that deep down I'd suspected something wasn't right but I chose to ignore my fears."

Her tone was so haunted Grace had no choice but to believe her. Still… "But, Mom, you're Puri Dye. You know everything."

Her mother's silver hair, worn loose today, shifted about her shoulders as she shook her head sadly. "When you're a mother, you'll understand. The intensity of your focus shifts to your children during their formative years. Your husband has to bear the burden of providing shelter, food, safety, as well as planning for the future. Some men—even the most honorable—can become so caught up in the challenge, they make choices they later regret."

Grace forced herself to ask, "Charles was right, then? Dad took a bribe?"

Yetta's chin lifted. "Yes. At the time, he said the money was winnings. I knew he'd been gambling more than normal. I wasn't happy about it because the chances of losing are equally great, but the money seemed to keep pouring in. Ernst always said that when you were on a roll, you didn't dare turn your back on Lady Luck."

Grace nodded. She'd heard him say that many times.

"We declared the money as income and paid taxes on it. Ernst hired an estate planner to set up the trusts for you girls. I ignored any niggling hint of doubt by allowing my life to keep me distracted."

"When did you find out the truth?"

"Just before he died. I knew his time was near and I could tell that he was in great pain—not physical, but emotional. I sang him a song that my mother sang to my father before he passed on. I don't even know what the words mean, but I believe it conveys forgiveness for one's sins."

She hummed the tune softly, then closed her eyes and said, "He only wanted what was best for his family. He never intended to cheat Charles. He planned to make up the difference in time, but Charles was impatient. Ernst's biggest regret was that we would be inheriting

Charles's antipathy, and his illness left him unable to do anything about it. He'd failed to protect his family. The humiliation, I believe, was what killed him."

Grace's eyes filled with tears. The memory of those months between her father's stroke and his death came rushing back. So often, she'd sensed his frustration and had attributed it to not being able to walk and talk well. Maybe he'd been agonizing over what he knew his wife and daughters would be facing down the road—Charles, his greedy, pissed-off ex-partner.

No. Charles killed him.

Grace reached across the table and gripped her mother's hand. Yetta didn't need to relive the horror of that day. Nor, as Charles said, was there any way to prove that he had caused her father to fall and hit his head.

"Mom, Charles is threatening to make this public if I don't hand over the money. Dad's reputation will be ruined. He worked so hard to improve the Romani image. I can't let that happen."

Her mother frowned. She didn't speak for a good minute. "I need to think about this, Grace. So much is happening on other levels…" Her voice trailed off.

Grace felt a shiver of awareness. She studied her mother's face. "Mom, you're not telling me something."

Yetta looked over Grace's shoulder toward the coatrack and smiled. "Yes, dear, you're right. Now, I need to go pick up Maya. She and I are going fish shopping."

"Fish? Like halibut? Salmon?"

"Goldfish. I've decided to buy an aquarium. Maya's been asking for one ever since she saw *Finding Nemo*."

Grace wasn't surprised. Her niece had made her

watch the DVD about a dozen times. "Good. That will make her happy. But, what should I do about Charles?"

Her mother was already halfway out the door. She glanced over her shoulder. "Perhaps you should ask Nikolai for advice. There's more to him than you think."

More to him than I think? I think about him more than I should. I want to know more— She consciously broke off the thought. Turning to Nikolai for advice or anything else was not a good idea. She couldn't allow him to influence her decisions. Especially when her life was such a mess.

Suddenly feeling light-headed, she stumbled to her feet. *What just happened?* Her mother had confessed knowing a secret that could blow their world to bits, then blithely trotted off to buy fish. "Fish," she muttered, as she exited the house through the patio door.

Oh, Daddy, how could you do this? Suddenly blinded by tears of grief, loss and disappointment, she bumped into a lawn chair that wasn't pushed up to the patio table.

"Damn. Damn. Damn," she swore, kicking the chair so hard it fell over and nearly skidded into the pool.

"Whoa. Somebody's pissed off."

She spun about to locate the voice. Nikolai. Head and shoulders peering at her above the cinder-block fence that separated the two yards. "Are you spying on me?"

"Why would I do that?"

She ignored the question and marched to the door of her little trailer. She opened it with such force the aluminum screen slammed against the metal siding and bounced back, hitting her shoulder.

"Stupid thing," she shouted, yanking it closed behind

her. Once inside, she bent over like a marathon runner who'd just finished a ten-K meet.

"The past is past," she whispered out loud. "Dad did what he thought was right. Well, maybe not right, but necessary." Her stomach churned. An acrid taste filled her mouth. She wanted to weep but was afraid if she started she might not be able to stop. "Just let it go. Let it go," she repeated like a chant.

She picked up a glass she'd left on the counter, filled it from the tap and took a tentative sip. The door behind her opened after the softest of knocks. Grace spun around, spilling water down the front of her top.

Nikolai loomed in the doorway. "What's wrong?"

Grace set down the glass behind her and crossed her arms. This was her home. Her sanctuary. "None of your business. Go away."

He stepped across the threshold, ducking his head to clear the doorway.

"No," Grace cried, glancing about for a weapon. She grabbed the only thing handy. A plastic wand adorned with silver and purple tassels. She'd bought it for Maya and had forgotten to give it to her. She pointed it at his chest.

Nikolai stopped. He looked at the toy then lifted his head and gave her a sardonic smile. "Are you going to turn me into a toad?"

"Or worse. Now, please leave me alone. I've had a bad day."

"So, tell me about it. Isn't that what friends—and family—are for?" he said, leaning one shoulder against the open doorframe.

Grace heard the hint of sarcasm in his tone. She

poked him harder, this time bending over the card-board stars at the tip of the wand. "We're not related, remember?"

His fingers closed around the wand and he tugged, making her take a step closer. "That's right. So pretending you're not feeling this chemistry between us is a bit cowardly for a princess, isn't it?"

Grace didn't want to talk about the attraction she felt toward him. She let go of the wand and walked into what she euphemistically called her living room. It consisted of a three-sided couch that she'd covered with fake fur. Accent pillows adorned with spangles and plastic jewels matched the multihued scarves that made up her curtains. She'd repapered the walls in a metallic gold foil.

She sat down, pulling a persimmon-colored pillow onto her lap. "I'm not a princess. And my dad sure as heck wasn't a king."

His eyes narrowed, but he didn't move closer to her. "What does that mean?"

"Nothing. Forget it. I don't care what my mother says—I'm not talking to you. For all I know, you have some ulterior motive for being here."

"What are you talking about? I'm here because your mother invited me."

"True, but you have a hidden agenda, and, frankly, I'm sick to death of secrets."

He closed the door and tossed the wand on the table. Resting his hip on the table of her built-in dining nook, he said, "I have no idea what you're talking about."

Grace hugged the pillow to keep her heart from spilling out of her chest. "You came here for payback. On the Romani."

He looked baffled. "That's ridiculous. I don't have any gripes against your family."

Grace moved to her knees. "Oh, really? You don't think my family let you down when you were a child?"

He shook his head and threw out his hands as if words failed him. "No."

"Even after your sister convinced you we were a bunch of marauding thieves?"

His lips flattened in a frown. "All kids have fantasies. They outgrow them."

"Right, but can you honestly say that you came here expecting to like us?"

He opened his mouth but no words came out. Which answered Grace's question.

"I thought so."

Nikolai pulled out a chair from the small table and turned it backwards and sat down. "Listen. I might not have thought much about your family when I first got here, but that's changed. I know that your mother is a good person. If she could have done something to stop my f…birth father from giving me away, she would have."

Grace clutched the pillow. His tone sounded sincere, but her ability to trust had been compromised almost to the breaking point. She sank back against the cushions and closed her eyes. "You're right. She would have. But you were probably better off being raised by the gaujos anyway."

A sudden thought struck her. "Wait a minute. If you were adopted, then your name isn't Sarna, is it?"

He didn't answer at first. "No. My name is Nick

Lightner. Sarna was the name on my birth certificate. When I decided to move here, your mother thought it would easier to explain my connection to your family if I used my birth name."

"Lightner," she repeated. "Nice, middle-America name. No ethnic vibes. And with your coloring, I bet no one ever suspected you of being a Gypsy."

Although outwardly he showed no emotion, Grace could feel his anger simmering below the surface. "My adoptive parents gave me their name—after my Romani father washed his hands of me."

Grace heard pain beneath the cynicism and she welcomed it. Honesty. That's all she was asking for at the moment. "He was in jail."

"For three lousy months."

She tossed up her hands. "So who died and made you judge and jury? You're convinced that your father was a worthless piece of dog doo who didn't care about you. Never mind that he'd just lost the woman he loved. Never mind that he was shook up, mixed up and grieving. Alone in jail. Unable to reach you. Probably being sold a line of goods by some overzealous social worker who had an eager, upstanding middle-class family dying to adopt a little boy."

His mouth opened but no words came out.

"Fathers sometimes make mistakes. They're not perfect," she cried, wondering who she was really trying to convince—Nikolai or herself.

He cursed loudly and stood up. "Stop trying to get inside my head. You don't know what happened. You weren't there."

His words hit hard. They were true. She didn't know

what had made her father compromise his rigid code of ethics.

"Maybe not, but I can feel for him just the same," she said softly. Happy to let Nikolai think she meant his father, not hers.

"Well, I can't."

His response angered her. She got to her feet. "That's it in a nutshell, isn't it," she declared. "That's the difference between us. It's not Mars/Venus, Gypsy/gaujo. It's more basic than that. The fact is I feel. You don't. Men like you ought to come with warning labels. Danger—emotional vacuum."

He let out a low growl, but Grace ignored it and walked past him toward her bedroom. She pulled aside the thick curtain of beads that separated her private space from the living area. Pausing, she looked over her shoulder. "I thought, for a brief moment, that we had a connection, but ask my sisters—" she said, shrugging her shoulders. "Heck, ask anyone—and they'll all tell you I can't pick men worth squat. Now, if you'd please leave, I'd like to—"

He caught her arm. "Damn, you piss me off."

Then he pulled her into his arms and kissed her. Hard.

Grace fought back for the space of one heartbeat, then she wrapped her arms around his neck and plastered herself against his warm, very male body. He might not be her ever-after man, but he was here and now. And he was offering just what she needed.

CHAPTER SIXTEEN

"WAIT." She pushed on his shoulders and he let her go. She stepped backward until she could no farther. "We can't do this," she said, panting. "*I* can't do this. I don't just have sex for the sake of having sex."

Nick almost groaned. Her words said *go,* but her eyes said *come.*

"Why not?" He kept his tone casual, but there was nothing casual about how he felt. He wanted her—to hell with Charles Harmon and the case. She wasn't Charles's patsy or cohort. She was a gorgeous, desirable woman. Forget the dozen or so reasons they shouldn't be together.

He closed the distance between them, which wasn't difficult in the cramped quarters of her trailer. "We don't have to do this, but don't pretend you don't want to. You don't have to be a fortune-teller to know there's something between us. Something hot. Significant. And from the number of cold showers I took this past week, I'd say it isn't going away any time soon."

"You've been thinking about me?"

"Day and night." Nick covered her mouth with his and tasted her.

After a few moments of mutual exploration that took

his breath away, she pulled back slightly and said, "I love the way you kiss. You could give lessons." She ran her hands across his biceps to his shoulders.

Nick nuzzled an intriguing hollow where her neck and jaw met. There was a voice in his head that said, *Step away from the princess,* but it was being drowned out by the roar of blood on its way past his conscience headed right to his penis.

"Okay," Grace said in a guttural whisper. "I give up. Let's do this now, before I remember what a mistake I'm making."

He kissed her again. His tongue plunged deeper, tracing her teeth, the roof of her mouth and underside of her tongue. She made a slight whimpering noise and transferred some of her weight to her arms, which were resting on his shoulders.

The angle opened the way for him to slide his hand under her white shell, which he discovered included a built-in bra. The stretchy material made it easy to pull down the elastic neckline and touch her skin. Hot and soft.

She shimmied against his palm, inviting him to explore. His fingers raked along her rib cage to the underside of her breasts.

She went still and opened her eyes. "This really is going to happen, isn't it?" she asked. He saw her nervousness, but she didn't flinch when his hand covered her breast and he gently squeezed.

He looked down at the fullness and felt his knees tremble. He couldn't wait to see her naked. To taste every square inch of her body, but he felt honor-bound to say, "It's not too late to call it off if you don't want…"

She took his hand and pressed it to her crotch. Even

through her black hip-huggers, he could feel the heat and moistness. "If I backed out now, there are parts of me that would never forgive me. Including where your hand is."

A pivoting motion of her hips made him think of a belly dancer. She stepped back and walked to the beaded curtain. The sparkling doorway led to a room unlike any he'd ever seen before. The vivid colors of the be-jeweled pillows on the couch were replicated every-where—walls, ceiling and curtains. Sheer pink scarves were draped over the two hanging light fixtures on ei-ther side of the wall-to-wall bed, which was covered in scarlet satin.

"Wow."

The long strands of beads gave a tinkling cackle after Grace followed him in. "A little over the top, I know," she said, shrugging one bare shoulder. "Liz says the decor panders to the stereotype people have of Gypsies. But I like it. I was going for the *I Dream of Jeannie* look."

Nick looked around as he unbuttoned his shirt. He found the surroundings slightly titillating. Campy and fun. Could he sleep there every night? That would de-pend on the company.

Grace leaned across the bed to close the curtains. The hue went from sunshine to mellow amber. She made a global gesture. "Welcome to my magic bottle."

He laid his shirt on the dresser—the only freestand-ing piece of furniture in the room, taking care not to top-ple any of the ornate frames she'd assembled. "Can you make all my wishes come true?"

"No," she said, shaking her head. Her gaze stayed on his chest and she licked her lips in an unconscious way that made him instantly hard. "Nobody can do that. But…" She unzipped her slacks and wiggled free of the stretchy material. "I might be able to satisfy one."

She held up her index finger, then put it in her mouth and slowly pulled it out. Nick swallowed hard. He clawed at his buckle in a frantic effort to get out of his pants, but Grace stepped closer and did it for him. With a flourish that would have done Zorro proud, she whipped the belt free.

Nick undid his jeans and stepped out of them. "This isn't going to be a hearts-and-flowers kind of thing, Grace."

Her hand flattened against his hard-on and she leaned into him. Her breasts brushed against his chest. "We can do it standing up for all I care. Just satisfy me. Now."

He slipped her panties over her hips. Pink lace, he acknowledged vaguely. He was more interested in the smoothness of her skin and the sculpted shape of her backside.

The stretchy fabric of her top molded to her figure, skimming her hips. He caught the edge and tugged upward. Grace lifted her arms. The elastic inched over her breasts, then suddenly they were free and visible.

Nick's jaw dropped and saliva pooled in his mouth. "Grace, you're beautiful."

She blushed like a virgin, but she didn't shrink from his scrutiny. "Thank you. Now, what's good for the gander, or some such thing."

He took off his shorts and faced her. He was glad for her speechless scrutiny. It gave him time to ask "Condoms?"

"Built-in hidey-hole by the lamp." She gestured vaguely in the direction of the headboard.

As she reached out to touch him, she ran her tongue over her bottom lip. Nick's body reacted as any red-blooded male's would. The point of no return was history.

Grace sensed the instant he was committed to making love to her. Some people might have considered the end result a sure bet, but Grace didn't take anything for granted where Nikolai was concerned. "Can we skip the foreplay and get right to the good stuff?" she asked.

He looked shocked. Grace didn't blame him. She wasn't sure where she'd left her rational mind, but this new, wholly sensual side of her had taken over. "It's been a while for me and I'm pretty much ready when you are, which by the looks of it was ten minutes ago."

She touched the head of his penis and ran her nails down the rock-solid shaft.

Nikolai let out a sound, something between a growl and a groan. "You," he said, gently pushing until the backs of her knees touched the mattress.

She sat down, legs spread in pure wantonness. Nikolai took in her pose, his left eyebrow lowering rakishly. "You could provoke a saint. My blood feels like it's going to shoot out the top of my head."

"I know a better way to blow off a little steam."

She leaned forward and put her lips on him. Her hands cupped her breasts as she rocked forward and back, drawing him in and out of her mouth. His stomach muscles tensed in a well-defined six-pack and she could see his toes curled against the carpet. He let out a low, painful-sounding moan. "Woman, that's torture. You're torture. You're not supposed to do that."

"I'm not?" she asked, letting her hand take over so she could look up at him.

"You're…a…princess."

The words sounded ripped from his gut.

"You mean like a royal pain in the ass?" she teased, grabbing his left cheek and squeezing.

Nikolai's head was back and the muscles in his neck stood out. "Yeah. That, too."

She leaned forward until her breasts were almost touching him, then she rubbed the tip of his penis between them. Nick let out a choking sound and pushed himself against her chest. Her flesh surrounded him and he hunched over as if fighting for control.

"Oh, Grace, you…" His voice broke as he threaded his fingers into her hair and made a fist. The tug on her scalp increased the molten heat between her legs.

He pulled her to her feet then switched places with her, so she was straddling his knees. He buried his face in her chest, filling his hands with her and breathing deeply.

Grace had never made love to a man who was half-Romani. The thought made her shiver.

Nick looked up. "Are you afraid all of a sudden?"

"N…no. I guess not, but—"

He nuzzled one breast, blowing softly on the wet trail left by his tongue. The rest of her thought flew out the large gaping hole in her mind. When he took one nipple into his mouth and suckled, she arched her back, grinding against his knee.

She squirmed with a powerful need until she found just the right placement for his knee. She ground her hips in a circle, reveling in the quick, hot flicker of ecstasy.

He kept her from going too far, too fast, by lifting her hips and bringing them toward his waiting erection.

Grace went up on her toes, then she lowered herself with agonizing slowness that had Nikolai letting out a jerky breath.

"Oh, baby," he said. "You're sweet, tight and wet."

Grace took a few seconds to thank heaven for this amazing connection; then she moved her hips in an ageless dance. She pushed harder and harder.

"Don't worry, Grace," Nikolai whispered in her ear. "We're getting there. Trust me."

She opened her eyes and saw his wicked, sexy grin. "But this damn satin bedspread doesn't give a guy any traction," he added.

A second later, she was on her back with Nikolai poised above her. Arms stiff, he looked down at her and said, "Do you mind? The way my butt kept sliding, we were going to wind up on the floor."

She laughed. *When was the last time I laughed in bed?* She couldn't remember.

He didn't wait for her answer. He lowered himself, filling her. She wrapped her legs around him and they rocked together until they found a rhythm that worked for both of them. Grace felt her climax building.

"Oh, oh, oh," she cried, becoming lost in the sensation.

He was making noises, too. Sounds that told her he was close to coming. She clung to his neck and lifted herself up, up. They met at the same place. He poured into her with a raw cry that seemed to come from the depth of his soul. Grace vaguely realized that they'd shared an emotional release neither could have predicted.

"Sweet," she said softly, tears slipping past her lashes. "Oh, Nick, that was nice."

"Nice?" he said gruffly. "Doughnuts are nice. That was freaking amazing."

She agreed.

He crushed her to him and rolled so they were side-by-side in a nest of rumpled bedding. With a tenderness she didn't expect, Nikolai swept her hair from her eyes and ran the back of his hand along her cheek. "You are breathtaking in every sense of the word."

She smiled. Oddly embarrassed by the flattery, but not by what they'd just done. "You're not too shabby yourself, Mr. Sarna. I mean Lightner."

He closed his eyes and pushed his head into the pillow. "Not yet, Grace. Please? Let's keep the real world at bay for a little longer."

She let out a sigh and curled up beside him. "Smart idea. Sex always turns my brain to mush. I swear that's the only reason Shawn and I lasted as long as we did."

"Good, huh?"

"Nothing like this, of course," she said, truthfully, although she kept her tone light and teasing.

"You're wicked."

"I know."

He ran his hand up and down her back as if drawing a map. Grace closed her eyes and threaded her fingers through the small triangle of wispy chest hairs between his pecs. Most of the men in her family were wooly bears compared to him. As she idly wondered whether hirsute genes skipped a generation, a sudden thought made her let out a gasp. They'd forgotten the condom.

"Damn."

"It hasn't been a minute."

"Sorry, but…"

He opened one eye.

"Look down," she said, pointing in the direction of his groin. "Do you see a used raincoat on that big boy?"

He didn't look. Instead, he muttered a low, rather appropriate expletive.

"You're not on the pill, I take it?"

"No, but even if I was, what about AIDS and STDs?" she asked, swallowing. "Pregnancy isn't the only thing to worry about."

"I give blood once every couple of months. It's a c...common thing when you've been in jail." He blushed. "I'm pretty sure I'm clean."

She found his embarrassment endearing. "Me, too. Clean, I mean. Not the blood-donor thing. I get queasy just thinking about needles, but I was tested after I broke up with Shawn. I haven't been with anybody since."

Neither spoke for a minute then Nikolai cleared his throat. "Going back to the subject of pregnancy, I've heard about a pill you can take after the fact."

Grace pushed back to gain some space. The flatness of his tone disturbed her. She stared at the ceiling to avoid seeing that other Nikolai, the one who was too much a part of the real world. "I could probably ask Liz," she said, feeling the warmth they'd shared start to slip away. Faking a smile, she added, "At least, we've established that we're not related. No potential pollution of the gene pool."

Nikolai's lips didn't flicker. He looked dead serious. "I'd expect to be told if anything came of this."

An edict, not a request.

Suddenly feeling naked and exposed, she grabbed the loose end of the bedspread and hugged it to her chest. "Um...okay."

Neither spoke for a minute, then Nikolai let out a long, deep breath. "I didn't mean that to sound like an order," he said, sitting up to face her. "I'm sorry."

The apology pushed her over the edge. The emotional roller coaster she'd been riding crashed. Tears backed up into her sinuses. She wadded up the corner of the blanket and pressed it to her face. "I think you should go."

She managed to hold herself together while he dressed and kissed her goodbye, but once he closed the door, she gave in to the grief, pain and disappointment that had been dogging her all day. The lovemaking—wonderful as it had been—hadn't changed her reality. She knew, deep inside, that her life would never be the same again. Nikolai or no Nikolai.

NICK LEFT Grace's snug, sensual little haven feeling more conflicted than ever. Her scent lingered on his body and made him crave her. Despite the low note that he'd left on, Nick had never felt more complete after making love.

He wanted to be with her. Which made him mad.

He didn't form strong attachments to people this fast. He wasn't a love-at-first-sex kind of guy. Not that he used women then abandoned them. In the past, he'd made sure his affairs were easygoing, mutually beneficial. He went out of his way to pick women he wouldn't fall in love with. And who wouldn't fall in love with him.

Never in a million years would he have chosen someone like Grace. Someone who put family first. Who led with her heart. Who couldn't fathom a father willingly giving up his child. At least she got that right. If Grace was pregnant, Nick would be on the first plane back. Leaving your kid for someone else to raise was the kind of thing Jurek Sarna did, not Nick Lightner.

Suddenly, Nick needed to talk to his dad. His *real* dad, Pete. He jumped the fence and let himself into Claude's house to use the phone.

When no one answered at home and Pete failed to pick up his cell phone, Nick tried the office. "Is Pete Lightner around by any chance? This is Nick Lightner calling."

"Hey, Nick, it's me, Roxy," the voice on the other end of the line said. "How's Vegas?"

After exchanging small talk for a few minutes, Roxy told him, "Pete isn't here. Hasn't been back since you left. I think your mom's keeping him busy. I heard their house sold in like six hours."

Nick thanked her and hung up. *Six hours?* That meant they'd be leaving sooner, rather than later. And he'd be alone. Just him and his dog.

Before today, he probably could have handled that. He wasn't looking forward to his parents leaving, but he was an adult. He'd be okay. But, now, after making love to Grace, Detroit felt a world away and the word home had taken on new meaning.

CHAPTER SEVENTEEN

AFTER HE SHOWERED and changed clothes, Nick tried Yetta's house, but there was no answer, although her car was parked under the carport beside Grace's. She could be out with one of her daughters or she might be at The Dancing Hippo, he decided.

He made the two-block walk with growing trepidation. Kids were an interesting phenomenon that hadn't played a huge role in his life until his sister gave birth to two beautiful baby girls. He'd held them as infants and watched them grow into intriguing little people, but he'd been a somewhat distant uncle and certainly hadn't given a lot of thought to what it would be like to have a child of his own.

Until now.

A kid. With Grace. If he closed his eyes, he could almost picture a toddler with dark curls and a flashing smile.

The toe of his boot caught on a knob of concrete and he stumbled. A reminder to stop daydreaming—for everyone's sake.

He studied Alex's house as he approached. The building was situated on the corner lot and sat at an angle so most of its backyard was sheltered from view. From all the horror stories he'd heard about sexual predators, Nick could appreciate the wisdom of that.

He rang the bell.

Alex, holding a small child in her arms, opened the interior door. The heavy metal screen door remained closed. "Hi, Nikolai, what's up?"

"Looking for your mother."

"She isn't here. Maya was having a bad day. There's been a lot of that going around lately." Her wide smile reminded him of Grace, although the two didn't look very alike. "Mom and Liz took her to the park." She opened the door. "Do you need to talk to her? We can try her cell."

He walked inside and was immediately engulfed by a mob of kids. All shapes, sizes and colors. Nick found he had to fight for balance because he couldn't move forward without stepping on tiny toes.

"Rita," Alex called. "Quick. Save him."

A young Hispanic-looking woman wearing an apron adorned with dancing pink and purple hippos corralled the youngsters by promising them a treat. "Who wants to make ants on a log?"

The collective squeal hurt his ears. Alex set down the cherub she'd been carrying, then picked up the phone. Nick only heard her side of the conversation, but he gathered Yetta was returning within the hour.

Alex put her hand over the receiver. "She wants to know if you could stop by the house later this evening?"

Nick nodded. He had a couple of errands to run.

She relayed the message then hung up. As he turned to leave, she put her hand on his forearm and said, "Could we talk?"

A minute later, after Alex had removed her apron and redirected two quarreling youngsters, she joined him on the front stoop. A steady stream of traffic played stop-and-go at the intersection.

According to Grace, Alex was thirty-five. Today, she appeared older. She used her index finger to rub a spot between her brows. "Headache?" he asked.

"A reaction to my new medication, I think. But I'll live." She looked at him. "I heard you were at the hospital the other night. I guess that means you know all about my ongoing minidrama."

"It doesn't sound very small to me. Your sister was quite upset."

She rolled her shoulders. "Yes. Grace is the baby of the family. We tended to shelter her from the everyday disappointments most people experience when they're growing up. That's why she takes it so personally when a person—or fate—messes with her plans."

"I've noticed," he said drily.

"Anyway," she said, scratching at a dab of purple paint on the knee of her jeans, "I just wanted to say thanks for helping out. She said you were a calming force in the waiting room. Grace is a pacer. We love her, of course, but she has a tendency to drive the rest of us crazy."

He understood completely. He waited, sensing there was something else she wanted to ask him.

"Do you smoke?"

The question took him by surprise. "No. Why?"

Her olive-colored skin changed hue slightly. "I used to. Before I got sick. Even a little bit afterward until Grace went ballistic one day and accused me of undermining my body's ability to defend itself." She smiled sadly. "Now I like to hang out with people who smoke so I can smell their clothing. God, that sounds really pathetic, doesn't it?"

"Yeah, sort of, but I understand."

"You do?"

"I smoked in my twenties. Then my mom had a scare and she asked my dad and me to quit. It was no big deal for me, but my dad went through all kinds of hell. The gum. The patch. Hypnosis. He still sneaks a puff or two when he gets the chance."

She gave him a smile that told him she did, too. Maybe knowing they shared a secret gave him permission to ask, "Do you know where Jurek Sarna lives?"

"Laughlin. But I don't know where in Laughlin. Mom knows, though. Are you planning to see him?"

"Maybe."

"Cool. Mom didn't say so, but I believe that was her ulterior motive in asking you to come stay with us."

"It was?"

She nodded. "She feels sorry for him—being sick and an outcast from the family."

"An outcast? You mean he's not welcome here?"

Alex shook her head. "I don't have anything against him. Whatever happened took place a long time ago. When Mom was a baby, I think. I don't know the whole story. Maybe you should ask her."

Nick left shortly after that. He returned to Claude's and tried his parents' number one more time, but only the machine picked up. Nick knew it was foolish to worry. They were moving into a new phase of their lives and everything would be fine. He'd be home soon. His dog was waiting for him. All he'd be leaving behind was a family he'd come to care about, a woman he most probably loved and a man he thought he hated.

What if Grace was right? Maybe it was wrong to condemn Jurek without ever bothering to hear his side of the story. But first, Nick had to finish the job he'd come to Vegas to do. A job that didn't include falling for Grace.

GRACE WAS FOLDING menus when a voice said, "You did it, didn't you?"

Grace looked up to find Kate staring at her. Her tall white chef's hat was cocked in a rakish tilt that made Grace want to smile. "Did what?"

"You know what. I can tell. You've got a dreamy, state-of-grace look. Did you have sex with Nikolai?"

No. We didn't just have sex. We made love. At least it sure felt like love to Grace. "Go away."

"An admission of guilt if I've ever heard one."

Grace had arrived late and had been playing catch-up ever since. Which, she told herself, was a good thing. She'd been too busy to think about what she'd done. Or the possible consequences.

Unfortunately, this had turned out to be family night at Romantique. Every other table she seated had at least one, if not two, adorable youngsters and/or babies.

She shoved the menus into their compartment and turned to face Kate. "Why aren't you in the kitchen? You never leave mid-rush. Is the power off?"

"Very funny. I'm letting Jo finish up. I covered for her at lunch so she could eat with her son after our meeting."

"Right. Your new lawyer. Is he a keeper?"

"He's a man," Kate said sharply. "We only talked about Ian and Maya. He seemed qualifed to handle my case."

Grace sensed there was something Kate wasn't sharing. "Is he handsome?"

Kate grabbed the menus from her and stuffed them away. "Why would that matter? I hired him for his law degree not for the color of his eyes. What's wrong with you?"

Yep. Something was up with Kate, but Grace was still too emotionally drained to ponder it. The nap had helped, but it hadn't erased the memory of Charles's revelation, nor could sleep mute the passion she and Nikolai had shared. "You're right. Sorry I asked. My brain is elsewhere."

"With Nikolai?" Kate didn't give her time to answer. She put her hands on her hips and gave Grace a stern look. "If you've fallen for him, you'd better hope he plans to stay in Vegas. Your work, your commitments are here. You can't just fall in love and leave."

Grace's temper flared, but she swallowed her reply when one of their servers—their cousin Enzo's daughter, Babette—appeared with a question. Apparently she'd mixed up an order. The guest had eaten the meal but was now refusing to pay.

Grace heaved a sigh. Had it been one of their regular patrons, she'd have comped the cost in a heartbeat. But the two men that Babette pointed out were strangers, and her gut told her they were only after a free meal.

"I'll handle it," Grace said.

She took her time walking to the table, greeting regulars to show how warmly her patrons were treated. The two men appeared agitated by the time she reached them.

"Gentlemen," she said, employing one of her well-practiced, superficial smiles. "I'm Grace Radonovic. My sister and I own Romantique. Babette tells me you have a problem."

"No, you have a problem, lady," said the older of the two. Probably in his midforties, his bulging belly displayed by a much-too-snug golf shirt, his florid face was an unhealthy shade of red. "Your girl brought my friend here the wrong food."

"Yeah," his buddy said. "I ordered the veal. She gave me some chicken thing."

Grace looked at the computer-generated receipt. "I can see that. Chicken Saltimbocca instead of Veal Picata. You're right. The mistake is ours, and I will gladly comp your meal."

She took her pen and crossed out the chicken. Her personal favorite.

"Not good enough," the vociferous speaker said. "I want our whole meal comped, including the wine. Your lousy service, which you just admitted to, ruined our dining experience," he said in a way that proved to Grace he was well-practiced in this kind of scam. "Besides, the food was only so-so."

Grace had been dealing with the public for a long time. She took a deep calming breath. "I'm most sorry that we've been unable to serve you to your satisfaction. It's always Romantique's aim to provide our patrons with—"

He rudely interrupted. "Yeah, whatever. I don't give a shit about that. You screwed up, lady. We're leaving."

He reached for his jacket, which was draped across the adjacent chair, but Grace used her hip to pin it in place as she pulled her cell phone from its clip on the waistband of her slacks. "Feel free," she said, pushing buttons with slow determination. "This young lady's father, my cousin, Enzo, will meet you at your car. Did I mention that his World Wrestling Federation name was The Barbarian?"

The men looked at each other.

"Enzo doesn't take insults to his daughter too kindly. Nor does he appreciate it when some low-life scum tries to cheat his cousins out of the price of a meal."

"Hey," the man barked, "if your crummy food—"

Grace reached past him and picked up his empty plate. "The food you devoured?"

"I was hungry enough to eat shit—that doesn't mean I have to pay for it."

She glanced around, aware that other customers were following the drama. "Yes, actually, it does. It's the law." She put down the plate and pressed the final two numbers. "I just know he'd love to meet you, wouldn't he, Babette?"

The girl nodded nervously.

"Now, listen," the man started, his voice sounding pinched. "I don't want no trouble. I just—"

Grace glared at him. "You just wanted something for nothing. But my sister and I work very hard to make this place a success. We don't take it lightly when a couple of two-bit bottom feeders show up and try to take advantage of a small, very human mistake."

The murmur of crowd approval swelled.

"Yeah," said a man from a nearby table. "Especially

since I overheard you two talking about how you could screw the place out of a freebie."

Grace smiled her gratitude to the customer. She couldn't remember his name but would be sure to send a bottle of wine to his table the next time he came in.

The loudmouth jumped to his feet and pulled his wallet from his hip pocket. "Fine. Whatever." He threw four twenties on the table. Enough to cover the price of dinner and his bar tab. "We're outta here. And, believe me, we're gonna tell people about how we were treated."

Before he could turn away a hand grabbed his shoulder, freezing him in place. "You forgot the tip."

Grace nearly dropped her phone, which she'd turned off to cancel the call to Liz. *Nikolai?* She hadn't noticed him come in.

"You've gotta be kidding," the man complained.

"Do I look like the type who kids?" Nikolai asked. "Y'see, me and Enzo used to wrestle together. He taught me everything I know about getting the most hurt for the least amount of effort."

The man's mouth flapped soundlessly. His friend hastily tossed down another twenty. "There. That's enough, isn't it? She really did mix up my order."

Grace handed the money to Babette, who was staring at Nikolai as though he were her knight in shining armor. "And had you brought that to our attention at the time, we would have fixed it," she said. "Now, please leave and don't come back."

The men grabbed their jackets and left. The room erupted in applause. Grace made a what-can-you-do sign. "I think this calls for champagne. On the house."

Nikolai caught up with her at the bar. "We have to talk."

After she directed her servers to offer a glass of either champagne or sparkling apple juice to every guest, she pointed Nikolai to the staircase that led to her office. "I'll meet you upstairs in a minute. I need to sign off on the drink order." She turned away, then stopped. "Oh, and thanks for your help."

"It was nothing. You had it under control, but since Claude told me Enzo is in Mexico at the moment, I thought I'd try Plan B," he said, reaching for her hand.

Grace couldn't bear to touch him. Not yet. She still felt too fragile, too off balance. "I'll be right back."

"Grace, I'm sorry for the way we left things this afternoon. What happened probably shouldn't have, but—"

"Not here," she said, stepping away. She wasn't ready to dissect what had gone on between them. She knew she couldn't avoid the conversation for long, but was one night to sleep on it too much to ask? "Can we save this for later? At home. Or—"

Before she could complete the sentence, Kate appeared with a big smile on her face. "Nice save, Grace. I loved the clean-plate bit. Brilliant. And I really enjoyed the way Nikolai went after the tip. Maybe we should hire him as our bouncer. We could even come up with a diabolical name. Like Brutus."

Nikolai gave her a get-real look, then said, "Do you mind, Kate? I need to talk to your sister."

"Me, too, but I can see you've got dibs. When you're done, come to the kitchen. There's a cannoli with your name on it."

Grace gave in. "Fine. We'll talk. Kate, will you sign off on my bar tab? I just bought the house a round."

"So I noticed. Smart way to put a positive spin on

what happened. I think I'll go have a glass myself. It's been one of those days, hasn't it?" She gave Grace a wink and left.

"How 'bout you?" Grace asked, stalling. "Do you need a glass of champagne before we get into this?"

"No, thank you."

"Ooh, nice manners. One might think you were housebroken."

She marched up the flight of stairs, thankful that she'd dressed in a simple black pantsuit, instead of her usual skirt and heels. Once in her office, she put her desk between them and sat down.

She kicked off her shoes without thinking and dug her toes into the thick pile of the carpet.

"Nice office," Nikolai said, looking around. "I think it's bigger than your trailer."

"I share it with Kate," she said, indicating a portioned-off workspace just beyond the filing cabinets. Adjacent to that was a large, square red-blue-and-yellow alphabet rug where Maya had spent her days as a toddler.

A small bookcase and beanbag chair had replaced the toy box and safety gate.

"That's Maya's space," she explained as Nikolai headed toward the play area. "It's in transition until she's ready to take over for me."

He laughed softly. Grace liked his laugh. Too bad she heard it so rarely.

"So? Are we discussing what happened in my trailer or my flakiness when it comes to birth control?"

"Neither. Like I said, I came to apologize."

"Are you serious?"

He meandered back to her desk, pausing briefly to look at the family photos on the wall.

"I acted like an ass," he said, placing his palms flat on her desk.

She didn't know what to say. In all the time she and Shawn had been together, he'd never apologized—sincerely.

"I have a bad temper," he added.

"You had a right to be upset."

"I'm as much to blame for what happened as you are."

She swallowed the lump in her throat. "I called my doctor. She said there's something I can take if I'm worried about a potential pregnancy. I have seventy-two hours."

He sat down and put his right foot on his left knee. He was still in jeans and boots, but he'd changed into a long-sleeved shirt. One she hadn't seen before. It looked new.

"I really was a jerk," he said softly. "I suppose partly because I know what it's like to be an unwanted child."

Grace's self-pity turned to contrition. Why hadn't she guessed that was what was bothering him? So much for her highly tuned intuition. "But, Nikolai, from what Mom told us, your parents were very much in love when you were born. What if your assumption that your father didn't want you is wrong? He was grieving. People do crazy things when they're in pain. I know, because Mom did something stupid, too, after Dad died."

"Did she give away one of her kids?"

"We were too old for that," she said, trying to smile. "But she gave nearly every dime of Dad's life-insurance money to Kate's husband to invest. Unfortunately, Ian's elaborate pyramid scheme collapsed. Then, rather than face up to what he'd done, he pocketed what was left of the money and headed for the border. Mom never would have made it so easy for him to steal the money if she'd been thinking straight."

"Money can be replaced, but a kid…"

Grace heard his bleak tone. She sat forward and looked him in the eyes. Such beautiful eyes. *If our child…* She shook her head and ordered herself to stay focused. "Is everything so black-and-white in your world?"

"Not everything, but—"

She didn't let him finish. "Listen, I know you've had a brush with the law. You've paid your debt to society, and you probably want to move on with your life. That's great, but don't you think the same should apply to your father—your birth father? Hasn't he paid for his mistake by not watching his son grow up?"

"I remember the day when no one came to pick me up from the babysitter. She started calling around. I was a little older than Maya, but I remember hiding because I knew something bad had happened to my mommy. Strangers came for me, Grace. A man and a woman. He pulled me out from behind the couch and carried me to a car. He was chewing Juicy Fruit gum. To this day, that smell makes me nauseous."

He took a breath and let it out. "I never saw either of my parents again. Don't try to cloud the issue with sympathy."

She sat back. "I'm sorry, but I'm not made that way. I can't look at George and not feel sympathetic. It's how I was raised." She tried to smile. "Growing up Gypsy, you see things differently. People aren't perfect. They make mistakes. Stealing is still stealing and it's wrong, but we don't throw people in jail for slipping up, like writing a check that needs an extra day or two to clear."

His brow knitted severely. He didn't like what she was saying, but she went on anyway. "In the Rom world, if you didn't have the money, someone would cover for you. If the police came knocking on your door, someone would keep them distracted until you had time to clear up the confusion. We look after each other because we know that in the gaujo world bad things happen when you don't have family around." She wanted to reach out and touch him but kept her hands folded on the desk. "You're a perfect example of that. If my mother had been there when your mother died, you would have come home with us. Period."

He didn't say anything for a few seconds. When he spoke, his voice was contemplative. "Does that mean you'd never leave the comfort and security of your family?"

"Where would I go?"

"Detroit, maybe."

Grace sank back in shock. "You're leaving? I thought you liked it here."

"I'm pointing out that you have choices. Just like those two jerks tonight. They chose to try to beat you out of the price of dinner, instead of doing the right thing."

The right thing? This from a guy who spent time in jail for getting into a bar fight?

"Nikolai, sometimes you baffle me. I don't think I know you at all. Who are you really?"

He didn't answer for a minute. Grace watched his eyes closely and saw the battle going on inside, but when he answered, his tone was resigned. "I'm a half-Gypsy freak with no idea where I belong. Satisfied?"

No. But she knew what would satisfy her. "I kind of like freaks. Wanna take me home? I promise to do the right thing this time and use a condom."

"Better safe than sorry, huh?"

"Always been my motto."

"Mine, too," he muttered softly. "Which is why I have to go." He started to reach out to touch her, but appeared to change his mind. A moment later, he was gone. Grace put her head on her desk and let out a long troubled sigh. *Detroit.* No way she could conceive of moving there.

CHAPTER EIGHTEEN

THE NEXT MORNING, Grace awoke from a fitful night's sleep. Before leaving Romantique, she'd finally confided in Kate about her interlude with Nikolai. She couldn't bring herself to talk about Charles or his claim about their father. She could only deal with one catastrophe at a time.

Kate had lectured her about communicable diseases and advised her to see her doctor the next day.

"But what if this was supposed to happen, Kate?" Grace had asked, letting the stillness of the empty kitchen calm her. She and her sister often had their best talks at two in the morning. "You and Ian took precautions, and Maya found a way past them."

"My daughter has defied odds all her life. According to Mom, Maya picked the time, place and parents she wanted. Why? Considering all that's happened, I have no idea."

Grace knew. Kate was a great mother—loving and creative. She'd learned from the best. The only other person—in Grace's opinion—who came close to being as devoted to her children was MaryAnn. Which, Grace thought, was why—after hours of tossing and turning—she'd decided to talk to her cousin's wife. She was absolutely certain MaryAnn wouldn't want to continue working for Charles once she learned the truth about his involvement in her father's death.

She pulled on a ball cap so the wind didn't wreak havoc with her hair. Her Lycra Capri's, sports bra and loose T shirt were all black, like her mood. But her hot-pink socks matched her running shoes.

Today was going to be warm, she realized as she made a show of stretching—just in case Nikolai was next door watching. But last night, she'd seen on the Weather Channel that a big storm was headed their way, thanks to a low-pressure area in Baja.

In the desert, that usually meant flash floods, an anomaly of nature that Grace and her father had loved to experience together. She still got weepy on stormy days, missing Ernst.

After making a purposeful loop around the neighborhood, she arrived at MaryAnn and Gregor's baby-blue ranch-style home—similar to the ones on either side of it, except their house still retained its original roofing material—coarse white rock.

The place had changed very little since MaryAnn and Gregor had taken it over from MaryAnn's mother. Grace had never cared for MaryAnn's mother, who now lived in Hawaii. She didn't understand how any grandmother could stand to live so far away from her grandchildren and never make any attempt to visit.

Nor had the woman ever invited MaryAnn and her family to come see her.

Grace was positive that kind of rejection had to hurt, but MaryAnn always defended her mother by saying, "It's her way."

As she knocked on the door, she observed MaryAnn's faded Toyota sedan parked beside the overflowing garbage cans. Gregor's car was gone. That was odd. Normally, Greg didn't go to work until much later in the day.

She looked around. Weathered boxes of junk were lined up along the concrete wall that separated the younger family's yard from Claude's. Broken toys. Dog-food dishes—even though their beautiful but ancient cocker spaniel had recently died, after a long, costly illness.

She'd considered organizing a communal work detail to spruce the place up, but when she mentioned the idea to her sisters, Liz had told her to mind her own business.

"MaryAnn?" she called, knocking again. *Maybe she walked Luca and Gemilla to The Dancing Hippo.*

She'd just turned to leave when the lock clicked and the door opened a crack. "Grace? What are you doing here?"

"I wanted to catch you before you left for work. What's wrong? Are you sick?"

The door opened all the way. MaryAnn's rumpled nightshirt came to the middle of her shins. Her hair was matted down on one side of her head. "No. Today is Charles's monthly breakfast meeting at the Insurance Center. I don't go in until noon. Gregor must have taken the kids to school, then gone out for breakfast," she said, yawning. "Want some coffee?"

MaryAnn turned and walked into the kitchen.

"No thanks, but a drink of water would be nice." Grace had wrestled with how much to tell her cousin and his wife about her father's involvement with Charles and had come to the conclusion that Ernst would have wanted her to warn Gregor and MaryAnn about how deceitful and cruel Charles could be.

"Actually, I'm here to talk about Charles."

MaryAnn took a can of Folgers from the cupboard. "You mean about your plans for the new restaurant?"

"No. I mean blackmail."

The can clattered loudly against the countertop. "What?"

"MaryAnn, Charles has threatened to expose some past indiscretion of my father's if I don't give him the money in my trust account. He doesn't plan to use it to remodel the coffee shop. He says he needs it for something else. He also claims the money is rightfully his because of some agreement between him and Dad."

After a slight hesitation, MaryAnn finished measuring the ground coffee into the filter, added a carafe of water then turned on the switch. Only then did she look at Grace and say, "Did Charles tell you what he needed the money for?"

"No. And I really don't care. He was horrible, Mary-Ann. He said he'd ruin Dad's reputation and prove once and for all that the Romani are nothing more than liars and thieves."

"Like he's some kind of saint," MaryAnn murmured. "What are you going to do?"

Grace sat down on the white vinyl stool. "I…I'm thinking about going to the police." She held up a hand, anticipating MaryAnn's response. "I know. I know. Dad didn't trust them, but I'm not going to let Charles extort money from me, no matter what happened in the past. It's just not right."

"But Grace, Charles has a lot of connections. I…I wouldn't cross him, if I were you."

The slight wobble in MaryAnn's voice caught Grace's

attention. "You didn't know about this, did you? Charles didn't brag about getting gullible me to hand over my trust fund?"

"No, of course not. Charles doesn't confide in me. I'm just his secretary. I make sure he's at court on time and I referee his arguments with his partners. Other than that, I'm practically invisible."

Grace heard the bitterness in MaryAnn's tone and was confused. In the past, MaryAnn had bragged about what a great boss Charles was. "What about Gregor?"

"Do you mean is he close to Charles? Don't be ridiculous. First off, Charles isn't close to anybody, but if he were, he wouldn't pick Gregor. Haven't you noticed that Charles only hires the Romani for low-level jobs?"

Grace had never given it any thought. "What about Uncle Claude? He doesn't sweep floors."

"Of course not. Why work for a living when you can get paid for making up lies?" Her tone was laced with barely concealed spite.

"MaryAnn," Grace exclaimed in shock. "What's going on? This doesn't sound like you."

Her cousin-in-law's eyes narrowed to an unfriendly squint Grace had never seen before. "How would *you* know, Grace? You're a princess. I'm just one of the peasants, remember?"

Grace was too stunned to speak. Where was the sweet, kindhearted, wouldn't-hurt-a-fly woman she thought she knew?

"The truth hurts, doesn't it, Grace?" MaryAnn asked with a laugh. The brittle sound drove a shiver up Grace's spine. With it came an odd tingling, like déjà vu, but she was positive nothing like this exchange had ever taken place.

Grace shook her head. "The truth? Have you looked at my life, lately, MaryAnn? My oldest sister just got out of the hospital. Liz is hanging on to her house by a thread. Kate and I are working our butts off to keep the restaurant going. Does that constitute royalty in your book?"

MaryAnn poured herself a cup of coffee. "It beats playing dumb while the man you work for exploits the poor, the lazy and the greedy to feather his own, twisted bed by making up bogus accident claims."

Grace's pulse jumped erratically. "What are you talking about? I thought his insurance operation was completely pro bono."

MaryAnn made a rude sound of contempt. "Of course you did. That's what he wants people to think. But I saw a file on his desk one day. Less than half of the claims are legit. People like Claude recruit suckers who need money. This is Vegas. They're easy enough to find. He and Greg help them stage accidents. Charles gets a kickback from his referrals to a couple of doctors and chiropractors, including the one Liz works for."

Liz? Oh, God, no. She can't be involved.

"Plus," MaryAnn went on, "if any of the claims go to court, he winds up hauling in big money."

"If you know this, why haven't you told anyone?"

MaryAnn shrugged. "Because Charles is too clever to get caught. If I called the police, you know who would wind up in jail—patsies like Gregor and Claude. Not Charles," she said with conviction. "People like him never pay for their crimes."

MaryAnn despised Charles, Grace realized. Deeply.

Passionately. But why? "There's something else you're not telling me. Have you been involved with him? Romantically?"

MaryAnn made a gagging sound. "Of course not. He's a freak. I wouldn't let him come near me." Her look of revulsion convinced Grace she was telling the truth.

"So why do you hate him? Does it have something to do with his past? If you know something, we could go to the police—"

Coffee sloshed over the rim of MaryAnn's cup. "No. Forget it. Charles is untouchable. Give him what he wants, Grace. Before it's too late."

"Cave in to his blackmail? No way. He thinks this information he has about my dad can hurt us, but he's wrong. We've weathered worse as a family. We'll survive this, too."

"He won't stop at ruining your dad's reputation. He'll find a way to ruin you, too. And your mother, your sisters, even me and my family. I knew someone who threatened to cross Charles. She didn't live very long after that."

Murder? Charles was capable of murder? Grace didn't believe it. MaryAnn was clearly overwrought.

"If that's true, why do you still work for him?"

MaryAnn wiped up the spill, never meeting Grace's eyes. "Better to keep a snake where you can see him than wonder where he might strike next. Your father taught us that, remember? Ernst was always spouting little bits of wisdom."

Her sunny "MaryAnn" smile returned, but Grace didn't buy the quick turnaround. Her intuition told her MaryAnn was keeping something from her.

Grace stood up abruptly. "I have to go. Mom needs me to drive her to Liz's. Catch you later."

Grace had no idea where her mother was. Nor had Yetta asked Grace to play chauffeur. But the voice in her head said Yetta was the person she needed to talk to. She had to hope her mother's visions wouldn't fail them this time.

"MOM," GRACE SAID, dashing into her mother's bedroom. "You won't believe what just happened. I can't make sense—" She stopped speaking to stare at her mother, who was wearing her best suit and skirt...with heels. "You're all dressed up."

"I have some shopping to do, then I'm meeting someone for lunch." Yetta was seated at her vanity. The gold velvet upholstered stool had always reminded Grace of a small, regal throne. As a child, Grace had sat on it to give her royal speeches. Yetta's cosmetic jars and perfume bottles had served as her loyal subjects.

"With Liz?"

"No, Elizabeth is going to the bank over her lunch hour to see about refinancing her house."

Grace sat down on the bed and hunched forward, still breathing hard from her sprint. Liz was refinancing? Grace hadn't heard that. Of course, she wasn't terribly surprised. Liz was the secret-keeper in the family. "I hope she gets it. She's been pinching pennies more than usual, lately."

Yetta gave her French twist hairdo a shot of styling spray then swiveled to face Grace. "Elizabeth will be fine. But you are in trouble. I can tell."

Grace took a deep breath. "Actually, we might all be

in trouble. As much as it pains me to say this, I think we need to call the police."

Yetta sat back. "I beg your pardon?"

"I just left MaryAnn's. I went there to tell her that Charles tried to extort my trust-fund money from me. She wasn't surprised. In fact, she told me that his insurance operation is basically a scam. Some of our family members might be involved. I know this is gaujo business, but I think it could hurt us, as well. If Dad were alive..." Grace watched her mother's facial expression change from concern to resignation.

"Grace, dear, I have something to tell you. You aren't going to like it."

Grace's breath caught in her throat. "What?"

"I contacted the authorities several weeks ago because of a disturbing dream I'd had. It was Jurek's idea. He suggested I call someone he knew. Someone we could trust to uncover the truth from the inside."

Dream? Jurek? Inside? A sick feeling swept upward from her belly. "Mom? What are you trying to say?"

"Nikolai is a policeman in Detroit. He came here to assist the Metro police to find out why Charles was suddenly so interested in you and your inheritance. It was the only way to keep my family from being devoured by the serpent."

The truth hit on several levels at once. She might have fallen if she hadn't been sitting down. Nikolai wasn't an ex-con, he was a cop. Working undercover. Using her family to get to Charles. *He was a cop.*

"Oh, my God," she said, fighting tears that closed off her windpipe. "He lied to me. You lied."

Yetta reached out and squeezed Grace's knee. "He

had to keep his identity a secret, Grace. And you have to promise me you won't tell anyone. Even your sisters. If word gets out, his life will be in jeopardy."

"It already is," Grace seethed. "Because I'm going to kill him." He'd made love to her as one man when he really was another. "Mother, how could you? Because he has a few drops of Romani blood, you welcomed a cop into our midst without talking to anyone? My God, Mom, what would Dad think?"

"Grace, I was—"

Grace was too angry to listen. "It's bad enough that you gave all of Dad's insurance money to Ian, but this is crazy. You're Puri Dye. You're supposed to *see* into the future, not to reshape it by involving gaujo police in Romani business."

Yetta shot to her feet. "Stop it right now. I'm through apologizing for the mistakes I made after Ernst died. I wasn't myself then. My sight hasn't returned fully. It might never come back, which is why I have to try to interpret my dreams. But I *saw* Charles. He was a snake and he was slowly devouring this family. I had to find a way to stop him."

"And the only way you could do that was to invite a cop into the compound?"

"He's not just a cop. He's Romani. He's Jurek's son."

Grace stood up, too. "Oh, really? Well, maybe somebody should have told *him* that because he thinks his family is back in Detroit. If anyone has an ax to grind with the Romani, it's Nikolai Sarna. Or should I say, Nick Lightner. That's his real name, you know."

"I do. I also know that you're upset about being kept in the dark about this, but Nikolai's boss—the person

I'm meeting for lunch today—insisted on secrecy. He felt Nikolai would be accepted more easily by the men in the family if he had a criminal record."

Grace stared at her mother, still not completely able to comprehend that Yetta had gone behind their backs like this. "I can understand you trying to help, Mom, but how could you not tell us the truth? What if one of us was involved in something shady? You might have sent your own child to jail."

"That wouldn't happen. I know my daughters."

Grace shook her head sadly. "But even Puri Dye miss things. You thought you knew your husband, too. Didn't you?"

Before Grace could take back the punishing question, a voice called from the hallway. "Anybody home?" *Liz.* "You'll never believe what happened at DesertWay this morning. We were raided."

THE RAID WENT exactly as planned. Almost.

Nick had taken tremendous satisfaction in showing his badge to Charles. "Busted," he'd said, savoring the moment.

Charles had cooperated without much of a fuss. In the end, fifteen people were taken into custody at the insurance center, including Gregor and Claude Radonovic.

The only snag arrived when a second team descended on Charles's office at the casino and discovered Mary-Ann missing.

When asked about his wife's whereabouts, Gregor had seemed genuinely baffled. "I haven't seen her since this morning. Maybe one of the kids got sick. Did you check at home?"

"Of course," Nick lied. It hadn't occurred to him to send a car to the house. An oversight. Proof that he'd lost his edge. Something that never happened to Nick Lightner but seemed to be chronic for Nikolai Sarna.

He'd gotten too close to the people he was supposed to be investigating. Shared meals. Basketball games on television. He and Claude had laughed and cussed. Nick and Greg had shared many a beer together.

Claude had remained his jovial self throughout the booking process. "Been here, done this," he'd said when an officer loaded him into the back of a patrol car. "Don't forget to feed the cat when you get home, Nikolai."

That comment had earned Nick a sharp look from Zeke. In their haste to plan the raid around Charles's monthly breakfast meeting, they'd neglected to make any changes in Nick's living arrangements.

While Zeke accompanied the suspects back to the department for questioning, Nick went to the casino to interview Charles's staff and secure videotapes and computers. He went through MaryAnn's desk, where he found handwritten notes indicating MaryAnn was fully aware of what Charles was doing in his bogus insurance operation.

Unfortunately, Charles had protected himself quite cleverly. Taken at face value, one might think Claude was the mastermind behind the scheme. Nick knew that wasn't possible, but proving it was something only MaryAnn could do.

And there was still the question of who was blackmailing Charles? Usually the motive was money, but from the employment records, MaryAnn appeared to be making a decent salary. Why mess with the golden goose?

He decided to ask her husband. An hour later, he was seated across from Gregor in a small but functional interrogation room. "So, Greg, what's the deal with MaryAnn and Charles? Anything going on between them you want to get off your chest?"

Gregor turned a sickly shade of gray. He shook his head and looked up from his hands, which were clasped in front of him as if in prayer. "You mean sexual? No way, man," he said with feeling. "She hates him. Calls him a pig. A…a…what's the word for a guy who diddles little kids?"

"Pedophile?"

"Yeah, that's it."

Nick wasn't buying it. "We've got two women downstairs who have been servicing Chuck for the past month or so. They're definitely not children."

Gregor shrugged. "Maybe he's changed. That was when he was younger."

"Did he do something to MaryAnn?"

That gave Gregor pause. "No. God, no. It was with his sister." He had to think a minute to come up with a name. "Amy. She and MaryAnn were friends. In high school."

"How do you know this?"

"She was a crackhead. One night she showed up when MaryAnn was out. I was a little drunk. We…uh…hung out. Talked. She told me what Charlie-boy did to her. It was sick. She wasn't much older than Gemilla when it happened. He was a grown man."

"And you decided to use that information to blackmail Charles," Nick said.

Gregor looked confused. "Huh?"

Nick's gut told him Gregor wasn't his man. "Did you and MaryAnn discuss this?"

Gregor's expressive face looked utterly appalled. "Are you nuts? She'd have killed me. To tell the truth, I was kind of relieved when Amy died. I know that's a terrible thing to say, but you can't trust addicts to keep anything secret."

"So, even though MaryAnn knew the truth about Charles and what he did to her friend, she still went to work for him."

"We needed the money. And Amy was dead."

And being close to Charles could provide a golden opportunity to hurt him when he was the most vulnerable.

But there was one other suspect to consider. "Did Liz know about Amy's history?"

Gregor shrugged. "I don't think so. She wasn't around much after Amy got bad. If Amy called anybody, it was MaryAnn."

"You gave her money?"

"Yeah. When we could." He looked down. "'Cept the last time. We were broke. She was dead a week later." He shook his head sadly. "MaryAnn was really bummed. Like it was her fault, you know? I tried to tell her it wasn't. If anybody was to blame, it was Charles."

Bingo.

"So, Greg, how could you work for a guy like that? Knowing what you know about him?"

He shrugged. "I needed work, man. Gotta feed my kids." *And support your gambling habit?* "Grace is the one who told me Charles was setting up a new office. When I went to apply for a job, Chuck said he could use both me and my dad."

Poor Grace, Nick thought. Instead of helping her

family, she'd set them up to fail. *No good deed goes
unpunished.*

"So where's your wife now?"

Gregor looked up sharply. "I don't know, man. I'm
worried. She wouldn't just leave the kids at day care
without calling me. What if Charles did something to
her? She knows a lot about his business."

Nick had a hunch that wasn't the case. Someone
knew where his prime suspect was, and he was betting
that someone was Grace.

"It was crazy," Liz said, pacing from one end of the
room to the other. "The guy who was breaking down the
computer was sort of friendly. He told me the hospital
was part of a pretty widespread scam involving cops and
everything."

"Cops?" Grace choked. "How?"

"I guess these people called 'runners' would give a
list of staged or bogus accidents to these cops. The cops
would file reports, then the runners would pick up the
police report and file a claim. They had people called
'jump-ins' who would provide personal information.
This is where DesertWay Med. came in. The jump-ins
would pretend to be injured and someone in the hospital would order tests, treatments, medicine, follow-up
doctor visits—all stuff that never happened."

"You weren't affected? They didn't ask you to fake
a treatment?" Grace asked, her heart in her throat.

Liz gave her a dark look. "Of course not. I handle
mostly geriatric patients and home visits."

Grace let out a sigh. "Thank God. One less Rom to
worry about."

She told her sister everything—except for Charles's claim that he'd killed their father. That was something she had to talk over with all her sisters before sharing with Yetta.

"So Nikolai is out there arresting people even as we speak?" she asked. "I didn't see him at DesertWay."

"I assume he was confronting Charles, but who knows?"

The phone rang. Grace bounced to her feet but stopped short of answering it. Her mother picked up the receiver. "Hello?"

She listened for several very long seconds then said, "I understand. Thank you for calling." She hung up.

"That was Zeke. The man I was supposed to meet for lunch," she added for Liz's benefit. "He's Nikolai's superior."

"You're dating a cop?"

"Don't be silly. It wasn't a date. We were meeting to discuss what was happening between his officer and my daughter."

Liz looked at Grace, who felt her cheeks flush with embarrassment. "What did he say?" she asked.

"Gregor and Claude have been arrested."

"Arrested?" Grace sputtered. "On what charges?"

"I didn't ask. After listening to Elizabeth, I have to assume they were both involved to some degree with this jumping runners thing."

Grace studied her mother closely. Yetta was sharp, despite being upset. Even finding out her brother-in-law and nephew were in police custody, didn't seem to faze her. "What do you want us to do?" Liz asked.

"Grace, find me the number of the lawyer Katherine

went to see the other day. She seemed quite taken with him. I'm sure he'll be able to help us." She stood up. "Elizabeth, I'd like you to drive me downtown."

"You bet," Liz said. "I want to see if I can find out if the hospital is closing or what. No work, no income, right?"

Grace called Romantique. She filled Kate in and got the number her mother wanted. She also asked her sister to call in their backup hostess to cover lunch. Grace was in no condition to play the role of gracious business owner.

What she really needed was someone to talk to, so she changed clothes and packed a few things in the car, then drove to the cemetery. She hadn't visited her father's grave since the first day Nikolai arrived in town. Considering all that had happened, it was time to bring Ernst up-to-date.

She spread a blanket on the ground in front of his headstone and piled three squishy couch pillows on top of each other. With legs crossed under her, she sat down and closed her eyes.

"I'm meditating, Dad. Liz said it helps quiet the mind. My head is ready to pop off my neck and roll into the desert."

A faint puff of wind made her wish she'd added a sweater atop her sleeveless blouse. Her feet and shins were bare, too, but they were protected by the blanket.

She tried to quiet the voices in her head, but thoughts from the morning slipped past her defenses. MaryAnn's inexplicable antipathy toward Charles. Yetta's amazing confession that she'd asked the police for help. Nikolai's identity as a gaujo policeman. Then Liz's news.

The slow, meditative breathing she'd been trying to

achieve turned choppy and shallow. Other questions flooded her mind. What would happen to Charles? What would Charles do when he learned Nikolai was an undercover cop? Would he hold Grace and her family responsible? Reveal her father's secret as payback?

She opened her eyes and stared at the headstone, her gaze drawn to the bright silver dollar winking in the dappled sunlight. *Why, Daddy? Why'd you do it? Was it just about the money?*

No answer came to her. She listened hard, but the only sound came from a blackbird pecking at the ground a few feet away. Its iridescent, blue-black feathers reminded her of her father's hair when he was younger. He'd tame the thick dark waves with a grooming product that came in a tube. She could picture him combing his hair with a small comb he kept in his hip pocket with his wallet. A wallet that always bulged with dollar bills: tens, twenties, hundreds.

Money had been important to her father, but surely not more important than family. "You take care of your family and your family will take care of you," he'd always said.

She'd never doubted that maxim until she started dating Shawn, who'd grown resentful when she'd tried to pull him into the Radonovic fold.

"That's *your* life, Grace, not mine. I have a family. Why would anybody want more than one?" he'd told her.

And she'd done the same with Nikolai, hadn't she? Only with him, she'd assumed that since he was part Romani he'd jump at the chance to immerse himself in her world. Her crazy, mixed-up world.

"Who in their right mind would take on this kind of

mess?" she muttered, shaking her head, frustrated that her thoughts had focused on Nikolai when they should be on the more practical concerns facing her family.

Instead of throwing herself into the fray, trying to help, she was hiding out fretting over Nikolai—the mostly gaujo cop who wouldn't think twice about arresting the Romani he'd recently befriended.

Is that what he's doing right now? she wondered.

She closed her eyes and tried to picture him. No image came to mind. Unnerved, she tried again, focusing intently. Suddenly, the sound of the wind disappeared. A chilly mist crept across the blank screen in her head. A moment later chaos erupted, as if someone had suddenly turned on a radio. She couldn't make out the muffled voices, but instinct told her people were arguing. Suddenly, the sound of turbulence was clipped by a thundering crack that made Grace cover her ears. A gunshot? she wondered.

Grace squinted at the foggy haze in her mind, picking out shapes that moved and swelled. MaryAnn came into focus. Her arm was outstretched as if she were pointing her finger accusingly. No, not a finger. A gun. She was aiming a gun at Nikolai.

"Stop," Grace cried. "He's not to blame for this. I am."

They both looked at her. MaryAnn's eyes were glassy and blank. Nick's were filled with concern.

He cares, she thought. But a moment later, the gun sounded a second time. The gray mist turned red. The color of blood.

She opened her eyes, surprised to find her cheeks wet with tears. Her whole body was shaking. A vision or her imagination? Which was it?

Her mother would know. Grace started to get up, but the loud thump of a car door startled her. Off balance, she fell onto her elbow and let out a small whimper. Enough to catch the attention of the man storming her way.

Nikolai. Grace barely registered the fierce look on his face. Her only thought as she jumped to her feet was, *You're alive.*

She must have cried those words aloud because he stopped abruptly and gave her a questioning look. She raced to him and hugged him fiercely. "Thank God you're okay."

Nick pushed her back then yanked off his sunglasses. The piercing intensity she read in his eyes made her flinch. "What the hell are you talking about?" he growled.

"I had a vision. MaryAnn shot you. I saw blood."

He made a disparaging sound. "MaryAnn has disappeared, Grace. Your mother said you were the last person to talk to her. Where is she? What did you tell her?"

Grace couldn't feel her fingers. "N…nothing. I don't know. Why are you being so hostile? My God, if anyone should be mad, it's me. You lied to me about who you are, and you have the audacity to give me grief about my cousin's wife's whereabouts? What's the big deal? She's only a secretary."

He snorted. "Nice try, princess. But she's much more than that. She's the key to keeping Charles in jail. We also suspect that she was blackmailing Charles."

"MaryAnn? Don't be ridiculous. She's—"

"Romani?" His tone dripped of contempt. "In this case, that defense won't fly. She's in this up to her eyeballs, just like her husband and father-in-law. And if I find out you aided and abetted in any way…"

Grace looked away. She didn't need to hear the rest of his threat. The worst he could do to her had already been done. He'd chosen sides. Nikolai Sarna was gone. He'd never really existed. The person gripping her arms as if she might attack him was Nick Lightner. Gaujo cop. Not a man she could ever love.

CHAPTER NINETEEN

NICK KNEW what she was going to say. He could read it in her face. She'd done something to warn MaryAnn. He didn't know what—Yetta had insisted she hadn't told Grace about his real purpose for being here until after Grace had talked to her cousin's wife. But Grace looked guilty. And resigned. As if she knew their relationship was over.

Which it had to be, right? She'd made it clear how she felt about cops.

"I told MaryAnn that Charles was pressuring me into giving him the money in my trust. That he'd made threats against my family. I didn't think she'd want to work for that kind of person."

"What did she say?"

"That she knew he was a bad man, but she needed the job. She said she was a glorified paper pusher. That's all."

"She lied. I have handwritten notes incriminating her. Plus, the statements of her own husband and father-in-law."

"Claude and Gregor turned against her?"

The how-could-you? look in her eyes made him want to punch something. Or someone. Preferably Charles. "They're trying to help us find her because they're worried that Charles will get to her first. Chuck has always been the big fish, but he's clever. He knows that the only way we can make these charges stick is if we have MaryAnn to tell us where the bodies are buried, so to speak."

She swayed slightly as if her knees might give out. He softened his tone as he added, "Things are under control at the moment. Alex is going to keep Gregor's kids until your mother can arrange bail. Kate's lawyer showed up. He'll represent Claude and Gregor, and MaryAnn when we find her. Liz is helping Zeke process the foreign prostitutes."

"The women I met in Charles's apartment?"

He nodded.

"So there's nothing for me to do?" she asked in a little-girl voice.

"You can tell me where MaryAnn is."

"I don't know."

"Then give me the names of her friends. Family. Anyone she'd turn to for help."

"Did you check at the ranch?"

"Yes. She's not there," Nick said, looking around. He'd been so caught up in finding Grace that he hadn't noticed the headstone bracketed by two rosebushes. So this was where the patriarch of the Romani was buried.

The grass was just starting to turn green. Trees were budding. A sanctuary of several acres squeezed between some warehouses and the highway. Except for a smattering of shrubs, some neatly trimmed, some overgrown, the only ornamentation Nick could see was a number of artificially bright plastic flower arrangements.

"Listen, Nikolai…I mean, Nick. I'm sorry. I can't tell

you where she is because I don't know, but even if I did, she's family. And—" Her shoulders rose and fell in a gesture he'd seen many times.

"And family trumps everything, right? The law comes second. Personal responsibility is a distant third. You can overlook breaking the law because she's married to your cousin."

Her dark eyes flashed with emotion. "I don't know where she is."

"Oh, come on, Grace. I overheard your sisters talking before I came looking for you. You're heir apparent to your mother's powers. Didn't you just say you'd had a vision? Something about me getting shot?"

"I saw MaryAnn. With a gun."

"Well, there were no guns drawn during the raid, so maybe what you saw is something that's going to take place in the future." He grabbed her hand and tugged her to sit down beside him on one of the pillows. "Try again. Give me some kind of clue. Is it MaryAnn in the conservatory with a lead pipe?"

Her cheeks turned as red as the silk binding on the blanket. "Why are you being so mean?"

"Because I'm pissed off. I can't leave town until this case is wrapped up. Now, I've got a fugitive. An *armed* fugitive according to your vision."

Her eyes went wide with distress. "You're making her sound dangerous. This is MaryAnn we're talking about."

"You're the one who said you saw a gun."

"I thought I did. I heard a sound and I...I..." She blinked back tears. "I don't want to talk about it."

Nick flopped to his side and stretched out. "Grace,

she's your cousin's wife. If I post an APB, someone else might find her first. Charles's goons are looking for her, too, you know. If he hired one hit man, you can be sure he'll hire another if it serves his purpose. If you want to keep her safe, go into another trance and find out where she's hiding."

She threw out her hands. "It doesn't work that way."

"Selective sight?"

"I…I don't know. It comes and goes. I don't have any control over it."

"How do you know if you don't try?"

She swallowed and looked down. "You don't believe in visions so why are you baiting me?"

He sat up sharply. "This isn't about what I believe. MaryAnn is a fugitive. People on the run make impulsive decisions. They get hurt. If you really care about your cousin and his family, you'll help me find her before something bad happens."

Grace knew she was being played. This wasn't the man she'd fallen in love with. This was the stranger who'd stepped off the plane with the squint of a hit man.

But he did have a point. She still felt the lingering uneasiness from her vision. MaryAnn *could* have a gun. Gregor had collected pistols for years before the kids were born. He only had a couple left, but MaryAnn knew how to use them. Not that Grace planned to tell Nikolai that.

"Okay, I'll try. But I don't guarantee anything."

She settled back on the cushion and closed her eyes. In her mind, she pictured herself sitting in the cemetery across from Nikolai. She saw her father's grave site. Ernst was shaking his head at her current conundrum.

Hi, Daddy. Fine mess I've made of things, huh?

Oh, Princess, you always did worry too much. Things have a way of working out, now, don't they?

She imagined her father sitting atop the marble headstone. Relaxed. Legs dangling. The way he looked when they were fishing off the side of their houseboat. He never caught anything, but he loved to "annoy the fish," as he laughingly called the sport.

He smiled at her and winked.

A horn honked from the side street; Ernst disappeared. Hot tears clustered behind her lids.

"Well?" Nikolai demanded.

Grace shook her head.

"You saw something. I sensed it."

She blinked. "You did?"

"Your face changed. Your smile turned soft and indulgent like when…never mind."

"When what?"

"Sometimes you use that smile when you look at me. Like when we were gambling and I called your bluff. I felt a connection."

Grace was surprised by his perception. "I saw my dad," she admitted. "He was fishing. On our houseboat."

Nick's eyes narrowed. "What houseboat?"

"Well, it's nothing elaborate. More like an RV on pontoons. The main deck has a couple of bedrooms, a kitchen and living room. The top deck is open. The kids sleep there on air mattresses. It's moored at Lake Mojave. Nobody's used it in a long time, but Mom won't hear of selling it. Dad loved the place."

"Lake Mojave? Where's that? The only lake I've ever heard of is Mead."

She explained about the less well-known reservoir produced by Davis Dam, also on the Colorado River but seventy miles south of Hoover. "Lake Mead is closer and more popular. The marina is also more expensive. Cottonwood Cove, where we keep our boat, is directly east of Searchlight."

Nikolai stood up and took his cell phone from his belt. "Give me the specifics. How do I find the boat?"

"Now, that's a little tricky," she said truthfully. "The last time I talked to the marina people they said they were going to move all the boats in our section to do some repairs. I could show you."

"Or I could call the marina and ask."

Grace shrugged. "You can try. But this is the off-season. And midweek. The owners are probably working in the dry-dock shop. When I need to communicate with them, I leave a message and they call me back. Eventually."

He gave her a look that said he didn't believe her, but after a few minutes of placing calls and waiting, he lowered his phone. "Damn."

She could tell he didn't want to spend any more time with her than absolutely necessary. Which was fine with her. She wasn't all that keen to spend time with him, either. She glared at him…and her heart softened, remembering the afternoon they'd made love. Dammit, they had feelings for each other. Sure, their problems were huge. Their differences enormous. So was their passion. Didn't that count for anything? "I have the key," she said, pulling her key ring from her pocket. She was *pretty* sure the small silver key opened the boat door.

"Damn," he repeated. He punched in another number

on his cell phone and started walking toward his car. Grace scooped up her blanket and pillows and followed. She could only hear bits and pieces of his one-sided conversation.

"…a long shot."

"She didn't actually see…it's more like a hunch."

"Fine."

"I will."

"What about backup? Fine. Got it."

She was breathing hard by the time she caught up with him. "Well?"

"You can come, but only to show me where the boat is. Zeke's sending a couple of Nevada State Troopers to meet us there. You will have no interaction with the suspect if she's present. Do you understand?"

Grace nodded. But beneath the blanket, her fingers were crossed. There was still the matter of the gun. If what she'd seen was a vision, then MaryAnn was armed. And very, very upset. Grace wasn't going to lose Nick to a bullet, even if she lost him eventually to his other life in Detroit.

YETTA HAD BEEN waiting in Zeke's office for what felt like hours. His small courtesy of allowing her some privacy had done little to appease her anger. Jurek had assured her that if family members were involved in Charles's scams, the police would treat them compassionately until the truth could be sorted out. Too bad nobody had told Zeke and his henchmen.

"I must demand that you stop interrogating my nephew and brother-in-law until our attorney has a chance to talk to them," she said, the moment Zeke opened the door. He'd left to get her a cup of coffee, which she didn't want, but the space had given her a few moments to collect herself. The man's no-nonsense manner bothered her, as did his occasional display of humor. She hated to be teased, although Ernst had loved to get her all riled up then kiss away her ire.

"He's with them, now. Kate brought him in. Your other daughter volunteered to talk to the two women we removed from Charles's suite. Apparently, she speaks a little Hungarian or some Slavic language."

That was news to Yetta, but Elizabeth had always been the most private child. The one with the hidden diary, friends she didn't bring home to meet the family, problems she wasn't willing to share. "Good," Yetta said, staring at the watery brown liquid in the disposable cup that he'd handed her.

The moment she'd received Zeke's call, Yetta had understood the gravity of the situation. In taking Jurek's advice to contact his son, she'd expected only Charles to be arrested. She hadn't thought about needing a lawyer to act on the family's behalf. Thank heavens Jo's son was licensed to practice law in Nevada, as well as California.

"I should be with Claude and Gregor. I've never met this attorney. Katherine said he's very young."

"Sorry. No family allowed. There will be an arraignment. It doesn't take Perry Mason to ask for bail."

"What are they being charged with?"

"That's up to the D.A. If your family members cooperate with our investigation, their lawyer might be able to cut a deal. Probation. Fine. Maybe a little jail time with community service."

Yetta couldn't tell if he was being patronizing or not.

"Are you married?" she asked. Married men spoke to women differently than single men did, she'd noticed.

He looked up from the stack of papers on his desk. "I was. A hundred years ago. She decided being a cop's wife wasn't her cup of tea."

Yetta could see why. Bad hours. Risky profession. An inability to trust people. She sensed that about him, even though they'd had very little direct contact. He was like a desert tortoise Elizabeth once brought home from school. Cautious and intensely focused, it took care of business but closed up shop when people got too close. Its hard shell was strangely beautiful and broke Yetta's heart, even though she knew that solid barrier was the only thing that had kept the animal safe for so many years.

"By the way," Zeke said, "just so you don't think I'm withholding anything, I got a call from Nick. He and Grace are on their way to Lake Mojave."

Yetta's fingers went numb. "Why?" she asked in a voice that seemed to come from a far-off place.

"Something about a vision and a houseboat."

The still-full cup tumbled to the floor. She looked at the stain on the floor. Instead of brown coffee, it looked red. Like blood.

NICK HAD strict rules about involving civilians in police business. Particularly when he cared about the civilian in question. He wasn't happy that Grace was standing at his side as they surveyed the horseshoe-shaped cove where the Lake Mojave Marina was located.

As Grace had predicted, the place was relatively quiet. Nick could tell that most of the people scattered about were fishermen. The motel to his right seemed pretty empty. The parking lot contained mostly pickup trucks and a few RVs. MaryAnn's car was not there.

Only one artery led to the floating marina. At the shoreline, a father and three youngsters were tossing bread to a gaggle of geese. Competing for food was a school of carp just below the surface. Huge fish that churned up the water like a boat propeller.

Nick stopped Grace before they reached the floating plywood dock. "Point out your boat, then go back and wait."

She kept walking. Her sandals made a *shush-shush* sound against the weathered decking that was wide enough for two people to walk abreast. Nick was glad he'd worn soft-soled shoes. He was even happier that Zeke had given him back his gun.

"It's either the second or third from the last in this row. I can't be sure from this angle. The Petersons' boat looks identical to ours, except for the name above the door." She looked at him. "Ours is called the *Gypsy Moon*."

Nick turned to see where she was pointing. A wide variety of vessels bobbed in slips evenly spaced along a shared dock, twenty or so berths on each side. The loud drone of a compressor came from a tin-roofed shed two rows over. The dry dock Grace had mentioned, Nick figured.

"How come your boat is moored in a slip while most of the ones like it are tied to anchors in the harbor?"

"Convenience." Her tone was put out. They hadn't talked much on the drive from Vegas. His one-word an-swers to her questions had had the desired effect. Nick wasn't deluding himself. He'd crossed the line professionally when he'd slept with her. He was involved emotionally and the only way he could get back on solid ground was to cut his ties with her, do his job and get the hell out of Vegas. Anything else would be disastrous.

At the end of the gangway, he got his first clear view of the two-story houseboats. They did resemble floating recreational vehicles. White aluminum siding. Skeletal frames on the second story where some kind of awning might go. They were bigger than he'd pictured, each filling its entire allotted space.

Grace pointed. "The third from the end. That's ours. The last one is new. I've never seen it before."

He stopped her when she would have kept walking. "Go back."

She paused but didn't turn around as he'd ordered. Instead, she appeared to be studying her family's vessel. "Everything looks just like we left it. I don't think she's here. Nobody's seen her. Can't we just leave?"

A woman from the boat-rental place had returned Nick's call just as they'd turned south on Highway 95 toward Searchlight. She'd told him she hadn't noticed any activity on the Radonovic boat, but she'd been away on vacation.

"I don't expect to find her here," he said shortly. "She's probably in Mexico by now, but I plan to check this out since we're here. Go back to the shore and wait."

Their face-off only lasted a few seconds. Grace gave in. She blew out a huffing sound and stormed off. Nick's satisfaction was cut short, however, when she stopped about halfway down the gangway and turned, hands on her hips, as if daring him to make her take another step.

He sighed and shifted his focus to the boat. White

with blue-and-teal trim, it bobbed innocently on the calm water. Withdrawing his gun from the holster at his side, he approached cautiously, stepping over the thick chain that had been painted nautical white but was beginning to rust.

A covered patio took up the back quarter of the boat. Bristly green artificial turf made a squeaky sound as he walked to the sliding patio doors. Although his view into the living room was blocked by white vinyl vertical blinds, he could make out a built-in couch and table to his right. Counters and shelves—the kitchen area, he presumed—were to the left.

He tried the door. Locked. The key Grace had given him was for the swinging door at the prow of the boat, which was facing toward the open water. He strained to listen for any kind of noise from inside, but the sound of a revving motor coming from the dry-dock area made it difficult to hear.

Adrenaline kicked in as he moved toward the starboard side of the vessel. A walkway about a foot wide allowed passage to the rear of the boat, where Nick had spotted a circular staircase. The boat bobbed slightly. He thought he detected a movement somewhere else on the vessel, but then decided the rocking was caused by his own shifting weight.

He gripped his gun a little tighter. There wasn't room between the boat and the dock for him to fall into the water, but the same couldn't be said for his gun.

At the first window, he bent down to look beneath the curtain. The sun-bleached oilcloth fluttered slightly. Nick thought he spotted something. A figure crouching or a pile of towels heaped on a bench? He couldn't be sure.

With his back to the wall, he inched to the next window. Its curtain was pinned shut as if something was leaning up against it.

The next two windows were stacked, one a foot and a half above the other. They were ten-by-twelve-inch rectangles that could be opened to allow ventilation. They were considerably lower than the other windows, directly below a patio area that was encircled by a blue-and-teal-striped canvas strung between metal railings.

Sleeping bunks, he guessed.

He bent over to peer into the lower of the two. His heart rate spiked when he spotted a body sprawled on the unmade bunk, but a second later, he realized the form was a neoprene body suit draped over a couple of pillows.

Letting out a sigh mixed with relief and disappointment, he stood up.

As he did, his head connected with something hard. Pain erupted under his skull. Silver spots danced across his vision. Reeling backward, his foot slipped over the edge of the boat and he went down heavily on one knee. He grabbed the railing to keep from falling face forward, but in doing so, his gun clattered to the Fiberglas deck.

Fighting nausea and very close to blacking out, Nick pressed his free hand to his head, trying to figure out what he'd hit. The loud thumping of shoes on the deck made him understand that what had happened wasn't an accident. He'd been attacked.

Acting instinctively, he lunged for his gun but was too late. A hand snatched it up. Nick closed his eyes and waited for a shot to follow.

"MaryAnn?"

Grace.

No, Nick tried to shout but the only sound that came was a low, desperate-sounding groan.

"You shouldn't have come here, Grace. I just needed a few days to figure out what to do. Is that asking too much?"

Nick recognized the voice of a person on the edge. He and Grace were both in danger.

He struggled to get up, but a wave of blackness forced him to lie still. He unintentionally let out a low moan.

Grace appeared at his side. "Nick, are you okay? Nikolai, answer me. Please."

"Get…" He tried to push her away. "Back up. Shore."

Her fingers pressed against his scalp. When she neared the spot that felt as if it was about to burst through his skin, he swore.

"My God, MaryAnn, you could have killed him."

"I just wanted to knock him out so I could leave."

Grace sat down and gently rolled Nick over so his head was resting in her lap. He couldn't see her clearly, but he felt her tension. He had to make her leave him. Every movement threatened to take him over the edge of consciousness.

"Go where, MaryAnn? Your family is here. Your kids are waiting for you in Vegas."

"So are the police, Grace."

Nick knew what hysteria could do to a person. Grace didn't appear to be afraid, but Nick wanted her to be. MaryAnn was desperate and obviously unbalanced. And, thanks to him, armed.

He opened his eyes, and although he had to squint to see past the haze of pain, he whispered, "Go. Please."

She looked down at him and tenderly moved a lock

of hair from his forehead. Her smile said, *You can't be serious.* Nick saw her take a breath and brace her shoulders as if preparing for war.

"MaryAnn, I brought Nikolai here to help you. I had a vision. A real, honest-to-goodness vision. I saw you crying. You were alone and frightened and confused. You wanted to run away, but the mother in you—the wife in you—couldn't leave your family behind."

"They're better off without me. They're Roms. I'm an outsider. I always will be, Grace."

"No. That isn't true. You're a part of us. We'd never desert you. If you let me take you back home, I'll prove it to you. We'll hire you the best lawyer and get you some counseling."

Nick silently groaned. *Don't tell a crazy person you think she's crazy.*

He couldn't see MaryAnn, but he heard her defeated tone when she said, "That's what Charles told Amy."

"Who?" Grace asked.

"Amy. Charles's sister. He told her she was crazy. That none of the things she remembered him doing to her when she was a little kid had ever happened. That's called power, Grace. Money buys you power. If you have enough money you can rewrite history."

His guess had been right—MaryAnn was the blackmailer, but the knowledge brought him no satisfaction.

"I know Amy was your friend, MaryAnn," Grace said, "but…"

"It happened to me, too."

"Charles molested you?"

"Not him. But I was raped."

"By whom? When?"

"Before I married Gregor. While I was a cocktail waitress at the Sands. He was a whale. A big tipper. I went to his room—for a drink. I thought he liked me, but when I tried to leave, he threw me on the bed. Said nobody would believe me because he was rich and I was nothing. In fact, I was less than nothing."

Nick groaned softly. He knew what recalling deeply harbored resentment could do to a person. He needed to bring her back into the present, but before he could speak, she said, "I got tired of being less than nothing, Grace. Charles was counting on either marrying you for your money or talking you out of your trust fund, but you wouldn't have had anything to do with him if you knew what a sick pervert he was. That gave me power."

"But you went to work for him."

She motioned wildly with the gun. "Somebody has to pay the bills after your cousin blows his paycheck at the casino."

Nick could tell that all of this baffled Grace. She reached out a hand. "Why didn't you tell me, MaryAnn? We're family. We could have helped."

"Ask him," she said, pointing the barrel of the gun Nick's way. "He'll tell you how reliable family is when push comes to shove. I heard Yetta talking. His mother was like me, an outsider. She never fit in, and she was miserable here. That's why they moved. You're Rom royalty, Grace. Your daddy's little princess. The rest of us are supposed to grovel at your feet."

Nick felt Grace start to move. He put his hands out to stop her from getting up, but his effort proved useless. She carefully lowered his head to the deck. "It'll be okay," she told him. "You're safe."

But you're not, he tried to cry. His words came out in a garbled slur. He rolled to his side and tried to sit up, but the effort left him panting and dizzy.

Shit. Shit. Shit, he silently swore. Where was his backup. The answer came to him immediately. Their position wasn't visible to the cops on the shore because of the taller houseboat moored beside them. He needed to send a signal, but with his gun in MaryAnn's hands, there was nothing he could do.

"MaryAnn, that isn't true," Grace said, stepping away from Nick's side. "We're just people. And we love you and your children."

Nick reached deep for the strength to move. He made it into a sitting position, his back against the wall of the boat. Yellow dots flashed across his vision and his extremities tingled in a way that told him he might pass out.

"Stay where you are," MaryAnn warned, shifting the tip of the gun barrel from Grace to him and back.

Grace took another step in MaryAnn's direction, her hands out imploringly. "What about Luca and Gemilla? Are you going to run off and leave them behind?"

The sympathetic tone triggered a response Nick hadn't expected. MaryAnn started to cry. Tears streamed from her eyes. "They're better off without me," she sobbed. "Everyone is."

Nick sensed the moment the thought hit her. A gun. A hopeless situation. He grabbed the rope railing and tried to stand up. He made it to one knee, but he wasn't fast enough to stop Grace from rushing forward.

"No," she cried, grabbing MaryAnn's arm with both hands.

What happened next was a blur to Nick. Two women in a macabre dance. He pulled himself toward them, using the side of the boat for support but they moved out of his reach. The pain in his head kept time to the pulse in his veins. Nausea left a coppery taste in his mouth. He staggered toward them just as a shot went off.

The pair froze. Then MaryAnn opened her mouth and let out a terrible cry of anguish. Grace had a surprised look in her eyes. Her gaze sought his. *I'm sorry,* she mouthed. Then her lashes fluttered like wounded butterflies against her too-pale cheeks. She would have fallen if not for her cousin's wife, who slowly eased her to the deck.

A violent red smear made a check mark against the white plastic wall.

"No!" Nick bellowed at the top of his lungs. "Help! Somebody call an ambulance."

CHAPTER TWENTY

"SHE WAS VERY LUCKY," the young, disheveled emergency room doctor who came to greet the family said. "If you gotta get shot, she picked the right place to do it. We're only worried about the chance of infection. Since the gun was fired at such close range it might have left microscopic pieces of clothing in the wound. We're keeping her a couple of days."

A couple of days. Nick would be gone by then. He'd already cleared his departure with Zeke.

His new friend wasn't happy to let him go, but he claimed to understand. Which probably wasn't true since Nick himself didn't understand completely why he felt such an urgent need to leave. At some level, he figured his motive was tied to the fear he'd felt as he'd watched the trooper who'd raced to the scene apply pressure to Grace's wound. While the second officer radioed for help, Nick had been unable to do anything but stare in horror as Grace's blood seeped between the man's fingers.

He hadn't let himself imagine what would have happened if she'd stopped breathing, but the despair that had lurked at the edge of his consciousness had served as a warning. To stay would mean becoming a hostage to fortune. Grace's well-being would always be the controlling motive in whatever he did. The thought terrified him.

"Can we see her?" Liz asked, walking up to the doctor. The two were exactly the same height and the man seemed a bit surprised when he glanced up from his chart to find her right in front of him. He didn't step back, though.

"As soon as Admitting finds her a bed. I've got her sedated at the moment. She was a little agitated."

"Well, she'd just been shot," Kate said, getting to her feet. Liz and Kate had been playing gin rummy together at a low table. "Who can blame her?"

Kate had arrived with her mother about half an hour after Nick got there. Apparently, Alex was at home with Maya and MaryAnn's children.

The doctor didn't answer Kate. Still talking to Liz, he said, "She keeps asking how Nikolai is. I checked the patient list. No one by that name was admitted. Should I be worried about brain damage?"

"I would be," Kate muttered, giving Nick a damning look.

"I'm Nikolai," Nick said, stumbling over the name. For the first time since he'd assumed the identity he felt like a fraud. "Nick Lightner. I've been on assignment with Metro. We had a suspect go missing. I got whacked on the head," he said, lightly touching the knot on his skull. The drums were overshadowing the painkillers he'd taken. "The EMTs on the scene checked me out and said I'm fine."

The doctor frowned. "You really should have that X-rayed."

Nick started to shake his head, but settled for a dismissive tone. "I have a hard head. Just ask these ladies."

"Very hard," Liz agreed.

"Rock solid," Kate said, dismissively.

The man shrugged, then walked away.

"Why were you so grouchy to him?" Liz asked Kate, crossing her arms over the logo on her UNLV sweatshirt. "He was cute."

Kate scowled at her. "Since when did you start noticing handsome doctors? I thought you were prejudiced."

Liz shrugged but didn't reply as the two sat back and continued their conversation in private. Nick walked to the window and watched the flow of traffic on the street. If he strained just a bit, he could see the outline of the Stratosphere. He'd never look at that icon of the Las Vegas skyline without remembering Grace's life-affirming whoop of triumph when they came to a stop after their thrill ride.

"She's going to be fine," a voice said to his right.

Nick stepped back and turned to face Yetta. "I know. The paramedics told me that. I guess I expected her to open her eyes and talk to me, but she didn't."

"The body helps out when there's too much pain to process. I fainted when my husband died. I was at his side, holding his hand. When I felt him leave us, I told my children, 'Daddy's gone, now.' Then I stood up and that's the last thing I remember until several hours later."

She frowned as if disgusted with the memory. "I wanted to be strong for my family, but the pain was too much for my mind to deal with. Grace thinks she's stronger than she is."

Her expression turned wistful. "Ernst named all the girls. He said it was his right since I'd had them all to myself for the first nine months."

Nick had to smile. "Did you offer to let him carry the next one?"

"Always. He said he would in a heartbeat, of course." Her smile held the same look his mother's did when she was thinking about his father. "Anyway, when he told me that the newborn, who had kicked my ribs till they were black-and-blue, was going to be Grace, I laughed out loud. 'This child is strong and invincible. Shouldn't she be an Isabella or an Isis?'"

Nick couldn't picture Grace as either. "What did he say?"

Yetta took a deep breath and appeared to reflect on the question. "He said, 'Grace Kelly was the strongest of them all. She left the life she knew to recreate herself as a princess. Can you imagine what strength that must have taken?'"

Nick wondered if she was trying to tell him something. But he didn't ask. He didn't even dare to hope. Grace had risked her life to save a member of her family. Nick admired her. Hell, he loved her. Which was why he wasn't going to make her choose between her beloved Romani family and him.

"I'm leaving in the morning. I hope Grace will be awake before then so I can talk to her, but if not, I'm asking you to make my goodbyes for me."

"You're going back to Detroit."

Nick nodded. "It's time. Zeke has things under control here even though his primary witness's mental state might be problematic when this comes to trial." Mary-Ann had been taken to a facility for a psychological evaluation. According to Zeke, she had apparently borrowed a car from her brother-in-law before heading to the marina. Investigators had found pills on the boat, leading them to assume she'd been considering suicide all along. They also found boxes of Charles's files. "Fortunately, she'd squirreled away a ton of paper evidence to use as protection in case Charles figured out she was the one blackmailing him. That ought to keep the D.A. on Charles's case for months."

"MaryAnn will recover," Yetta said with confidence. "Gregor is standing beside her. This might be just the thing to make him grow up. As for Claude, he'll probably move back to the ranch for a while. We'll help him find a renter for his house."

"Do you mind if I stay there tonight? I could get a motel near the airport, if you'd rather."

Yetta's smile looked sad. "No, of course, not. You're always welcome here, Nikolai. You're a part of this family, too."

He didn't say anything.

"I know you don't believe that, but it's true. None of this was your fault."

Even if that was true, Nick knew he'd never forget the look on Grace's face as the gun went off. When he'd watched her sink to the deck of the boat, he'd felt as though someone had yanked his heart right out of his chest.

"She isn't going to take your leaving lying down," Yetta said. "You know she doesn't give up on people she loves."

Nick's heart reacted to the word *love,* but he kept his expression blank. "Then, it will be up to you to remind her that she's supposed to be looking for a prince. That lets me out. Would a prince go off and leave his princess in the hospital?"

Yetta frowned. "Hmm, that's a very good point."

Nick faked a smile and started away. He paused and added, "Listen, if I don't see her before I leave, be sure to tell her that I hope she finds her prince someday. She deserves somebody worthy of her."

Yetta's smile surprised him, but he didn't dwell on it. He had travel plans to make.

"HE'S LEAVING."

Jurek let out the breath he'd been holding. His gut still burned where the staples had been. His surgeon had been right. The little sample he'd taken from Jurek's bowel had been cancerous, but the oncologist insisted the variety was slow-growing, and once they had the tumor removed, the prognosis was good.

He wanted to believe the man. He needed to live long enough to hear the final outcome of what was happening in Las Vegas. Which was why he'd been sitting up waiting for Yetta's call instead of sleeping as the visiting nurse had insisted he try. She'd even given him a sleeping pill, but he'd hidden it under his tongue. He would use it later.

"When?" Jurek asked, adjusting the lamp beside his recliner.

"Tomorrow. Early."

"You haven't told him anything about my...situation, have you?" Jurek had finally shared bits and pieces of his health saga with Yetta, but he'd asked her not to tell his son.

"No, but I plan to as soon as I get home. I've said it before and I'll say it again, you need to talk to him. Tell him what happened. Explain why you gave him up for adoption. He's never going to heal if he doesn't hear the truth from you."

Was she right? Was he making matters worse for his son by keeping his distance?

"Let me bring him to you, Jurek. Before it's too late."

"He'll think I'm trying to play on his sympathy."

She gave a small chuckle. "I'm not totally convinced he has any. Nikolai has built a wall around his heart, and believe me, if Grace couldn't pull down that barricade, you probably don't stand a chance, either."

"When would you come?"

"Tonight. The doctors have told me Grace is going to be fine. Elizabeth is taking me home, then coming back. Katherine will remain here in case anything happens. I'll pick up my car and your son."

My son.

"Okay," he said. He hung up the phone and closed his eyes. The hum of the heating unit filled his ears. In a few short hours, Jurek would see the boy he'd turned his back on thirty years earlier. He swallowed the lump in his throat and closed his eyes.

A thousand images flashed on the screen in his head, but none was clearer than seeing his son holding Lucy's hand as they boarded a city bus. Not the bus that had cost Jurek the love of his life. Just an ordinary day when Lucy and Nikolai were going exploring.

His bold, adventurous child with curly blond hair and a smile that could make a believer out of the most damaged soul. Like Jurek's. He'd seen too much, experienced the worst life had to offer. He'd given up on hope until the day he'd met Lucy and fallen in love.

Rosy cheeks and a laughing smile that breathed life

into his jaded heart. He'd believed her when she said anything was possible. Of course they could have a home and a family, even while she pursued her dream.

But it had been a fantasy. An outright lie. And he'd been so damn angry, so consumed by bitterness, after learning that his wife had died while he was stuck in jail, he'd let his fury and grief blind him to the gift she'd left behind.

Now, he had to face his mistake. The child who had haunted his dreams all these years. And in his son's face, he knew he'd see Lucy.

"YOU AREN'T GOING to like this, Grace. Nick's leaving."

Grace heard her sister's voice, but the words didn't mean anything. *Who's Nick?*

She opened one eye and looked around. Hospital. MaryAnn. Gunshot. A surprisingly loud gunshot. Nikolai. *Nick.*

She tried to speak, but her mouth felt as if someone had packed her cheeks with cotton balls. She looked with longing at the dull pink plastic pitcher on the movable table and almost as if someone read her mind, a cup and bendable straw appeared in front of her lips.

She took a sip. "Uck," she said, grimacing as she swallowed the water. "Leaving?" she asked. "The hospital?"

Kate took the cup away and sat down. She looked serious. Dead serious. "He's leaving town, kiddo."

The dryness in her throat came back. "When?"

"In the morning."

Liz, who was sitting on the end of Grace's bed fiddling with the television remote control, looked over her shoulder and added, "Mom said he's staying at Claude's tonight then catching a flight home in the morning."

"No way. He can't leave without talking to me first. My God, we made love. Doesn't that count for anything?"

Liz dropped the remote. Her gaze went to the other bed in Grace's room. Grace craned her neck to peek around the curtain at her neighbor. A white-haired woman with a protruding belly winked at her.

Grace blushed and smiled, then carefully turned onto her good side. Every movement set off knife pricks of pain, but these were a mere nuisance compared to the gnawing fear in her belly. "I need to see him. Take me home. Now."

Liz started to laugh. "You really believe that princess nonsense, don't you?"

Grace tried to pull back the blankets. Her sister's expression turned serious. "Whoa. Stop." Liz hurried to Grace's side. "You can't leave. Doctor's orders."

She gently pressed Grace's shoulders flat to the mattress. "You just had surgery to repair a bullet hole in your side, Grace. People die from those kinds of things."

Grace knew she wasn't going to die. Not from what happened at the lake, but a broken heart could be fatal, too. "He can't leave, Liz. He's the one. My p...p...prince," she admitted raggedly.

"Oh, come on, Grace. That's what you said about Shawn. How do you know Nikolai is any different?" Kate asked.

Normally, Grace would have found a more convincing way to answer her sister's question, but her mind was still fuzzy from the drugs she'd been given. "I saw it. While I was in the helicopter that picked me up at the marina."

"You had a vision?" Liz asked. "Like Mom's?"

Grace turned the hand that wasn't attached to the IV palm-side up. "Maybe. I saw myself walking on a path. Alone. All of you were calling me to come back, but I knew if I kept going I'd run into Nikolai."

"Him specifically?" Kate demanded.

Grace nodded. "I couldn't see him, but I knew he was somewhere up ahead. Waiting for me to choose."

Her sisters looked at each other, their skepticism obvious.

"Before this happened, Nikolai asked me to go back to Detroit with him, and I said I couldn't."

"Which is true," Kate said firmly. "You can't."

"But what if he really is my prince, Kate? My soul mate?"

Her sister didn't answer, but Grace suddenly discovered she had no energy to go anywhere. She closed her eyes, calling to mind one of the other visions she'd experienced during the flight to the hospital. She and Nikolai. Dancing. At a wedding. Their own? She could only hope.

CHAPTER TWENTY-ONE

NIGHT ON THE DESERT was a formidable thing—the vast blackness, broken only by scattered pockets of lights belonging to homesteads, that reminded Nick of a movie where aliens took over the planet. Mountains, illuminated by the smidgen of starlight and slice of moon, encircled the vast basin, like the hulking monsters that had lived just outside the glow of Nick's childhood night-light.

The drive from Vegas to Laughlin had been strangely peaceful. Nick figured after the life-and-death drama of the afternoon, he and his passenger were both suffering from a type of post-traumatic letdown.

Nothing like a smooth road in unbelievably wide-open spaces to make you feel small and insignificant, he thought.

"Grace mentioned that you have a dog?"

Nick was caught off guard by the question. "Um...yeah. His name is Rip."

"As in Rest In Peace?"

He laughed. "If you were a basketball fan in Detroit, you wouldn't have to ask."

"Oh." A second later, she said, "I suppose your parents are taking care of him while you're gone."

He nodded. It struck him that he'd have to put Rip in a kennel next time he needed a dog-sitter. The thought saddened him.

"This is the first time our family has been without a pet since before Alexandra was born," Yetta said conversationally. "The girls offered to buy me a little dog after Ernst died, but I couldn't risk it."

"Risk what?"

"Loving and losing. The two go hand in hand, of course, and I was too cowardly to try again."

Nick shifted uncomfortably. He'd expected some kind of lecture. That was part of the reason he'd resisted her offer to introduce him to his father. But after ten minutes of arguing with her, he'd realized that Yetta had a lot in common with her youngest daughter. Grit and determination.

"You strike me as a pretty brave person. I would say your daughter came by her daring quite honestly."

She sighed softly. "Actually, Grace is more like her father. Kind, generous, optimistic and, yes, brave. I'm the worrier. The one who cautions against change. My mother blamed this on what happened to me when I was a baby. Have I told you this story?"

"I don't think so."

"There was a tragic accident shortly after I was born. A fire. Two of my sisters were badly burned—one fatally—and I suffered smoke inhalation. My lungs never have worked quite right. Cold moist air is particularly hard on me, which is why we moved to the desert. Ernst was terrified that I would die before him. He always said he could handle anything but that."

Nick almost smiled, thinking he understood the feeling. He wasn't prepared when she said, "I would have died in that fire if not for your father. Jurek—or, George, as people call him—saved my life."

"What happened?"

"I only know what I've been told. My sisters were playing by the camp's cooking fire. One of their skirts caught alight. The fire spread to the wagon where I was sleeping. Your father, who was only about nine or ten at the time, was a hero, but he also was the one who took the blame for what happened. And has paid for that mistake ever since."

Nick's curiosity made him ask, "What do you mean?"

"He was left in charge to watch over me and my sisters while my mother stepped next door for some herbs. He became distracted by a couple of his older cousins, who enticed him away for a moment. When the girls started screaming, he rushed back and pulled me from the burning wagon. Sadly, my sister Alba died from her burns and Beatrix was severely crippled."

"What happened to George…uh, Jurek?"

"He was sent to Poland to live with his grandmother. Not long after that, Hitler invaded the country and closed the borders."

This must have been the story Grace's sisters had alluded to. The deep, dark secret.

"Perhaps you've studied history," Yetta said. "Hitler regarded Gypsies as subhuman." Her voice was low and bleak. "In 1934, he ordered the sterilization of the *racially* inferior, mostly Gypsies, African-Germans and patients in mental institutions."

"How did George survive?"

"By his wits. He was young and strong. And handsome. Like you. He was the fairest of his family, I've been told. Although you also have your mother's Scandinavian genes."

Nick watched the glow of lights in the distance start to take shape. They would be in Laughlin soon. He would meet for the first time the man who both gave him life and gave him away. Anger and resentment, the two coping strategies that had served him well most of his life, suddenly didn't seem to be working.

"Are you telling me this so I will feel sorry for him?"

She turned toward him. "No. Jurek is a proud man. He wouldn't want your pity. I told you so you might begin to understand that some of the decisions we make as adults are based on what happened to us as young people."

"Is that his excuse for giving me up for adoption?"

Yetta made a soft sound that seemed slightly reproachful, but all she said was, "You can ask him that yourself."

Nick glanced around as they joined the traffic in this booming river town. Laughlin wasn't Las Vegas, but it was the place where he'd finally meet his father.

CHARLES IGNORED the noises and smells of the holding cell the same way he'd blocked out the coarse reality of his childhood. The ugly sound of punches being thrown. Of angry voices and foul language. His mother's crying. The revolting odor of his father's drunken breath when he collapsed on Charles's bed.

They'd lived in a tiny three-room apartment at the time. Charles's bed had been located on what was euphemistically called the screened porch, although the curled and rusted screen wouldn't have kept out a hummingbird, much less a mosquito.

There'd been better times, but inevitably something had gone wrong. Maybe something he'd done. No one would say. If Charles asked, he'd either get a lecture from his father or his ears boxed by his mother. He'd learned to keep his mouth shut.

That night, when he heard his father staggering toward the back door, Charles slipped out of bed and hid beneath it. It was a small bed and he was a big boy, but he pressed the length of his body against the wall and hoped his father was too drunk to notice.

Charles was tired of providing comfort when his mother wouldn't. In his heart of hearts, he knew what his father did wasn't right. The way he touched Charles and wanted to be touched. It made Charles sick, but to refuse meant something even worse. It meant being called "a worthless sack of shit that no one would ever love."

That might have been true. He hoped it wasn't but even if it was, he didn't feel like being a good boy tonight. Instead, he'd make himself invisible.

His father was too drunk to even make it into the bed. He stumbled and crashed to the floor an arm's length away from where Charles was hiding. His invisible self watched his father's chest go up and down for the longest time. Then, for no reason that Charles could see, it quit moving. His father twitched for a little while and white stuff came out of his mouth, but then that stopped, too.

After his father's death, life improved. Until his mother hooked up with another loser. There were tears to deal with when the asshole left. And a baby. But Charles never resented his new sister. Amy was a tiny, perfect gift.

Charles loved his sister with all his heart. She turned ten the year he graduated from college. He'd worked his way through law school and still had managed to give his mother money to help make Amy's life easier. When he began working for a law firm that served three of the largest casinos in Vegas, Charles could afford a nice apartment. Sometimes Amy came to visit him, to spend the night.

Charles had never intended to let history repeat itself with Amy. But she was such a docile child. With the softest skin. The brush of her tiny fingers made him feel healed. He couldn't help himself when he touched her the way his father had touched him.

She never complained. She never told their mother. She'd taken his secret to the grave with her, or so he'd thought. But, no, the ungrateful little bitch had blabbed to MaryAnn, who'd told Grace.

Charles heard the whole story from Nick, who had flashed his badge when Charles was arrested. "A fucking cop," Charles muttered under his breath.

He'd been blindsided because he knew how much the Romani disliked and mistrusted the police. That Yetta would have the balls to go behind her daughters' backs and invite a cop into the family boggled his mind. He'd underestimated Yetta. He should have been on his guard. He'd counted her out because of the way she'd gone to pieces after Ernst's death. An understandable—if costly—mistake.

But how could dull, bland MaryAnn, who followed orders like a drone and never questioned the ethics or legality of his actions, have come up with a plan to blackmail him? How could he have misread her so completely?

The district attorney who'd been in earlier had alluded to stacks of damaging evidence that MaryAnn had squirreled away. The bitch. He fully expected to be released on bail after his hearing. When he got out, the first order of business was payback. He still had connections. Favors to collect. People who feared the dirty laundry he could air. By the time he got done with Grace and her family, the name Charles Harmon would become synonymous with apocalypse in Romani lore.

JUREK WAS GLAD he'd taken a pain pill right after Yetta called. Normally, he would have toughed it out. Lord knows he'd been through worse, but he needed to maintain his focus on the young man sitting across from him.

His son.

He'd waited thirty years to see his boy and he wasn't about to let pain rob him of the moment.

Yetta, who was in the adjoining kitchen making a pot of tea, called out, "We don't have much time, Jurek. Nikolai is leaving in the morning."

Nikolai—his son—shifted uncomfortably on the sofa across from him. Jurek's small, utilitarian apartment was part of a seniors-only complex. He'd purchased the unit at a time when he was temporarily flush from a string of wins at the craps tables. Instead of partying it all away, as was his usual style, he'd banked the majority of the money and looked for an affordable piece of property.

He'd qualified for a low-income loan. The one-story, stucco bungalow wasn't fancy, but it had tripled in value. It would be his only true legacy to his son when he died.

"You have to leave so soon?"

Nikolai nodded. "This was a job, not a vacation. Chuck, the snake, is in jail. My work here is done."

He said the phrase with a bit of humor. Jurek didn't get the joke, but he smiled anyway. It was hard not to smile. His son was so handsome and fit. His musculature belonged to his mother. Lithe and strong.

"Do you like being a policeman?"

"Yes, for the most part."

Jurek felt a nagging pressure around his wound. He made every effort not to wince when he shifted his upper-body weight to his left elbow.

Nikolai's eyes narrowed, telling Jurek he'd spotted the telltale display of weakness. Such a show would have gotten him killed in Sobibor.

"Tea?" Yetta asked, carrying a tray with three cups and a teapot.

"Tell me about your parents. How is Pete? Last I heard, he'd made chief of police or something."

Nikolai looked nonplussed. "You know my dad?"

"I *knew* him. He was one of the first people I met after your mother…er, Lucille and I, moved to L.A. The Lightners lived in the same apartment complex as we did. Had a cute little daughter, a few years older than you. They were real nice to us. A lotta people weren't back then."

Yetta handed them cups filled with pale golden liquid. Nothing she'd found in his kitchen, he was sure. Must've brought it with her. "Thank you."

"Green tea has therapeutic properties. It will help you heal," she said.

"Uh…um…what exactly is wrong with you?" Nikolai asked. "Yetta said you'd been sick."

Jurek didn't want pity. He wanted…he didn't know exactly what he wanted, but whatever it was didn't involve talking about his health issues.

"Nothing big."

Yetta set down her cup with a crack. "Oh, for heaven's sake, Jurek. Tell him. He deserves to know."

He gave her a frown that should have kept her silent but didn't. "If you don't, I will. Your father has cancer. Not that he told me about it, but his doctor gave me the truth because Jurek put me down as next-of-kin."

"What kind of cancer?" Nikolai asked, his brow crinkled.

"I didn't ask, but he told me they caught it early, and Jurek has an excellent chance of making a full recovery."

"That's good," Nikolai said.

Jurek was pleased to see the tension leave his son's face. Until Yetta made a huffing sound. "It would be good news for most people, but this man—" she pointed at Jurek "—prefers to believe that Hitler's henchmen planted some kind of poison in his bowels that is released slowly over time. Something his doctors can't detect."

Jurek felt a shiver run down his spine. He'd never told anyone, not even Lucille, about his fear. "How do you know that?"

Yetta sat back, as if the fight had gone out of her. "I…felt it. When I visited you before. I closed my eyes and we went back to that place. That awful place. And I…I…" Her voice dropped to a husky whisper. "I felt as violated as you must have."

She reached out, tears in her eyes. "They were evil men, Jurek, but their poison has long since left your system. Thanks to Lucy."

He closed his eyes and gripped her hand. He fought to keep his emotions under control. How could he let his adult son see him reduced to tears the very first time they met?

"Do you remember when I visited you in jail after Lucy died?" Yetta asked.

Jurek nodded. "We had a big fight," he said softly.

A smile touched her lips and she looked at Nikolai. "I was a lot like Grace back then. Passionate about family. I was incensed that your father had given you to a gaujo family. I accused him of robbing you of your birthright. Do you know what he said?"

Nikolai shook his head.

"Tell him, Jurek."

"I said being Romani never brought me anything but grief. That you were better off not knowing anything about us…me."

Yetta's smile was touched with sadness. "I didn't understand at the time. But I do now. And having met Nikolai, I agree, Jurek. You were right to do what you did."

"Huh?" Nikolai said, setting down his cup. "He was right to give me away?"

Yetta nodded. "Yes. You're a fine man, an honorable man. You grew up safe and loved. Not that you wouldn't have known acceptance and a sense of family with us, but Jurek gave you an opportunity most people never have. He gave you two worlds. What you do with that is entirely up to you."

She rose and picked up the tray. "I need to call the hospital and check on Grace. I'll be outside for a few minutes."

Nick watched her leave with a sense of panic. He was

alone again with a man he'd spent most of his life hating. He'd constructed elaborate fantasies about what he'd tell his birth father if their paths ever crossed.

But the man sitting in the cheap recliner didn't fit the image Nick had of a self-centered, low-life egoist who couldn't be bothered to raise the kid he'd fathered. This man, George, or Jurek, as Yetta called him, was old, withered, yet too proud to show that he was in pain.

"Do you prefer I call you George or Jurek?"

"George. Only Yetta calls me Jurek. When I first came to America, I found the name sounded too much like *jerk* to gain me any respect. George was on every dollar bill. I thought that would be a good omen."

Nick smiled for the first time since entering the small, tidy residence. He hadn't had any idea what to expect, but a white crushed-rock yard with two pink flamingos wasn't even close. Nor was the aluminum foil that covered the window near the door. An energy-saving technique, Yetta had whispered under her breath while they'd waited for permission to enter.

"Nice place you've got here, George. Have you lived here long?" he asked, hoping small talk could take the place of the important questions he was afraid to ask.

"Ten years. Before that, I traveled around a bit. California, Arizona, New Mexico."

"Warm states."

George nodded. "I had enough of the cold when I was a boy."

"Is it true about the concentration camp?"

George nodded.

"Which one?"

"Sobibor."

"Never heard of it."

"It wasn't famous."

Nick wondered if he would have survived if he'd been the one taken from his family and subjected to torture and abuse.

"The answer is yes."

"I beg your pardon?" Nick said.

"You're asking yourself if you would have been a survivor, and the answer is yes."

"How do you know?"

George smiled. "You survived being separated from the safety of the only family you ever knew. You survived losing your mother at a very young age. You survived moving from California to Michigan. That alone takes a very strong person."

The last was said with a wink, and Nick laughed. He decided he might have liked this man if things had been different. "I'm not complaining about my life. My adoptive parents have been good to me. I don't have any regrets."

"I've kept tabs on them…and you over the years. I knew when I asked Pete and Sharon to take you that they'd give you a better life than I could."

"Because you were an ex-con?" Nick asked, his throat tight.

"Because my heart was gone. Your mother was the light of my life. The only light I'd ever known, although I've always felt a special connection to Yetta. Unfortunately, I've never been able to look at her without remembering that awful day when she was a baby."

"The fire. She told me."

"Did she tell you that one of her sisters died? That

the other was disfigured for life, and that Yetta's own health was never the same? All because of me."

"She said it was an accident."

"There are no accidents. There are only choices. Take your eye off two happy, laughing children to look at your cousin's puppy and people die. Get off a bus and get hit by a car."

Nick had no idea what to say so he said nothing. A moment later, George shook his head as if coming back to the present. "We all make choices. I gave you to the Lightners because I didn't want to be responsible for ruining another life."

Nick felt as though a weight were pressing on his chest. This was his chance to tell the old man off. *I was your responsibility, you bastard. I was your flesh and blood and you gave me away without a second thought.* But now he knew that wasn't true. George's choice hadn't been random or frivolous.

He leaned forward and locked his hands together. "I spent a lot of time being pissed off at you. I still don't understand why you never contacted me when you knew where I was. But I don't hate you."

George's eyes didn't reveal much, but he nodded and said, "I wouldn't blame you if you did."

Suddenly, Nick needed to talk to Grace. To get her take on what just happened. To hold her. "We should probably be going," he said, standing up. "Will you be okay here alone? Yetta was talking about your moving into Claude's house for a while. Maybe you should consider it."

George shook his head. "My doctor's not done poking around inside of me. I swear he's the great-grandson of that bastard in Sobibor. Never happy if they aren't experimenting." He made it sound like a joke.

Nick smiled, but he was worried, too. Despite his cavalier attitude, George didn't look well. Impulsively, he leaned down and gave his birth father a hug. "Listen, I have to go. But I'm not ready to say goodbye to you just yet, okay? There's a lot I don't know about you and my mother. I'd like to talk again."

"Anytime," George said, his voice thick with emotion.

Nick walked to the door. "I'll call you from Detroit."

His father lifted his chin proudly and gave a curt nod. Nick knew the gesture well—it was one of his.

CHAPTER TWENTY-TWO

GRACE WAS DREAMING. A dream she'd had before. A favorite of hers…because he was in it.

In the past, he'd been faceless. Just a body. Hands, lips, a touch that made her dizzy.

"I missed you," she said, as she always did when he returned to her dreams.

"I'm glad."

They were walking along the ridge of a hiking trail in Red Rocks. She loved the dramatic vistas, the shadows cast by the rugged terrain. She relished the feel of the fierce wind that seemed to say, "If you stand in one place too long, I'll reshape you, as well."

"That's a very self-centered attitude," she said, dropping his hand crossly. "If you loved me as much as you claim, you wouldn't leave me."

Nick/Nikolai/the man in her dream shrugged as if her complaint meant little. "But, Grace, it's always safer to leave than to be left."

She heard raw pain in his voice and knew he hadn't meant to hurt her. For a moment, she saw the child that he'd been, hiding in fear that the Gypsies might appear in the night and take him away. She touched his arm. "But life doesn't come with guarantees and when you find someone who loves you—someone who is willing to overlook the fact that you're just a little bit crazy—you hold on to them for as long as the good Lord lets you."

"I wish I could do that, Grace. But…"

She watched in horror as he stepped back into thin air. He looked down, as if suddenly realizing his mistake, but it was too late to change his mind. His arms reached for her just as he disappeared from sight.

"No…" With a cry, she peered over the edge of the precipice. His body was sprawled far below. Blood seeping into the pale sandstone.

"Nikolai, come back. This is only a dream. It doesn't have to be this way. I promise. Come back."

But he didn't move. Maybe he didn't know it was a dream. Or, God forbid, maybe it wasn't.

"SHE HAD A pretty rough night," the nurse who'd accompanied Nick to the door of Grace's room said.

It was early, not quite five. He was wiped out—he'd only grabbed a couple of hours of fitful sleep after returning from Laughlin, but he figured he could nap on the plane. The only flight with a spare seat was leaving in an hour and a half. He had a cab waiting for him downstairs. Liz had offered to drive him to the airport, but he'd wanted to make a clean break.

Which didn't explain what he was doing here.

"We gave her a shot for the pain at three. She'll probably sleep for another couple of hours."

"That's good," he said. "I just wanted to check on her. She's going to be okay, right? No infection?"

"So far, her temperature has remained the same. I think she'll be fine."

He thanked her, then slipped into the room and walked to the bed closest to the door. The woman in the bed next to Grace's was snoring loudly. Assured of relative privacy, Nick took Grace's hand. "I'm sorry, sweetheart. I'm a coward for leaving like this, but I don't know how to handle messy goodbyes."

He kissed her knuckles. "That doesn't mean I'm not going to miss you. Every day. Probably for the rest of my life." He shook his head ruefully. "I've given this a lot of thought. You and me. We have a connection. It's not like anything I've ever felt, but our worlds are just too different."

And your family comes first in your life. He knew that now and could even understand it. His father's people were pretty special. Strong. Resilient. He was proud to be part Romani, but that didn't change anything. He still had to leave and he never expected to return—despite Yetta's prediction.

"We lost you once, Nikolai Sarna, and we're not going to lose you again," she'd said to him last night. "Mark my words."

He'd hugged her at the gate and joked about her putting some Gypsy spell on him. Maybe she had. Or was the magic all Grace's?

"The way I see it, Grace," he continued. "You've got Romantique, I've got my job. You and Kate are an awesome team. And I don't know if I told you, but I'm up for my dad's job. If I get it, there's no way I can transfer to Vegas. It seems the cards are stacked against us, kiddo." *Plus it would probably kill me if you chose Vegas over me.* "So, I'm doing the noble thing."

He snickered softly. *Noble. Not cowardly. Yeah, right.*

When the pressure against his sinuses made him squint, he bent over and kissed her lightly on the lips. Her mouth didn't respond, but her breath was warm and sweet.

"I love you, Grace."

Then he left, without looking back.

CHAPTER TWENTY-THREE

GRACE STABBED the hard soil at the base of the rosebush with her hand trowel. In the two weeks since being shot, life had spiraled downward with a speed that left her reeling.

For the first time in her life, she felt alone. Desperately alone.

Not literally, of course. She hadn't had a moment of privacy since being released from the hospital. Her sisters had done their best to keep her distracted so she wouldn't slip into a deep depression over the fact that the man she loved didn't love her.

After all, he'd disappeared into the great void of Michigan while she'd been flat on her back in the hospital.

"Completely unheroic," Alex had decreed.

"Definitely not a true prince," Liz had concurred.

"Another damn frog," Kate had muttered.

Grace had agreed—for the brief period when she was totally furious. But then she remembered her dream. The look of devastation on Nikolai's face as he fell. The regret.

A part of her knew that he was as unhappy about the way things had turned out as she was, but she couldn't forgive him. He hadn't even stuck around long enough for them to talk. Her ego felt as tender as the area around her gunshot wound. All she wanted to do was stay in bed and sulk.

Unfortunately, her recuperation/period-of-mourning had been cut short when a complaint of E. coli contamination made health department inspectors pounce on Romantique. Yellow caution tape blocked the doors. People in lab coats took swabs from every surface in the restaurant's kitchen and destroyed all the meat in the freezer. Damage control had turned into a full-time job for Grace.

Of course everyone knew who was to blame for the vicious, untrue allegation—Charles. Grace blamed herself. And her father.

She hadn't been to visit her father's grave since the day of the shooting. And the plants had suffered. All the beautiful blossoms were gone. Brown spots had attacked the leaves.

"Mom's in Laughlin, you know," she said, carefully raking the dead foliage into a pile. "She's decided George will never get back on his feet unless he moves into Claude's house where she can bully him."

Grace's first thought after hearing this plan had been purely selfish. *Maybe if Nikolai's birth father lives next door, I'll get to see his son again someday.*

She pounded a brittle lump of dirt. "He hasn't even called to see if I'm alive. He showed up, wreaked havoc, then left. I hate him."

The sound of her father's laugh mingled with the traffic noise behind her. *Oh, princess, you're well now. What are you waiting for? Go after him.*

"Leave Vegas?" She rocked back on her haunches

and stared at the headstone. Leave her family? Her business? Her life?

"I…I can't do that. I belong here."

Or did she?

Just that morning, Kate had pounded on Grace's desk and shouted, "Snap out of it, Grace. We're going to lose this place if you don't help me figure out a way to stop Charles from sabotaging our reputation. Don't you care if we go bankrupt?"

At the time, Grace's first thought had been, no, she didn't care about Romantique or any of the other problems that had recently cropped up. Liz's joblessness and the glitch at the bank that showed her several months behind in mortgage payments. Or the rumor that was circulating about one of Alex's aides. A totally false and potentially damaging allegation.

Grace didn't care because she felt numb.

Just like your mother felt after I died.

Grace started as if poked in the side with a stick. Her wound didn't appreciate the movement. Her conscience didn't like hearing a truth she hadn't wanted to admit. Was she avoiding life the same way her mother had after Ernst had passed away?

Grace opened the box of plant fertilizer she'd brought and sprinkled it on the soil, then grabbed her water bottle and unscrewed the cap. "Our world is falling apart, Dad, and all I can do is sit around feeling sorry for myself because Nikolai hasn't bothered to call. Pathetic, huh?"

"Awful."

Startled by the deep voice that came from behind her, Grace spun around. She had to grab the headstone to keep from falling. "Zeke," she exclaimed. "I didn't hear you come up."

"Sorry. I called out your name, but you were talking to someone." He looked around. "A ghost?"

"Just talking to myself," she said. "Cheaper than therapy, although I'm sure most people would say it's not as effective."

Beneath her fingers she felt the silver dollar recessed in the marble—a 1933 Walking Liberty. Her thumb circled the coin, as if reading the raised image. *Walking Liberty.* Was it a sign?

Zeke's normally severe expression softened. "I got your message. 'The snake still slithers.' Very cryptic."

After Kate's temper tantrum, Grace had called Zeke to see if he was aware of her family's sudden bout of bad luck. Since she knew her mother had used a reptilian reference to describe Charles, she figured Zeke would understand.

"Have a seat," she said, pointing to the plastic bucket. She spread the now-empty fertilizer bag at the base of the headstone and sat down, her back resting against the engraved marble.

"Your dad?" Zeke asked. "He must have been quite a man. I'm sorry I never met him."

"He was a great guy. Not perfect, but we all miss him a lot. Mom, especially, although I think she's finally moved beyond the worst of her grief."

He didn't comment. Grace had sensed something between the tall, thin cop and her mother, but had never stopped to contemplate it.

"Okay. Here's what I think," she said. "Charles is out on bail and he has an ax to grind. Given his contacts,

how tough would it have been for him to bribe someone to fake an E. coli scare at Romantique? The word
alone would send customers running, even if there
wasn't a trace of contamination on the premises."

Zeke nodded.

"We know he's the reason Liz lost her job, but it just
occurred to me that he might be the reason she hasn't
been hired someplace else."

"Blackballed?"

"Possibly. Plus, someone's tampered with her credit
history. She could lose her house."

He pulled out a small notepad and jotted something down.

"And yesterday, one of the mothers at Alex's pre-
school claimed someone called to warn her that one of
Alex's aides was a convicted child molester. The caller
wouldn't give his name. Naturally the charge is bogus."

Zeke made a few notes then he looked at her and said,
"You think like a cop. I'm not surprised Nick fell for you."

Her heart squeezed at the mention of Nikolai's name,
but pride made her lift her chin. "A person who's fallen
for someone doesn't generally skip town without saying goodbye."

Zeke made an offhand gesture. "Most of the guys I
know would rather take a bullet than watch someone
they care about get hurt." He nodded at her side. "I
know Nick was proud of you because he told me so."

His praise felt good, but it would have been better
coming from Nikolai. "Would it have killed him to stick
around until I woke up?"

"Maybe not." He shrugged. "But I don't know what
the big deal is. There are outbound flights to Detroit

every day. I haven't noticed your name on any of the manifests."

Grace started to list all the reasons she couldn't leave, but suddenly felt her father's hand on her shoulder. *We're Romani, Grace. We share the load so one person doesn't get stuck carrying too much.*

But my sisters need me.

She must have spoken aloud because Zeke said, "Nick's not the kind of guy to admit he needs someone in his life. I know because I was the same way. Cost me a wife and kids."

Grace suddenly had an image of a much younger Zeke walking away from a woman and two young children. Impulsively, she got up and walked to him. She leaned down awkwardly because of her bandage, but managed to hug him. "If you feel the urge to be part of a family, you can take my place," she said, only half kidding. "I'm not going to be around for a while. Who knows what will happen without my guidance and direction?"

He remained stiff in her hug, but he did gently pat her back. "Are you going somewhere?"

Grace stepped back. "Yes, I think I am. But there's one thing I have to do first."

YETTA LOOKED AROUND the waiting room of the clinic. She'd driven Jurek to his doctor's appointment. She hated hospitals as a rule, but this one wasn't that bad. And the nurses had all been warm and kind.

When Ernst had been hospitalized, Yetta had been so shattered and afraid, she hadn't truly appreciated the people around her. Not only had she lost the man she'd loved more than life, but her inner voice, the essence of her soul, had gone missing, too.

This time, she had her "sight" back. She knew with certainty that Jurek would recover, but convincing him of that was proving a challenge.

"Why don't you come back to Vegas with me? You said you're done with the doctors here so what have you got to lose?" she asked, as she drove them back to his place.

"I'm not a charity case, Yetta."

"I know that. You're family. And you've been through a rough time. You need a chance to recoup your strength so you can go visit your son."

He didn't say anything.

"Jurek, you may not believe this, but Lucy loved you more than she loved to dance."

He looked at her. "What'd you say?"

"You heard me. I was her friend, you know. Maybe her only friend, except for you. She was sweet but too pretty. The other women were afraid of her. And men adored her."

"She was never unfaithful," he said. His tone challenged her to say otherwise.

"Of course not. She loved you."

His eyes closed. "Not enough."

"What's enough? She gave you a son, even though her fellow dancers told her being pregnant would ruin her body, her timing and her equilibrium."

"She didn't want to stay home and be a wife and mother."

"She might have. Later on. After she'd gone as far as she could with dance. It was her dream, Jurek. And you never appreciated how much dance did for you."

"For me?" he cried. "All we ever did was fight about it."

"My point exactly. You should have embraced it. Without dance, Lucy never would have left Minnesota. Dance is what brought her to you."

He was silent for the rest of the drive. When she pulled into the lot marked Visitor Parking, he said, "She was a vision, wasn't she? 'Joy on two feet,' one of the critics called her."

"Yes, she was."

"Do you think she'd hate me for giving our son away?"

The mother in her made Yetta want to comfort him, but first she had to help him get past his guilt. "I think she would have understood how sad you were. That you blamed yourself."

His low grunt was accidental, she was sure. "She would never have been on that bus if I hadn't been in jail. What kind of dumb jerk goes back to the store where he'd written a bad check?"

"Someone whose little son needed milk."

"I was workin', you know. A real job. Selling cars. But the owner was a cocky son of a bitch. He tried to screw me out of a commission, and when I called him on it, he said he'd sic his police buddies on me."

He looked at Yetta. "I put the paycheck he gave me in the bank. I didn't know he'd stopped payment on it. I swear I thought the check I wrote was good. But with my record, the cops didn't have any choice but to haul me in."

Yetta believed him. "Jurek, did you point me to Nikolai because you believed his helping my family would even some old score you think there is between us?"

"Maybe."

"I thought so. Well, you were wrong."

"What?" Jurek started visibly.

"First off, there is no score to settle. But even if there was, bringing Nikolai here only made things worse. There's an ugly rumor going around that one of Alexandra's employees is a child molester. Kate and Grace's restaurant still isn't open, even though the health people can't find a drop of contaminated food. Liz is out of work. And Claude has moved back to the ranch, so the house next to me is empty. But worst of all, my youngest daughter is wasting away from a broken heart," she said. "Thanks to you and your son, my family is falling apart."

Jurek almost smiled. A part of him knew he was being played, but he still asked, "What can I do about it?"

"Come home and help me get things back in order. You can rent Claude's house."

"Why now?"

"Because I've lost enough. My daughters miss Ernst. They could use a father figure in their lives, and this would be a good way for you to stay in touch with your son. He's in love, too, you know."

Jurek realized she was right. He'd let fear and self-pity control his life for too long. Lucy would have been furious with him. He opened the car door and got out. The pain was there, but he'd dealt with worse.

"When do you want to leave?" he asked when she joined him to walk to his door.

"We could have left days ago if you hadn't convinced yourself you were going to die."

"I *am* going to die."

"We all are, but this isn't your time," she said, squeezing his arm.

"How can you be so sure?"

She tapped her temple and smiled. "I'm a Gypsy fortune-teller, remember?"

Jurek tried hard not to smile, but once the dam cracked, a loud guffaw followed. "You're a persistent old dame."

"I know. Are you ready to start packing?"

He paused to let the truth sink in. He was going home. After all these years, he was rejoining his family. It's what he'd always wanted but hadn't dared ask for.

Blinking at the tears in his eyes, he fumbled with his key and said, his voice gruff with emotion, "Yes, I think I am."

CHAPTER TWENTY-FOUR

GRACE ENTERED the room slowly, looking around to see if she and Charles were alone. She hadn't spoken to him since the day of his arrest. He looked…older, but still very much Charles. His suite, however, bore little resemblance to the apartment she'd visited that fateful day just a couple of weeks earlier. Moving boxes were stacked everywhere.

"Where are you going?" she asked.

"A condo that belongs to a friend," he said. "My assets were frozen by the IRS—nice touch, by the way."

"I don't know what you mean," she said truthfully.

"Don't be modest, Grace. You not only got Metro, the Clark County D.A. and the National Insurance Crime Board involved in my case, but the Mounties and Uncle Sam, too. Quite impressive."

Although outwardly he acted as pleasant and amicable as ever, Grace felt his fury like a pulse of red-hot electricity in the air. "I had nothing to do with any of that, Charles. The police used me, too. Nikolai—Nick—whatever his name is—was a plant. I didn't know he was a cop," she said, walking past him into the middle of the room. "Which is why I don't understand why you're attacking me and my sisters."

Charles appeared surprised by her directness. "I have no idea what you're talking about."

She set her purse down and crossed her arms. "I suppose you're telling me it's just a *coincidence* that the health department descended on Romantique's kitchen after someone phoned in an anonymous tip about E. coli."

He didn't react.

"And Liz can't get hired anywhere, and The Dancing Hippo is under investigation. All in a week's time. How is that possible?"

He put out his hands and shrugged. "Seems like we've all had a run of bad luck."

Grace stepped toward him. "Don't play games with me, Charles. I thought we were friends. I thought you liked my family. My God, you came to our Christmas parties and graduations and birthdays. How could you betray us like this?"

His eyes narrowed and he closed the distance between them. "Don't talk to me about betrayal, Grace. Not when you're the reason I might lose my license to practice law, not to mention everything I've worked my entire life for."

Her heart skipped a beat, but anger trumped fear. "Me?" she cried. "I'm not the one who imported prostitutes and scammed the insurance companies out of millions."

His hand came up but he made a point of relaxing his fist. "Alleged," he said softly.

She shook her head. "Fine. Great. You're innocent. This was all a big mistake. None of that matters to me, Charles. What I do care about is my family, and what you're doing to them."

He laughed. The sound sent a shiver down her spine, but she refused to be intimidated. "Oh, Grace, you're a fool if you think I'm going to admit to collusion or bribery or anything else for the benefit of your wire."

She wasn't an actress, but if Nikolai could pretend to be a hit man, she could pull this off. She shrugged off her leather jacket. "You think I'm here to get your confession and feed information to the cops?" His gaze went to her chest, where she unbuttoned the top button of her starched white blouse. "Well, you're wrong. I'm here to make a deal."

His upper lip curled back. "What kind of deal?"

"My trust money in return for your stopping this assault on my family."

His eyes narrowed. "I figured you'd show up sooner or later once you got my message."

He strode past her, knocking her purse, which had been strategically placed on the arm of the sofa, to the floor. The latch came open and the contents looked ready to spill out. She snatched it up, praying he hadn't noticed anything amiss.

Fortunately, Charles was facing the window, focused on something in the distance.

"Then you'll do it? You'll call your contacts at the health department and get them out of Romantique's kitchen?"

He turned and looked at her. "It was amazingly easy to close down your precious restaurant." His grin turned malicious. "This is the age of litigation. A complaint doesn't have to be real to ruin your reputation. Rumors alone will do that. Consumers are a fickle lot, Grace."

She stood up, purse in hand. "I knew it was you."

He shrugged. "Then you know I can undo it—for a price."

Grace took a breath to steady her nerves. "I'll give you the money on one condition. You sign a paper absolving my father of any involvement in the union bribes."

"Why would I do that?"

"For my mother's sake. I don't want her memory of my father tainted in any way."

He threw back his head and laughed. "Saint Ernst. Is that it? Rewriting history the Romani way. Forget it. That's my money and I want it back. Once it's in my bank account, I'll think about calling off the hounds of hell I've got lined up to piss on your family tree from now until the end of eternity." He snickered. "I had plenty of time in lockup to plot and plan, Grace. You'd be surprised at what a fertile mind can come up with when revenge is the motive."

Distress pulsed through her. Her fingers gripped her purse tighter. "Haven't you done enough? You pushed my father. You let everyone believe that the stroke caused him to fall, but it was really you. You killed my father."

Charles snickered softly. "Again, my dear, prove it. And as satisfying as it was to watch your dad lying there, slipping away…" He paused as if picturing the actual event. "I knew I couldn't let him die or I'd never get my money. That's why I called the paramedics. How was I supposed to know the stroke would make it impossible for him to conduct business?"

Grace flew at him, pummeling him with her purse. "You sick bastard. I hope you rot in jail."

He grabbed her arms and held her back. "Sorry, princess, but you're not going to get your wish. Even if the D.A. can prove that I masterminded the insurance fraud, the most I'd be looking at as a first-time offender is a suspended sentence and fifty-thousand-dollar fine."

He smiled smugly. "Your trust fund ought to cover that nicely. The rest will buy me a ticket to a lovely island that is renowned for its offshore banking."

Zeke had been right. Charles was the kind of man who had to brag to someone about his coup. Grace just had to nudge him a little further. "Offshore banking? What are you talking about? If you're so damn rich that you have offshore accounts, then why do you need my money?"

He sighed. "That's my nest egg. Money I skimmed off the casino when my doddering partners decided they wanted to play rather than work for their share. I ran a double set of books that even MaryAnn didn't know about."

Grace didn't say anything.

"Once I beat this rap—and I will—I plan to join my money on a sun-soaked beach."

She shook her head. "I can't believe I ever thought you were a decent person."

He threw back his head and laughed. "Oh, Grace, admit it. When you wanted Xanadu's restaurant space, you thought I was a prince. Life is full of people using people. Love is make-believe."

She put her hand on the doorknob. "Goodbye, Charles." She turned to give him one last look. "You know, you're a decent-looking guy. You should have no trouble finding all the make-believe love you've missed in your life in prison. Ta-ta."

She walked to the elevator on shaky legs. The door was open. Inside, she slumped against the wall and let out a long, heartfelt sigh of relief. Then, she handed her purse to the man who was smiling at her.

"How'd I do?" she asked.

"We could have used his offshore account number, but other than that, I do believe the D.A. will be very happy with this tape," Zeke Martini said. He opened the clasp and pulled out a tiny tape recorder—backup in case something happened to the wire she was wearing.

"Pretty gutsy. Now, let's see how brave you are when you get to Detroit."

Grace's extremities were starting to shake from the letdown. Tears clustered in her eyes. She sniffled. To her surprise, Zeke reached out and touched her chin. "You've got your ticket, right?"

She nodded. "Tomorrow."

"Good girl."

The elevator came to a stop and Grace stepped back. She looked at Zeke and gave him a watery smile. "By the way, in case you need to get hold of me, Mom will be around. She brought Nikolai's birth father to live in Claude's house."

"I know."

She frowned. "Are you still having us followed?"

His coloring changed enough for her to tell that he was blushing. "Just Yetta. I wanted to make sure she was okay."

So Zeke did like her mother. Whether Yetta shared those feelings, Grace couldn't say. She'd spent at least two hours that should have been devoted to packing on testing her "gift." Not only could she not predict what would happen to her loved ones while she was away, but she had no sense of whether or not Nikolai would welcome her arrival or close the door in her face. Which was why she'd decided not to call ahead and warn him of her plans. She wanted to see his reaction when he opened his door and found her standing there.

"YOU'RE A PAIN in the butt. You know that, right?" Nick bent over to pick up the ball Rip had just deposited at his feet, then sliced a grounder in the general direction of the blue spruce in his parents' backyard. Most of the snow was gone, but the temperature was only in the thirties.

He'd been home for two weeks. He and Rip had returned to their predictable schedule, except for the extra hours Nick had spent at the station. Work was therapeutic. It took his mind off Grace.

Helping his parents pack up their belongings was *not* therapeutic, but he was here to do just that. At least, that's what he assumed his mother's call had been about. He'd dashed home after work to pick up Rip and change clothes, but when he arrived at their house nobody was home.

"This is very poor form, wouldn't you say, bud?" he said when the panting dog returned. "Maybe they went for some KFC." He'd been living on fast food since his return from Vegas. Every time he walked into his kitchen he remembered what it had been like to sit in Romantique surrounded by members of the Radonovic clan and their friends.

Call her, a voice in his head said.

He ignored it. Just as he had for a fortnight. He knew that Grace was fine. He knew the case was going as planned. He knew that Yetta had just returned to Vegas with George. Knowing things was part of his job.

What he didn't know was whether Grace missed him. Or ever thought of him. Or wanted him to call and tell her he was a complete and utter idiot and that he was ready to quit his job and move to Vegas to be with her.

But he didn't call. Because he couldn't leave. Not now. His name was on the short list for his dad's job. The continuity appealed to him. He liked being a cop. He loved living in the Midwest. He was entrenched, which probably proved that he wasn't Romani. He was a civil servant, which meant he'd never be rich. What kind of prince had a mortgage and a truck loan?

"Nick," a familiar voice cried from the doorway of his parents' home. "Sorry we're late. We were at the airport picking up somebody. Come see who."

Grace? His heart rate jacked up to unhealthy. He dropped the slimy ball without throwing it and wiped his hand on his jeans as he dashed to the patio door.

"Hey, brother dear," his sister cried, rushing to meet him. She wrapped her arms around him and squeezed hard. "I bet this is a surprise."

Of course it's not Grace. Why would she come after the way you turned coward and ran away? He fought to keep his expression neutral. "Hey, Judy, what are you doing here? Where are the girls? And Randy?"

"At home. I needed a couple of days to myself and I found a cheap flight online, so I figured I'd help our parents make up their minds about this move."

"Huh? What do you mean? Mom, what's she talking about? You sold the house, right?" He took off his leather coat and threw it onto a chair.

Pete nodded. "Yeah. Escrow closes in a couple of

weeks, but your mom and I aren't sure we're ready to pull up stakes completely."

"But you said you never wanted to live through another Detroit winter."

"Exactly," Judy cried. She was dressed in a comfortable-looking pantsuit, but Nick thought she looked too thin. And more stressed than usual. "I'm afraid one of them is going to slip on the ice and fall," she said, directing her comment to Nick. "A broken hip could be the beginning of the end."

He frowned. "People don't fall in Oregon? Is it a law?"

His mother laughed. "Now, children, this isn't an either-or proposition. Your father and I have decided we're still young enough to do both. We're going to be—forgive the cliché—snowbirds. We'll winter in the west and spend our summers here."

"Then why sell the house?" Nick asked.

"Because it's too big for two people. We'd been hoping for a while that you might find a girl and settle down and possibly buy it from us but since that hasn't happened..."

Nick looked around. He could picture Grace painting the walls. Persimmon. Or purple. Bright colors and exotic plants, instead of white walls and potted ferns.

His sister let out a little yelp. "Oh, my gosh. Mom, look at him. Nick's in love."

He stepped back and nearly tripped over Rip. "What are you talking about? I'm...I'm..."

"You may be right, Judy. I noticed something was different when he came back from Vegas, but I let your father convince me it was work related."

"Stop. Right now. You are not fortune-tellers. You

can't look at a person's face and know whether or not he's in love."

His sister and mother exchanged a glance, then Judy said, "But we know *you*, little brother. I don't suppose her name is Grace, is it?"

Nick felt his jaw drop a good foot. He blinked twice and looked from his mother to his father, who appeared completely baffled by the conversation. "How do you know that?"

Judy crowed in triumph then walked to him and put her hand on his arm. "You don't remember?"

He shook his head. "No. We haven't spoken since I got back from Vegas."

She tilted her head and smiled a gentle smile that he associated with her daughters. "On my thirteenth birthday, I had a slumber party and one of the girls brought a Ouija board. You were hanging around being a pest and I was jealous of all the attention you were getting, so I did something mean." She looked down. "I told my friends that you were adopted and your real parents were Gypsies."

"Judy!" their mother exclaimed.

Judy looked truly repentant. "I was a brat and he was this adorable little boy that everybody loved. But my plan backfired because one of them—Bettina, I think— said, 'Hey, if he's got Gypsy blood then he's probably really good at seeing into the future.' So they made me invite you to play the game with us. Is any of this coming back?"

Nick shook his head, but a hazy memory glimmered just beyond reach.

"So what happened?" Sharon asked.

"Well, we each asked the board who we were going to marry and when it was Nick's turn, the board spelled *G.R.A.C.E.*"

Nick couldn't hold in his expletive.

Judy reached out. "I remember because that was the name of Bettina's cat. We teased you for weeks about being a cat lover. Every time we'd cross paths, I'd meow and say, 'Marry me, Grace, I love you, Grace.' Don't you remember?"

"You're making this up, Judy. I'm outta here. Come on, Rip."

His dog—the dog that obeyed his every command—just looked at him.

Judy smirked. "Even Rip knows I'm telling the truth."

"I don't want to hear any more."

She looked at him and grinned her most annoying big-sister grin. "Come on. 'Fess up, little brother. Who's Grace? She exists, doesn't she? Are you in love? When do we get to meet her?"

Nick felt the air leave his lungs as if he'd been socked in the stomach by the bouncer at the Pit Stop. He shook his head but couldn't catch his breath to speak. His mother swooped in and put her arms around him. "Oh, honey, is it true? Did you meet her in Las Vegas? Is she Romani?"

For weeks he'd felt torn in two—his past and his real life battling for supremacy. He couldn't win, so he gave up. "Yes."

"You love her?"

"Yes."

Judy slugged him in the shoulder. "Then what the heck are you doing in Detroit?"

"This is where I belong. With you guys. You're my family."

His mother shook her head. "Oh, sweetheart, who said you can only have *one* family?"

Nick looked at his father. "My job is here. Grace's life is there."

Pete smiled. "There's such a thing as compromise, son. Look at your mom and me. One day we were all set to move, the next we're bi-coastal…well, you know what I mean."

Nick swallowed the lump in his throat and hugged his mother. "I love you guys. Even you, Jude." She made a face that he remembered from their childhood. "I still don't know if I believe that story about the Ouija board or if you're just an incredibly lucky guesser, but you're right. Her name is Grace. And I think I have some apologizing to do."

"Why?" Judy asked.

"The last time I saw her, she was in a hospital bed recovering from a bullet wound that was pretty much my fault."

His mother groaned.

His father grimaced.

Judy laughed. She was his sister. What did he expect?

"Come on, Rip, time to eat crow."

He looked around for his dog, but the animal was no-where to be seen. A bark made them all turn. The collie was waiting by the front door, his whole body wagging with excitement.

CHAPTER TWENTY-FIVE

NICK TRIED Grace's cell again.

Still no answer. He didn't have any of her sisters' numbers programmed in and didn't want to take the time to use directory assistance.

"You've reached…" the prerecorded voice said.

"Grace," a bright, happy voice inserted.

"At the tone—"

He threw the phone on the passenger seat with such force it bounced sideways and cartwheeled to the floor. He started to go after it, but must have drifted into the adjoining lane because a loud, impatient honk made him overcorrect.

"Good grief, I'm driving like Grace," he muttered, and put both hands on the wheel.

Rush-hour traffic in Detroit started around three. He used surface streets to miss the worst of it and managed to turn onto his street about half an hour after leaving his parents.

He slowed down. Kids were often around this time of day, even though spring seemed to have been shoved out of the way by the remaining dregs of winter. A gray cloud hung low, like a misty blanket.

Rip, in the back seat of the extended cab pickup

truck, barked excitedly. Nick looked around but saw neither child nor four-legged animal—the only things other than a ball that Rip ever got too animated about.

Half a block from his home, though, Nick took his foot off the gas. There was a strange car in his driveway. A white compact. It appeared empty.

He parked across the street and closed the door before Rip could weasel past. His friend wasn't happy about being left behind, but Nick's cop's instincts were on alert.

He left his gun locked in the glove box since there didn't appear to be any immediate danger and pressed the alarm on his key bob to lock the doors.

Looking around as he approached the vehicle, he saw nothing out of the ordinary. Today was garbage day and the majority of his neighbors' plastic containers were still sitting in front of their respective houses. The homes on his block were thirty-year-old post-war ranch-style homes. Most had double garages that had been converted to living space…which meant cars in the driveways and on the street.

But not Nick's house. His garage was as neat and orderly as his home. His lawn was mowed in the summer and his walk shoveled in the winter. Generally, crime didn't happen on his street since people were aware that a cop lived here. But that didn't mean it couldn't.

He memorized the car's license number and was just reaching for his cell phone when he remembered that he'd dropped it on the floor of his car.

Taking a deep breath of cold air, he stepped close enough to look inside. The first thing he saw was a neon-pink wool scarf. It still had the price tag on it. And it was wrapped around the neck of the woman who was curled up asleep in the back seat.

His knees went rubbery and he had to grab the hood of the car to keep from going down. His breath came in short, shaky puffs and a roar that sounded like a giant ocean wave filled his ears.

"Grace."

He tapped the window with his knuckle. "Grace," he said again, finding his voice.

She stirred. Her eyes opened and she sat up, blinking, obviously confused about where she was. Then she looked at Nick. And smiled. "Finally," she cried, scrambling to unlock the door.

"You're here," she cried, bursting to her feet. "I was afraid I had the wrong address. But then I thought, what's the worst that could happen? The home owner calls the cops and you arrest me."

Nick hugged her without speaking. There was so much to say. So much that had been said. "How did you find me?" he finally managed.

She blinked as if the answer to his question was obvious. "George, of course. Mom moved him into Claude's house yesterday."

George. Jurek. His father.

"And MapQuest," she added. "Only took me about an hour longer than it should have. I got lost a couple of times, but notice," she said, pointing to the car, "not a single bent fender."

He chuckled softly. *Grace. Oh, God, how he loved her.* "How are you?" he asked trying to keep his emotions under control until he figured out why she was here.

She sobered. Her shoulders straightened. "Do you

mean how's my side? The bullet wound?" Her eyes danced with humor. "I love saying that. It makes me sound so dangerous and kick-ass."

He forced himself not to smile. "How is your bullet wound?"

"Healed. Mostly. Wanna see it?" Her eyebrows waggled. "Perhaps we could go inside first. It's kinda nippy out here. I had to run the heater twice and I was afraid I might get asphyxiated."

"Not outdoors. You could run out of gas, though."

"Oh. Then I froze for nothing?"

He studied her. Jeans. Long-sleeved white blouse. A T-shirt of some kind underneath. And the scarf. Not the right clothes for Michigan's variable spring weather. "Yes. Of course. Inside." He pointed toward the house, but turned on his heel and dashed the other direction. "Rip. I gotta get my dog. I'll be right back."

Nick realized he probably sounded like an idiot. But his mind was struggling to process this amazing event. Grace. Here. Smiling at him with tenderness and something else. Something he recognized, but didn't dare put a name to until he heard the words from her.

Rip had slobbered all over the driver's-side window by the time Nick got the door open. He reached for the animal's collar but the collie shot past him, squeezing through a much-too-small space. "Rip," he called, but the dog bolted. Across the street and straight into Grace's path.

Nick slammed the door and charged to the rescue.

Grace wasn't sure exactly how she ended up on the wet, stiff grass. She tripped, that was a given. And she must have rolled to avoid landing on her sore side. But the rest was a blur. Probably because a very determined furry animal was covering her face with kisses.

"Help," she peeped, half laughing, half dismayed that her carefully applied makeup was now shot.

"Rip. Dammit. Sit."

The licking stopped.

"I can't believe he did that. I'm sorry, Grace. Did he hurt you?"

She opened her eyes. Her prince was kneeling over her. She folded her hands across her chest and sighed loudly. "Kiss me."

"W…what?"

"Kiss me."

"Here? Now?"

She opened one eye. "Come on. Do I not look like Snow White? Rip could be one of the dwarves." She turned her chin just a bit. "Dopey?"

The dog actually looked offended.

"Happy," she offered instead.

His ears cocked and his rear end waggled.

Nick rocked back on his haunches and shook his head. "You've got to be kidding."

She sat up on her elbows. Her side ached but she wasn't about to tell him that. "No, I'm completely serious. I just flew two thousand miles to tell you that there's no way I'm letting you walk out of my life. In some people's book that might make me a stalker, but it's my version of tough love." She returned to her flat position. "If you don't love me back…tough."

She closed her eyes again. Not in jest but to keep her tears at bay. She hadn't really thought about what would happen if he *didn't* want her.

She started to roll to her good side to sit up, but she felt his presence. Close.

"I didn't mean to make you cry, princess. I just can't believe it's this easy. No dragons to kill. No overgrown vegetation to hack through or magical spells to undo. Just one silly dog standing between me and my future."

She opened her eyes. "What'd you say?"

"That was my less-than-eloquent way of saying I love you." He kissed her. Right there on the cold, damp grass of his front lawn.

A storybook kiss that might have gotten out of hand if not for Rip, who suddenly decided he deserved a kiss or two of his own.

She petted the exuberant collie and rewarded him with a peck on the nose, then said, "Thank you for that reminder. As your master and I both know, decisions made in the heat of passion aren't necessarily the best for either party."

She turned her attention to Nick. "I didn't mean what I said earlier about tough love. I'm not going to make you do anything, Nick. But I do think you love me, and I know I love you. So that means we have some decisions to make, and I don't want you to look back at this moment with any regret. Your birth mother gave up her career to marry Jurek and found being a wife and mother wasn't enough for her. I can't ask you to leave the job you love, and if I move here, it means giving up my family and my business."

TEN MINUTES LATER, they faced each other across his dining-room table, two mugs of microwaved cocoa between them. The furnace was running and Rip was sitting beside Nick's chair.

Nick couldn't believe his future had come down to a matter of geography. His first inclination was to open his heart and tell her he'd follow her anywhere. But the mention of his birth mother had reminded him that nothing was that simple.

"So how do we do this?" he asked. "Two thousand miles is a heck of a commute."

She gave a half smile. "But think of the frequent flier miles we'd accrue."

"That might work for a while, but what happens when we have kids?" He looked at her and decided to go for broke. "Marry me and move here. You could still do the books for Romantique via telecommuting. You just won't be able to do the hostessing."

"Well, Kate wouldn't be happy. And Romantique's in a real bind right now." Grace told him about Charles's vendetta and the reason why the restaurant was temporarily closed.

He swore and reached across the table to take her hand. "Sorry, Grace. But there's probably never going to be a perfect time to move. For either of us. The fact is, I love you. I want to marry you. And if that means moving to Vegas, then that's what I'm going to do."

She looked at him, her eyes filling with tears. "I love you, too, but this is so important and—" Whatever she'd been about to say was cut short by Rip, who suddenly jumped up, knocking her purse, which had been resting on the table, to the floor. The contents spilled out, including the deck of cards she'd brought on the plane to play solitaire with.

Grace welcomed the distraction. She was tempted to let Nick make this noble sacrifice. He was her prince. This is the kind of thing princes did, right? But her conscience wouldn't let her. As she reached for the cards, a shiver of awareness raced up her spine. Out of the corner of her eye, she spotted the ghostly image of her father. Grinning, Ernst said, "Luck or destiny? Life is a gamble, Gracie. Sometimes you have to risk everything to win."

She stared at the splashy "Play Las Vegas" logo on the deck she'd impulsively purchased at the gift shop in the airport. Suddenly she knew what to do. She quickly shuffled the cards, as her father had taught her, then held the deck out, face down, on her palm. "We'll let the cards decide. If you pick the high card, we live in Detroit. If I get it, we make Vegas our home."

"Princesses first," he said, not hesitating for a second.

She quickly made her cut.

"The queen of hearts," she said softly.

Nick pushed his cup to one side and scooted closer to the table. After drawing in a deep breath, he reached out, his hand hovering over hers for just a moment. When he flicked his wrist, he revealed his pick.

NICK STARED at the ace of diamonds and was speechless. He'd won. Grace would be his. She'd marry him and move to Detroit. A sense of joy so powerful he couldn't describe filled him up, making him want to laugh and cry at the same time. "I love you, Grace."

She was in his arms in a heartbeat, and he couldn't stop kissing her.

They stumbled into the bedroom, bouncing off the wall in a tangled ball of arms and legs. The bed made a creaking sound. Grace, who was on top, lifted her head and looked around. "A man's room. Nice, but needs color. Will that be a problem?"

He buried his hand in her hair and kissed her. "Nope."

She worked her hands under him and pressed her body flat. Jeans and friction. Soft to hard in a way that blocked conscious thought. "Clothes off," he thought he heard her say.

Nick rolled them to their sides and did his best to oblige as quickly as possible. "Love, honor and obey. I like that," she said, licking her lip in a sexy way that cost her a nip on the belly button.

Her laughter made him want to slow things down. They had so much to talk about.

"Later," she whispered in his ear. "Sex now. Talk later."

He didn't ask how she knew what he was thinking. She was a Gypsy princess. Her mother was Puri Dye. Besides, although he didn't plan to mention it, he knew what she was thinking, too. Because he felt exactly the same fire.

They were linked. Somehow. By fate. Through time. He didn't understand it, but neither did he doubt it.

She reached between their bodies and touched him. "Do we need…?" he asked, looking into her eyes.

Her lips curved in a smile. "Not if you trust me. I'm not pregnant. My period started the day I came home from the hospital. And I've been taking the pill faithfully."

He thrust lightly against her hand. "I was an ass about that. If you want to know the truth, I was hoping you were pregnant, so I didn't have to worry whether or not you loved me. We would have gotten married because it was the right thing to do."

"Me, too."

She guided him into her and he closed the gap. Her body welcomed him home, and he let out a small cry. "Thank you for loving me, Grace."

She moved her hips, up and against him. "You're welcome. Now, dazzle me with brilliance. I flew two thousand miles and just lost at cards. It's the least you can do."

He scooted downward until his lips brushed against the credit-card size bandage on her side. "Does this hurt? Do we need to be careful of reopening it?"

"A mere scratch," she said breathlessly, but he was so attuned to her feelings he knew she was lying.

"R...right," he said, moving lower. He brought her close to the edge then backed away as she writhed with yearning.

"You...do that...again...and..."

Her threat was lost in a gasp of pleasure as he thrust into her, putting his own needs aside until he felt her pulsating waves of pleasure. The signal for his own release.

Afterward, Grace wasn't sure she could move. Her body had traveled into a sphere that she didn't recognize. Another world. A beautiful place, warm, safe and filled with peace. She never wanted to leave, but a small child, a boy, was sitting just outside the light. She couldn't quite see him, but she knew he was there. Alone. And frightened.

She went to the edge of the circle and waited for him to look up. When he did, she smiled and held out her hand. "I'm Grace. I'm here. You don't have to be alone anymore."

He didn't come to her right away, but she was patient. She knew this was important. Maybe the most important thing she would ever do in her life. She waited, and finally he reached out and took her hand.

And stepped into the circle.

"You're home," she said, returning to the world where a solid chest was under her cheek, moving up and down with each breath.

What did it mean? She didn't know, but the vision filled her with peace and a sense of wholeness. That was enough for now. She might think about it later.

"Do we need to talk more?" Nick's voice was husky.

She snuggled a little closer. "What more is there to say? You won. Me. My future. Our future." She lifted her chin and turned her head to look at him. "Although you do understand that doesn't mean I'm some kind of chattel. This is the twenty-first century."

His chuckle rumbled under her ear. "I didn't think it meant you were my sex slave. You're my princess. I'm only sorry you didn't get your prince."

Grace gave him a look that said he'd lost his wits. "How do you figure that? The man I'm going to marry is noble, gallant, generous and kind. He takes care of the people in his life and the citizens of the world at large. He's handsome and dashing and he loves me. What more could a princess ask for?"

"Gold? Treasure? A palace?"

She looked around. "This place has potential. It just needs...me."

He laughed and kissed her. His kingdom was complete, or would be when they had a passel of children around them.

"I love you, princess."

"Thank goodness. There's big money riding on this, you know."

"There is?"

She nodded somberly. "Apparently, Claude set up odds at one of the small casinos. So far, bets are running heavily in my favor, but a few silly people thought I'd come back alone."

Nick shook his head. Only a fool would throw his money away like that. When it came to love, Nick was—now and always—betting on Grace.

Everything you love about romance...
and more!

Please turn the page for Signature Select™
Bonus Features.

BETTING ON
GRACE

BONUS
FEATURES
INSIDE

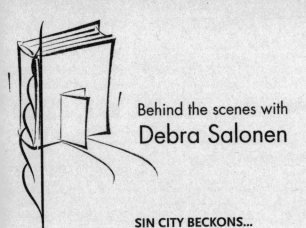

Behind the scenes with
Debra Salonen

SIN CITY BECKONS...

As you approach Las Vegas from the west by car, be sure to look for the billboard that says, "Seven Deadly Sins? We demand a recount." I took that to mean, "Be prepared for anything—you're in Vegas, baby."

But given my advanced age—I'm not in my twenties...or forties, for that matter—and my proclivity to thriftiness (okay, I'm cheap), I wasn't looking for strippers, booze and high stakes poker. I was interested in a more holistic approach that would take me beyond the neon glow of The Strip and give me a look at the "real" Las Vegas.

Well, yes...um, there is one, but it's, uh, not all that interesting, so this travelogue is a mixture of the marvelous, the miraculous and the mundane.

The highs: The Stratosphere, obviously. A must-see because of what you can see from the

1,149-foot observation tower. Built in 1996, the hotel/casino has been called a "mad phallic fantasy" and is located in an area between "Downtown" and "The Strip" that was once known as the "Naked City" because showgirls who lived nearby sunbathed in the afternoons in the buff. Nowadays the view is different, but you can observe the panorama for a full ninety minutes if you choose to dine at Top Of The World, the revolving restaurant that offers an excellent, although pricy by Vegas standards, Sunday brunch. Or you can screw up your courage and try one of the thrill rides crowded atop the flying-saucer-shaped building. If Grace and Nick can handle The Big Shot, why not you?

The lows: The Shark Reef at Mandalay Bay. If you have kids in tow, this might be an acceptable diversion, but for anyone who has visited a—how should I say—less petite aquarium, you might want to save your fifteen bucks for something more interesting. Like a gondola ride along the subterranean canals at The Venetian. It's twelve dollars, but the serenade from your gondolier is free. Romance level? Alas, low. Blame it on the smell of chlorine or the tourists snapping pictures from the Rialto Bridge, but I found the experience far too public to qualify as romantic.

Although you will find mention of a wedding at The Venetian in Kate's book.

The How-Did-They-Do-That?: Hoover Dam. An amazing piece of history and engineering. The sheer numbers are staggering: 726 feet high, 660 feet thick at the base, 1,244 feet wide at the top. It weighs approximately 6.6 million tons. Sadly, since September 11, the underground tours have been curtailed, but the trip to see this modern marvel is still worth your time. And to reach this man-made wonder, you pass through Boulder City, a charming little nongaming community with a gorgeous public golf course and free parks that often host wild bighorn sheep that wander down off the mountain for a snack.

On the cheap: So you put your money on lady luck and she backed someone at another table. Whatcha gonna do? Believe it or not, there are inexpensive venues in the Las Vegas area. The Clark County Museum, which is located on Boulder Highway in Henderson, is one example. No glitter. No glamour. Just an unassuming building set well off the road. But the excellent exhibits follow the history of the Las

Welcome to Paradise

Vegas basin from prehistoric footprints, odd-looking camels and a gnarly-looking extinct wolf to the present. There are exhibits displaying the native tribes, the padres, the miners, the railroad and, of course, the gamblers. Tip your hat to Bugsy Siegel. View The El Rancho, precursor to the hotels of today. Naturally, you can't miss Elvis. And the Rat Pack. The romantic in you won't pass up the celebrity weddings. Did you know Paul Newman and Joanne Woodward were married here? Outside, you can stroll down memory lane (if your vision of memory lane is post WWII). Five original homes are decorated in vintage memorabilia of the period, including a mobile home not unlike Grace's.

Another inexpensive side trip is the Ethel M chocolate factory. It's not exactly Willy Wonka, but the self-guided tour is free and there's a complimentary piece of chocolate waiting for you at the gift shop, which is where you end up, of course. Outside is a peaceful oasis stocked with more than 300 species of cacti, succulents and desert plants. The perfect place to eat your chocolate so it doesn't melt before you get back to your car.

If you're only here for the food: Welcome to paradise. Again you have your choice of going high, low, fantastic or cheap.

High: there are fabulous restaurants in Las Vegas staffed with world-famous chefs or chefs trained by world-famous chefs. If you're a seafood lover and you've done well at the tables, you might want to try AquaKnox at The Venetian.

Low: perhaps your taste runs to mile-long smorgasbords. Our local friends suggested we try the Santa Fe Station, but apparently this culinary anomaly is everywhere. The premise is simple—a lot of food for the money. If that means trading flavor for abundance...well, visit the dessert buffet first. If you like a little entertainment with your dinner, there's always the sacrificial virgin at Jimmy Buffett's Margaritaville. I don't know for a fact that the limber young lady was a virgin, but she walked away unscathed, so that must mean something, right? For a more prosaic view, I'd suggest a stop at Whole Foods grocery on West Charleston to pick up a picnic lunch to enjoy at Red Rock Canyon National Conservation Area, a twenty-mile drive due west of town. The commanding vistas make you utter, "What casinos?" The scenic loop, which costs five dollars and comes with a map of hiking trails, is well worth the price of admission. You can hike...or not. And while you're in the neighborhood, leave time to visit Bonnie Springs Old Nevada. The shoot-out is a bit hokey and the petting zoo quaint, but the beer is cold and the cowboys are happy to show off their six-shooters.

Las Vegas truly is a phenomenon that invokes a certain state of mind, sinful or otherwise. They say that if you were looking down at earth from the space station, Vegas would be the brightest spot on the planet. A beacon of sorts. And if visitors from outer space landed here first, what would they think about our inhabitants and culture? Interesting question, but while people-watching in Vegas I often found myself wondering, "What if the aliens have already arrived...and stayed?"

Recipes: Romantique's House Specials
by Debra Salonen

Our appetizer:

CRAB CAKES COLLEEN

1 lb. crab meat
1/3 cup mayonnaise blended with
2 tbsp. Dijon mustard
2 eggs beaten with a dash of cayenne pepper
1/2 cup onion, 1/4 cup sweet red pepper,
1/4 cup celery, 1 clove garlic (all finely
minced)

Mix all ingredients together.

Use a serving spoon to shape into patties; fry one or two patties at a time in butter at a low temperature, 4-5 minutes per side. Keep warm (covered) in oven until all patties are done. Serve with slices of fresh mango, drizzled with lime juice.

Our house salad dressing:

LEMON SESAME DRESSING

1/4 cup canola oil plus 1 tsp sesame oil
1/2 cup rice vinegar
2 tbsp organic cane sugar
1/4 tsp salt and pepper
Half a lemon
*2 tbsp toasted sesame seeds (important to
use toasted, which are found in most Asian
food sections of the grocery store)*

Whisk together oil, vinegar, sugar and seasoning.

Sprinkle sesame seeds atop your favorite salad greens, squeeze lemon on greens just before serving, then coat with salad dressing.

At Romantique, we serve our fresh vegetable du jour (typically asparagus, sautéed chard and beet greens, or summer squash mélange) with this sauce:

LIME DILL DIJON SAUCE

The juice of one lime
1/2 cup plain yogurt
1/4 cup Vegenaise (or mayonnaise)
1 tbsp Dijon mustard
1/2 tsp sugar
1/2 tsp finely chopped fresh or dried dill
Salt and pepper

Mix together. A piquant addition to vegetables or roasted pork, lamb.

Our fabulous rice pilaf is served family-style:

PISTACHIO PILAF À LA JPS

1 1/2 cups pistachio meats
1 onion, chopped
4-5 cloves of garlic, diced (optional)
1/2 cup olive oil or butter
Any or all of the following vegetables for color and taste:

1 can artichoke hearts, chopped (these are NOT the marinated kind)
1 can Heart of Palm, chopped
1-2 stalks of celery, chopped
1 carrot, diced
1 cup rice
2 1/4 cups water
1/2 cup brewer's yeast
2-4 tbsp Ume plum vinegar (this replaces salt, so amount varies by taste)
One bunch organic greens such as kale, spinach or collards, washed and loosely chopped

Sauté pistachios in heavy, dry skillet, browning on each side. Turn down heat and add onions (and garlic) for 1-2 minutes to lower pan temp, then add oil or butter. Stir to coat, return heat to medium. Add vegetables and cook over medium to medium-high heat until onions are translucent and vegetables slightly browned. Add rice, stirring to coat in oil. Cook for two minutes, then add water and bring to high simmer. Add yeast and vinegar. Add greens on top, but don't stir into mixture. Turn heat to low and cover. Simmer until water is absorbed and rice is tender. (Serves 6-8 as a side dish, 4-6 as a main meal.)

As a main course, try a family favorite:

MAMA'S CHIOPPINO

1 yellow onion
1 green pepper
1 red pepper
6 cloves garlic
1/4 cup olive oil
2 large cans of stewed tomatoes
1/2 tsp dried basil or 1/4 cup fresh basil,
finely chopped
3 large bay leaves
Salt and pepper to taste
2 cups water
4 cubes Knorr's fish bouillon
1 can tiny shrimp
1 can crabmeat
1 can clams
Any combination of fish: shrimp, scallops,
firm white fish, such as halibut, snapper
(deboned) or rockfish, clams and/or mussels
in shell, crab legs

In a large pot sauté vegetables and garlic in oil
until just tender; add tomatoes in juice, cutting
up any whole tomatoes. Add seasonings. In
microwavable container dissolve four cubes of

Knorr's fish bouillon in water, add to soup pot. Next add the canned fish with juices. Simmer for several hours, stirring occasionally. Just before ready to serve dinner, add fish. Cook until fish is no longer translucent. Serve with lemon wedges and warm sourdough bread.

Or our:

HERBED PORK TENDERLOIN

1 3-pound boneless pork loin roast
2 tbsp coarse cracked black pepper
2 tbsp grated Parmesan cheese
2 tsp dried basil
1 tsp dried oregano
2 tsp dried rosemary (Kate prefers to drape
3-4 sprigs of fresh rosemary over the roast,
and she uses a twist of fresh rosemary and
lavender as a garnish.)
2 tsp dried thyme
1/4 tsp garlic powder
1/4 tsp Kosher salt

Pat pork dry with a paper towel. In a small bowl combine all rub ingredients well and apply to all surfaces of the pork roast. Place roast in a

shallow pan and roast in a 350°F oven for
1–1 1/4 hours, until internal temperature,
measured with a meat thermometer, registers
155°F. Remove roast from oven and let rest for
5-10 minutes before slicing to serve. This, too,
is wonderful with our lime dill sauce.

*Leave room for dessert, which is sinfully delicious.
The cake itself is dense, but not overly sweet. The
glaze is purely decadent:*

CHOCOLATE-GLAZED COCOA CAKE

1 3/4 cups flour
1 cup granulated sugar
2/3 cup unsweetened cocoa powder
1 tsp baking soda
1/4 tsp ground nutmeg
1/4 tsp salt
1/2 cup canola oil
1/4 cup honey
2 egg yolks
1 cup skim milk or soy milk
1 1/2 tsp vanilla extract
6 egg whites
1/2 tsp cream of tartar
1/2 cup raspberry preserves (not used in the
shortcut bundt-pan version)

For the glaze:
> *1 cup confectioners' sugar*
> *1/4 cup unsweetened cocoa powder*
> *1/4 cup skim milk or soy milk*
> *1 tbsp honey*
> *3/4 tsp vanilla extract*
> *Half a bar of organic dark chocolate*

Preheat oven to 350°F. Lightly grease two 8-inch round cake pans and dust with flour. (Shortcut version: lightly grease and dust one bundt pan.) In a large bowl sift together flour, sugar, cocoa powder, baking soda, nutmeg and salt. Make a well in the center and add the oil, honey, egg yolks, milk and vanilla. Use electric mixer on low to stir until combined and smooth.

In medium-sized bowl beat the egg whites on high speed until foamy. Add cream of tartar and continue beating until mixture forms stiff peaks. Stir 1/4 of the egg whites into batter, mixing completely, then gently fold in the remaining egg whites. Divide mixture between the prepared pans or place in bundt pan.

Bake 35-40 minutes or until toothpick inserted in center comes out clean. (The bundt pan may

take a few minutes longer, but don't overcook.)
Let cool on wire racks five minutes, then invert
on serving plate. Place strips of waxed paper
under the edges to protect from glaze. When
cake is completely cooled, spread preserves on
bottom half, then top with second layer.

To prepare the glaze: In a small saucepan or
double boiler, combine sugar and cocoa
powder. Whisk in milk, honey and vanilla. Chop
chocolate into small pieces to facilitate
melting. Add to mixture and over low heat cook
for 1-2 minutes until smooth and chocolate bits
are melted. Using a spatula, work quickly to
frost the sides and top of the cake. If applying
to bundt cake, drizzle frosting, making sure to
get both inside and outside. With a sharp knife
score a line around the bottom edge of the
cake and remove waxed paper.

Serves 12.

Here's a sneak peek...

One Daddy Too Many
by
Debra Salonen

*The Radonovic sisters' stories continue in a new
three-book miniseries coming from Harlequin
American Romance—Sisters of the Silver Dollar.
Watch for Kate's story, One Daddy Too Many,
available May 2006*

CHAPTER 1

KATE RADONOVIC GRANT took a long draw on the straw that was stuck in her can of decaffeinated, desugared, de-everything soda, then glanced at her watch. He should be here any minute. She'd caught him on his cell phone just as he was leaving his Lake Las Vegas home.

She'd terminated dozens of employees over the years. The restaurant business thrived on short-term hires, and while not her favorite aspect of the job, she didn't lose much sleep over the prospect of letting someone go. Until now.

Of course, this time she wasn't talking to a crack-addict dishwasher or a chronically late bartender. This time she was firing her attorney. Robert James Brighten. Rob. A great guy, who'd really come through when her family needed him. But Kate knew the best way to reciprocate for all that he'd done was to fire him.

With any luck, this *thing* she felt for him was entirely one-sided. A figment of her sexually deprived imagination. But even if Rob was attracted to her, he'd change his mind once he heard the latest development in her family's saga.

The distinctive sound of a sports car's engine intruded into her thoughts. Seconds later a sleek silver status symbol pulled into the parking lot of Romantique, the restaurant she owned with her sister, Grace.

Her heart rate sped up. From what she had to do, not from Rob's presence, she told herself. Unsuccessfully. Only a liar would try to deny what Rob Brighten did to her libido. And Kate was honest—brutally so, her sisters often claimed.

His Lexus coupe purred to a stop and the driver's door opened. Rob unfolded his long legs and got out with the amazing fluidity of the young and fit. He was only four years Kate's junior, but she felt decades older.

Once standing, he leaned over to retrieve something and her gaze zeroed in on his derriere. Elegantly sculpted in a tailored navy blue pinstripe suit. She tried not to ogle, but a person who had been without sex for as long as she had could muster up only so much willpower.

Belying the conservative cut and color of his suit, his pale plum shirt and vibrant red-and-silver tie had a Gypsy flair, although she knew his heritage was Romani-free. Like Kate, her ex-husband was Romani, and she'd vowed that if she ever got involved with another man, he wouldn't carry a drop of Romani blood in his veins. Rob fit that criterion. Too bad he was wrong for her in every other way.

He tossed his fashionable sunglasses on the seat of his car, then closed the door. "'Morning, Kate," he said, turning to face her. "I'm glad you caught me before I got to the office. I was going to call you at home. I have some interesting news."

"Really? Does it have to do with my felonious family? We won't be on the clock, will we?" she asked, only half teasing. She still hadn't gotten a bill from him, and her reserve cash was running low.

"There's no charge for good news," Rob said, offering a smile to ease the tension he felt percolating between them. From the first day he and Kate met, he'd felt a hum—something intriguing and rich with potential, even though they'd both politely ignored the connection for the sake of professional ethics. But now that their legal business was nearly concluded, he hoped other aspects of their relationship would change, too.

"I haven't heard good news in so long, I'd probably need subtitles to understand it," she said, as she brushed a wind-whipped hunk of hair out of her eyes. Her gorgeous mocha-brown eyes.

He wasn't surprised by her cynical tone. This woman had been through hell the past couple of weeks. Make that the past couple of years. "What if I told you I have something that will guarantee hordes of new customers?"

She crossed her arms and gave him a get-real look.

"Here." He held out the hardcover book he was carrying. "This is for you."

She recoiled slightly at first, but took it and read out loud "'Prowess: Loving the Older Man.'"

Her lips, slick from a clear gloss, puckered for a moment, then curved into a smile. She glanced up, and the smile threatened to become a laugh. "I don't have a lot of free time to read, but, um…thanks?"

Rob's heart double-thudded, and he had to step back to keep from touching her. According to his mother, who had recently been promoted to Romantique's assistant manager, Kate ran the kitchen like a submarine commander under fire, and she didn't hug.

"You're welcome. But don't worry. You don't have to read it. I just wanted you to see the picture on the back."

Her elegant brows flickered. She flipped the book over. "Adam Brighten. Your father?"

Rob nodded. "It's Dad's new bestseller. He's coming to Vegas for a book signing and…to get married."

"Does your mom know?"

Rob was touched that her first concern was for his mother. "Yes. He called Mom before he called me."

His parents had divorced—officially—just weeks

after Rob graduated from high school, but he'd known for years that they'd stayed together only out of an obligation to him. Yet even after going their separate ways, they'd remained friends. Which had bugged his ex-fiancée to no end.

"Is Jo okay with this?" Kate asked.

"Absolutely. We both think Dad's been lonely and dissatisfied with his life for a long time." Not that Rob talked to his father often. They had little in common, except golf.

She took a key from the pocket of her snug faded jeans. Her gray UNLV sweatshirt had seen better days, but on Kate it looked good. Her running shoes were thick soled and functional, albeit slightly tattered, as well. "So how exactly is this book going to change my life?"

He moved close enough to get a hint of her fragrance. Not perfume. Never perfume that he'd been able to detect. Just soap and a crisp, citrus-scented shampoo.

"As best man at my father's wedding, I get to pick where to have the reception. Naturally, I thought of Romantique." She seemed pleased but not overly impressed until he added, "Did I mention that this will be a rather high-profile event, since both the bride and groom are minor celebrities? Dad said something about a crew from *Entertainment Tonight*."

She swayed as if the possibility made her knees

weak. They bumped body parts. Mostly elbows and forearms, but a little skin. A little warmth. Enough to make his throat close.

"Here?" Her brown eyes were so wide and fathomless he felt momentarily lost in them. He saw her embrace the possibilities. A hint of the light he'd noticed when she was watching her daughter sparkled to life. "This could be big."

Her grin made him want so badly to kiss her that he grabbed for any distraction. "Before I forget, you asked me to stop by, remember? What did you want to talk about?"

A blush inched up her neck. A second later her chin rose. "I'd planned to fire you," she said softly.

"I don't blame you."

"You don't?"

"You hired me to make sure your ex-husband didn't come near you or Maya after he's released on parole, but I just got a call from the associate I had working on the case. Turns out your ex is…" His mouth went dry. He knew how much this was going to upset her.

"Moving next door into Uncle Claude's house," she finished for him. Her tone was bleak. "Mother told me this morning."

"I'm sorry, Kate. I dropped the ball. I should have gotten a restraining order or—"

"You couldn't have prevented this, Rob. Mom can

be very determined. Especially when she thinks she's *seen* the future."

His mother had explained about Yetta Radonovic's so-called abilities. "But Yetta was one of Grant's victims. Surely she doesn't think that by taking care of him now, he might leave her something if he dies. There *is* no money, Kate."

"That's not it. Ian is sick. He's family. It's a Romani thing, I guess you could say." She made a halfhearted attempt at a smile.

Although her tone sounded very matter-of-fact, Rob sensed an undercurrent of pain in her voice. "This has got to be tough. I'm sorry." He put his hand on her arm. Lean muscles flexed beneath his touch. His fingers closed of their own accord. "I could go to court. Get an injunction. I'm sure we could prove—"

She pulled away. "No. I can't fight this. Mom lost her ability to see into the future after Dad died—from a combination of grief and drugs the doctor gave her—but now her visions have returned. She believes that Ian needs to be here. For Maya's sake. I don't know what that means exactly, but what if she's right?"

Rob's hand closed into a fist. He wasn't a violent man, but at the moment he would have loved to punch something. Preferably Ian Grant's face. But he heard the resignation in Kate's voice. This wasn't any of his business.

He pulled out his checkbook from the inside pocket of his suit jacket and quickly scribbled an amount and his signature. "Will this work as a deposit?" he asked, handing her the check.

Her gasp told him she was surprised. And pleased.

"Dad gave me carte blanche. He wants the best. I know I can trust you to deliver that."

Kate managed to keep her emotions together until Rob left, but when Rob's mother, Jo, arrived ten minutes later, Kate could barely speak. "I can't b-believe it," she said, showing her the check. With all those lovely zeroes.

"Oh, honey girl, don't cry. I've been telling you all along, good things happen to good people. Sometimes it just takes a while to prime the pump." Jo gave Kate's shoulders a robust squeeze.

"But this is too much," Kate said. "Rob must think I'm some kind of charity case."

"My son is in love with you, you idiot. He'd give you every dime in his account if he thought you'd take it."

The check Jo had been in the process of handing back slipped through Kate's suddenly numb fingers and fluttered to the tile floor, which was covered in dust. "He... You... No... Don't kid about something like that," she said once her power of speech returned. "Rob's a great guy. The best. But no way in the world would he be interested in someone like me."

Jo, who'd grabbed a broom from the utility closet, leaned on it and said, "Someone like you? You mean someone who puts family first, who works twenty hours a day and still manages to be a great mom and fabulous boss? And who would look like a model if she ever wore anything but jeans and a chef's uniform?"

Kate shook her head. "Very funny. I'm skinny, burned-out and emotionally bankrupt. If you see your son before I do, tell him he really truly is fired. For his own sake." *And mine.*

Jo resumed sweeping. "Yeah, sure. You two are going to be together a lot over the next couple of weeks planning this reception. They say love is infectious. Maybe, with luck, we'll hear more wedding bells down the road."

Kate started to laugh. She didn't believe in luck. Or love. She was about to say so when the back door burst open and Rob dashed in. "I forgot something." He barely spared a glance for Jo—"Hi, Mom," he said—as he hurried toward Kate.

The intensity of his look set her nerves racing. Had he changed his mind? Did he want his check back?

He didn't stop until he was right in front of Kate. So close his scent enveloped them, drawing her into a world made up of two people. A man and a woman.

This wasn't about business. It was personal.

"As I was driving away, it hit me that maybe the

BONUS FEATURE

reason your mother invited Grant to live next door is so the two of you would patch things up and get back together."

The possibility had occurred to her, too, although she knew that would never happen. "Maybe. So what?"

"So...this." His kiss started out light, curious, but it deepened in a way Kate couldn't have predicted and didn't understand. Like old souls, reunited at last, a voice in her mind whispered.

"No." She pushed ever so gently on his shoulders. She didn't believe in such things. Ian had taught her that love was a farce. An excuse to use people and leave them. She had a daughter to consider. She couldn't... wouldn't run that risk again. "We have to work together." A feeble excuse, but the best she could come up with.

Rob smiled as if she'd given him a gift. "You're right. We do." He dropped a sweet, tantalizing peck on her lips, then left.

Kate grabbed the stainless steel counter for balance. Once she was certain she wouldn't embarrass herself by swooning, she called out, "And you're fired."

But, of course, by then it was too late. He was long gone and so was her heart.

...NOT THE END...

Watch for Kate's story, One Daddy Too Many, *available May 2006.*

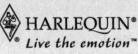

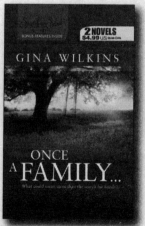

SHOWCASE

The first book in the
Roselynde Chronicles from...

Beloved author
ROBERTA GELLIS

ROSELYNDE

With a foreword by bestselling historical romance
author Margaret Moore

One passion that created a dynasty...

Lady Alinor Devaux,
the mistress of Roselynde,
had a fierce reputation for
protecting what's hers. So
when Sir Simon Lemagne
is assigned as warden
of Roselynde, Alinor is
determined to make his life
miserable. Only, the seasoned
knight isn't quite what
Alinor expects.

Plus, exclusive bonus features inside!

If you enjoyed what you just read,
then we've got an offer you can't resist!

Take 2 bestselling love stories FREE!

Plus get a FREE surprise gift!

COMING NEXT MONTH

Signature Select Spotlight
IN THE COLD by Jeanie London
Years after a covert mission gone bad, ex-U.S. intelligence agent Claire de Beaupre is discovered alive, with no memory of the brutal torture she endured. Simon Brandauer, head of the agency, must risk Claire's fragile memory to unravel the truth of what happened. But a deadly assassin needs her to *forget*....

Signature Select Saga
BETTING ON GRACE by Debra Salonen
Grace Radonovic is more than a little surprised by her late father's friend's proposal of marriage. But the shady casino owner is more attracted to her dowry than the curvy brunette herself. So when long-lost cousin Nikolai Sarna visits, Grace wonders if *he* is her destiny. But sexy Nick has a secret...one that could land Grace in unexpected danger.

Signature Select Miniseries
BRAVO BRIDES by Christine Rimmer
Two full-length novels starring the beloved Bravo family.... Sisters Jenna and Lacey Bravo have a few snags to unravel...before they tie the knot!

Signature Select Collection
EXCLUSIVE! by Fiona Hood-Stewart, Sharon Kendrick, Jackie Braun
It's a world of Gucci and gossip. Caviar and cattiness. And suddenly everyone is talking about the steamy antics behind the scenes of the Cannes Film Festival. Celebrities are behaving badly... and tabloid reporters are dishing the dirt.

Signature Select Showcase
SWANSEA LEGACY by Fayrene Preston
Caitlin Deverell's great-grandfather had built SwanSea as a mansion that would signal the birth of a dynasty. Decades later, this ancestral home is being launched into a new era as a luxury resort—an event that arouses passion, romance and a century-old mystery.

The Fortunes of Texas: Reunion
THE DEBUTANTE by Elizabeth Bevarly
When Miles Fortune and Lanie Meyers are caught in a compromising position, it's headline news. There's only one way for the playboy rancher and the governor's daughter to save face—pretend to be engaged until after her father's election. But what happens when the charade becomes more fun than intended?